Praise for Kerry Greenwood's

'Independent, wealthy, spirited and possessed of an uninhibited style that makes everyone move out of her way and stand gawking for a full five minutes after she walks by—Phryne Fisher is a woman who gets what she wants and has the good sense to enjoy every minute of it!' —*Geelong Times*

'Phryne . . . is a wonderful fantasy of how you could live your life if you had beauty, money, brains and superb self control.' —*The Age*

'Fisher is a sexy, sassy and singularly modish character. Her 1920s Melbourne is racy, liberal and a city where crime occurs on its shadowy, largely unlit streets.' —*Canberra Times*

'The presence of the inimitable Phryne Fisher makes this mystery a delightful, glamorous romp of a novel—a literary glass of champagne with a hint of debauchery.' —*Armidale Express*

'Impressive as she may be, Phryne Fisher, her activities and her world are never cloying thanks to Greenwood's witty, slightly tongue-in-cheek prose. As usual, it's a delightfully frothy, indulgent escape with an underlying bite.' —*Otago Daily Times*

'Greenwood's strength lies in her ability to create characters that are wholly satisfying: the bad guys are bad, and the good guys are great.'—*Vogue*

'If you have not yet discovered this Melbourne author and her wonderful books featuring Phryne Fisher, I urge you to do so now . . . In a word: delightful.' —*Herald Sun*

'Elegant, fabulously wealthy and sharp as a tack, Phryne sleuths her way through these classical detective stories with customary panache . . . Greenwood's character is irresistibly charming, and her stories benefit from research, worn lightly, into the Melbourne of the period.' —*The Age*

'The astonishing thing is not that Phryne is so gloriously fleshed out with her lulu bob and taste for white peaches and green chartreuse, but that I had not already made her acquaintance.'
—*Bendigo Advertiser*

KERRY GREENWOOD is the author of more than fifty novels and six non-fiction works, and the editor of two collections. Previous novels in the Phryne Fisher series are *Cocaine Blues*, *Flying too High*, *Murder on the Ballarat Train*, *Death at Victoria Dock*, *The Green Mill Murder*, *Blood and Circuses*, *Ruddy Gore*, *Urn Burial*, *Raisins and Almonds*, *Death Before Wicket*, *Away with the Fairies*, *Murder in Montparnasse*, *The Castlemaine Murders*, *Queen of the Flowers*, *Death by Water*, *Murder in the Dark*, *A Question of Death: An Illustrated Phryne Fisher Treasury*, *Murder on a Midsummer Night* and, most recently, *Dead Man's Chest*. The books have recently been made into the ABC TV series 'Miss Fisher's Murder Mysteries'. She is also the author of a crime series featuring Corinna Chapman, baker and reluctant investigator; the first five novels of which are *Earthly Delights*, *Heavenly Pleasures*, *Devil's Food*, *Trick or Treat* and *Forbidden Fruit*. In addition, Kerry is the author of several books for young adults and the Delphic Women series. When she is not writing Kerry is an advocate in magistrates' courts for the Legal Aid Commission. She is not married, has no children and lives with a registered Wizard.

UNNATURAL HABITS

A Phryne Fisher Mystery

Kerry Greenwood

First published in 2012

Allen & Unwin
Sydney, Melbourne, Auckland, London

83 Alexander Street
Crows Nest NSW 2065 Australia
Phone:(61 2) 8425 0100
Email:info@allenandunwin.com
Web:www.allenandunwin.com

Cataloguing-in-Publication details are available
from the National Library of Australia
www.trove.nla.gov.au

ISBN 978 1 74237 243 3

Set in 11.5/14 pt Adobe Garamond by Bookhouse, Sydney
Printed in Australia by McPherson's Printing Group

10 9 8 7 6 5 4 3 2 1

The paper in this book is FSC® certified.
FSC® promotes environmentally responsible, socially beneficial and economically viable management of the world's forests.

All names in this book are fictional. No real person was intended. If someone has actually been named, it is a fault of my impoverished imagination.

This novel is dedicated to my sister Janet. My hero. Sisterhood is powerful.

With thanks to David, an angel in wombat form. Jenny P and Ika, Helen, Jan and Henry Gordon-Clark, my formidable researcher Jean Greenwood, Michael Warby of the keen historical mind and refusal to be defeated by the guardians of any hidden store of documents, Susan Tonkin, who outfaced the National Library to obtain the only extant copy of *The Woman Worker*, and the Bacchus Marsh Historical Society.

But man, proud man,
Drest in a little brief authority,
Most ignorant of what he's most assured,
His glassy essence, like an angry ape,
Plays such fantastic tricks before high Heaven,
As would make the angels weep.

William Shakespeare
Measure for Measure

CHAPTER ONE

'Do you believe in clubs for women, Uncle?'
'Yes, but only after every other method of quieting them has failed.'

Punch cartoon,
1890

The attack came suddenly. Out of the hot darkness in the notorious Little Lon came three thugs armed with bicycle chains. The tallest lashed his against the crumbling side of a building. It hit a metal sign advertising Dr Parkinson's Pink Pills for Pale People, which rang like a drum.

'An ominous noise,' commented Dr Elizabeth MacMillan.

'The natives are restless,' agreed her companion. She was the Hon. Miss Phryne Fisher, five feet two with eyes of green and black hair cut into a cap. They were not the target of this assault. They were blamelessly approaching the Adventuresses Club bent on nothing more controversial than a White Lady (Phryne) and a dram of good single malt (Dr MacMillan) and an evening's exchange of views on weather, politics and medicine. But Little Lonsdale Street was always liable to provide unexpected experiences.

However, the person who was fated for a good shellacking appeared to be lone, female and unprotected, which could not be allowed. Phryne turned abruptly on her Louis heel and, putting both fingers in her mouth, whistled shrilly.

'Look out, boys!' she yelled. 'Cops!'

Usually, this was a sound strategy. As police always entered Little Lonsdale Street in parties of four, the thugs would be outnumbered. It was just their bad luck, this evening, that they were led by a foolhardy tough with no sense of self-preservation. News like Phryne got around. He should have recognised her. But instead of a tactical withdrawal, he swung the chain again and struck a sign advertising Castlemaine Bacon (none finer). He advanced on Phryne and the doctor. She looked at her companion.

'You can't say I didn't give them a chance to get away,' said Phryne apologetically.

Dr MacMillan waved a Scottish hand. 'You did,' she admitted.

Phryne raised an arm and made a circling movement. Men dressed in blue cotton appeared out of the darkness. They fell on the chain wielder and his satellites. To the noise of crunching bone and flesh hitting walls and pavement, Phryne and the doctor walked through the lesson (do not attack the concubine of our master Lin Chung unless you have a tank and a Lewis Gun and probably not then) and spoke to the intended victim, who was still cowering against a dustbin with her arms protecting her face.

'Hello,' said Phryne. 'Did they hurt you?'

'Didn't get started,' said the victim in a cultured voice. Not a working girl, then. 'What did you do with them?'

'Over there.' Phryne directed her attention to the melee, which had almost resolved into three untouched Chinese men and a heap of damaged thugs, groaning for burial or at least a stiff drink and a few bandages. The young woman boggled at the sight.

'Who are the Chinks?'

Phryne winced. 'The Chinese,' she said coldly. 'They follow me when I wander around this bit of the city. Their master is concerned for my safety. Not that I cannot look after myself. What have you done to attract this kind of attention, I wonder?'

'Asking too many questions,' replied the girl. She was small and plump. Her hair was shingled as short as the doctor's and her clothes were expensive. And not what they had been, sartorially.

'Always unwise in Little Lon. Can we offer you a drink and a new pair of stockings? I'm Phryne Fisher, and this is Doctor MacMillan of the Queen Victoria Hospital, and our club is just over there.'

'Oh, Miss Fisher!' the young woman gasped. She pinkened. 'Of course. Thank you! I am a bit of a wreck.'

Phryne caught the eye of the blue-clad warriors. She bowed with both hands pressed together in front of her breast and indicated the stone entrance of the Adventuresses Club. They nodded and bowed deeply in turn.

'Of course, having a bodyguard does endow one with a certain insouciance in dealing with the denizens of Little Lon,' Phryne told the girl. 'Might we know your name?'

'Oh, sorry. Kettle,' said the young woman. 'Margaret Kettle—but everyone calls me Polly. I'm a reporter.'

'You are not, I understand, hoping to write any stories about this club?' demanded Dr MacMillan.

'No!' protested Polly. 'No, certainly not, that was not what brought me to Little Lon.'

'Lips sealed?' asked Phryne.

'Buttoned,' promised Polly earnestly. She could see her drinks and her stockings vanishing just as she thought that they were hers. And she really needed a drink. Gently brought-up girls seldom met thugs in noisome alleys and she was shaken.

'All right, then. My guest, Molly,' Phryne told the female giant sitting in the porter's chair. 'Bung over the book and I'll sign her in. Quiet night?'

'Until you got here,' grinned Molly. 'I expect cops'll be along to scrape up the remains soon. Better get inside before anyone starts asking questions.'

They ascended the stairs. Outside, a ragged boy settled down under the verandah. He attracted no attention whatsoever, except from Molly, who gave him a pie left over from her dinner. It was a good pie, though he did not eat it with the golloping ferocity of the truly starved. But he ate it. It was a good pie.

Phryne watched Dr MacMillan settle Miss Kettle into a padded chair while she ordered drinks and a brief lease on the Withdrawing Room. This was kept supplied with first-aid equipment and the means for repairing or replacing clothes, plus emergency brandy and a young woman who could be summoned for comforting the bereaved or supplying new garments, whichever was required. Her name tonight was Annie. She thought this the best job she had ever had, as emergencies were not common in the club. Annie spent most of her time in the kitchen, being fed tidbits by the cooks and drinking as much tea as she could hold. Summoned, she conducted Miss Kettle into the Withdrawing Room. There she sat the reporter down, sponged the mud of Little Lon off her knees and palms, provided her with new hosiery, and allowed her to wash her face and comb her hair while Annie attended to her clothes.

Polly Kettle had not been so tended since she was six and had fallen out of a tree which she had been expressly forbidden to climb. She drank her sal volatile, her hot sugared tea and then her brandy obediently. Annie smiled at her.

'There you are, Miss; no harm done,' she told the patient. 'I just caught up the split seam and put back the hem.' She surveyed Polly critically. 'You'll do.'

'Thank you,' murmured Polly, in a medicated haze. 'Are you a ladies' maid?'

'No, Miss, they call me an attendant,' said Annie. Polly saw that she was a meagre underfed creature, perhaps eighteen years old, with a scarred face. No one else, perhaps, would employ her. There were plenty of unemployed girls. Annie noticed her look.

'Burns,' she explained. 'I fell into the fire when I was a child.'

'Do you like working here?' asked Polly, her reporter's instinct asserting itself.

Annie broke into a pleased smile, strangely distorted by the scars. 'Oh, yes, Miss, the ladies are very kind, the pay is good, and no one objects to the way I look.' She opened the door to admit Polly again to the Sitting Room. Polly went where directed, still bemused.

Dr MacMillan and Phryne Fisher were ensconced by an open window. Phryne was sipping from a frosted glass. Polly licked her lips.

'Come and have a drink,' invited Phryne. 'And if you sit there you will share our cooling breeze. What would you like?'

'Gin and tonic, please,' said Polly. 'Thank you so much for looking after me.'

'Not at all.' Phryne waved her unoccupied hand. 'We are expecting you to enthral us. Serena, a G and T for Miss Kettle, if you please.'

Serena obliged, and minutes later Polly was clutching a frosted glass of her own.

'Now,' said Phryne cosily, as she drew Polly down to sit next to her, 'do tell!'

'Girls are going missing from the Magdalen Laundry at the Abbotsford convent,' said Polly. Her hearers failed to gasp or exclaim. Polly, a little disappointed, took a deep gulp of her drink. It was strong and shocked a little pink into her pale cheeks.

'Yes?' prompted Phryne.

'Three of them so far. Mary O'Hara, Jane Reilly, Ann Prospect. Sent out to stay with a pious widow in Footscray and vanished.'

'Not just run away? I would, if I was sent to a pious widow,' said Phryne.

'Pregnant,' said Polly baldly, disdaining euphemism. 'Very pregnant. Within a month of delivery. The pious widow runs a nursing home in Footscray. My newspaper's Mr Bates interviewed her and she was unable to tell him what had happened to the girls, or why they should run away when they were so close to their time. Ann Prospect has relatives. They have not heard from her. The same for the others. No one has heard from them. The police are not interested.'

'But you are?' asked the doctor.

'I am,' said Polly.

'Why?'

'I'm a reporter,' said Polly defiantly. 'I work for the *Daily Truth*. They only want female reporters to write about fashion and food and babies and turn in reports of flower shows (getting all the names correct). I want a scoop.'

'In order to prove to your proprietor that you are a real reporter?' asked Phryne.

'Yes!' said Polly.

'A laudable ambition,' said Phryne.

'No one cares about bad girls!' Polly burst out indignantly. 'They make one mistake and they are shut up in the laundry doing hard work. Their babies are adopted out. They are ruined. We ought to have got beyond that. What use is freedom—they told us that we fought that war for freedom—when the women are still punished and the men go on to seduce another girl?'

'Indeed,' said the doctor gravely.

'The cops told me that they had just run away to go on the street,' said Polly. 'Who is going to buy your body when you are eight months pregnant? It's ridiculous.'

'Certainly,' said Phryne. 'Have you enquired at the morgue?'

'The morgue?' Polly took another gulp of her drink.

'Well, the three girls are either dead or somewhere else, alive. That is the first thing you need to ascertain. I believe that there is a register of unclaimed bodies. Then, if they are not there, you need to ask at various hospitals. You keep a proper account of your patients, Elizabeth, do you not?'

'Of course,' said Dr MacMillan. 'Come to the front desk and I will arrange for you to search the records. Of course, some of our patients do not use their real names. We discourage this but we understand it.'

'That is . . . very kind of you,' faltered Polly. Life was becoming extremely real at present, she thought.

'And I will ask about who sent your assailants,' said Phryne. She finished her drink and sauntered out. Polly looked at Dr MacMillan, who seemed reassuringly normal.

'Does she mean to go and . . .'

'She does,' said the doctor comfortably.

'Is she always like that?' asked Polly.

'When she was sixteen she was an ambulance driver on the Western Front. I don't think she's been daunted by anything since then,' the doctor told her. 'She flew me into Hebridean crofts during the flu epidemic when she had to land on shingle and strand with sea on one side and cliff on the other and never turned a hair. Miss Fisher is a force of nature and there is never anything you can do about her. Have another drink and appreciate the show. That's what I do. I wonder, now, could any of your girls be at the Queen Vic? Do you have a description of each of them—or, better yet, a photo?'

'They were photographed when they entered the care of the convent,' said Miss Kettle, still bemused. 'I have them here.'

'Show me,' said Dr MacMillan. 'There will be a reasonable explanation, I'm sure enough of that.'

'And if there isn't?' asked Polly.

'Then we will hand the matter over to Miss Fisher,' said the doctor, sipping her whisky. 'She's very good at the irrational.'

'Oh,' said Polly.

'But none of this is for publication without our permission,' added Dr MacMillan severely. 'Death may be a public matter, but birth is a female mystery. What was your last line of enquiry, m'dear?'

'Brothels,' said Polly, eschewing euphemism again.

The doctor seemed unmoved. 'Few brothels would employ women in their last trimester of pregnancy.'

'Yes, that's why I wondered if . . . They say there are brothels that have special interests. You know, boys, small children, women with one leg, that sort of thing.'

'The depth of male depravity is indeed bottomless,' said Dr MacMillan. 'And after thirty years in the medical profession nothing now astounds me about evil and the temptations of the devil. But I suspect that I would have heard of such a place. And I haven't.'

Polly had never met anyone like the doctor—or Phryne. Among women of her nice respectable middle class she herself was considered unacceptably bold and even immoral for insisting on a career which did not include reporting on garden parties. Next to her was a group of ladies discussing strange tribal rites in New Guinea. And others were talking about a durbar where the elephants had got drunk and fallen over while curtseying to the governor. And a further group, rather elevated by cocktails, wondered aloud whether taking a lover is permissible only after one's husband has acquired a mistress, or if one could venture on a suitable man before, if the occasion seemed to warrant it. She took refuge in her drink.

Dr MacMillan was examining the three photographs. She put on her wire-framed glasses and stared.

'No, can't recall seeing any of them,' she commented. 'Plain girls, aren't they? Not good prostitute material, though given those dreadful smocks and difficult situation I suppose they cannot look their best. The brothel market is rather overcrowded at present, you know. Employment is hard to get, even in the pickle factories and the dangerous trades, and so many young men didn't come home from the Great War. Girls who would have expected to marry some respectable tradesman will find no candidates except amongst the damaged and ruined, and that really only exchanges one set of cares for another. They have to work, but female wages are still much lower than men's, as though all of them were just finding a little piecework for pin money, not struggling for survival. So brothels are only accepting the young and pretty and winning. The poor drabs on the street are having a parlous time, I fear. They don't last long.'

Polly was shocked. Fortunately Phryne returned before she had time to burst into tears at the cruelty of female fate.

Miss Fisher was giggling. 'Miss Kettle, did you really ask about pregnant girls in the Blue Cat Club?' she said, sitting down and crooking a finger at the bartender for another White Lady.

'Yes, I heard they had strange tastes,' explained Polly. Phryne patted her hand.

'Yes, indeed, but exclusively male. You have been followed around town tonight by at least three fascinated observers, all watching, I fear, to see which of them was going to get you. The Blue Cat is far too soigné and careful of their manicures to inflict violence, luckily. But two others were dangerous. I should not go anywhere near Corsican Joe's in the near future. The far future, either. Or Madame Paris. I shall talk to her. It was the Corsican's men who tried to beat you. I am fairly confident that they will not attempt that again. And I will take to you meet Madame Paris in due course, if you like. But your enquiries need to go in another direction.'

'Why?' asked Polly. 'And why are you helping me?'

'Well, darling, one does not like to watch a nice little woolly baa-lamb go leaping and gambolling into a field full of large bitey wolves. It has a certain morbid interest, I agree,' said Phryne, sipping deeply. 'But it is basically a blood sport and I don't even like fox-hunting.' She gestured to the photos Dr MacMillan was holding. 'Have you seen the girls, Elizabeth?'

'Not a one,' said the doctor.

'I thought as much. One of the Corsican's little pals mentioned that there is some sort of farm where pregnant whores have been sent. It sounds like it might be dire. Since even Lin Chung's minions couldn't get anything more out of him, I suspect that is the extent of his knowledge. Asking around,' warned Phryne, 'will be perilous.'

'I don't care,' said Polly stoutly, buoyed by company and gin. 'I'm a reporter with a name to make.'

'Up to you,' shrugged Phryne.

'A little advice?' suggested the doctor.

'Yes, of course,' said Polly.

'Sew your name and address into your undergarments,' said Dr MacMillan. She observed Polly's look of incomprehension and did not smile.

'Makes it easier to identify your body,' explained Phryne. 'Assuming that they don't strip you naked, of course. Perhaps a tattoo might be better,' she added.

'Yes, dear, but think of the trouble when you changed addresses,' objected the doctor.

Suddenly it was all too much. Polly rose, straightened her new stockings, took her leave, and left. Phryne and Dr MacMillan exchanged a speaking glance.

'How long do you give her?' asked the doctor in her soft, exact Edinburgh voice.

'Maybe a week,' said Phryne, signalling for another drink.

'Perhaps two,' agreed Elizabeth MacMillan. 'Be generous. Now, tell me about your new bathroom.'

'I have a malachite bath,' said Phryne. 'And I have acquired another follower.'

'Indeed?'

'Tinker,' said Phryne. 'Apprentice detective. Here for six months on trial. From Queenscliff. He appointed himself my acolyte. Wants to be a cop. Father's a sailor, he's from a big hungry fishing family. Eldest child. About fourteen, I think.'

'A likely lad?'

'Many abilities, but he's finding it hard to settle down in my house.'

'Too big?' asked the doctor.

'Too female,' said Phryne. 'But he's only been here a week. We shall see.'

'Indeed we shall,' said the doctor, and sipped her single malt.

Phryne started the great Hispano-Suiza with a roar which would have startled Little Lon if it was liable to be startled, which it wasn't. Alarums and excursions were commonplace and a large engine could not compete with the crowd exiting from Little Chow's all-night cafe to settle a small difference of opinion with broken bottles and bricks. To the merry accompaniment of crunches, shrieks and thuds, Phryne drove decorously enough out of Little Lon and on to St Kilda Road, heading for home in the two am chill of a hot day. Not even a tram on the wide stretches of the highway. Presently she spoke aloud.

'You can come out now,' she said. She heard a muffled curse behind her and suppressed a smile.

'How'd you smoke me, Guv'nor?' complained Tinker. 'I was real careful.'

'Next time you are being real careful, do not stand entirely still. Entire stillness doesn't happen in nature. Just practise melting into the landscape, as though you are a tree. Besides, the porter told me about you. Why are you following me, Tink?'

'Are you mad at me, Guv?' he asked.

'No, just curious.'

'Can't sleep inside,' confessed the boy. 'It's too . . .' He groped for a word which would not be insulting to his benefactor. 'Too womany.'

'I thought that might be the case.'

'And it's not as though they ain't nice to me, but I don't belong. There's Miss Ruth and Mrs Butler in the kitchen and Miss Jane in the library and Mr Butler in the pantry and you and Miss Dot upstairs and me nowhere . . .'

'I see,' said Phryne.

There was a long silence as St Kilda passed under the streetlights. Tinker ventured, 'You gonna sack me, Guv'nor?'

'No, I'm going to give you a little house of your own,' said Phryne. 'Now if you will be so kind as to get out and open the gate so that I can drive in, we will fix this right now.'

Tinker, mouth agape, did as ordered. Phryne entered her own bijou dwelling, picked up an electric torch and led the boy straight through the house, out of the back door, and into the garden. This had been laid out by Camellia, the wife of Phryne's Chinese lover, Lin Chung. It had jasmine bowers and bamboo fences. It smelt, in the cool darkness, bewitching.

'Shed,' said Phryne, very quietly. Tinker looked.

It was a small stoutly constructed building in which a previous inhabitant had been wont to indulge a diseased passion for fretwork. It had carpenter's tools hung on the wall, a stout bench and block for cutting wood, and a lot of sawdust on the floor. One window. One door, which could be shut. Tinker stood in the darkness and inhaled the scent of cut wood and realised that he could hear the sea. It was not the roar of the real ocean, to which he had been born and had heard all his life. It was the half-hearted lazy slopping ashore of the bay. But it was the sea and he released a breath which he had not known he had been holding. For about a week, it seemed to Tinker. He put a hand on the wall to steady himself.

Phryne said nothing. She played the light around the unlined walls and the dusty floor.

'Yes?' she said.

'Oh, yair,' replied Tinker fervently.

'Then it's yours. Tomorrow you can sweep up a little and move in some furniture. Or you can sleep on the ground, if that suits. Now we are going inside for the sandwiches which Mrs B always leaves for me and I seldom eat, and then you are going to bed in the house. All right?'

Tinker did not know what to say. This angel, this goddess, had broken open his prison doors and given him a priceless gift. His own place. No more listening to Miss Jane talking about mathematics, no more feeling like an awkward lump always in the way in the kitchen. No more sitting gingerly on the edge of the sofa hoping he wouldn't break something.'

He did not know what to say and had never hugged anyone. He extended a grimy, calloused hand. 'Thanks,' he said, and Phryne shook, gravely.

Phryne woke to the noise of activity downstairs. Not the usual late-breakfast preparation-for-lunch buzz and occasional clank in the kitchen, but thuds of furniture being moved. Tinker had relayed her instructions and someone was trying to move something heavy—a cast-iron bed frame, perhaps—without making any noise. This was not working. Phryne put out a hand and pulled a bell rope. Dot appeared as though summoned up on a breath of sea wind.

'Going to be a nice day,' she said, putting down the tray on which reposed Miss Fisher's Greek coffee, roll and butter, and the little pot of Seville orange marmalade which she favoured. Phryne sat up in bed.

'Good morning,' she said. 'I gather that Tinker is moving his furniture?'

'Yes, Miss, he said you told him he could have the shed. I've given it a good sweep out. But he won't let us decorate it at all. He was real short with Jane offering him books and Ruth saying she could find him some paint. Just the hessian lining is good enough for him, he says, and we only just got him to accept a bed to sleep in. Not even curtains.' Dot sounded mortified. 'People will think we're mistreating him.'

'Two points,' said Phryne, reaching for the coffee. 'One, if the nice ladies from Children's Protection come around, refer them to me. And, two, it's what Tinker needs. Everyone will be more comfortable with him sleeping in the shed, especially him. Make a note to buy another bed for the spare room. And ask him if he would like electric light or a hurricane lamp. He'll be safe enough; he's used to them. He'll be wanting to read, I hope.' She took another sip of the life-giving fluid. 'It will be all right, Dot, I promise. Lovely day, you said?'

'Yes, Miss,' said Dot, accepting the orders with great relief. It would be nice to have someone guarding the back gate. It would also be nice—though she hated to admit it, it seemed so uncharitable—to have Tinker out of the house, where he was so awkward and uncomfortable that he disrupted the peaceful routine which Mr and Mrs Butler had imposed on Phryne's rather chaotic life. Dot liked routine. It made her feel safe. It wasn't as though Tinker wasn't a good boy, Dot was sure, at bottom. He was respectful, cheerful, likely to be of great use to Miss Fisher. But he was so patently a boy. Not a man like Phryne's friends or Mr Butler; a boy, and he disturbed the girls. He didn't know how to treat them, although he had sisters, he said. Also he hadn't got used to the length of his arms and legs, so he knocked things off tables, tripped over rugs, and broke china, which upset Mrs Butler. He was alternately cheeky and depressed. And that made Dot feel that she should do something to help him, having little brothers of her own. It was clear that the family were getting on Tinker's nerves as much as he was getting on theirs. The whole house had been uneasy since his advent.

Much better, Dot considered, that he should have a refuge in the shed. When he felt like joining the family, he would probably be better company.

There was a loud crunch as the bed frame was squeezed though the back door, a cry of triumph from Tinker, and a grunt from Mr Butler. Phryne smiled and ate her roll.

Dot handed her the hairbrush and Phryne got out of bed and stood herself before the big mirror, garlanded with art deco vines in green enamel and gilt. There was Miss Fisher, a pale oval face, red lips in a cupid's bow, green eyes staring directly at her reflection, doll-like except for the decisiveness in the bone structure. Behind her stood Dot, mousy, in her favourite shade of brown with her hair in a long plait wound round her head; devout, delightful, and always a little worried about Phryne. Phryne blew a kiss to her own reflection and put down the brush. Her short black hair, snipped into a bobby-cut, was as shiny as a crow's feather.

'Bath,' she said, and went into her new bathroom. It was magnificent. The bath was made of green malachite. The walls were scarlet. Dot thought the whole thing very garish. Bathrooms ought to be white, or at the most a very pale pink or blue. But, she had to admit, it suited Phryne's flamboyant personality. Dot made sure that there were sufficient moss-green bath sheets and went downstairs to see what domestic disasters had occurred while she was away. Behind her, Phryne lifted up her voice in one of her favourite bath songs, 'My Canary Has Circles Under His Eyes'.

Dot smiled. It was pleasant to be home.

By the time Phryne descended to the main house, the move had been accomplished. Tinker had allowed that he had got used to sleeping in a bed, so he had his iron one, and bedding. The sawdust had been swept out of his little home and he had nailed a flour sack across the window to provide privacy. All of the rest of his possessions reposed on the carpenter's bench. Sexton Blake novels, string, stones, shells, fishhooks stuck in a cork, a magnifying glass, matches, a notebook, a pencil, useful bits of wire. His hurricane lamp was filled and trimmed. Phryne surveyed Tinker's domain, smiled, and held out a heavy wrought-iron key.

'No one will come in, Tink, but you have to put your sheets and dirty clothes into the laundry basket on Wednesday night, and remake the bed yourself. New shirt and underwear every day, remember. I shall have this checked. And a wash every night and a bath at least every week. You can use the Butlers' bathroom.'

'Can't I wash in the sea?' asked Tinker, who was used to Queenscliff and its clean waters. He had gone for a swim every morning since he could walk.

'No,' Phryne told him. 'Walking naked into those waters might expose you to unpleasant things, the least of which is prosecution for public indecency. You can go swimming when we buy you a suitable costume. Sorry, Tinker, it's indoors and fresh water for your ablutions. Agreed?'

'Agreed, Guv,' said Tinker, and received the key as though it were a medal. He had never known a space which was his own. He would have agreed to any conditions. Washing, though he was at a loss to understand why the guv'nor thought it was so important, was a minor concession.

'But keep your raggedy clothes separate. They smell just right. You may need them for my investigations.'

'Right you are, Guv,' said Tinker.

'And Mr Butler will give you a key for the back door when he has another cut. Just in case you need to come in during the night.'

Phryne wondered how Tinker would like isolation, now that he had it, and was gracefully providing a refuge in case Tinker found himself subject to night terrors. He had lived in extremely cramped conditions all his life and might find privacy threatening, in the black night of a strange garden. He just said, 'Thanks,' and vanished into the shed. Phryne heard him testing the lock.

'Good,' she said to the door, and went inside for a cup of tea and a ginger biscuit and the accumulated mail, which overflowed the silver salver on which Mr Butler presented it. Dot joined her in the sea-green parlour, bringing her embroidery. Phryne slit envelopes and discarded letters into a wastepaper basket.

'Rubbish,' she commented over the noise of crumpling. 'Dross. Invitations to events long past. Appeals for charities.'

'Nothing interesting?' enquired Dot, stitching a boronia flower.

'This one is from the Socialist Women,' said Phryne. 'And here is an art show which might be intriguing; proceeds to go to feeding the unemployed. Here is my copy of *The Woman Worker*. That is always worth reading. Invitation to a levee at the . . . damn. I wasn't expecting any callers. I wonder who that can be?'

The doorbell had chimed. Mr Butler paced to the door with magisterial speed. Phryne listened. She was not in the mood for entertaining visitors. However, this one was admitted without delay. Few people had automatic entrée to Phryne's house. She stood up to shake hands with her favourite policeman.

'Jack dear,' she greeted him. 'What brings you here on such a clement day?'

John 'call me Jack, everyone does' Robinson looked glum. This was his usual expression. He was a tallish man with an instantly forgettable face which had served him well in his career. Even people he had repeatedly arrested didn't really remember what he looked like, which allowed him to arrest them again. He sat down heavily in the offered chair and accepted, unusually for him before lunch, Mr Butler's offer of a whisky and soda as well as tea. Phryne diagnosed a particularly difficult case, probably involving society people, which had compelled him, much against his inclination, to ask for Miss Fisher's help.

'You interfered in a fight in Little Lon last night,' he said to Phryne.

'Certainly. Some nasty people were about to beat a young woman reporter. An action in very bad taste. Why do you ask about it? Has someone had the nerve to complain?'

'No, though two of them thugs are still in hospital. Said they were routed by some Chinks. Nothing to do with you, Miss Fisher,' said Jack meaningly; he knew all about Miss Fisher's bodyguard. 'It's the victim.'

'Polly Kettle? What about her?'

'She's been kidnapped,' said Jack, and gulped down the whisky and soda in one draught.

CHAPTER TWO

All successful newspapers are ceaselessly querulous and bellicose. They never defend anyone or anything if they can help it; if the job is forced upon them, they tackle it by denouncing something or someone else.

HL Mencken
Prejudices, First Series

'Oh, dear,' said Phryne. 'So soon.'

'What?' asked Robinson.

'I mean, she was pursuing a very perilous line of enquiry and appeared to have the sense of self-preservation of a chocolate Easter egg in a blast furnace. Dr MacMillan and I gave her very low odds of surviving. Even so I expected her to last longer than this.'

'What was she trying to find out?'

'What had happened to three girls who absconded from a nursing home just before they were due to give birth.'

'Yes, they were reported missing. By Mrs Ryan, the woman who runs the home. Bit of a harridan but very religious.'

'Did Polly speak to her?' asked Phryne.

Jack sipped at his tea and reached for one of the ginger biscuits.

'Yes. Interviewed her. Looks like the girls all took off together. Though they might not have stayed together. None of their families have heard from them. Though they wouldn't expect to; very traditional families, turned their daughters' pictures to the wall and cast them from their door, the mean bastards. Sorry, Miss Fisher.'

'I couldn't agree with you more,' Phryne told him.

'Miss Kettle talked to Mrs Ryan, told her that she was going to the morgue to look at the unclaimed bodies, which we had already done and they ain't there. Then Mrs Ryan's son Patrick saw three men grab Miss Kettle and shove her into a big black car and that's the last anyone has heard from her.'

'I see,' said Phryne. 'What do you make of Patrick?'

'Big bruiser, not too bright. Idle. Bludger. Lives off his mum and probably steals from her. But she dotes on him. The father took off for Adelaide years ago. Dead, now. The grog got him. He's her only child. Doubt he has enough imagination to make anything up.'

'No other description of the car but big and black?'

'No, he doesn't know anything about cars.'

'Or the men?'

'Men in suits wearing hats. Average size, medium build, wasn't close enough to see their faces.'

'Ah, the perfect witness.'

'Yeah. Trouble is, I hear that Miss Kettle had been asking around all the . . . er . . . houses . . . about the missing girls. That wasn't wise. Any of them might have resented it and wanted to shut her mouth. I haven't got the time or the manpower to investigate all the brothels in Melbourne. Sorry, Miss Dot.'

Dot nodded. She knew the term.

'So you want me to enquire and expose myself to the same danger?' asked Phryne teasingly.

Jack Robinson bridled, which is difficult to do sitting down with a teacup in your hand. But he managed it.

'You won't be in any danger,' he protested. 'Everyone knows about you.'

'Do they? And what do they know about me?' asked Phryne.

'That you're not to be trifled with,' said Robinson. 'Look, this is really unofficial and if you don't want to do it I'll understand.'

'Oh, I didn't say that,' said Phryne. 'I liked Miss Kettle. I'll start with talking to her editor. He might know what she was intending to do. Then, perhaps, the convent where the girls had been working. Dot will accompany me there so I don't offend any local religious rules. Then the pious widow. Then—a few of the more strong-minded businessmen. But I fear, Jack dear, that all I will ascertain is that poor Miss Kettle is no longer with us.'

'Just find the body,' said Jack callously. 'Then we can take her off the books. My boss is going crook at the number of open files. And while you're at it, you can find those girls, too. If you can spare the time.'

'Piece of cake, Jack dear. And with my other hand . . . Oh, by the way,' said Phryne artlessly, 'how did you know about that attack in Little Lon? There were no cops around while it was happening. I didn't see any, at least.'

'Information received,' said Jack Robinson. He wilted a little under Phryne's gaze. 'We were keeping an eye out for that girl,' he admitted. 'She was getting into dangerous waters.'

'Yes, seriously shark-infested,' agreed Phryne. 'Huge, swarming, heavily toothed sharks. Where did she go after she left the Adventuresses Club?'

'Home,' said Robinson. 'As far as I know.'

'So she was abducted this morning from Mrs Ryan's house,' said Phryne.

'Yes. About eight. Here's the address and all. I hope you can find her before . . .' Jack did not complete the sentence. 'Of course, we've got alerts out for her. But we've got nothing to go on. You might have more luck.'

'I hope so,' said Phryne.

The conversation continued amicably. Jack Robinson's orchids were blooming fabulously in the still-hot summer. Phryne told him about the treasure hunt at Queenscliff. When he arose to take his leave he was a more contented policeman.

'Well,' said Phryne. 'Ring my sister Eliza, if you please, Dot, and ask her and Lady Alice to lunch. I need her insight into the Unfortunate class. If she says yes, warn Mrs B there will be two extra at the table. And then come upstairs. This is going to be intriguing. What does one wear to talk to an editor?'

Mr Trevelyan was a much tried man. The exigencies of getting his paper out every day had thinned his greying hair and furrowed his brow and, by the redness of his nose, either ruined his digestion or driven him to the bottle for consolation. The last thing he needed, he conveyed, was an aristocratic visitor to ruin his day further.

But he was relatively polite, asking Phryne to be seated, removing some spills and files so that she could do so, before offering tea and asking her business.

'Miss Kettle,' said Phryne. She had chosen a light green suit and a primrose silk shirt for her encounter with the fourth estate, with a matching spring green hat. 'She's been abducted. I'm looking for her. Have you any idea what she was working on?'

'Polly Kettle! That girl is a nuisance! I've already had the police here, two reporters out sick after that banquet last night, and the printers screaming for copy.'

'Your life is hard,' sympathised Phryne.

'No one knows what an editor's life is like,' complained Mr Trevelyan, inspired by her unexpected kindness. 'Reporters and printers and newsboys asking for more money, all of them with their grubby hands in my pockets, and scarce worth trying because I'm just breaking even—and that's on a good day. Kettle wanted to be an Ace Newshound. Good ambition for a young man, not so good for a young woman. There are places where she can't go. I told her that. I told her! Places where she would be in danger.'

'And danger seems to have hold of her,' said Phryne.

'So the cops said.' Mr Trevelyan had the grace to look momentarily sorry. 'She didn't tell me anything about what she was working on. She did her garden parties and her cooking column and her society news and then she went waltzing out on some frolic of her own.'

'You didn't guess anything about her line of enquiry?'

'Girls missing. Nothing unusual in that, not in this city.'

'Could she have left any notes?'

'We can look,' said the editor. He led the way out of his small crowded Spencer Street office into a large crowded Spencer Street newsroom. Desks were set at random across the floor, surrounded by balls of paper which had missed the wastepaper baskets. Several people were working hard, as is common in the presence of the editor. Copyboys and copygirls stood poised to run written pieces off to the typists or down to the printers in the basement. The grimy windows looked out onto a cheerful view of the railway shunting yards. People were shouting into telephones, scribbling notes, demanding tea, and tearing pages out of typewriters and crumpling them. It sounded just like a newsroom ought, Phryne considered. It smelt of ink, cigarette smoke and impatience. She was pleased. But it was no sort of environment for a delicate young woman, and Miss Kettle must have had a certain amount of fortitude to survive it. Even now a crippled man had dropped a crutch as he tried to stand up and was swearing the air blue. No one was rushing to help him.

Phryne found this interesting but the unimaginative repetition was getting on her nerves. Phryne admired inventive profanity. This was not original. She bent with a flash of garters which drew gasps from behind her, retrieved the crutch, shoved it neatly into its requisite armpit and said into the angry, snarling face, 'Be civil, or I shall provide you with a nursemaid, a spanking and a dummy. You should have grown out of this sort of tantrum when you were four years old. For shame. And there is a lady present,' she reminded him. 'In fact, me.'

Total silence fell. One of the copygirls said, 'Jeez,' in an awed voice. Then, one by one, the newsroom began to applaud.

Phryne bowed. The crippled man glared at her with furious eyes. Then, as the clapping went on, he turned and limped out of the room.

'It's not altogether his fault,' said a youngish man with a scarred face. 'He had a bad war.'

'So did you,' said Phryne. 'Flyer?' She had seen those flat, angry scars before. Aviators often had burnt faces.

'Not too bad. Had to ditch the old bus in the Channel and that put out the fire, d'you see? I was lucky. Still see out of both eyes. But he was army all along, spent four years in the trenches. Came back damaged. Left a leg somewhere on the Somme. Othello's occupation gone. He never wanted to be a reporter.

'But he's a bad-tempered bastard,' added the scarred man. 'And they say he also brought back his service revolver. Threatens to kill people all the time. No one's had the nerve to stand up to Sergeant Bates. Miss . . . ?'

'Fisher,' said Phryne. She held out her hand. 'Mr . . . ?'

'Downey,' said the youngish man. He pumped her hand enthusiastically. 'You're asking about Polly?'

'I am,' said Phryne. 'Does anyone know anything about her?'

'Nice girl,' said one older man, putting down his racing page. 'Ambitious. I reckon she had the stuff too. Was after a big story.'

'Anyone know what?'

'Her lips were sealed,' grinned Mr Downey. 'We've all been like that. Well, except for poor old Bates.'

Mr Trevelyan, in a hurry to get Miss Fisher out of his office, introduced his reporters.

Mr Coffin, also known as Zeno, racing and horses. Mr Thompson, crime beat. Mr Bates, senior reporter. Mr Downey, general news. Mr Pribble, political news. Mr Simpson, leaders and assistant editor. Mrs Simpson, advertising. Mr George, photography. Mrs Fiskin, in charge of the typing pool. Mrs Howard, fashion, food and home management. She was a thin middle-aged woman in a very fashionable suit who was noting down every detail of Miss Fisher's garments, shoes, hat, hairstyle and even leaned close enough to sniff at her scent.

Phryne bore this without complaint until Mrs Howard sniffed for the second time, then she said crisply, 'Floris Stephanotis, only available from London by mail order, suit and blouse by Madame Fleuri of Collins Street, shoes hand-made by the excellent Mr Lowenstein in Flinders Lane, hat by Firielle's on the Boul Mich, Paris, and the stockings are indeed pure silk. I decline to describe my undergarments in mixed company.'

'Not even if we say pretty please with sugar on it?' asked Mr Downey, entranced.

'Not even then,' Phryne told him firmly. Mrs Howard looked as abashed as a hardened fashion reporter can manage, which is to say, very slightly embarrassed.

'I'm so sorry, Miss Fisher, but you are quite famous, you know. I've never seen you close up. Only in the crowd, you know, at openings and bazaars and so on.'

'You may look all you like,' said Phryne generously. 'The back view is also rewarding.'

'My oath,' agreed Mr Downey, not quite sotto voce. He had been behind Phryne went she bent over to retrieve the crutch. She decided not to hear this remark but spoke to Mrs Howard instead.

'And, by the way, I quite agree with your last column. Hemlines are definitely going up.'

'You read my column?' gasped Mrs Howard, overcome.

'Of course,' said Phryne, who had once glimpsed it over Dot's shoulder in the morning room. 'Miss Kettle's notes?' she asked Mr Trevelyan.

Recalled to his duty, the editor indicated a desk and Phryne sat down in the chair. A mess of papers burdened the desk. Spills, she was told, from published articles. Cooking—a thrifty new recipe for shepherd's pie (more potato, less meat). Account of an azalea growers' conference with all the growers' names spelt correctly. An experiment in fruit growing in Bacchus Marsh. High tea with the lady mayoress in aid of charity, with another list of attendees. Phryne leafed through them. Nothing to the purpose. The fruit growers looked interesting because their spokesman was a woman whose name sounded vaguely familiar. Phryne kept that one. The drawers contained exactly what she expected them to contain. Pencils with their requisite sharpener, several leads from a propelling ditto, a new bottle of ink, a half-empty bottle of same, drawing pens, typewriter ribbon tangled beyond any but an Alexandrine solution, hairpins, a comb, a compact with Rachel *poudre de riz*. At the bottom were a couple of loose cough sweets which had stuck, in their immemorial way, to two rubber bands, an eraser and chain of paperclips. There was also a bottle opener, which hinted at office parties, a kit for repairing runs in stockings, a packet of Ladies' Travelling Necessities, and a bottle which proved to contain aspirin. Phryne summoned Mr Downey. He attended eagerly.

'Anything missing?' she asked.

Breathing in her scent, he leaned over the desk. 'No,' he said regretfully, hoping to prolong his contact with this delectable woman. 'Her notebook, of course. But she would have had that with her. Her notes on the missing girls would have been in that. No, our Polly played her cards close to her chest. I hope nothing's happened to her. Nice girl,' he said.

'How nice?' asked Phryne, her face very close to his.

He grinned. 'Not that nice,' he told her. 'I'm engaged.'

'Ah.' She stood up. 'Mr Trevelyan, thank you so much for your attention,' said Phryne. 'Can I borrow your Mr Downey for an hour or so? Just to guide me through the newspaper process,' she added.

'Half his luck,' said Mr Trevelyan, and opened the office door for his distinguished visitor and Mr Downey, who was trying to preserve a solemn countenance. And not succeeding very well.

Followed by whistles, Phryne left the office and led her captive out into Spencer Street.

'Where's your pub?' she asked.

'The Fleet Street, but you really can't go there,' he protested. 'Rough sort of place.'

'Watch me,' advised Phryne. He watched. Phryne walked through the doors of the Fleet Street as though she owned the freehold, and he followed her into the beer, cigarette smoke and sawdust fog. There was a chorus of cheers and whistles, followed by a strange silence. When he found Miss Fisher, she was sitting at the bar, had already ordered a gin and tonic, and the populace had decided that she was neither a whore nor an avenging wife and was engaged in wondering, as so many had wondered before them, who and what, exactly, she was. Mr Downey wondered the same thing.

He sat down next to her, planted his feet on the familiar brass rail, and ordered a beer. Barney the barman, a tough ex-boxer, brought it. On his face was the same astonishment that Mr Downey felt. He looked a question at Downey. Downey shrugged. Everyone went back to his beer and his own concerns. Phryne was too difficult a problem for this early in the day.

'That,' Phryne told him, 'is what usually happens. Assume the rules do not apply to you and they don't.'

'Impressive, Miss Fisher,' said Mr Downey.

'Thank you. Now tell me what you didn't want your editor to hear about Miss Kettle.'

'That obvious, was I?' he said ruefully.

'Only to the educated ear,' said Phryne, sipping. 'Excuse me,' she said to Barney. 'Can you take this back and mix me one with the real gin? The stuff out of a bottle marked "gin",' she clarified.

Barney, who was known for his ferocious suppression of bar brawls and his ability to bite off ears and remove crown caps with his teeth, took the glass without complaint, poured away the drink, and concocted a new one, using gin from a marked container and a new flask of tonic water with a yellow label.

Miss Fisher sipped and approved. 'Thank you so much,' she said graciously. 'Mr Downey?'

'You're amazing,' he commented. Then he recollected himself. 'Yes, you want to know about Miss Kettle. Our Polly was ambitious. She went after a story like a terrier after rats. She thought she was on to something with this missing-girls story. And she was right. No brothel is going to want girls in the pod. Something very nasty is going on. She might have been going to talk to the pious widow.'

'She did,' said Phryne. 'She was abducted outside her house by three men in a big black car.'

'Oh,' said Mr Downey. 'Then it sounds like she was indeed on to something. Her next appointment was with the convent. The Mother Superior. They run the Magdalen Laundry. But I doubt that Polly got to see her. Or that she'd get anything out of her if she did. And the girls didn't vanish from the convent . . .'

'Did Polly talk to the parents or relatives of the missing girls?'

'All of them. No family knows—or cares—where their erring daughter went. Or so Polly said. She was pretty wild about that. Called them cruel canting hypocrites.'

'Polite language considering what I might have said,' commented Miss Fisher.

'Yair, I can imagine. Just. Batesy used to pinch her notebook, you know, and read it. Never forgave her for stealing his story. Some coots really hold on to a grudge. Anyway, looks like someone resented her questions.'

'That means a trawl through the brothels,' sighed Phryne. 'Again.'

'Can I report on this?' he asked. 'I mean, private eye the Hon. Miss Fisher investigates missing news reporter?'

'Not yet,' said Phryne, laying a scented hand on his arm. 'But I promise that, should I find her, you shall have the scoop all for yourself.'

'Bonzer,' said Mr Downey.

The conversation strayed into other channels. Mr Downey's intended, Ariadne, seemed to be a model of girlish kindness, style and intelligence. The last was not a common desideratum. She was a solicitor's clerk, however. Not a reporter.

'One in the family is enough,' he said. 'And I need a wife who doesn't fret if she's left alone while I'm chasing a story. Give Ariadne a book and she's happy. Can't cook or housekeep worth a damn so we'll live in a serviced flat. We ought to be happy,' said Mr Downey.

Phryne thought that indeed they might. She finished her gin and tonic, paid her score, and went home for lunch. Polly's only enemy in the newsroom looked to be Mr Bates, who hated everyone. He would bear investigation.

CHAPTER THREE

Don't be afraid of cold meat . . . there are hundreds of appetising ways to serve it . . . some men like it, but cold mutton has wrecked many a happy home.

Blanche Ebbutt
Dont's for Wives

Lunch was going to be excellent, as usual. But Mrs Butler always made a special effort for Miss Fisher's sister Eliza and her titled companion. To the cold steak and kidney pies with homemade tomato sauce and green salad she added a potato salad of particular succulence, the sliced tomatoes and onions laced with olive oil which Miss Fisher liked, and egg and bacon pies made with their own eggs and Castlemaine Bacon (none finer).

Tinker, Jane and Ruth were to eat their lunch in the kitchen with the Butlers, as the conversation was likely to be of topics which nice young ladies should not discuss. Although they were confident that Phryne would tell them about it later, if she needed their help. They were reconciled and, in Tinker's case, relieved not to have to look to Jane for an indication of which fork to use.

The Hon. Miss Eliza Fisher had been flung out of her family, to her great relief, by a father unimpressed by her socialism (and he didn't even know about her devotion to Sappho). In Australia she had found many persons of like mind and also had set up house with her close companion, Alice Harborough, a woman who had relinquished her own title and dedicated her life to Doing Good among the lost, stolen and strayed. Melbourne had an ample supply of waifs. They were very happy.

But, Phryne thought, regrettably, frumps. She had never managed to persuade her sister into anything more becoming than the brightly printed shift dress she wore, made of cheap sea island cotton printed with macaws. Phryne was sure that no natural macaws, in themselves a brilliant bird, came in quite those shades of baby's bottom pink and shrieking green. The hat was orange straw, to add insult to injury. Lady Alice was no better, in washing blue with eye-watering yellow stripes. They had evidently attended the same sale at Coliseum Treadways. Phryne felt positively underdressed by comparison.

'Well, this is very nice,' observed her sister, after she had engulfed half a pie and a lot of salad. 'But to what do we owe the honour of this invitation?'

'The pleasure of your company, of course, and my need for some insight into the underworld.'

'For a lunch this sumptuous,' said Lady Alice, 'you have our undivided attention.'

'I am looking into the disappearance of three girls from a lying-in home sent there from the Abbotsford Convent,' said Phryne, 'and the kidnapping of a reporter who was trying to find out what happened to them. The reporter is a young woman with all the sense of self-preservation of a concussed dormouse. The girls were very pregnant, which rather rules out brothels, unless there is one which caters to very peculiar tastes.'

Lady Alice dabbed at her lips with her napkin. 'There are some of those,' she said. 'Base exploiters of the working class. Very young girls, or girls who can seem very young. One-legged women are strangely popular. Very fat women, too. And dwarves. The slang name for that house is the Freak Show, and it is. I suppose they are providing employment for women who might otherwise be homeless or in some institution. But I never heard of one which wanted women in . . . such a state. Have you, darling?'

Eliza swallowed her mouthful of potato salad. The only thing she envied about her sister's life was her employment of such a marvellous cook.

'No, never,' declared Eliza. 'Of course, no one has ever plumbed the depths of male depravity, but even for the male sex that seems extreme.'

'I agree,' said Lady Alice. 'You say they were at the convent?'

'Yes, the convent sent them to a lying-in home,' said Phryne, allowing Mr Butler to pour her another glass of South Australian riesling, which was young but rather sophisticated for its age.

'The only reason I can think of for them leaving before they gave birth is—'

'They wanted to keep their babies,' capped Eliza.

'Sorry?' asked Phryne, who had gone to considerable lengths to avoid the whole question of fertility.

'The convent will allow them to work there until they reach term,' explained Eliza. 'And will care for them when they give birth. But they never leave that convent with their babies. The baby is taken away and they never even see it, never hold it. It is adopted out as soon as it is born. Or kept in the orphanage, as there are so many spare children. These girls wanted to keep their children. While this is unusual, it is perfectly understandable. There are many women still in mourning for the babies they never saw.'

'They seem to have left their lying-in home together,' said Phryne.

'Which argues that they had somewhere to go,' said Lady Alice. 'Collectively. They must have had a destination.'

'Why do you think that?' asked Phryne. 'Do have some more wine.'

'Thank you, Mr Butler.' Lady Alice sipped deeply, her plain face distressed. 'Because otherwise they would have been found.'

'Not in hospital, not in the morgue,' Phryne confirmed.

'You see, then. They knew that once they went into labour at that place they would be helpless and their babies would be stolen. So they left as soon as they could.'

'And where would they go?'

Lady Alice thought about it, taking another celery curl and crunching it. But in a very aristocratic manner, as Dot observed. She took a celery curl herself and tried to eat it in the same way.

Finally Lady Alice answered, 'Do you know, dear, I haven't the faintest idea. Not to one of the shelters; they would do the same as the convent. And not as nicely. Certainly not to a . . . house of ill-repute. Not to their relatives?'

'No,' said Phryne. 'The police have enquired.'

'Then I really can't offer any advice,' said Lady Alice. 'Eliza?'

Eliza Fisher swallowed more egg and bacon pie. 'No,' she said regretfully. 'I can't think of anywhere either. And you'd think that if there was a shelter taking in pregnant girls, we would have heard of it.'

'There being so many,' agreed Lady Alice.

'And we haven't,' said Eliza. 'We have thought of starting one,' she added. 'But there is the expense, and I am running out of sapphires and I won't get my money from the family for some time.'

'And even then you will need something to live on,' Phryne pointed out. She believed in charity. Up to a point. Not if it deprived her of her house and her staff and her beautiful clothes and good food. That was taking virtue too far, she considered.

'Well, yes, there is that,' agreed Eliza. 'Now as we haven't been able to help with the girls, how about this reporter? When you say no sense of self-preservation, Phryne, how naive is she?'

'She asked Mr Featherstonehaugh at the Blue Cat if he was harbouring pregnant girls.'

There was a gale of laughter, which died away into crumb-spattering coughs. When Mr Butler had poured Miss Eliza a glass of water, and her lover had pounded her on the back, Phryne continued, 'And she threatened to set the police on Corsican Joe.'

Dot had never heard of this person, but she saw both dowdy ladies exchange significant looks.

'Oh, dear,' said Eliza.

'Quite,' said Phryne. 'She was abducted in a big black car from outside the lying-in home. By three big men, though that may be the witness's excuse for not doing a damn thing about it. Jack Robinson was not impressed by his valour.'

'Big black car,' mused Lady Alice. 'Do we know anyone with a big black car, my sweet?'

'There is the mayor,' said Eliza. 'Probably not him. Though I wouldn't put it past him, mind. But he'd never use his own car. Big black cars are not common. Most people prefer colours—like your red Hispano-Suiza, Phryne. I have a feeling that I have seen a big black car about . . . but I can't remember where. Sorry. I'll telephone if I can recall it.'

'Good. Then may I tempt you to a little lemon meringue pie?' asked Phryne.

'Always,' said Eliza.

Phryne left the lunch table to usher her visitors to the door feeling full but unsatisfied. If Lady Alice and Eliza didn't know of a shelter, then it didn't exist. Where, then, had those girls gone? Phryne picked up the telephone and ordered a notice to be put in the 'absent friends' column of both *The Age* and the *Daily News*. Then she sat down in her parlour. She got out her file and looked at their photographs. Mary O'Hara. Probably had blonde hair, pale skin, possibly blue eyes. Pretty. She looked like a child in her school uniform. Couldn't be more than fourteen years old. She checked the date of birth. Yes, barely fourteen. Julie Reilly was plump, brunette and possibly sentimental—she had the look of a girl who cherished lost dogs and rescued forlorn kittens. And Ann Prospect had a very firm chin and gaze to match. Nothing at all in common except that they were pregnant. And unmarried. And missing. Phryne sighed. She opened the police briefs and began to read.

Mary O'Hara. Characterised by her mother as a good girl, very fond of the children. She had—Lord help us—eleven siblings. Characterised by her father as a liar and a bad girl and good riddance. Interesting. Phryne took up the next file. Ann Prospect. Eighteen years old. A self-willed girl who worked in the pickle factory and turned over her wages to her father, as was only right, but objected to him spending her money on drink. Which was not her place. When found to be in a state of disgrace she refused the perfectly reasonable marriage offered to her and went to the convent saying very blasphemous things about the Church. Would not be welcomed back to her family's bosom. Sounded like a very prickly bosom, Phryne thought. She herself would not want to repose in it.

She looked at the last file. Julie Reilly. Seventeen. Studious. Had been very upset when her father refused to allow her to stay at school, though she had won a scholarship. She wanted to become a teacher. Instead her father had required her to work in the woollen mills. Obediently she went to work there, but had fallen pregnant and been banished to the convent as her father said he wouldn't pay good money to support bastards. And he didn't want her back, either. Charming.

Phryne thought about it, then summoned her minions.

Tinker, Jane, Ruth and Dot came into the parlour and took their seats. Phryne laid a hand on the police briefs and delivered a concise summary of their contents. Then she asked for comments.

'They don't seem to have known each other before the convent,' observed Jane. 'I mean, different suburbs, different ages, different jobs.'

'Yes,' said Phryne. 'They must have met in the Magdalen Laundry.'

'They must have been desperate,' said Ruth.

'Why do you think that?' asked Phryne.

'Because however bad the convent was, there was food and a bed and a roof,' replied Jane. 'The same goes for that home.'

'I agree.' Dot nodded. 'They would have been scolded all the time for being wicked and sinful, but you can get used to scolding.'

'Not even notice it after a while,' Tinker put in. His mother had seldom communicated with her children except by nagging. He had long ago learned to block out the sound of her voice until she reinforced some order with a clip over the ear. And she had a punch like a heavyweight. Ruth grinned at him. He grinned back.

'Remind me not to scold you,' said Phryne. 'Continue, Ruthie, please.'

'I mean, even though there was hard work and nagging, they were fed and lodged. Outside there ain't no one to look after them. Isn't. Anyone,' she corrected herself. Remembering being cold and overworked and continuously yelled at had taken her back to the language of her childhood.

'But someone got to them,' said Dot. 'And there aren't many outsiders in a convent.'

'Who could get in?' asked Phryne. 'Men?'

Dot's shocked glance replied before she actually said, 'Oh, no, Miss!'

'But what if something went wrong with the water supply in the Magdalen Laundry and they had to bring in a plumber?'

'Then the girls wouldn't be there when he came, and two nuns would be with him until they walked him out the gate. Old nuns. Tough ones.'

'They are that cautious, eh?'

'Oh, yes, Miss. And the whole convent is surrounded by that really high wall. And they have big dogs. Convents have to be careful. Some men have . . . real strange ideas about nuns.'

'And, of course, the high wall works both ways. It keeps the nuns and the girls in, as well as keeping the lustful out.'

'I suppose so, Miss,' conceded Dot, who hadn't thought of it that way.

'So the girls couldn't have got out of the convent,' said Tinker. 'If the wall is so high and there are dogs. Which is why they had to wait to make their getaway until they were sent to this place in Footscray.'

'Quite right. They could have been plotting for months,' said Phryne.

'Waiting for their chance to flee,' said Ruth, clasping her hands. She loved romances and this sounded like a romance.

'And once they were able to—make their getaway, was it, Tinker?—they went. Promptly. Neatly. Leaving no clue. Arguing either amazing luck or very good staff work,' said Phryne.

'I don't reckon them poor girls are that lucky,' said Tinker gloomily.

'Me neither,' said Ruth.

'What would you like us to do, Miss Phryne?' asked Jane, who considered that enough time had been spent in idle speculation. She was a scientist and preferred experiment to theory any day.

'I think,' said Phryne slowly, 'I think that we will hire Bert and we will take a little taxi ride. We need to visit all of the families, and then we need to visit the lying-in home kept by the pious Mrs Ryan.'

'Shouldn't we be going after Miss Kettle first?' asked Dot. 'She might be in danger.'

'The cops are looking for her,' said Phryne. 'They have methods and people which we don't have. We shall augment their efforts. I suspect that if we find the girls we will find out why someone kidnapped Miss Kettle. So we shall pursue the whole enquiry. One at a time. We shall use our advantages.'

'What do you want us to do?' asked Ruth.

'I propose letting you out of the car, two on the street at a time, to talk to the local kids. It's school holidays, there will be kids around. One of you I shall take in with me. On some pretext I shall send you off with the other children, and you need to find out what the mother or father isn't telling me.'

'What sort of thing?' asked Jane, who liked precision.

'Could be anything,' said Phryne. 'Find out if the girls had boyfriends, if they had political affiliations, if they had friends and who the friends are and what sort they are. Especially try to find out why Mary O'Hara's mother says she is a good girl and her father says she is a liar.'

Tinker, Ruth and Dot exchanged a glance. Dot crossed herself. Phryne knew what they were thinking because she was thinking it herself.

'Yes, but we can't leap to the conclusion that it is incest,' she told them. Jane looked a little startled. She had been thinking about Fermat's Last Theorem until someone gave her some data. She was about to ask for clarification when Ruth nudged her.

'Tell you later,' she whispered. Jane accepted this.

'What would you like us to be?' asked Dot.

'Shabby genteel,' said Phryne. 'That fits in everywhere. That means you wear cotton trousers and a clean shirt, Tink, but the shirt Dot mended for you, not a new one. Cotton dresses, girls, clean but worn. Those straw hats that got caught in the rain. You will wear what your own good taste dictates, Dot dear, and I shall stay in this suit. With a different hat and flat shoes I will look enough like a district visitor.'

Dot grinned privately. Nothing was going to make Phryne look shabby, genteel or otherwise. She could be dressed in a hessian sack and still look superb. And few district visitors had their clothes made to measure by Madame Fleuri of Collins Street.

The company scattered to change. All Dot did was replace her modish jacket with a cardigan which had sagged out of shape in the wash. She stuck her rosary in her pocket, in case she might be asked to join in some act of devotion. And said a brief prayer for the lost and strayed as she did so. Dot, a true daughter of the Church, desperately hoped that the convent had done nothing wrong, and would cheerfully unleash the fires of hell—or Miss Phryne, a reasonable earthly substitute—on them if they had fallen from the grace expected of them by God and the saints.

Mrs Butler was asked to provide a hamper. Mr Butler was instructed to summon Bert and his bonzer new taxi, which Phryne had bought for them early in their partnership. Phryne inspected her troops.

Tinker looked just right. He could have been a good boy from a good family who had fallen on hard times or a child of the working class whose parents had Aspirations. Jane had brushed her hair back under the slightly drooping brim of the straw hat and pulled it down hard, so that she looked like a mushroom in an outgrown blue shift. But she had mended gloves and her sandals were clean but had one strap replaced with string. Ruth had braided her hair very tightly, donned a yellow dress on which she had spilled orangeade which had never entirely washed out, and had cheap yellow cotton gloves, which clashed with her ensemble. Dot twirled to exhibit her saggy cardigan. Phryne beamed.

'You are all very, very worthy minions,' she told them. 'Now you take the files, Dot, and you grab that hamper, Tink. I can hear Bert at the door. Have you all got your emergency money?'

They all nodded. Six pennies jingled in every pocket.

'If something goes wrong, run. Don't fight unless you have to. Get back to the taxi or call a cab or get on a tram or summon a policeman. Then find a telephone and call the house. Mr Butler will be here and will advise you. Clear?'

They nodded. Even Mr Butler bent his stately head in butlerine acquiescence.

'Then let's go,' said Phryne. 'The game's afoot!'

CHAPTER FOUR

Laws grind the poor
And rich men rule the law.

Oliver Goldsmith
'The Traveller'

The nearest house was that of Ann Prospect in Collingwood. It was a nice respectable wooden house in good repair, painted recently. Someone had planted red geraniums in the miniscule front garden. Someone loves this house, Phryne thought. She had brought Dot and Jane with her. It seemed a good fit. Tinker and Ruth might betray their working-class origins. They hadn't yet learned the sophisticated hypocrisy which Phryne found so useful in prosecuting her enquiries.

The door was answered by a small girl in a maid's uniform. Someone had done their best with the lace, which had been trimmed and mended where it had frayed. Phryne knew that Dot would be able to tell her all about the girl's clothes when they were back in the car. The servant bobbed a terrified curtsey. Phryne gave her the card which said *The Hon. Miss*

Phryne Fisher: Enquiries. She reserved this one for the snobbish. It always worked.

And so it proved. After the girl had scurried off, the mistress of the house herself appeared in moments and ushered them into a parlour darkened by plush curtains and littered with ornaments. Inherited, Phryne diagnosed. This family had come down in the world.

'Tea, Miss Fisher?' asked the woman, a tall rangy redhead, who had introduced herself as Mrs Edward Prospect. The daughter favoured her mother. Mrs Prospect wore a beige suit of no imagination or fit and great respectability. Second-hand, Phryne decided. Too proud to shop at the cheap shops, too poor to shop at the expensive ones. She was rigid. You could have measured angles with Mrs Prospect. Phryne smiled at her, however.

'No, thank you. I have come to make some enquiries into the fate of three missing girls. Your daughter Ann is one of them. But before we speak further, perhaps you could send my daughter to join your children? This conversation might not be fit for tender ears.'

'Of course,' replied Mrs Prospect. It had apparently not occurred to her that if the conversation was likely to be indelicate, Miss Fisher should not have brought her daughter. She rang the bell and Jane was sent away with the little maid. 'Do sit down, but I am afraid I cannot tell you anything about . . . Ann's whereabouts.'

'You haven't heard from her?' asked Phryne. Mrs Prospect linked her fingers in a knot.

'Not a word. We did not part on good terms.' The tone of voice could have been used in the fishing industry for freezing prawns. 'I have no interest in her fate.'

'Then we have nothing at all to talk about,' said Phryne equably.

Mrs Prospect saw her aristocratic visitor about to rise, collect her bag and escape. This could not be allowed to happen. Phryne's visit would endow Mrs Prospect with boasting powers hitherto unknown and would agreeably squash the pretensions of that common woman next door, who had once entertained a bishop. Besides, she had caught a look of disapproval from the plain young woman who had accompanied the Hon. Miss Fisher. A devout young woman, with the beads of a rosary trailing out of her cardigan pocket. Mrs Prospect hastily assumed her company smile.

'Let's not be hasty, Miss Fisher. What do you want to know?'

'What was Ann like?'

'Like?' Mrs Prospect frowned. 'She was a girl. Tall and slim like me. She had to work in a—well, we all have to work, don't we, in this modern postwar world?'

Phryne assented. 'We do indeed. Did she object to working in the factory?'

'No, not at all. I thought she ought to try for a job in an office—the company at the factory is very rough—but she said that she liked it. She was being considered for a promotion to leading hand. She was doing well. Though one could not approve of her tendency to socialism. She was a member of the union, you know. Then—she fell.'

'Yes,' prompted Phryne.

'And of course she couldn't stay here. I have young children who could be corrupted by her evil example. She was wilful. She would not say who was the father of her child of shame. We came to an agreement with an old family friend who said he would rescue her good name. And she turned around and rejected him! Flat! I was so embarrassed.'

I bet you were, thought Phryne. You never liked your daughter and then she shamed you. So you got rid of her, and you don't miss her at all.

'How . . . wilful,' she agreed tautly.

'It was shocking!' said Mrs Edward Prospect, groping for her smelling salts.

'Certainly,' said Phryne. 'Did she take anything with her to the convent?'

'Only the clothes she needed.'

'And she hasn't been back to collect her other things?'

'Certainly not!' said Mrs Prospect. 'Her father has forbidden her to enter the house.'

'I see. And where is Mr Prospect?'

'At his work,' she said stiffly. 'But I am sure he cannot add anything to my account of this . . . distressing affair.'

'Indeed,' said Phryne. 'Did Ann have any friends?'

'She never brought them here,' responded Mrs Prospect. 'I believe she associated with some of the girls from the factory. But I don't know them,' she said with leaden finality.

'Well, I'll just collect my daughter and pursue my enquiries through other channels. Thank you for your time, Mrs Prospect.'

The lady of the house rang for the little maid and Jane was produced. She looked rather white and pinched, Phryne thought, as though she had seen something horrible. But she said nothing and they left the house in good order.

They returned to the cab, where Bert was lounging against the door, smoking one of his aromatic roll-ups and contemplating the street.

'All right?' he asked Phryne.

'In a way. Call back the others, will you, Bert dear?'

Bert put his fingers in his mouth—at no time disturbing the cigarette—and whistled. Ruth and Tinker came running.

They all piled into the taxi and Bert started off for the next destination.

'Phew!' said Dot.

'I second your "phew!" and raise it,' said Phryne. 'Dot, pour us some tea, please. How did you go, Jane? You look upset.'

'I am,' said the young woman. She gulped sweet tea from the thermos Dot produced. 'That woman has four more children. They're all locked in a bare back room with the maid. No toys. No books but the Bible. They are forbidden to play or even move much in case they dirty their clothes. They argue and fight all the time. And the poor little maid—she's only twelve, an orphan—they got her from the convent. She sleeps in the kitchen on a pile of rags. But they say that Annie left and never came back. They haven't seen her again.'

'But she has been seen,' said Tinker, puffed up with triumph. 'The kid next door said he saw her go in when no one was home and leave again with a suitcase.'

'Aha,' said Phryne. 'Nice work, Tink.'

Tinker glowed.

'Was anyone with her?' asked Phryne.

Tinker was immediately dashed. 'I didn't ask,' he muttered.

'Never mind, you will next time,' said Dot comfortingly.

Ruth frowned. 'I talked to the kids on the other side,' she said. 'They hadn't seen Ann. But they say that Mr Prospect is a big bad-tempered bruiser and yells something chronic. They reckon that he beats his family. He drinks a lot.'

'Ah, I suspected as much,' said Dot.

'Why?' asked Phryne.

'She was wearing a high collar—in this weather!—and long sleeves. To cover the bruises.'

'God have mercy,' said Phryne.

Dot chose to believe that this was a prayer and crossed herself.

'Next address, Guv'nor,' said Bert.

'Ask about socialism if you can,' Phryne said. 'Ann Prospect was a socialist. Her mother disapproved, of course. Do you know anyone in the Manufacturing Workers' Union, Bert?'

'I can find someone,' said Bert. 'They'll help when I tell them that a daughter of the working class has disappeared. They know a lot of people.' He chewed his cigarette. 'And there's the sheilas, the Militant Women. You know about them, Miss.'

'I read their magazine,' said Phryne. 'A good notion, Bert. Where are we now?'

'Still in 'Wood,' said Bert. 'You watch yourself. This ain't the nice bit. Not that Collingwood has a lot of nice bits.'

'I rely on your vigilance,' said Phryne sweetly.

'I'll be vigilant all right,' Bert assured her. 'Or they'll have the wheels off the cab before you can kiss yer 'and.'

It wasn't a nice bit of Collingwood, even among the available bits. The streets were unpaved, the dust endemic and the smell indicated that the sewerage commissioners had not explored this far into the wastelands. It was poor, mean, dirty and overcrowded. The arrival of the car produced immediate interest. A scurry of grimy children appeared as if by magic, and their grimier elder brothers left the wall and bench where they had been slouching outside a barber's shop and hulked across to ascertain whether this taxi might provide prey. Phryne wished she had brought her little gun. The situation looked ominous. But she had been in worse places. She got out of the car.

The emergence of Phryne was greeted with whistles and crude comments. The emergence of the driver, however, produced a profound silence which was only broken when a thin, tow-headed young man said meekly, 'G'day, Bert.'

'Fraternal greetings, Comrade Scott,' said Bert. 'How's it goin'?'

'There ain't no work,' said Comrade Scott. 'No money, neither.'

'Just as usual, eh?' Bert smiled. 'This is Miss Fisher. Friend of the workers, and not bad for a bloated capitalist. Now, we're looking into the disappearance of one of the daughters of the working class. She used to live 'ere. Mary O'Hara. You know 'er?'

'Nice little girl,' said Comrade Scott. 'Real quiet. Used to help her mum. We couldn't credit it when she got into trouble. None of us got close to her. She'd shy away from any man. Like she was frightened.'

'This true?' demanded Bert of the assembly.

They all nodded.

'What about the family?' he asked.

'The old man's out of work,' said Comrade Scott. 'Took ill. Used to be a brickie. The old woman's a cleaner and takes care of the children. Eleven of them—well, ten now that Mary's gone. Dunno how they makes ends meet. The old man can't do much anymore.'

Phryne reflected that there was one thing he could still do and it might be better if he couldn't do that either. Eleven children! In a house no bigger than the Prospects' and a good deal more rundown.

'They home?' asked Bert.

'Yair,' said Comrade Scott. 'He's home. She's at work. Poor cow.'

Leaving Bert to continue the interrogation, Phryne waved at her minions to stay in the car and took Dot to knock on the unpainted front door. No one had planted anything in this front garden apart from corned-beef tins.

Knocking on the blistered door produced only a scamper of footsteps, then silence. Phryne called out, 'Anyone home?' and the door creaked open an inch or two. A small worried face peered out.

'You the bailiffs?'

'No, I'm Phryne Fisher,' said Phryne. 'I want to talk to your father.'

'Jeez,' commented the voice, and the door gaped, half off its hinges. A bellow came from down the hall and the voice fled. A small girl, Phryne thought, in a calico smock made from a flour bag. She had *Fine Flour* stencilled across her bony shoulder-blades.

The house stank of frying fat, filthy humanity and cigarette smoke, with an undernote of beer. Surprisingly prosperous smells for such a sty, Phryne thought. Dot was fingering her rosary, uneasy. They walked down the hall into the kitchen, from whence had issued the bellow.

It had come from a large man. He was sitting in an armchair. He had a packet of cigarettes in his hand and had clearly been drinking from a beer bottle. Otherwise the room contained no furniture but a table and three chairs. To the leg of the table a small child was tethered with a leash around its waist. It was crying in a low voice, as though it had been unattended for a long time and knew that no relief was in sight. Phryne was instantly disgusted. Dot swooped and grabbed the leash, untying the child.

'Who're you?' growled the man. He was a revolting sight. He was wearing ragged khaki shorts and a filthy blue singlet. He was unshaven, greasy and more than three parts drunk.

'I'm Phryne Fisher,' she said again. 'Are you Mr O'Hara?'

'What's it to you?'

'Could be money,' said Phryne evenly. Beating this monster around the head with that unwashed skillet and tethering him to the table would be satisfying but not productive of information. She could put off proper retribution until later.

'Yair?' he asked, faintly interested.

'First we had better do something about this baby,' said Phryne. 'Do you have any milk?'

'Beer's better,' he said.

The cupboard was empty and the ice chest had neither ice nor milk in it. A flood of children had come into the room. Dot selected the oldest, who was perhaps thirteen, and gave her six pennies.

'Go get some milk and bread,' she ordered. 'And lollies all round. Come back quick and you shall have threepence for yourself.'

The girl grabbed and ran, pursued by the others. Dot found a clean nappy and changed the baby. Another could be heard crying on the back porch. She took the toddler outside with her to attend to it. As she did so, she prayed very hard for control of her temper. Did poor Mrs O'Hara have no relatives who could care for her children apart from her brute of a husband?

'Tell me about your daughter Mary,' said Phryne.

'Liar,' said Mr O'Hara.

'Really? What did she lie about?' asked Phryne, lighting a gasper in defence against the smell.

'How she got into trouble,' said Mr O'Hara fuzzily. 'Said it was Don. Don's a good bloke. He wouldn't do a thing like that. Brings me beer and smokes. Pays the rent. I got a bad back and leg. A wall fell on me.'

He looked up for sympathy and found none in Miss Fisher's stony eyes.

'So who is this charitable gentleman?' she asked.

'Don,' explained Mr O'Hara. 'Donald Fraser. Lives down the road. He likes to come 'ere because he's all alone since his mum died last year. He took a fancy to our Mary. But he wouldn't have . . .' He was falling asleep.

Phryne did not interfere with the benevolent action of the Forces of Alcohol. So Mr O'Hara had sold his virgin daughter to his neighbour for beer, smokes and rent. It probably struck the neighbour as a bargain. She looked at Dot.

'God have mercy,' said Dot, hefting a filthy baby. The tethered child was clinging to her leg. It was howling. They were all howling, now. Phryne went out into the backyard to get away from the noise and found the earth quite bare of grass. Worn barren by the children's feet. What a universe, she thought. She had seen battlefields in France with more amenities. What could she do to ameliorate the situation? Money would go straight to Dad and Dad's beer and Dad's smokes. Of course, she could castrate Dad with that blunt knife on the scullery sink. That would solve one problem, at least. It was a very tempting idea.

Thinking about this, she went back inside to find that Dot had worked her household magic. Every child had had his or her face and hands scrubbed with green soap. Every child was sitting on his or her patch of floor with a basin, cup or plate of bread and milk. Babies had been provided with bottles, which suppressed their justifiable complaints. Silence had fallen. Mr O'Hara snored.

Phryne waited until the eldest child had eaten her bread and milk. Then she said, 'What's your name? I'm Phryne and this is Dot.'

'Katie,' said the child. She was not as grimy as the others and had bright, famished eyes like a sparrow. And was as light on her feet as a sparrow, too, which would serve her well, as long as she could outrun Mr Fraser.

'Have you seen Mary since she went away?'

'No,' said Katie. 'She ain't come back 'ere. Would yer, if yer ever got away?'

It was a good question. Phryne wouldn't.

'Tell me about Mr Fraser,' she coaxed.

'He lives up the road in the big blue house. Friend o' Dad's. Brings us lollies. I useta like him but he made Mary cry. She made me promise not to be alone with him.'

'Did you promise?' asked Dot.

'Yair,' said Katie.

'Then keep your promise,' Dot told her.

'But he's got books,' protested Katie. 'That's why Mary went to his house.'

'I shall send you books,' said Phryne. 'What do you like to read?'

'Adventures,' said Katie wistfully.

'Adventures you shall have. When does your mother get home?'

'Six,' said Katie. 'It's all right, yer know, when we're all at school. But it's holidays,' said the child, who had never associated holidays with swimming and beach picnics.

'I shall speak to your mother,' said Phryne, putting threepence into her hand. The recently scrubbed fingers clutched tight. 'And I shall have a word with Mr Fraser,' she added grimly.

'Dad'll be real crook if he don't come with beer and smokes no more,' warned Katie.

'He shall come,' said Phryne.

Dot mopped the children and distributed lollies from the bag Katie had bought. Then they wrestled the sagging door shut behind them. Dot took a deep breath of relatively clean Collingwood air.

'Mr Fraser?' asked Dot. 'That brute sold her to Mr Fraser for beer and cigarettes?'

'Yes. See why we shouldn't jump to conclusions? Now I shall call on him—alone.'

'You're not going to . . . do anything rash, Miss?' asked Dot.

'I never act rashly,' said Phryne.

Dot, who disagreed, did not reply.

After a quick word with Bert, Phryne obtained admittance to the big blue house, which was in an excellent state of repair. The hallway was polished and extremely tidy. Just, no doubt, as Mr Fraser's mother had demanded. He was a soft, smiling little man, with an agreeably warm handshake. When he smiled, he had dimples. Phryne was not enchanted.

She allowed him to usher her into a parlour which had been decorated—presumably by himself, for it was all cool surfaces and Charles Rennie Mackintosh furniture. The walls were covered with bookshelves. What a magnetic attraction this place must have had for an intelligent, print-starved child like Mary O'Hara! A fine literary web, and in the middle sat Mr Fraser, smiling, like a spider waiting for prey. She handed him her card. He read it and raised his eyebrows.

'The Hon. Miss Fisher! To what do I owe the honour of—'

'Two things,' said Phryne. 'First, I am looking into the disappearance of three girls. One of them is Mary O'Hara. Have you seen her since she was sent away in unmerited disgrace to bear your child?'

'Miss Fisher . . .' he protested.

'Do not waste my time, Mr Fraser,' she warned. 'You bought her from her frightful father for beer money. Not an uncommon transaction. I just need to know whether you have seen her.'

'No,' he said. 'But it wasn't like that, Miss Fisher. I really loved her. My little Mary! So sweet, so kind!'

'And you let her be sent away to that convent,' she said.

'I . . . couldn't admit it,' he faltered. 'She was under sixteen.'

'And that's how you like them, eh?' asked Phryne, smiling a wicked smile which knocked Mr Fraser back on his heels.

'Er . . . yes,' he said. 'And she loved me, too.'

'Then why didn't you offer to marry her?'

'I . . . don't know,' he said.

'I see,' said Phryne.

'What must you think of me?' he cried.

'Oh, I already know what to think of you,' she told him. 'Katie O'Hara is about ready for your attentions. If you so much as lay one finger on her, I will arrange to have you killed.'

'Miss Fisher!'

'Outside your house,' she said, 'there are men who would skin you alive for sixpence. I will supply the sixpence. But you will be safe if you continue to provide for the O'Hara family, and allow Katie and the others to read your books. Look on it as the wages of sin,' said Phryne, and left.

CHAPTER FIVE

There's no scandal like rags, nor any crime so shameful as poverty.

George Farquhar
The Beaux' Stratagem

Phryne jumped into the car and swore.

'Bert, get us out of this accursed place,' she said, and Bert engaged some gears.

'Next address, Guv'nor?' he asked.

'Next address,' said Phryne. 'God bless my blood pressure! This,' she added, 'is not going to be an agreeable day.'

'Who's next, Miss Phryne?' asked Jane.

'The last missing girl, thank God. Julie Reilly. Seventeen years old, wanted to be a teacher, sent to work in a woollen mill, not welcome home again in her shameful condition.'

Dot considered it fortunate, in view of Miss Phryne's disintegrating temper, that the Reilly house was locked and there was a To Let sign on the front fence. The children scattered in search of information. Bert got out and leaned on the cab door, smoking his rollie and staring at the horizon. He was thinking. Phryne found the flask she always popped into any picnic basket and poured herself a tot.

'I might just go into that milk bar,' suggested Dot. 'See if they know where the Reillys have gone.'

'Why not?' asked Phryne. She was dealing with a rush of hatred. This always gave her a headache. Had she been armed, she thought, which luckily she was not, she might have shot that appalling little man in his too-neat house. That would have caused comment, even in Collingwood. And she had heard that the appointments of the Womens' Prison were not in the least comfortable. Bert had caught her mood.

'So he's the father?' he said. 'That bloke in the big house?'

'Yes,' said Phryne.

'I could just mention it to the comrades,' suggested Bert. 'People like that have accidents. Quite often. Sort of terminal ones.'

'Don't tempt me,' growled Phryne. 'He's paying the rent for that family. They need him. But I would be obliged if a watch was kept on him. If the comrades detect any funny business, then the accident should proceed on schedule.'

'Right,' said Bert. When Miss Phryne spoke in that tone, it was time to salute. He had known officers like her. They could be trusted. They led from the front. And they knew their own mind.

'What did the comrades say about the situation?' she asked, a little mollified by the good cognac and the gasper she had lit.

'The old man is a bludger,' reported Bert. 'The old woman works all the hours there are. Comrade Scott reckons O'Hara could work if he liked but he don't like.'

'He's a leech,' said Phryne.

'Too right,' agreed Bert. 'I reckon this family have run off on the rent,' he added.

'Moonlight flit?' asked Phryne.

'Yair, not an eviction, there's no notice on the gate. I'll just have a dekko at the letterbox.'

He was about to open it when the postman's bike appeared. Bert greeted him. 'Gidday.'

'Gidday,' replied the postman. 'You visiting the Reillys?'

'Lookin' for 'em,' said Bert easily. 'Any ideas?'

'They was gone from one delivery to the next,' said the postman. He pushed back his cap. 'And I got a couple of letters for 'em, too. If they ain't here I have to take 'em all the way over to dead letters.'

'I'll take 'em,' said Bert, and held out his hand.

The postman looked doubtful. His freckles darkened. 'There's twopence due,' he warned.

Bert felt for a coin, found sixpence, said, 'And keep the change,' and the postman handed over several letters.

'Well, hooroo,' and the bike was pedalled onward, fortunately not being challenged by rain, hail or gloom of night.

Bert dropped the letters into Phryne's lap. 'That's interferin' with His Majesty's Mails, that is,' he said complacently.

'So it is, well done,' agreed Phryne. She surveyed the envelopes. 'This looks like a personal letter, and this is her copy of *The Woman Worker*,' she told Bert.

'I read that,' said Bert.

'So do I, a splendid production. And this is definitely a bill. We can put that into the letterbox. And the magazine. I'll steam the letter open when we get home, it might contain a clue. Anything else in that box?'

'Just this,' said Bert, holding out a folded note. It bore a scrawl in black ink and a confident, sprawling hand. Phryne read it aloud.

'*Julie, remember the revolution SS 5.10. BM.* Cryptic,' she said. 'Ah, here are the troops.'

A very proud Ruth was escorting a badly dressed girl of about twelve. She stood in front of Phryne, scuffing her boots in the dust and sucking the end of her plait. Ruth gently removed the hair and said, 'Tell the lady all you know about the Reillys, and she'll give you a penny.'

'Twopence,' said Phryne. 'Hello. What's your name?'

The child replied haltingly that she was Mary. There were a lot of Marys in Catholic Collingwood, Phryne thought. This Mary began to speak in a rush. She really wanted that twopence.

'They went away in the middle of the night, all their furniture went too. In a cart. Landlord came next day for the rent and swore something cruel. Mum says they had bad luck. Their Julie lost her job and they couldn't carry on without her. The missus is sick and the baby too.'

'Any idea where they might have gone?'

'She had a sister in the country somewhere . . . Shepparton, that was it.'

Having told all that she knew the girl put out her hand. Phryne gave her twopence, and Mary abruptly lost her nerve and ran, clutching the coins in a death grip.

'Well, minions?' asked Phryne.

'I heard the same,' said Tinker.

'And me,' said Jane.

'And me,' said Dot, who had come back from the shop. 'They left owing on the tick. The shopkeeper's not fazed. Said they'd been going downhill since they lost Julie and she wasn't surprised that they vanished. No idea where they went.'

'Righty-ho,' said Phryne. 'Now on to the pious widow and then home—I've had just about enough for one day.'

The minions agreed. This detecting was more tiring than he had imagined, Tinker thought. He accepted an egg sandwich and ate wolfishly. He still wasn't used to the liberality of Phryne's cuisine. All that food, he said to himself. And always enough for me, too.

Food made Tinker sentimental. He smiled on his new family and they smiled back.

The Barkly Street home of the pious widow was very clean. That was about all that could be said for it. The doorstep was scrubbed, the windows sparkled. The paint on the door was recent. When the door was opened a gust of carbolic made Dot sneeze. The small servant, doubtless from the same orphanage, was painfully scrubbed and starched and very thin. There was no smell of cooking in the house. Just disinfectant and, when Mrs Ryan came in to receive her distinguished visitors, naphthalene. Phryne looked at the parlour. It was bare. Hard chairs, no carpets, no ornaments but a large picture of the Sacred Heart, with added thorns. Phryne had never liked this depiction of Christ. It was disturbingly anatomical. The space above the empty fireplace, which contained not even a fan of red paper or a bunch of dried flowers, was occupied by a wooden cross on which an agonised figure was writhing. It was beautifully carved. Phryne wished that it wasn't.

'Mrs Ryan, I am looking into the disappearance of three girls from your house,' she said. 'And the abduction of a reporter. What can you tell me?'

Mrs Ryan was tall and skeletal. Her hair was dragged back into a punitive bun under a white cap. Her cotton dress was clean and grey, almost like a nurse's uniform. She wore a white apron which crackled with starch. She did not sit down but folded her hands in front of her waist and said stiffly, 'Does the convent know that you are here?'

'I have not yet visited the convent,' Phryne told her.

'Then I am not at liberty to tell you anything,' snapped Mrs Ryan.

'As you wish,' said Phryne gently. 'But it will be my unpleasant duty to convey your refusal to help to Detective Inspector Robinson. He will have further questions, I am sure.'

Mrs Ryan paled. 'Very well,' she muttered. 'Ask your questions and go away before the neighbours see you.'

'Delighted,' said Phryne, really meaning it. 'When did the girls leave your house?'

'At night,' said Mrs Ryan. 'That's all I can say. They were in their beds at curfew—they go to bed at eight—and not there in the morning.'

'Did they have any visitors?'

'Visitors are allowed between the hours of three and five in the afternoon. They have to be received in this parlour. They had no visitors.'

'And any letters?'

'None. I open and inspect all the patients' mail.'

I bet you do, thought Phryne. Prison must be like this. Or hell.

'Were they friends? Did they leave together?'

'They talked, when allowed. We impose a Holy Silence but they are allowed to speak at meals. I don't know if they were friends. We don't encourage friendship between the patients.'

Mrs Ryan's voice was scraping on Phryne's nerves. It was like the voice of a machine. A cold, flat, disapproving machine. Dot had taken out her rosary for comfort. Mrs Ryan's chill gaze noted it and passed on.

'Did they take their belongings?' persisted Phryne.

'Yes, such as they were. And several things belonging to the house. Towels and so on. They are thieves and when they are found I want them prosecuted. I have a list.'

'I see,' said Phryne. 'Show me.'

Mrs Ryan went to a plain deal desk and produced a list. Phryne and Dot read it. Three towels, some underclothes, a sewing kit, soap, toothbrushes, stockings. Value, perhaps five shillings. Mrs Ryan had put down five pounds. The pious widow, it seemed, was greedy. That might be useful.

'I would be willing to offer a reward for any information,' said Phryne silkily. 'Perhaps your son might know more?'

'I doubt it,' snapped Mrs Ryan. 'In any case, he isn't here.'

'What a pity, we will have to come back,' said Phryne. 'Now, about this abduction.'

'I didn't see anything,' said Mrs Ryan. 'All I know is that she came here to ask impertinent questions, I was busy, and my son received her into the house, which he should not have done. Then, he said, as she was leaving, she was dragged into a big black car. Now, if you are quite finished, I have important work to do.'

'Of course,' said Phryne graciously, and was escorted out by the little maid, into whose hand she slipped a sixpence. The child gasped, grabbed, and instantly cached it in her knickers.

'What's she like?' asked Dot gently.

'Bitch,' whispered the child, opening the door. 'Bloody mean bitch.'

The door closed and Phryne drew in a breath of air which was not contaminated with the smell of mothballs. Dot dived into the car and poured herself a cup of strong sweet milky tea. Phryne had a tot of the good cognac. Both were shaken.

'If I had been sent to the pious Mrs Ryan,' said Phryne after an interval, 'I would decamp if I had to crawl.'

'Over broken glass,' agreed Dot.

The minions returned. Bert came back and leaned into the car.

'I got the office that the son's down the pub,' he said. 'You want me to talk to him?'

'Yes, please,' said Phryne. 'But we have to go home. Come to dinner later—and bring Cec. Can you manage if I take the cab?'

'Don't you dent it,' warned Bert, and strolled off.

'Miss Phryne, you don't have a licence to drive a taxi!' protested Dot.

'No, isn't that lucky,' said Phryne, taking her place at the wheel and revving the engine.

'Why is it lucky?' asked Jane.

'Because I cannot be assumed to know the rules,' replied Phryne, and set off for St Kilda as though, Dot thought, devils were after her.

On the other hand, that was the way she usually drove.

Once arrived home, the party scattered to write down their impressions and information in their notebooks. Thereafter Tinker retreated to his shed with a plate of gingerbread and a glass of milk; the girls to their room ditto; Dot to the sitting room with a strong cup of really hot tea, which tea in thermoses, however welcome, never was; and Phryne to run a scented bath to get the combined odours of naphthalene and filth out of her nostrils. She lay and soaked luxuriously in a slick of cypress oil. The pine scent was perfect. Too late to visit a convent, even if she had any tact left. And Detective Inspector Robinson was going to call to hear what she had to report. Phryne wondered if he had found the big black car.

A short time later, dried, powdered and dressed in a silk

gown, she sat in her own room to read *The Woman Worker* with care. There was a socialist link. One girl had had a copy of this magazine delivered, another was in her own trade's union.

It was, as usual, a Gestetner duplicate, with a hand-carved depiction of the Woman Worker in Russian social realist pose at the head. But the content was ferociously passionate and made stirring reading.

'What is the position of women in the advanced capitalist countries? And what is the position of the millions of working or peasant women in the colonial and semi-colonial countries?' it asked, and proceeded to tell Phryne.

'. . . it is lower than a slave. She is nonexistent politically, she is frightfully exploited economically, she has no standing socially, she is isolated culturally. Read the reports on labour conditions: fivepence a day, no Sunday, no holiday, giving birth to child at the loom in a textile mill or in the hell of a match factory . . . such is her lot.'

Phryne nodded sadly.

'Here she is also a second-rate citizen. If she is not the slave of the boss (who exploits her at half the wage paid to men for the same work), she is the slave of the so-called "home", where she bears the brunt of the economic dependence of the male "supporter" on capitalism. Unemployment, starvation, the burden of rearing and educating children, etc., all this is the lot of the working-class woman.'

Phryne read of a splendid display of solidarity at the Perdriau Rubber Company where, after thirty-seven girls had been dismissed for refusing to make more heavy shoes than they had agreed, the whole workforce of two hundred had sat idle at their benches for a week until management had given in and re-employed the dismissed workers.

The paper noted with delight the creation of a women's fruit-growing collective in Bacchus Marsh. Such things were essential until the revolution came and the workers triumphed. The name of the woman in charge was Isobel Berners. They had already planted an acre of nectarines and apples and had inherited a lot of stone fruit, including white peaches. They were also making jam and jellies.

Phryne approved of the Militant Women. And white peaches were her favourite fruit. She thought that she might motor down to visit and perhaps acquire some fruit in the season. Who better to purchase it from? Militant peaches would probably be very tasty.

Phryne dressed for dinner in a loose cotton frock patterned with sea anemones. The weather, as seemed usual in Australia at this time of year, continued hot. Fortunately Mrs Butler had risen to the challenge, constructing wonderful salads. Jane was discussing one with Ruth—or, rather, Jane was reading a thick book and Ruth was talking—when Phryne came in.

'Salmagundi,' said Ruth.

Phryne had never heard the word before. 'What on earth is that?' she asked, sitting down in her chair as Mr Butler brought in the jugs of iced lemonade for the children and Dot, and White Lady for Phryne. She sipped. Icy, lemony and perfect.

'That hits the spot, Mr Butler, thank you. Ruth?'

'It's a very complicated salad, all in jelly,' replied Ruth, whose sworn ambition was to be a very good cook. 'Only possible in this climate, Mrs B says, with the invention of the American Refrigerating Machine. She didn't trust it to start with but she really likes it now.'

'One must have a way of making ice in this hot place,' said Phryne. 'Jack? Beer? Jane? Lemonade? What are you reading?'

One of the things Jane loved about Miss Phryne was that she did not object to reading at the table, and had indeed caused a bookstand to be made for Jane.

Mrs Butler strongly disapproved, but that was because she wanted people to appreciate her cuisine. Jane very often had no idea what she had eaten. Only that she had cut it up into small pieces, whatever it was, so that it could be eaten with a spoon and not interrupt her concentration. On the other hand, there was nothing that Jane didn't eat. You could not call her picky, the cook told her husband. And that Tinker was so thin that he'd fight the dog for her bone if Mrs Butler didn't keep up the supplies. It was lucky Miss Fisher was so rich, or Tinker would eat them out of house and home.

'Eugenics,' said Jane. 'It's interesting. Restricting the breeding of the unfit. There is a basic flaw in their argument, I believe.' She forked in some potato salad.

'Which is?' asked Phryne.

'Who decides who is unfit?' asked Jane.

'There you have put your finger exactly on the nub,' Phryne informed her. 'Keep reading and I think you will find that the unfit will cover any group which the writer does not like—Catholics, Chinese, Jews, Presbyterians, Aborigines—and any group he is afraid of—the poor, for instance, who seem set to out-breed him. The only people allowed to breed freely will be—'

'Him,' said Ruth, proving that she had been listening.

'And his mates,' thus Tinker. Engulfing massive quantities of ham and salad evidently did not slow his mental processes, though it didn't improve the clarity of his speech. Ruth leaned forward and wiped mayonnaise off his chin with a napkin. He flushed but did not resent the action as he might have done a day before. He had his own refuge now, where he could be as messy as he liked. He said, 'Thanks,' took the napkin, and cleaned his own face. Phryne was pleased and Ruth was amazed.

'Just another way of doing down the workin' man,' observed Bert, who had been listening as well. 'Cuttin' down on the numbers which might rise when the revolution comes.'

'On the other hand,' said Phryne, 'we have Mr O'Hara and his eleven starving children.'

'Yair, he ought to have tied a knot in it all right,' said Bert.

Dot blushed. Bert apologised.

'But contraception is not sterilisation,' said Jane calmly, almost causing Mr Butler to drop his tray. The code of his profession, stern as it was, had not accustomed him to such language in a lady's house. The glasses tinkled, but nothing fell. Mr Butler had his standards. He adhered to them rigidly.

'True,' said Phryne. 'If Mr O'Hara knew about such things, would he have used them?' Phryne favoured the Socratic method of education.

'No,' said Ruth, after deep thought. 'He doesn't care. It would have to be something Mrs O'Hara could do without him knowing. To protect herself.'

'Poisoning her old man leaps to mind,' said Bert.

Cec laughed.

'And she can't use those . . . things,' objected Dot. 'She's a Catholic! The Pope has declared all such things anathema!'

'Really? Why is it his business? Isn't he celibate?' asked Jane. She would have questioned Dot further but Phryne raised a hand. Theological debate in her household was best done in private.

'Jack dear, I'm sure you can't find this diverting. How are things with you?'

Detective Inspector Jack Robinson had been silently working his way through a superb egg and bacon pie and thinking about his own problems. He came to with a start to find everyone looking at him.

'Sorry, wasn't listening,' he said.

'Never mind,' said Phryne. 'I'm sure eugenics are the last thing on your mind. Have you found the big black car which took Polly Kettle away?'

'Not so much as a sighting of it,' he said as gloomily as so full fed a man could manage. 'Funny, that. It's not a main street and there aren't a lot of cars around that bit of the suburb. But no one's seen it, and it's school holidays, too. Cars like that usually attract the kids. I bet you draw a crowd everywhere you go in that big red monster of a thing.'

'I certainly do,' said Phryne. 'So, no sighting of the car? Odd.'

'I thought so.' Jack Robinson crossed to the buffet to remedy his *salade russe* deficiency. 'I've put Collins on to tracing every big black car in the area, but that's a bit of an ask. I'm talking to the girl's parents and her friends. She might have had a sweetheart.'

'I recommend you have a conversation with Mr Bates of the newspaper office,' suggested Phryne.

'Why? You think he had something to do with it?'

'Not necessarily, but he hates everyone and will therefore tell you the things about Polly which a tactful or affectionate person would omit or soft-pedal. Those may be things you need to know.'

'So they might.' He spooned some potato onto his plate.

'But we will have a full briefing after dinner,' Phryne told him. 'For now we appreciate the cuisine and make polite conversation. What do you think of this Bradman as a batsman?'

'Ugly style,' commented Jack, willing to do the civil.

'So they say,' said Phryne.

'But effective,' said Jack, relaxing a little. Missing persons made him nervous. Especially missing girls. They might have run away with a lover or taken a job on an outback cattle station or emigrated to New Zealand. Or they might be lying in a shallow grave in the Dandenongs. They could not be ignored and most of the time they turned up a year or two later with a new baby and an unacceptable husband. But every tenth one didn't. Girls, thought Robinson sourly, were pests. They ought to be safely locked up somewhere until they were twenty-five and had reached the age of discretion . . .

They adjourned to the sitting room, each with his or her favourite drink, and the children produced their notebooks. One by one, they recounted what they had seen and heard, and Phryne made notes in her own book on the case.

'Ann Prospect,' she announced. Information flowed in. 'Bert? Did you speak to Mr Prospect?'

'Yair,' said Bert. 'He's not like his missus. Brute of a bloke. Hands like shovels. Y'know, the kind of bloke who butts out his ciggie in his palm to show you how tough he is. He didn't care that the girl had a bun in the oven. Wanted to keep her because she was earning. But his missus wouldn't hear of it. I think he liked her all right. Asked me to tell her he'd have her back if I could find her. I reckon he gave his missus a belting when he found out she had sent the girl away.'

'I thought so,' exclaimed Dot.

'Had he any idea where she might have gone?'

'Nah,' said Bert. 'Didn't know anything about her friends. Said she was a commo and maybe the commos stole her and sold her to a brothel. I put him right about that,' he said complacently, looking down at a few new cuts on his scarred knuckles.

'Had she any relatives?' asked Phryne, eschewing comment.

Mr Prospect handed out enough beatings, it seemed only just that he received a little of his own medicine.

'He said his sister hadn't seen her,' Bert told them. 'She wouldn't go to any relatives on his wife's side. They're all like her.'

'Poor girl,' murmured Dot.

'And the father of the child?' asked Phryne.

'He didn't know, or he would have put the black on the bloke.'

'Lovely,' said Phryne. 'Well, we shall have to go to the factory and ask some questions there. Associates?' she asked the children.

'I reckon she was well out of there,' said Tinker. 'The kids think Mrs Prospect's cracked.'

'Gentility,' said Dot. 'She's mad about it.'

'And those children and the maid in that filthy back room,' said Jane. 'Disgusting.'

'Yes, I agree. All right. How about Mary O'Hara?'

The associates detailed everything they had learned about Mary O'Hara's miserable situation. Phryne and Dot added their description of the household.

Jack whistled. 'What are you going to do about them, Miss Fisher?' he asked.

'I've set the Children's Protection Society on them,' said Phryne. 'And Bert has mentioned the matter to the comrades. I suspect they will be all right. I still have to catch poor Mrs O'Hara. She might know where Mary would go. She must have known, however, about her husband's foul transaction with that appalling little man.'

'Maybe not,' said Dot. 'She isn't home much.'

'She's on the interview list,' agreed Phryne. 'Now, how about the Reillys?'

'Poor,' said Ruth.

'Dirt poor,' said Tinker. 'Poorer than I used to be. No wonder they run.'

'Ran,' corrected Jane automatically.

'Left owing rent and money at the milk bar,' said Dot.

'Possibly to Shepparton, according to their young neighbour,' said Phryne. You might enquire there?' she suggested to Jack Robinson, who made a note of his own. 'Very well. Mrs Ryan, the pious widow?'

'Mean bitch,' said Tinker.

'True, but we don't say "bitch" in company,' instructed Phryne. 'Only here with us. And she was indeed. Formaldehyde in her veins. What a cold vicious woman for poor labouring girls to have attending them. But not exactly a fount of information. What did you get from the son Patrick, Bert?'

'He's a lout,' said Bert, lighting a cigarette. 'Soft as butter, a mummy's boy, all mouth. Never worked a day in his life. Would make a good bludger, though, keeping the door at a brothel. Big. Strong. Don't know nothing about the missing girls. Stuck to his story about the big black car. I filled him up with the old juice and he still stuck to it, then he said, "But she's mine." I thought that was crook. I was about to give him a good belting—he'd spew all he knew, I know them blokes—but then he passed out and fell off his stool. So I left them to sweep him out with the sawdust and come here. I'll get back to him,' said Bert meaningfully.

'All right,' said Phryne. 'You keep an eye on him, and administer the said belting when you feel it would do the most good. I don't like this, friends. Perhaps the reason why Jack can't find that big black car is that there is no big black car. Perhaps Polly Kettle is still there.'

'In that nursing home?' asked Jack, startled. A straight-line thinker, he was frequently surprised by Phryne's reasoning. 'I'd need a search warrant.'

'But I wouldn't,' said Phryne sweetly. 'And I wouldn't have to telegraph that I was coming, allowing them to hide her somewhere else. Should she still be alive, of course. I think I shall call on Dot's parish priest. He has a right to inspect the nursing home. No, that won't do; he would be too polite. How about some government person? Can you lend me a policewoman, Jack?'

'Yes, but she'd need a search warrant, too.'

'Oh,' said Phryne. 'Well, any suggestions?'

'The Welfare,' said Jane, and shuddered, as did Ruth, Tinker, Dot and Phryne. All of them had spent childhoods haunted by the threat of the Welfare, who could take children away to an unspecified but dreadful fate.

'Good idea,' said Phryne, taking a strengthening swallow of her drink. 'Can you speak to them? Do you know anyone?'

'I know just the person,' said Jack, taking a gulp of his beer for the same reason. 'Miss Steel, and you're going to love her. In a way,' he added.

The evening continued with Jack, Bert, Cec, Dot and Phryne listening to the gramophone, and the children scattering to their own rooms.

Tinker had his wash and changed into his pyjamas—a novelty, as he had previously slept in his shirt when he had one. He took his evening cocoa and biscuits to his shed, and shut himself in. He sat down at his carpenter's bench, lit his hurricane lamp, and opened a new Sexton Blake. The sea shushed outside. In all of St Kilda, there was probably no one as solidly content as Tinker.

CHAPTER SIX

O, it is excellent
To have a giant's strength; but it is tyrannous
To use it like a giant.

William Shakespeare
Measure for Measure

The day began as usual with Greek coffee, a croissant, and a letter on her breakfast tray. Phryne opened it once the coffee had done its stimulating work and she could coordinate the letter opener without peril. The envelope was addressed to The Hon. Miss Phryne Fisher. It contained one half-sheet of pale blue notepaper, in very good style, with an engraved (not printed) address in Flinders Lane. It was headed *The Blue Cat Club* and was written in elaborate script in elegant dark blue ink.

If Miss Fisher would call this morning at eleven, Mr Featherstonehaugh would be much obliged.

'Well,' said Phryne.

'Well?' asked Dot.

'The Blue Cat Club,' Phryne explained, 'is a very elegant, very well-run establishment for practitioners of—how shall I put it? The love that dare not speak its name, as Oscar Wilde said.'

'Sorry?' asked Dot. 'Would you like cypress or roses in your bath?'

'Cypress,' said Phryne. 'I shall smell like Aphrodite. Which would be entirely inappropriate. In this case. Interesting. Polly Kettle went to the Blue Cat just before she disappeared.'

'Do you think they had anything to do with that?' asked Dot, still puzzling over 'the love that dare not speak its name'.

'Possibly,' said Phryne. 'You're going to talk to the parish priest about various matters?' she asked Dot.

'I'll go directly,' said Dot. She was feeling in need of some spiritual consolation herself. 'You do know, Miss, that you have to have the bishop's permission to talk to the nuns?'

'Then I shall get it,' said Phryne.

Phryne bathed and dressed. She chose a severe navy suit, as close to masculine dress as she could manage without wearing trousers (which might be construed as satirical). These clothes would also be useful for overawing the multitudes should that be necessary. Today should contain Miss Steel and her inspection of Mrs Ryan's lying-in home, an interview with Mrs O'Hara, and the Blue Cat Club. A day full of contrasts and just to Phryne's taste.

She was beginning to be anxious about Polly Kettle. If she had just been quietly strangled in a back alley the body should have turned up by now, found by some couple seeking privacy or by an inquisitive dog. If she was dead there was no hurry. But if she was alive and at the mercy of, say, an over-muscled mother's boy with a mouth, then she needed to be rescued and right speedily.

When Phryne came down Miss Steel was waiting for her. She had refused Mr Butler's offers of refreshment, to his evident distress, and was only barely sitting on a chair in the hall. She leapt to her feet as Phryne approached.

'Miss Steel.' She held out a muscular hand.

'Miss Fisher,' responded Phryne.

'Shall we go?' asked the woman.

Phryne looked at her. A tall, energetic brunette with bright eyes and a hard mouth; not a woman to be lightly crossed, especially when armed with a clipboard.

'You have a car?' she asked of Miss Steel.

'Outside,' said Miss Steel.

Not one for idle chatter, thought Phryne. She gathered gloves and handbag and bade her household be good in her absence. She seemed to hear the populace draw a deep breath of relief as she took Miss Steel of the Welfare out of the house.

'Jack said you were all right,' said Miss Steel, as she folded her length into a smallish car of indeterminate make. The driver did not speak or smile, but started the vehicle as soon as Phryne had shut her door.

'I am,' said Phryne.

'I have met Mrs Ryan,' said Miss Steel. She had an exact, precise way of speaking, which cut off her words with a decisive snap of white teeth. Phryne began to feel she was in some sort of fairy tale. Possibly Miss Steel was the Big Bad Wolf. And her driver was as unresponsive as one of the living dead in a novel she had just been reading about Haiti. He drove very well, however. For a zombie. Footscray loomed.

'Lying-in homes are not as regulated as hospitals,' Miss Steel informed her. 'But they can be inspected at any time without notice. Jack says that you suspect a girl might be being held prisoner there.'

'It's a possibility,' said Phryne.

'Then we shall find her, if she is there,' said Miss Steel. 'I am entitled to unlock any door. If they have conveniently lost the keys, then Willis will break it down.'

'He can do that?' asked Phryne.

'Oh, yes,' said Miss Steel.

Phryne looked at the driver. He still showed no expression. Phryne's identification of him as a resurrected cabbie was firming. 'Oh, good.'

There seemed nothing else to say. Miss Steel checked her clipboard. Phryne looked out the window at the docks flying past. The pickets were still there, the huge iron doors shut fast. Soon they arrived at Mrs Ryan's house.

Still unspeaking, Willis opened the gate for Miss Steel and her companion. He marched up the steps and rang the bell. There was silence. Then he knocked like thunder. Nothing happened.

Miss Steel and Willis exchanged a glance. Willis returned to the car and came back with a sledgehammer.

'One moment,' said Phryne. It was an old lock, of no complexity. She picked it in a moment with her hatpin.

'Jack said you had valuable skills, Miss Fisher,' observed Miss Steel without a smile. 'Willis?'

Willis preceded them into the house of the pious widow. It still stank of carbolic and naphthalene. No one in the front rooms, which bore marks of a hasty exit. The picture of the Sacred Heart stared Phryne in the eye. They went down the hall towards the back of the house, where someone was crying.

Several somethings, in fact. Four beds were packed close together in a cramped room. Four women lay there with four new babies. All of them were crying, including the small maidservant, who was standing at the doorway with a burnt saucepan in her hand, weeping like a funeral. The smell was almost a character in itself. One of the beds was soaked with blood and the coppery tang overbore the other unpleasant smells: excrement and despair and burnt milk.

'Call an ambulance,' Miss Steel told Willis. Phryne inspected the bleeding woman. She was still alive. She grabbed at Phryne's hand.

'An ambulance is coming,' Phryne told her. 'Lie still.'

'You, girl,' ordered Miss Steel. 'Take that object back into the kitchen, put on the kettle, wash your face and return for orders.'

The child gaped. Then she did as she was told. Miss Steel picked up each baby, looked disinterestedly into the screaming face, joggled it expertly and gave it to its mother. Silence began to fall. Cradling the last baby in her blue-clad arms, Miss Steel turned her gaze on the most conscious patient, a woman with sweat-soaked blonde hair and haunted blue eyes.

'Tell me what happened. Where is Mrs Ryan?'

'Bloody went off this bloody morning. Bloody early. Dunno where. Bloody bitch. Bloody rotten bitch! Damn her to hell. Left poor bloody Ellie there. Bloody knew she was bleeding.'

'Why didn't you go out and get help?' asked Phryne.

'She's got our bloody clothes,' said the woman. 'So we won't bloody run away. And I'm a bit bloody wobbly on me pins.'

'You, girl,' snapped Miss Steel to the servant, who had returned. 'Your name?'

'Mary, Miss.' The girl was mopped up and as lucid as she ever was. Probably it was a relief to hear someone give unequivocal orders. And she had put down her milk saucepan.

'Don't you bloody bully her,' said the blonde woman. 'Poor bloody little scrap's been doing her bloody best.'

Miss Steel gave the woman a long look so full of cold venom that she faltered and buried her face in her child's meagre wrappings.

'Where are the clothes?' asked Miss Steel. 'Show me.'

Mary led the way to a large linen press. It was, of course, locked. Phryne produced her hatpin again. The lock yielded. Inside were bundles of shabby garments. Miss Steel loaded the maid with them and ordered her to assist the mothers to dress.

'Where are they going?' asked Phryne.

Miss Steel tried the poisonous look on Phryne, who smiled sunnily and repeated the request. Miss Steel recognised a nature as adamant as her own and finally replied, 'Back to the convent. They cannot stay here.'

'They're in no state to walk,' said Phryne. 'Do you know a nice nurse who could care for them for a week or so?'

Miss Steel sneered. 'And who should pay for such a nurse? Wages, food, fuel? The government? I don't believe I could authorise such expenditure.'

'Me,' said Phryne. 'Do you know such a nurse? I'm looking for a pleasant efficient lady. These girls have suffered enough.'

Miss Steel was not used to this sort of benevolence; it was like a slap in the face. Jack Robinson had told her she would find Miss Fisher educational. She was beginning to think that this might be so.

'I shall telephone,' she said, and for the first time since she was six beat a retreat from another person.

Returned, Phryne told the patients that they need not try to rise and dress. The blonde woman shoved her hair back from her eyes and said, 'I bloody heard all that. Can you bloody do it?'

'Oh, yes,' said Phryne. 'What's your name? I'm Phryne Fisher.'

'Oh, jeez,' said the blonde woman. 'I bloody know your sister. I'm Phoebe. Miss Eliza really bloody admires you. Now I can bloody well see why.'

At that point the ambulance arrived to take Ellie to hospital. Her baby went with her. Phryne instructed them to take her to the Queen Victoria and tell the admitting doctor that Phryne had sent her.

The small maid brought in tea. Phryne waited until they had eaten Mrs Ryan's private store of shortbread. They were weak, she thought, because they had been starved. Every face was hollow and hungry. The babies were thin and wailed because their mothers didn't have the spare calories to make enough milk. Phryne was disgusted with the human race. Wolves, between ravenings, treated their pregnant and nursing females better than this.

Willis returned. He stood at ease, perfectly composed and expressionless, waiting for another order from his hougon, Miss Steel.

'Now, I need to know if there is anyone else here,' Phryne said to the patients. 'I'm looking for a woman reporter who came here yesterday. This is the last place she was seen. Anyone know anything?'

'We weren't bloody allowed out of this room,' responded Phoebe.

'But you used to listen,' said Phryne.

'Of course. Nothing else to do here but bloody wait for the next bloody bowl of gruel and read the bloody Bible. Not the whole Bible, mind. Just the nice bits. Nothing bloody exciting.'

'And? What did you hear?'

'Just a bit of talk. Then the bloody door slamming.'

'Drat,' said Phryne. 'I am sending you a nurse, ladies, who

will care for you until you recover. If you want to leave, you can leave. Stay here for a little while longer,' she added and, collecting Willis, went out to explore the rest of the house.

'I'm tired of picking locks,' she told him. 'If a door is fastened, break it down.'

He hefted his sledgehammer. For the first time she saw a trace of emotion on his face. It seemed that Willis really liked knocking down doors.

The other bedroom belonged to the son, Patrick. It had been wrecked, evidently by someone in a hurry to collect their belongings. Phryne picked through the rubbish. Lone socks, horrible underwear, a few discarded wrappers, bottles, butts and newspapers. No letters, cards or directions to the post office. Nothing to her purpose. The next room was locked and Phryne stepped back to allow the zombie room to swing. The cheap deal splintered very satisfactorily.

Inside was a camp bed, a chamber-pot, a copy of the Bible and nothing else. The small window was boarded over. It was dark and as hot as hell. Phryne directed Willis's attention to the window. He actually grinned at her. The boards cracked and fell away and light streamed in. Willis swung again and smashed the small window, where the glass was already broken. He was clearly enjoying his day. Phryne wasn't.

The chamber-pot was empty but smelt stale. The camp bed was barely more than strings. Prisoners had been kept here. Phryne sat down on the stretcher and looked at the plaster wall. It was scribbled over with names, pleas and rather crude anatomical drawings. Phryne went back for her bag, a pen and paper, and a further interrogation of the patients.

'She locked us in there if we answered her back,' offered the dark-haired woman, who said her name was Louise. 'Or stole food.'

'She bloody did,' agreed Phoebe. 'And I bloody kicked her bloody son a bloody good one in the shins when he shut me in there. Pity I had bloody bare feet, but.'

'Didn't do you any good,' observed Louise.

'Ah, yes, the son,' said Phryne. 'Did he rape you?'

Phoebe raised an eyebrow at this plain language.

'No,' she replied. 'He didn't bloody like pregnant women. He bloody pinched and slapped, though. Mean bloody bastard.'

'Enjoyed cruelty?' said Phryne.

'He bloody did,' agreed Phoebe.

'What did you write on the wall?' asked Phryne.

'Die you bloody bastards,' said Phoebe.

'Very restrained of you,' said Phryne.

Thereafter Phryne took a large sheet of butcher's paper and traced every legend on the cell wall. Position might prove important. Then she searched the house. The kitchen was clean. It contained enough food to feed the patients for the rest of the day, though judging by the porridge pot and the supply of oats they had been existing on gruel. There were also liberal supplies evidently meant for Mrs Ryan and her repulsive son. The yard was clean and orderly and bare. There were no more doors for Willis to smash and he returned to his resting trance.

Mrs Ryan's office had to be the place where she might find a clue. Miss Steel had replaced the telephone and was writing notes for her report in a fast, efficient shorthand. Phryne nodded to her and began to take drawers out of the desk.

After an hour she had gleaned that Mrs Ryan's paperwork was all in order, that she had an unexpected passion for Turkish delight flavoured with rosewater, her son smoked Capstan cigarettes, her sister lived in South Yarra and she had stolen the patients' letters. They had been opened and thrown into the bottom drawer of the desk. This piece of gratuitous cruelty made Phryne want to borrow Willis's sledgehammer and break something. Preferably Mrs Ryan's head. Pointless to shove that sharp letter opener through her heart as she clearly didn't have one. Phryne gathered the envelopes and began to sort.

The most recent were on the top. She took them back into the patients' room.

'Phoebe?' she said. 'There's a letter—two letters—here for you. Sorry, nothing for you, Louise. And what is your name?'

'Annie,' muttered the woman who had not spoken. Her voice was dead. With this sort of neglect, a recent birth and nowhere to go, Annie might just give up and slide down into death herself. Her baby was not even crying. Phryne located a letter for Annie Jordan. She held it out. Annie did not even reach for it.

'There's nothing out there for me,' she mumbled and closed her eyes.

'You bloody beaut,' said Phoebe. 'Me sister's gonna take the baby. And I can go back to bloody work.'

'On the streets?' asked Phryne. Phoebe sat up straighter.

'That's me bloody place. I'm all bloody right on the streets. And I won't get bloody caught again, falling in bloody love with a bloody client and believing his bloody lies. Come on, love,' she said roughly to Annie. 'Pull yourself together! Gimme the bloody letter, I'll bloody read it to you.'

Phryne watched as Phoebe laid aside her baby, unfolded the letter, and read it to herself. She gave Phryne a sharp glance and handed it back.

'Not for this poor bloody Annie after all,' she said. Phryne took the letter away.

It was a brief and cold announcement that her father had barred her from his house. She was not to try to speak to her sisters or her mother. But she was enjoined to pray God for forgiveness for her sin. And for her false accusation against that good man, Father Kennedy. Phryne folded the letter into its envelope and shoved it into her bag. This would repay further investigation.

Miss Steel had returned.

'Mrs Chappell lives just around the corner and is on her way,' she said with faint astonishment, aware that she was reporting to Phryne. 'If you will guarantee her wages and the girls' board then she is happy to stay for two weeks. She is between engagements.'

'Did you tell her about this situation?' asked Phryne.

'Yes. She just wanted an assurance that Mrs Ryan had gone. She seems to have taken against her.'

'I can't imagine why,' said Phryne, and led Miss Steel to the cell. Miss Steel's cold face became colder. She went from the colour of good porcelain to vanilla ice cream.

'I've made notes of all the graffiti,' said Phryne. 'If Miss Kettle was here, she might have written on the wall. I shall have to puzzle it out in a better light.'

'When I find Mrs Ryan,' said Miss Steel, 'she will be in trouble.'

'And if I find that she has connived with her rotten son to kidnap a journalist, she will be in jail for many years,' said Phryne. 'So she will be in trouble with you and also really, really sorry.'

Unexpectedly, Miss Steel held out a hand. 'I believe that she will,' she said, and almost smiled.

Phoebe dragged herself out of bed, staggered a little, then actually left the cramped, hot room. She walked to the kitchen, steadying herself against the wall. There she opened cupboards and the icebox.

'Bloody bitch,' she remarked almost under her breath. 'She's had all this bloody food and let us do a bloody perish. You there, tall and handsome. Fetch me that bloody pot, will you? And the bloody butter and eggs and bacon and the milk. And bloody slice some of that bread. Girls, we are going to bloody have lunch.'

Willis looked at Miss Steel. She made no move. So he did as he was ordered, showing unexpected skill with the bread knife and today's loaf. Phoebe had sunk down in a chair, out of strength for the moment but fighting still. Phryne turned away to hide her smile.

'What can we do with all these letters?' she asked.

'Another crime to add to Mrs Ryan's list of offences,' said Miss Steel. 'Return to sender, I suppose.'

'I'll take them,' said Phryne. 'I'm going to the convent soon. Some of the women might still be working there.'

'Caught in the grip of an outmoded belief system,' said Miss Steel. Not a fan of religion, it seemed. Mind you, Phryne thought, she was rapidly going off it herself.

Nurse Chappell arrived. She was a small, plump, rosy woman of perhaps forty in a plain grey dress. Phryne saw that she had a carpet bag, a watch pinned to her bosom, an air of no-nonsense competence, and a faint scent of carbolic.

'Miss Steel,' she greeted the woman from the Welfare. 'And you must be Miss Fisher. I've heard so much about you. Now, what have we here?'

Phryne outlined the situation. She put a banknote into Mrs Chappell's hands.

'Food,' she instructed. 'Whatever you think proper. Hire a nursemaid if you like. They can stay or leave as they wish. And have a care to Annie. I think she might despair.'

'Not in my nursery,' said Mrs Chappell briskly. Phryne credited the statement. Annie would recover or Mrs Chappell would know the reason why. Miss Fisher consulted her watch.

'Right, now I must go into the city. Can you give me a lift or shall I summon a taxi?'

'I must stay here for a while,' said Miss Steel. 'Willis shall drive you wherever you wish to go.'

Willis handed over the bread knife, Phryne farewelled the patients, and she was carried into the city in the small unremarkable car.

'Have you been with Miss Steel long?' asked Phryne, settling her hat and trying to shake off gloom.

'Six years,' he said. 'She's all right. We see some dreadful things, but. Hard on a family man.'

'It must be.'

'A man just wants to take 'em all home,' he said. 'Like puppies. And it gives a man a bad view of his fellow man.'

'Oh, I can understand that,' said Phryne.

'All them kids have fathers,' he continued in a rush of words. 'Where are they? How could they just leave them poor girls like that?'

'A question I have frequently asked of myself,' replied Phryne.

'So a man just tries not to feel,' he explained.

'But it doesn't work,' she said gently.

'Nah,' he said, and lapsed into his zombie trance again.

CHAPTER SEVEN

I know not whether Laws be right
Or whether Laws be wrong;
All we know that lie in gaol
Is that the wall is strong . . .

Oscar Wilde
'The Ballad of Reading Gaol'

Bidding Willis farewell (he grunted, evidently regretting his loquacity) as they arrived at Flinders Lane, Phryne got out of the car and walked down to the discreet entrance of the Blue Cat Club. It was surrounded by tailors and furriers. On the corner of Calico Alley stood a respectable tall stone building in a style which could loosely be described as Victorian Gothic, with Palladian overtones. The newly finished Majorca Building, all Moorish lamps and coloured tiles, stood on the other side of the alley. At the Collins Street end of the lane, occupied by seamstresses, button makers, stamp collectors and sellers of bric a brac, was one of Phryne's favourite arcades. This was a part of the city which she always found intriguing.

The brass plate which proclaimed that this was her destination also bore the legend *Gentlemen Only*. Undeterred, she pressed the button and the door gaped. Inside, a tall, uniformed figure stared at her in amazement.

'Miss Fisher,' she said, and passed the portal. 'Mr Featherstonehaugh is expecting me.'

'As you say, Miss,' said the functionary stiffly, preceding her through a tiled hallway into a large room glittering with diamonds.

They were, of course, only crystal chandeliers and lamps with crystal drops, but the effect was dazzling. The room was empty at this hour. It was the Cafe Royale, writ large. Plush. Gold leaf. Marble copies of the Apollo Belvedere and the David. The scent of patchouli, so favoured by dear Oscar, and beeswax furniture polish flowed over her. She sniffed gratefully as it obliterated even the memory of mothballs. She softened her stance. Here, at least, she would meet no gentlemen who might contribute to Miss Steel's overflowing portfolio of misused children and abandoned women.

Mr Featherstonehaugh was waiting for her. He was a smallish, rounded gentleman wearing an impeccable evening suit with just a hint of the velvet and silk of the eighties. He had abundant white hair in a Neapolitan style favoured in the old days. He smelt bewitchingly of amber essence. His hand, as she took it, was smooth, plump and white with one gold signet ring. He seemed altogether charming and harmless until her eyes met his: dark, penetrating and stern. Oh, Lord, thought Phryne, another strong character. That makes two in one morning. I do hope he is going to offer me a drink.

He conducted her to a positively indecent chair and snapped his fingers. A waiter brought a silver tray on which reposed a tall glass jug, tinkling with ice, two glasses, and a small plate of

Kalamata olives. Phryne settled into the chair, which embraced her tired limbs with fervour. The contrast between this luxury and Mrs Ryan's house could hardly be greater. Mr Featherstonehaugh murmured polite observances about the weather and ordered the waiter to pour the distinguished visitor a drink.

This, on tasting, proved to be cider cup. But not entirely cider and lemonade. She considered the taste.

'Pear,' she observed. 'A little cognac. And something else.'

'Indeed,' her host said gravely. 'The secret is guava jelly. Just a touch of the tropics. We go through gallons of it in the summer. The gentlemen find it agreeably cooling.'

'And not too intoxicating,' she said.

'Indeed. Thank you very much for coming to see us, Miss Fisher.'

'My pleasure, I assure you.'

'I have . . . several of my gentlemen have told me . . . that you might be able to put my mind at rest,' he said, with uncharacteristic lack of clarity.

'Which gentlemen?' she asked, taking another sip of the cider cup. She must ask Mr Butler if he knew how to make it.

Mr Featherstonehaugh named several friends, whom Phryne had always regretted because they played so firmly for the other team.

She nodded. 'I would be delighted to reassure you,' she said gently. He really was *bouleversé*. 'Tell me all.'

'Some history, Miss Fisher?'

'If you please. I am very comfortable and I do not have to be anywhere else for some time.'

Mr Featherstonehaugh smoothed his hair and lit a rose-leaf-tipped cigarette. Phryne allowed the waiter to ignite her gasper. There was silence as the smoke drifted upwards like incense to some phallic god. Finally he spoke.

'When the Great Scandal broke in 1895, I was only a young man, but I realised that for such as myself England was finished. Most of us fled to France, along with the divine Oscar, who really was such a fool. He thought he was untouchable, when none of us are safe. He thought his position would secure him, and it didn't. He thought his friends would rescue him, and they couldn't. Or wouldn't. He went to Paris to die, and did, and I went to Paris, too. But I could not settle. It was so . . .'

'French?' offered Phryne.

He smiled. 'Just so. The police had found out their strength under the Criminal Law Amendment Act—Oscar taught them that, too, unfortunately—and were ranging for revenge with Até at their side. No one has ever approved of us. They have tolerated us at best. But you know this,' he said.

'I know.' Phryne drank more cider and the waiter refilled her glass.

'So I realised my assets and sailed for, well, as far away as I could go. Australia. Where no one really believes in men loving men, and don't particularly care if they do. Oh, yes, it is illegal—' he held up one finger in case Phryne should protest '—but the only cases which get to court are those which are visible. Soliciting in public toilets and public parks and so on, and a couple of notorious sailors' hotels in St Kilda. And schoolmasters and priests preying on pupils and choirboys, naturally—such actions are entirely reprehensible.'

'And not confined to one gender,' said Phryne, a letter about a certain Father Kennedy in her bag.

'Indeed. You do not consider one sort of predation worse than the other?'

'No,' said Phryne. 'I would happily execute all those who rape children. By evisceration,' she elaborated.

'I, too,' said Mr Featherstonehaugh. She looked into his eyes. She recognised truth. 'Do nibble at an olive. I believe they are considered rather good. I import them from Greece. We do not cater for that perversion here. We never have. I bought this building, equipped and furnished it, as a safe haven where we could be ourselves. And I have operated it since 1909 without incident. We have never attracted police attention. I have taken . . . certain precautions.'

'These olives really are excellent,' observed Phryne, knowing he meant that selected persons had been paid off. It probably also meant that the neighbours were paid a small amount to warn the club if a raid was gathering outside. And there was undoubtedly a safe way out, possibly through the cellar.

'I'm so glad you think so,' he said. 'Not all our members are . . . so,' he said, crooking his little finger in the universally recognised signal. 'Some are just gentlemen who are—well, perhaps one could say "over-womaned".'

'Married with sisters and aunts and cousins and daughters?' asked Phryne.

'Exactly. This is a place where they do not have to remember their manners. We also,' his voice radiated pride, 'have an excellent chef. Well, two. One for plain fare and one French. Though he's actually Calabrian. Downstairs they will see nothing which might offend them. Upstairs they will not be allowed to go. What goes on there never impinges on the ordinary Blue Cat members.'

'I understand,' said Phryne. 'Cafe Royale rules.'

'Quite. The ordinary ones consider that belonging to this club is a little daring, a little risqué; they like the frisson and they love the food. I brought with me a chef who was my dear friend at the time. He left me his recipes when he died—too young, poor chap. Such fare as cannot be obtained in Australia.

Even *ortolans en brochette.*' He winced for some reason. 'The members of the inner circle, as you might say, all know each other. So there is no chance that . . .'

'They might blackmail anyone, because they can be blackmailed in their turn,' said Phryne. 'Any scandal would reflect on all of you. I understand.'

'Good. So imagine how I felt when I saw this in the *Hawklet*.'

Phryne read the cutting.

CLEVELAND STREET IN MELBOURNE?

A little bird tells us that a scandal is imminent which will stagger Melbourne's high society. And it will happen in Flinders Lane at a club for gentlemen. Expect dreadful revelations!

'Oh, dear,' said Phryne.

'There is only one gentlemen's club in Flinders Lane,' said Mr Featherstonehaugh.

'This is dated March last year,' she observed. 'Nothing since then?'

'No. But I am worried. There can be no Cleveland Street scandal here. Here there are no miserable messenger boys obliging gentlemen for money. We do not even allow consenting—nay, eager—sailors of the merchant marine or soldiers who have discovered their true nature in the trenches, unless they are members already. We have no prostitutes here, Miss Fisher. Of that, I can assure you.'

'This must be a very well-conducted club,' said Phryne gently. The man was on the verge of tears and would never forgive himself if he cried in front of a woman. 'I don't think you have anything to worry about, really.'

'But this wretched missing reporter!' he protested. 'She was last seen here! I fear . . . I fear . . .'

'That some of your more enthusiastic members might have removed her? Because you all walk on a razor's edge, and any slip would be total, utter ruin?'

'Yes,' said Mr Featherstonehaugh softly.

Phryne signalled to the waiter, who had been a stolid earwitness throughout. 'Cognac,' she said. 'Fast.'

He vanished and reappeared, holding the glass, in a whisk of black and white. Obviously one of the Mr Butler school of Domestic Service. Phryne gestured to him to hold the glass. Now was not the time for her to come over all motherly, though she was deeply sympathetic. Mr Featherstonehaugh gulped, sobbed, turned it into a cough, and mopped his brow with an exquisite linen handkerchief.

'I'm so sorry, Miss Fisher,' he faltered.

'It's nothing,' she told him. 'Now, be comforted. Miss Kettle was seen at another place after your club. She vanished from Footscray. No one will investigate you. Not even as to where you find ortolans in Australia. Where no ortolans fly.'

'Are you sure of this?' asked Mr Featherstonehaugh.

'Certain. I am pursuing several lines of enquiry, but none of them concern you or your excellent establishment.'

He relaxed at last into the amorous embrace of the plush chair.

'Oh, I have been so worried,' he said.

The waiter patted his shoulder and offered him more brandy, which he sipped.

'But you can do something for me,' Phryne continued. 'Your members are used to keeping secrets, and they are everywhere. If anyone hears anything about Polly Kettle, I would be much obliged if they would tell me.'

'Of course, Miss Fisher,' said Mr Featherstonehaugh.

'Is any member of your club involved in any way with the press?'

'I trust you, Miss Fisher, but I cannot disclose any of the members' names.'

'Yes, quite. I meant, if any of them are, perhaps I could meet them? My word is my bond and I swear not to even write down their names.'

Mr Featherstonehaugh thought about this. He drank more brandy. He looked up at the waiter and said flirtatiously, 'The best cognac, my dear?'

'Only the best for you, Boss,' said the waiter in a broad Australian accent. 'I thought you were going to keel over.'

'Well, well, I applaud your generous spirit. Spirits. Hah! Very well, Miss Fisher. We shall invite you to lunch.'

'Gentlemen only,' Phryne pointed out.

'You shall be an honorary gentleman,' he said slyly.

'I have always tried to behave like one,' she responded.

'And if you solve this case without involving us, I shall tell you the secret of *ortolans en brochette*. In Australia.'

'Deal,' said Phryne, and held out her hand.

She returned home with the name of the book from which the delectable cider cup had derived, still wondering about the ortolans. Surely a man of Mr Featherstonehaugh's refinement wasn't cooking budgies?

Lunch was cold chicken and ham sandwiches and ice cream for dessert. Very satisfactory, Phryne thought, considering the Blue Cats' two cooks. One for rice pudding and roly poly and steak and kidney pudding, and one for *Mont-Blanc aux marrons* and *quiche lorraine* and *boeuf en daube*. Cunning.

After lunch she laid out her butcher's paper and displayed it for her minions.

'Ooh,' said Tinker, looking at the rude words.

'Interesting,' said Jane, looking at the diagrams. 'They've got the labia entirely wrong, you know.'

Phryne smiled. Thus the scientific mind.

'Yes, but that need not concern us here. This is the wall from Mrs Ryan's prison cell. I want you to sort out the entries. I want the ones which don't say the equivalent of "die you bloody bastards". I know who wrote that one.'

'Are you looking for a clue, Miss Phryne?' asked Jane. 'Should I get Ruth?'

'Where is she?'

'In the kitchen, Mrs Butler's making an ice-cream concoction. Something to do with egg whites. They weren't whipping properly so I thought I might take my book into the parlour to get out of the way.'

'Bombe Alaska,' diagnosed Phryne. 'Delicate work in this heat. No need to disturb her. Can you and Tinker make notes for me? I have to call a bishop.'

'Yes, Miss Phryne,' replied Jane. 'I'll take this side, you have that side, and we'll meet in the middle?' she said to Tinker. He nodded.

Phryne left them sorting out the invective from the anatomically incorrect and went to the telephone. The weather had turned humid and she found thinking difficult. Walking to her own hall was like wading through warm treacle. The limbs seemed to be weighted and the intellect fogged. How anyone ever gets anything done in the tropics I can't imagine, she thought. And there's going to be the mother and grandmother of a storm fairly soon. The black cat Ember's taken refuge in my wardrobe and Molly's as flat as a dogskin rug on the bathroom tiles. Nothing moving but her poor little panting tongue. And if this goes on I might join her.

She got through to the bishop's secretary fairly easily, but the bishop was not available. Phryne hadn't expected him to be. She made an appointment to see him the next day. She also mentioned that a certain Father Kennedy should be questioned under obedience about the pregnancy of a girl called Annie Jordan. And that if this was not done Miss Fisher would be reluctantly compelled to mention the matter to friends of hers at the *Hawklet*. This snippet caused the secretary to make comprehensive notes about the matter for the bishop's urgent attention. That being as much as she could do from the Catholic angle for the day, Phryne called Jack Robinson and told his sergeant all about Mrs Ryan's disappearance, emphasising that finding Patrick Ryan had become urgent, as it was possible that Polly Kettle was in his hands, and they were not reliable hands. She also asked for and got the address of Polly Kettle's parents in Camberwell.

By that time she had had enough of the telephone and went back to the parlour. Jane and Tinker were discussing what they had found, quite amicably. My, isolation had done that boy a power of good. He even looked more comfortable, sprawling over the paper and breathing heavily through his mouth as he untangled the prisoners' scribblings and wrote the important ones down in his notebook. He was wearing his new shorts and had even abandoned his boots and put on the sandals which he had previously scorned as girlish footwear. Of course, melting feet might have something to do with that.

Phryne still felt slow and stupid. She sat down, rang for Mr Butler and ordered iced lemonade, and read through her own notes. Then she selected the *Encyclopaedia Britannica* and read the entry on ortolans. It was so cruel and disgusting she was very glad that she had missed this gastronomic treat.

The birds, Emberiza hortulana, were identified with the Roman delicacy fig-peckers. Being foolish enough to migrate to France, they were captured alive, kept in a dark box and fed on millet, figs and grapes, then drowned in armagnac. They were then roasted quickly and eaten whole by a diner with a linen cloth draped over his head. The taste was amazing, apparently, from the ambrosial fat to the bitter guts. Revolting. One writer opined that the linen cloth was to allow the diner to hide from God. Sounded reasonable. From the picture, they looked a bit like finches. Phryne could not imagine Mr Featherstonehaugh allowing such brutality to occur at the Blue Cat. She looked forward to his secret.

Thunder rumbled overhead. Phryne drank lemonade and meditated on cruelty. There was such a lot of it about. She was sunk in gloom by the time Jane and Tinker called her over to the big table to receive the gleanings of their study.

'Mostly they're just things like "die you bloody bastards" and "fuck Mrs Ryan". Someone else wrote "only with yours",' giggled Tinker.

'But there is this,' said Jane. 'It doesn't seem to relate to anything else.'

Phryne read the legend *SS 5.10 BM Kollontai.*

'Interesting,' she said.

'What is Kollontai?' asked Jane.

'Alexandra Kollontai, a revolutionary Russian woman. Good work, minions. This is definitely significant,' Phryne told them. They beamed.

'Yes, but what does it mean?' demanded Tinker.

'Ah, there you have me,' said Phryne. 'I don't know yet. But we've seen it before. In relation to Julie Reilly. In the letterbox. I have it here somewhere. Ah, yes.' She exhibited the note. '*Julie, remember the revolution. SS 5.10, BM,*' she read.

'Whatever that means,' said Jane.

'That we shall ascertain. I wonder if it's a phone number? Might be scrambled, of course.'

'There are four hundred and fifty-six million, nine hundred and seventy-six thousand permutations of those seven letters and numbers,' said Jane after a brief calculation.

'Then you had better get started,' said Phryne serenely. 'Is Dot back yet?'

'Yes, Miss Phryne, she's in the garden,' said Jane, slightly dismayed. But it might not be as bad as she thought at first, she told Tinker as they went into the hall. 'The letters have to stay together, two letters for the exchange. So there's only six hundred and seventy-six thousand perms of that.'

'Oh, good,' said Tinker, who had always liked numbers. Especially when they related to how many fish he had to sell to constitute enough potatoes for seven people's dinner. 'Tell me about permutations. Sounds hard.'

'Not really,' said Jane, delighted to have an intelligent auditor. Ruth was only interested in numbers when it came to measuring ingredients. 'You just take the original number of variables . . . There are twenty-six letters in the alphabet, so you just multiply twenty-six by itself, which makes six hundred and seventy-six, for the total number of ways of arranging any two letters. There are three numbers, so you multiply ten by itself twice to make a thousand, and multiply the two together. But now I come to think about it, it won't be that bad, because if the number is a coded version of five hundred and ten then there might be only ten possibilities.'

'How does that work?' Tinker asked, feeling that Jane might not be as tedious a companion as he had thought. This was mind-stretching stuff. He found that he liked the feeling. Jane expounded.

'Let's say it's a code where you add a number to the original one. Say you add four to every number. Then the original telephone number would have been 176. So the ten possibilities would be 510, 621, 732, 843 and so on.'

'So how would the letters work then?' enquired Tinker, suddenly drowning in a sea of numbers.

'You might add a fixed number of letters. If it's four again, then instead of SS it would be WW. So there'd only be twenty-six permutations for the letters. So twenty-six times ten is two hundred and sixty.'

'Unless the numbers and letters you add changes every time?' suggested Tinker.

Jane frowned, while appreciating that this innumerate fisher boy had made a valid comment. Tinker might have his merits after all.

'I really hope they don't, or we'll be in a spot of bother,' Jane answered.

Phryne took her shady hat from its peg by the back door, passing through a cloud of culinary gloom. The egg whites, apparently, had completely declined to be whipped. Mrs Butler was of the opinion that there must have been a speck of grease in the mixing bowl. She was making an apricot cake instead, as Mrs Butler hated waste. Phryne nodded in passing and kept going. The most even-tempered of cooks became unstable when the ingredients rebelled.

Dot was sitting under the arbour, her sewing in her lap, a glass of her most sinful drink, a sherry cobbler, before her. She was always aware that she had signed the pledge when she was eight. A sherry cobbler was as far as her dissipation ever went.

'How goes it, Dot dear?' asked Phryne.

'Nothing useful,' said Dot. 'I was just sitting here, thanking

God for my own nice clean bed and safe roof and good clothes. I can have whatever I want to eat or drink. God has been very good to me. And you, too,' she added hastily, in case Phryne should be offended at being considered an agent of the divine.

'Indeed,' said Phryne, sitting down on the wrought-iron garden chair.

'I could have been one of those girls,' said Dot. 'Before I met you and you rescued me. If that creature had actually got to me. I would have been disgraced and in that convent. How was the lying-in home?' she asked.

'Just as frightful as you can imagine,' said Phryne. 'The Blue Cat Club, however, was palatial. I have suggested to Mr Butler that he buy Mr Terrington's book. He has the nicest concoctions. It's called *Cooling Cups and Dainty Drinks*. Worth buying it for the title. Sometimes civilisation lies in the outsiders, Dot. None of the Blue Cat's members would have anything to do with illegitimate children.'

'Because they aren't interested in women,' said Dot calmly.

'That's so,' agreed Phryne.

'I know they're committing a sin,' said Dot slowly. 'But at least it doesn't hurt anyone else.'

'Bravo,' said Phryne. 'We shall make a bohemian of you yet. What did the priest say?'

'He knows the Kettle family quite well,' said Dot. 'He says Mrs is very devout, Mr only turns up for Easter and Christmas. There's a brother, he never comes to church at all, and Polly used to be there a lot but lately she's been absent, too. He thinks she has a boyfriend. I never met an Anglican priest before. I thought they would be different from our priests but they're really not. I suppose a priest is a priest. He's an old man; seen a lot. I liked him. You ought to meet him, Miss. How did you get on with the bishop?'

'I haven't spoken to him yet, and until I do I can't go to the convent. But this afternoon we just have to pass away the time soothingly, while the minions ring a million phone numbers, the kitchen seethes, and you get on with your tea-cloth. And I finish this mystery, which has to go back to the library. Then we need to return to Collingwood and catch poor Mrs O'Hara. I have a little present for her.'

'Oh, Miss,' said Dot, clutching her embroidery to her bosom. 'Not . . . some of them . . . things?'

'No, just an appointment for a fitting with the Marie Stopes device,' said Phryne soothingly. 'Eleven children are enough for any woman. Wouldn't you agree?'

'The priest says it's a sin,' said Dot, not entirely convinced.

'There's a lot, as I remarked, of sin around,' Phryne told her. 'This way at least we can mitigate the damage.'

'I suppose,' said Dot, and got back to her stitching.

Phryne opened her book and sipped her lemonade. Agatha Christie. What a plotter. Phryne wished briefly that the real world was so amenable to being solved.

Phryne drove to Collingwood without more than the usual number of incidents. Dot kept her eyes firmly shut for the whole journey. The sky was darkening like an ink stain. There was going to be a huge storm soon, and Dot wanted to be alive to see it. Dot liked storms. Poor little Ember was tucked safely away in his wardrobe. And rain might reduce this humidity. Even in the open car Dot was soaked in sweat, which she felt was unladylike.

Mrs O'Hara was a meagre, underfed, overworked harridan. It would be surprising if she was not, Phryne thought. Phryne eyed her. It appeared that she was not presently pregnant. She could see the woman's hip bones through her washed thin dress.

'Yair?' she demanded. She was so tired that no real anger could be heard in her voice. Inside the house, babies wailed.

'We came to your house yesterday,' said Phryne. 'To ask about your daughter Mary.'

'She's not here,' said Mrs O'Hara, defending the doorway with her body.

'I know,' said Phryne gently. 'She's missing.'

'Yair,' said Mrs O'Hara.

'Where might she have gone?' asked Phryne.

'Dunno,' said Mrs O'Hara. 'The others is all still 'ere. You talked to my 'usband?'

'I did,' said Phryne.

''E says you said that Fraser's the father,' said the woman, leaning into the edge of the door and lifting one foot as though it hurt.

'I believe he is,' said Phryne. 'Come on, let us in. It's going to pour in a moment. Is your husband home?' she asked, hoping that a merciful heart failure had removed him from the suffering world.

''E's at the 'ospital,' said Mrs O'Hara, moving aside to let them in. ''E's been attacked.'

'Really?' asked Phryne, pleased. 'By whom?' There were so many possible contenders.

'Dunno,' said Mrs O'Hara, leading them into the hot, crowded, filthy kitchen. ''E says some nun came and 'e keeled over.'

'A nun?' exclaimed Dot, putting her basket of food down on the unscrubbed table.

'Sister Immaculata, 'e said. I dunno,' said Mrs O'Hara and sank down into a chair. Immediately a wave of children engulfed her. She tried to embrace them all. ''E sold Mary to 'im, didn't 'e?'

'Yes,' said Phryne.

'And now she's run away,' said the woman. Her hair straggled out of its bun and she tried to shove it away with a worn, calloused hand.

'Yes,' agreed Dot, distributing lollies with a liberal hand.

'Woman from Children's Protection came.' Mrs O'Hara accepted a cup of strong, heavily sugared tea from Katie. 'Said she'd be back. With food. But she's not goin' to take 'em,' she said fiercely.

'No, they're yours,' agreed Phryne. 'And if you keep this appointment, you need not have any more than you can feed.'

'Thanks, Miss,' said Mrs O'Hara. 'I didn't know,' she told Phryne. 'I never knew he'd do that.'

'No?' said Dot sceptically.

'But she might have been better off with 'im than 'ere,' said Mrs O'Hara, and began to cry.

Katie glared at Phryne. A small boy kicked her in the ankle. Dot grabbed the child and restrained him.

'We are all going to have tea,' she told the children, 'while Miss Phryne talks to your mum. I've brought sandwiches and cake.'

She was immediately mobbed. Silence fell, except for gobbling noises. Table manners were not taught, evidently, in the O'Hara household.

'I'm sorry,' said the woman, wiping her cheeks with both hands. 'I'm that tired.'

'I know,' said Phryne. 'Can you think of where Mary might have gone?'

'Nah. We don't have no relatives. He come 'ere from New Zealand. We've never met none of his family. And my brother was killed in the war, my mum and dad have passed on. I dunno where she might 'ave gone. If you find her, tell 'er that we miss 'er. Tell 'er if she come 'ome I'll deal with 'er dad. The bastard.'

'I'll tell her,' said Phryne. She handed over a parcel of books to Katie, and she and Dot left.

'Phew,' said Dot.

'Absolutely,' said Phryne. She took the time to put the Hispano-Suiza's top up. The sky was leaden and portentous.

They were almost home when the storm hit. Phryne left the big car at the kerb and they ran inside through raindrops as big as golfballs, which seemed to contain much more water than was physically possible. The mosquitoes vanished, the air cleared like magic, and standing on her own porch Phryne rejoiced in the wafts of cool air.

Then she bade her minions leave their phone researches in case of lightning strike and closed the outer door on a really very impressive storm.

CHAPTER EIGHT

Isabel: I will proclaim thee, Angelo; look
for't! . . .
Or with an outstretched throat I'll tell
the world aloud
What man thou art.
Angelo: Who will believe thee, Isabel?
My unsoiled name, the austereness of my
life
My vouch against you, and my place in
the state
Will so your accusation overweigh
That you shall stifle in your own report,
and smell of calumny.

William Shakespeare
Measure for Measure

The lights went out, as they usually did. A cool wind swept through the house from the open kitchen door as Tinker went to his shed to fetch his hurricane lamp. Ruth reported that the Butlers were having a lie-down until the power came back on, and brought iced lemonade.

'I hope the refrigerator doesn't melt,' she worried.

'That takes hours,' said Phryne. 'And if it does, we'll just have to eat all the ice cream.'

Tinker, returning with his lamp, said, 'You beaut!'

'Come in, Lucifer, Son of the Morning,' said Phryne extravagantly. 'Shall we play cards?' she suggested.

'All right,' said Jane. 'It's a bit too dark to read.'

'Snakes and Ladders,' suggested Ruth, who always lost patience playing even Vingt-et-un with Jane, who calculated the odds with every card.

'Good idea, get the box,' said Phryne, who had played far too many games of cards in exigent circumstances. A game called Texas Hold 'Em always reminded her of terribly young and grimy American troops in France in 1918. Poor dough-boys, she thought. Snakes and Ladders she had played with her own siblings. And Jane could have no odds to calculate.

Or could she? Mathematics were a closed book to Phryne. As long as her debits vastly exceeded her credits she was happy. Or perhaps the other way around. Phryne hired mathematical people to do such thinking for her. They seemed to be happy with the arrangement. Ruth found the box and unfolded the Snakes and Ladders board. It was an old one, with happy smiling tots climbing the ladders and gaping, fanged snakes—a Victorian child's toy. They settled down and began to play. One, two, three and up the ladder—joy. And four, five and down a snake, horror.

Molly, nervous, decided that the place to feel safest was lying on Phryne's feet. She was hot and heavy. Phryne slipped off her shoes and reversed the process, resting her own slim feet on the dog. Molly woofed companionably and licked her toes. Molly had always liked the taste of Phryne's skin. Lightning flashed, bleaching the cosy room with actinic light. Thunder thumped like an HE shell. Phryne closed her eyes against a sudden vision of the Western Front. That was thunder. Not high explosive; no stench of blood and sulfur and dead men. She was in her own house. In excellent company. But she shivered. Molly licked her feet to comfort her. Dot divined that something was wrong.

'Miss?' she asked.

'Mmm?' said Phryne.

'Miss, it's your turn,' Dot prompted.

Recalled to the present, for which she was immensely grateful, Phryne threw the dice, pushed her token and went down an exceptionally long snake. Ruth giggled. Tinker went up a ladder and glowed with pride. Jane frowned, attempting to calculate the odds of throwing the right number to get onto a ladder next time . . .

'So what are the odds of throwing a four?' asked Tinker, interested. 'I need a four.'

'One in twelve,' said Jane. 'There are two ways to get a four: a three and a one, or two twos.'

'Every time?' asked Tinker.

'Every time,' affirmed Jane.

'But that doesn't work in two-up,' objected Tinker. 'You can win by following the pennies. You bet on what came up last time. You almost never get a head, tail, head, tail, like that.'

'It shouldn't work like that,' said Jane.

'But it does,' said Tinker, sure of himself. 'My dad took me to a lot of two-up games and he always come—came—out ahead.'

'When we finish this game, we can try it,' said Jane, who was a firm empiricist.

'Meanwhile,' said Dot, 'it's your turn, Tinker.'

'Oh, yair, sorry.' He threw the dice. His one-in-twelve chance came in. And he rose triumphantly up a ladder.

Humanity, thought Phryne. Quite a good idea, after all.

Thunder crashed. Inside his wardrobe, Ember wailed in protest that a royal cat should be so tormented and affronted. Molly licked Dot's feet, too. Ruth concentrated on the game, Jane thought about probability. And the Somme campaign was half a world away in place and time.

The lights came back on in time to prevent an ice-cream orgy, and they separated: Jane and Tinker to throw endless coins before resuming their telephone ordeal; Ruth to the parlour to consult the *Britannica* on endive; Phryne and Dot to sip lemonade and read through the notebooks.

'We'll have to go to Camberwell,' said Phryne eventually. 'Talk to the parents. I'd better do that. Then perhaps another visit to the newsroom. Someone there knows more about Polly Kettle than they have told me, which is very obstructive of them. Where is that girl? If she's just romped off on a folly of her own I shall be cross.'

'She doesn't sound like a romantic sort of girl,' observed Dot, turning another page and puzzling over Jane's script. Tinker wrote neatly, though his spelling was not good, Ruth's recipes would never fail for confusion between 'add sugar' and 'seethe', but Jane's writing looked like an intoxicated inky spider had staggered across the page on the way to the bar for another drink. Which it really didn't need.

'No, she wasn't. Ambitious, innocent, driven by a sense of purpose, with no sense of self-preservation, but not romantic. And the Ryan family gone, leaving only a few odd socks behind. I hope Jack can find them. Storm's over. I'm going for a swim to clear my head.'

'Have a nice time,' murmured Dot, who only swam when the temperature was above one hundred degrees Fahrenheit.

Phryne flew upstairs for costume, bathing cap, towel and sandals, then put her loose shift back on over the ensemble. The cool air slapped her into wakefulness as she walked down her front steps and towards the beach. The air was rain-washed and clean.

As she walked down the beach she shed clothes and then waded into the water. No one there but a few dogs whose owners were calling unavailingly from the shore. One was a Newfoundland who was delighted to tow Phryne out into the deeper water, where she could swim freely, then circled her like a large furry shark, barking occasionally then spluttering with his mouth full of water. It was delightful, and by the time she and the dog beached again, her foul memories had been washed away. The dog trotted away to find someone suitable to shake water all over. A couple of sunbathers further up the beach looked like promising recipients.

On her return, there was news. Somehow the bishop's secretary had managed to insert a call in between the fruitless mathematical ones. The bishop would see Miss Fisher at nine in the morning. The matter of Father Kennedy, the secretary added, was under investigation. Jack Robinson reported that there had been sightings of the Ryans, which he was pursuing. And Mr Featherstonehaugh had invited her to lunch on the morrow, at one. Phryne was pleased and went back to her book. Perhaps Mrs Christie was right. It was just a matter of following the right clues.

Morning dawned for Tinker with the actual rising of the sun through his hessian blind. No one else was awake. He put on his shorts and shirt, found his fishing gear, collected Molly and slipped out of the back gate. It was going to be another hot day and his only chance of a catch was before the surface water got too warm. Then the fish would head for the depths, out of reach of his line. He joined the die-hard old men on the pier. They looked at him, grunted, and made room for him. Molly flopped down beside him. Silence fell. Molly woofed at a seagull who ventured too close. The sea slopped ashore.

'They bitin'?' Tinker asked ritually, after the correct interval.

'Not bad,' conceded the old coot next to him. 'Sea trout, a few.'

Which meant that the water was teeming with prey. He could tell from the sea birds in diving clouds and the occasional round, dog-like head of a seal rising with its whiskers bristling, mouth full of fish. The line jerked. One. Two. More.

Tinker strung his scaled and gutted fish onto his line, tipped his cap to the old men, and walked home with ten sea trout, whistling. Molly barked and frisked beside him.

Mrs Butler was pleased. 'Nothing better than fish straight out of the sea,' she told him. 'Good boy! Yes, you shall have some,' she remarked to Ember, who wreathed around her ankles, tail as straight as a taper. 'Thanks for cleaning them, I hate gutting fish. Have a wash, now, and be ready for breakfast.' She took a deep breath and wrinkled her nose. 'Oh, Lord, that dog! Did she eat all the insides?'

'And rolled in the rest,' admitted Tinker.

'Drat. Well, you know who is going to be washing her before she comes into a Christian household. Out you go, now,' she ordered, and Molly took the offered bone and accepted banishment. She could never understand what people had against delightful fishy smells.

Tinker shrugged. He didn't mind washing a cooperative dog on a hot day. And Molly had really enjoyed those fish guts. He had never had a pet before Miss Fisher's advent into his life. Molly's wholehearted gusto pleased him. And he liked being a provider. At breakfast, everyone would know who had caught the main dish.

Tinker accepted a large fruit bun and went out again to wash both himself and Molly in the obsolete bathtub next to the copper. The garden filled with the noise of splashing.

'I think he's going to be all right,' commented Mr Butler, who liked a piece of fresh fish, lightly fried, with a squeeze of lemon, for breakfast.

'I think so too,' agreed his wife, setting the big frying pan on the stove and decanting a scoop of lard into it. 'Pour me another cuppa, will you, love?'

'I'll do that, and I'll take the tea out to the breakfast room. Miss Dot will be down soon.'

'Good. And the bread, the butter, the toast, the scrambled eggs, the marmalade and the Vegemite are all on the trolley. Fish'll be ready soon.'

All was peaceful in the kitchen and the garden, where Molly was shaking herself, restored to sweetness and scented only with yellow soap, which she considered an inferior aroma compared to fish guts. Tinker dried both of them, dressed and went in for breakfast in a very happy frame of mind.

This continued as even Jane, forking in the white flakes while she read her book, remarked that the fish tasted very good today.

By the time Phryne descended the breakfast room was empty and they had all scattered: Ruth to the kitchen, Jane and Tinker back to the phone, and Dot to the garden. Dot was doing *The Age* crossword and trying to make sense of nine across when she saw what Phryne was wearing.

'Oh, Miss!' She jumped to her feet. 'You're going to see the bishop! Shouldn't you change?'

'Why?' Phryne looked down at her rose-coloured shift, embroidered with clove pinks around the hem. It had an enchantingly cut little jacket and did not show any immodest flesh, not even her elbows. With it went a dusty pink cloche. And she had handmade grey leather shoes. Phryne thought that the bishop ought to appreciate being able to look at such a spectacle of stylish female beauty.

'The skirt! It's so short!' protested Dot.

'Look, Dot dear, I've no further patience with the sensibilities of clerics. God made my knees and he had a purpose for them. Anyway, you can only see them if I sit down and I'm inclined not to sit with this bishop unless he shows signs of cooperating. There are girls missing and at least one priest who has fathered a child, and I'm out of all charity with him. Them. Are you coming or not?'

'I'll have to get changed,' said Dot.

'Then give me your crossword and I'll wait out here for you.'

Dot surrendered the puzzle and hurried away. Phryne perched on a white wrought-iron chair and did her best with nine across. She had just filled in *anarchy* for *State of chaos* when Mr Butler called her to the telephone, which had managed to squeeze in a ring while Tinker and Jane were taking a break for lemonade and shortcake. It was Jack Robinson, who reported that Patrick Ryan had hired a van. The number had been conveyed to all police stations across the state, and someone would probably see it. Enthralled neighbours had reported hurried packing and a hasty departure.

'What did you say to them?' asked Robinson, nettled.

'Nothing controversial,' replied Phryne. 'Their own consciences, assuming they have such a thing, supplied the terror. 'The wicked flee where no man pursueth, Jack dear.'

'Yes, I suppose so,' he grumbled. 'What are you doing today?'

'Going to interview a bishop, lunch at the Blue Cat Club, and visit some nuns,' said Phryne.

'The Blue Cat? You won't find anyone to enchant there, Miss Fisher.'

'No. Tell me, any complaints about that club?'

'None. They're very quiet, very discreet. We've got no trouble with the queans. They're not to be taken lightly, mind. Few years ago some bright public school oafs decided to crash one of their banquets. They didn't realise that some of the members were rugby players and boxers. The bad boys nearly completed their careers served up on a silver dish, baked, for supper. They stripped them naked and painted their, er, genitalia blue and threw them out into Flinders Lane, to the horror of all passers-by. Never happened again. You take care, Miss Fisher.'

'I am more likely to be in trouble with the nuns,' said Phryne, blew him an invisible kiss, and hung up.

The bishop proved to be a dessicated cleric of some seventy summers, which appeared to have baked him like a mummy. He was scribbling notes, consulting a thick book. He did not seem to notice his visitors, though they had been announced by his secretary.

Phryne was not in the mood to be ignored. She began to count aloud.

'In five seconds I am going to the newspapers. One, two, three, four . . .'

'Miss Fisher?' asked the bishop, putting down his pencil.

'The same. Good morning, Your Reverence.' Phryne managed to keep an ironic edge out of her voice.

'Good morning, good morning.' Even his voice was as dry as deserts. 'Your companion?'

'This is Miss Williams,' said Phryne.

Dot bobbed and kissed the amethyst on the dried talon held out to her. The fact that Phryne hadn't done this registered on the bishop.

'And you are not a daughter of the Church, Miss Fisher?'

'I am a daughter of the aristocracy,' said Phryne grimly. 'Which is not the same thing, but can come in useful.'

'This matter of Father Kennedy?'

'Quite. A young woman called Annie Jordan gave birth in extremely unpleasant circumstances, and that priest was the father of her child.'

'Do you have proof?' he asked.

'I have her word.'

'The word of a fallen woman!' he sneered.

'Ah. Well, if that is your attitude, I am sure that my friends from the *Hawklet* and the *Truth* will be fascinated.'

'They wouldn't dare . . .' he began.

'Because your John Wren bully-boys will drop in and break the press? Good heavens, I wonder what the archbishop will think of that. I shall ask when I see him.'

The bishop was really paying attention to her now. Phryne thought it was similar to being examined by a crocodile. In Darwin, as she recalled. It had lain on its sandbank and summed her up the same way: threat, landscape or prey. Phryne had never, since childhood, been prey. And was far too active to be landscape.

'You know the archbishop?' he grated.

'Oh, indeed, and he owes me a favour. Quite a large one, as favours go.'

'Father Kennedy is a very well-thought-of priest,' said the bishop.

'Indeed, I am sure that he is charming. Otherwise he would never have been able to seduce devout girls. Possibly he finds them more amusing than the bad girls—more of a challenge. However, let that be as it may, he is going to be punished and Miss Jordan is going to be supported, is she not?' Phryne said flatly.

'I shall summon him,' said the bishop. 'I shall take his confession. If matters are . . . as you say, then he will be called to the closed community in Daylesford. They spend all day in prayer.'

'No girls?' asked Phryne.

'No other people except monks,' he said. Was that a small evil smile lurking at the side of the lizard's mouth?

'And Miss Jordan?' asked Phryne.

'Leave her details with my secretary and we shall make suitable arrangements. She will be supported. And her child of shame. Her parents will be compensated for her care and the situation explained. The usual story is a hidden marriage and an early bereavement. Papers will be provided to prove this.'

'Neat,' said Phryne admiringly.

He gave her a long look and blinked his hooded eyes. 'It seems to be adequate. Was there something else, Miss Fisher?'

'I need to visit the Convent of the Good Shepherd in Abbotsford. I gather I need your permission to question the nuns.'

'You do,' he said.

Silence fell. Phryne did not break it. Dot fidgeted. This was no way to talk to a prince of the church! If lightning struck Miss Phryne, Dot would not have been surprised.

However, no lightning fell. The phone rang in the secretary's office. Outside the window a thrush disputed possession of a worm with another thrush who had seen it first. Still no one spoke. Dot was at screaming point. Phryne was perfectly composed, ankles crossed, knees on shameless display, hands in lap, seeming to be listening to the avian quarrel outside. She was thinking about something else and might easily sit there all day, occupying a part of the bishop's office which ought to be tidily vacant. She was detestably calm. Finally, he broke.

'Your reasons for questioning the sisters?'

'Three girls left the lying-in home. I want to know where they went. Also, a reporter is missing, and the proprietors of that lying-in home have done a very fast moonlight flit. I would like to know their destination, too. The young woman may be in danger.'

'And you think the sisters might know?'

'They might.'

'And you think that they might tell you?' The 'you' was emphasised with scorn.

'If you order them to comply, yes.'

Abruptly, the bishop gave up. 'Very well, Miss Fisher. Ask Jenkins for the letter of introduction. I shall telephone the Mother Superior myself. Is that enough for you?' He sounded ragged.

Phryne stood up. 'Yes, that will be all for now,' she said, and walked out. Dot fell in behind her.

They stood by Jenkins' desk while he typed the letter of introduction, had it signed by the bishop (who was repairing his outrage at being outfaced with neat gin) and left.

On the street outside, Dot drew in a deep breath. 'You're brave, Miss!'

'Nothing to be afraid of,' said Phryne, leading the way back to the big car. 'He's not my spiritual superior. Or anyone's. Now Mannix, he's a different kettle of fish. But I was a little disappointed,' she observed, getting into the car and pressing the starter.

'Why?' asked Dot, still amazed that something biblical hadn't happened to Miss Fisher and everyone around her.

'He didn't even notice my knees,' she said. The big car roared in answer.

At home, the telephone experiment had proved a failure. The few numbers which had been authentic had nothing to do with reporters, the Catholic Church, girls or escape, being an estate agent, a funeral home, several private houses of unexceptionable respectability and two police stations. But Jane was not downhearted.

'We have proved that the hypothesis was not valid,' she declared stoutly. 'Now we need another.'

'You are an example to us all,' Phryne told her. 'Why not think about another thing which the numbers might represent? I don't think they're a coincidence or I would not have set you to such labour. Take the rest of the day off, darlings. And ask Mrs B for a treat. What do you fancy?'

'Ice cream,' said Tinker and Jane in unison. They said 'snap' and grinned at each other. Phryne was pleased. Moving Tinker out of the house meant that he willingly spent more time inside. Odd but true.

She telephoned the lying-in home and found that Nurse Chappell had everything in hand. She had hired a helper, laid in reasonable food, and allowed Phryne to speak to Phoebe.

'She's let us bloody get up out of them stinkin' bloody beds,' said Phoebe. 'Grouse food and all, chicken stew not bloody gruel. I'm feelin' bloody better. The others is all bloody right. We heard that poor bloody Ellie is doin' all right as well.'

Phryne told her about the bishop and suggested that Annie was about to be rehabilitated.

'That's a bloody miracle,' said Phoebe.

Phryne was inclined to agree, told Phoebe to feel free to swear at the priest when he visited as much as she liked, and rang off with a feeling of a good job of blackmail well executed. She thought that it was a bit tough on the devout enclosed brothers to have a girl-seducing renegade foisted upon them, but perhaps he would be a challenge to their faith which they would effortlessly surmount. In any case, Father Kennedy would be as unhappy as anyone could wish. Phryne grinned.

Now to consider what on earth she was going to wear to lunch at the Blue Cat. What did a patently female person wear to a gathering of those who played so firmly for the other team?

She put this to Dot, who was considering the same thing, and had laid out several ensembles on Phryne's moss-green bed.

'I don't know, Miss, to be sure,' Dot worried. 'You could wear the boy's suit, of course.'

'That might be thought sardonic,' said Phryne. 'Or even satirical. No, I think the good old subfusc garments, Dot dear, the black—no, the dark green skirt, the jade blouse, the green hat with the peacock feather. Blue shoes and nude stockings. And find me the big jade ring Lin Chung brought home from his last voyage.'

Only Phryne, Dot thought, would consider such a costume to be subdued. But dressed in it she was magnificent.

'I am considering how well the colours will look against the red plush, the gilt and the marble,' she told Dot. 'Anything else and I might melt into the background, and that would never do.'

'No, indeed,' murmured Dot, who thought that most unlikely in any circumstances. Phryne had a way of claiming the foreground as if by right.

She left in a cloud of Jicky and Dot tidied a little, tried a couple of new perfume samples which had come from France, liked one called Délice d'Amour, and pottered down to lunch with the children, who seemed to be playing a loud word game of some sort.

The Blue Cat once again admitted Miss Fisher as though she weren't an alien, and the uniformed young man—Phryne wondered if they chose their waiters and attendants by height, they were all very tall—led her to the smaller dining room, Phryne trying desperately not to think of the manner in which Catherine the Great was reputed to choose her guardsmen. Such thoughts were not polite in this company. Or then again . . .

'Miss Fisher,' said Mr Featherstonehaugh, taking her hand.

'My dear Mr Featherstonehaugh,' she said, smiling.

'If you would like to come this way . . .' He led her to a high-backed, extravagantly carved chair at the head of a sumptuously dressed table. There were swags of linen and lace. There were also epergnes full of flowers. Tuberoses. Of course.

'Now, before the gentlemen come in, Miss Fisher, I must have your agreement. No names must be written down. Not ever.'

'I agree,' said Phryne. 'In fact, I swear.'

'It's not that we don't trust you,' he explained, as the attendant opened the far door and the company filed in. 'But things written down can be read by all.'

'I understand,' said Phryne. She rose from her throne to meet her guests.

Several gentlemen she knew from various encounters, some licit, some illicit. There was a barrister, a banker, a famous football player, two actors, Dr MacMillan of the Queen Victoria Hospital in her lounge suit (obviously another honorary gentleman), several merchants and . . . humping along, scowling, Mr Bates of the *Daily Truth*.

Well, well. One truly never knew.

Phryne murmured greetings and shook hands. The gentlemen sat. Wine was poured, a fresh, fruity riesling from the Barossa Valley. Mr Featherstonehaugh handed her a menu. On the club notepaper, it was written in exquisite calligraphy in the signature dark blue ink.

'*Gazpacho Andaluz*,' she read with interest. '*Caneton Rouennais à la presse*, *salade aux tomates*, *russe et verte*, *tartelettes aux fraises des bois*, *fromages*, *fruits*, *café*. Perfect for a summer's day. Light, tasty, cool. Not an ortolan on the page, which was a mercy, because had they been there Phryne would not have been able to resist trying one. And bringing on herself a few extra years in purgatory.

'Gentlemen,' she said aloud, raising her glass, 'a toast to discretion.' They drank. 'Mine, I assure you, is absolute.'

'We know that, Miss Fisher,' said the football player. 'Or we wouldn't be here. And neither would you. You know what I mean,' he added.

The atmosphere, which had been tense, eased a little.

'Quite,' said the banker. 'We know about you. We know you have assisted several of us to avoid . . . notice. Even talked a policeman out of prosecuting. Smuggled old Tom's friend in to see him when he was dying, to say goodbye.'

'We queans appreciate you,' said the fancy-goods importer.

The waiter giggled and subsided quickly under Mr Featherstonehaugh's glare, which could have been employed to flambé crêpes Suzette.

'So we've asked around,' said the barrister.

'And we may have something for you,' said the actor.

'But first,' said Mr Featherstonehaugh, 'the repast.'

Waiters brought in the soup. It was iced, spicy and delicious.

'Have you seen our *Measure for Measure*, Miss Fisher?' asked the actor.

'Not yet,' said Phryne. 'It isn't one of my favourite plays.'

'Wasn't mine either,' confessed the actor. 'When I was cast for Angelo I hadn't the faintest how to manage him. I just said the words as carefully as I could. But then Clarissa arrived and the whole piece took fire.'

'Clarissa?'

'You haven't heard of her?' The actor was aghast, almost choking on his gazpacho.

'I've been out of town,' apologised Phryne.

'She really is something surprising,' opined the barrister. 'Cold and determined, her Isabella the nun.'

'But in real life she's very warm,' said the actor. 'Been on the boards since she was a tot, of course. Born, as they say, in a trunk. Played fairies when she was four. Graduated to Juliet when she was fourteen—the age, of course, of the real Juliet. Got away with a lack of technique because she was so beautiful—long golden hair, blue eyes. Now she has the technique to play anyone, and she's still beautiful. Hardly fair, is it? And she's here for good, I believe. Fell in love with some lawyer stage-door johnny and married him.'

'But she's funny,' said the footballer. 'Saw her in that comic thing—something about earnest? Playing a sarky girl.'

'*The Importance of Being Earnest*, my dear,' said the banker.

'Yair, that was it. Funny,' said the footballer.

'Your Angelo is chilling—a study in twisted lust,' said the barrister.

'I've had such a lot of practice,' sighed the actor.

There was a general laugh as the *caneton* was brought in with the salads. The meal was sumptuous without being too rich for people who had to go back to work. Phryne's opinion of Mr Featherstonehaugh's acumen rose another notch. She allowed the waiter to help her to *salade russe*, for which she had a passion. Mr Bates did not eat, but confined himself to crumbling bread and drinking glass after glass of the white wine. He spoke to no one. Phryne caught occasional glances from the others. They looked on him with great compassion, even pity. She wondered why.

A heated discussion between the actor and the fancy-goods importer about colours attracted her attention.

'They're calling it "bugger's mauve",' objected the importer. 'No lady is going to buy it.'

'But Beaton says it is the colour which all fair women ought to wear,' said the actor. 'And who's going to tell the gently born what such crude characters as actors call it? It's the purest violet.'

'Couldn't put it on a footy jumper,' said the footballer.

The table paused and looked at him. Phryne was impressed that no one laughed at him.

'Agreed,' said the barrister. 'Now, what about these strawberry tarts?'

'Wonderful,' said Phryne. 'They taste like *fraises des bois*. Australia really does have excellent fruit.'

'The pineapples,' said the fancy-goods importer, a cockney by the sound of him. 'The mangoes! When I think I had to pay six shillings apiece for green African mangoes in London. I could buy up a bathtub of them here and just bathe in it for the same money. And pawpaw and bananas and nectarines and berries. Paradise.'

'White peaches,' said Phryne.

'There's an orchard in Bacchus Marsh to which I might direct your attention,' said the barrister idly. Phryne was alerted. None of this conversation was idle. 'They rather specialise in soft fruit. I'm sure they would welcome your interest, Miss Fisher. And your patronage, perhaps.'

'Indeed?' asked Phryne. 'What's the name of this excellent orchard?'

'Groves of Bilitis,' said the barrister, without emphasis.

'I shall make a note of it,' said Phryne. Bilitis, eh? Someone had been reading Louÿs. Might as well have called it Sappho's Orchard. Interesting.

'Coffee,' said Mr Featherstonehaugh.

The gazpacho had been superb, the tomatoes at their ripest, the *caneton* would have been happy to have such an afterlife in prospect, and the strawberries had been sprinkled with kirsch. The fruits were on ice and delicately frosted by some kitchen alchemy and the cheeses included Camembert and Stilton as well as Cheddar for the football player, who had simple tastes and had drunk Victoria Bitter throughout. Phryne took a bunch of dark grapes and picked them, one by one. She had received one clue. Time for another.

'Mr Bates?' she asked.

He grunted.

'What can you tell me about Polly Kettle?'

'Stupid bitch,' he mumbled.

'Agreed,' said Phryne. 'To a certain philosophy she would have appeared to be headlong, rash and foolish.'

'Too right,' said Mr Bates.

'But she is missing and I fear that she is in serious danger. Won't you help me?' she asked gently.

'Someone's stealing girls,' he said, quite clearly. 'Been on to it for months. It was my story. I was finding things out. But that silly bitch grabbed it and ran with it and now she's been nabbed. Paper won't touch it. Because it's her story now. She stole it from me.'

'I see,' said Phryne. 'Knowing that I will not quote you, what can you tell me?'

'Out of the convent,' he said, taking another gulp of wine and holding out his glass. Phryne caught the glance between the waiter and the proprietor. Mr Featherstonehaugh nodded and the glass was refilled. 'Bad girls.'

'Oh, I say,' objected the banker, and was hushed by the importer.

'But they haven't been turning up in the usual places,' said Mr Bates.

'You mean, brothels in the city?' asked Phryne.

'Not a sign of them. Bill said he's been getting enquiries about passengers on his boats.'

'I have,' said the importer. 'My boats don't usually carry people, just goods. To and from, you know.'

'To and from where, exactly?' asked Phryne.

'Here to London River,' he told her. 'Via Aden.'

'Oh, dear,' said the actor.

'Why "oh, dear"?' asked the footballer.

'The Middle East has rather a penchant for blonde girls,' said the actor. 'Boys, too.'

'White slavery?' asked Phryne. 'Surely not.'

'Why not? Just because it's a popular legend doesn't mean it isn't true,' said Mr Bates aggressively.

'Of course,' said Phryne soothingly.

'Employment agency called Jobs for All in Lonsdale Street, barked Mr Bates, not conspicuously soothed. 'Asked Bill for places for ten girls going to Aden. He smelt a rat. Refused to send them. But he isn't the only person with boats in Melbourne ports.'

'My oath,' said the importer. 'And some not as fussy as me. Thing was, the funny thing was, the funds were to come from a Catholic charity. Connected to the convent. Called Gratitude. I didn't like it, not one little bit.'

'How many girls have disappeared?' asked Phryne.

'Eighteen, counting the recent ones,' grunted Bates. 'All of them discharged to a "good Catholic home" as domestic servants from that convent. Poor cows probably on their way to an Egyptian brothel. And once there, how could they get away? Can't speak the language, probably kept doped. It's wrong.'

'And if these people have Polly Kettle?' asked Phryne.

'I reckon she's on her way there, too.'

Mr Bates hauled himself to his feet and stumped out. There was silence as they listened to his faltering steps, the opening and closing of doors, the gatekeeper summoning a taxi.

'Poor man,' said Phryne.

'He had a bad war,' said a merchant. 'Fell in love with a fellow soldier. Who loved him back. They were very happy together. For years. Then . . .'

'They found them both in the same shell hole,' said the barrister. 'Bates was mortally injured. And he was lying in the pieces of his lover, cut in half by shrapnel. A common tale. But Bates is one of those fellows who only has one chance at love. And it was gone. They say he spent months in a mental hospital, begging them to let him die. But he didn't die.'

'Horrible,' said Phryne.

There was another silence. Mr Featherstonehaugh served more coffee and liqueurs. Phryne took a green chartreuse.

'Some of our cast have been made offers,' said the Shakespearean actor. 'Travel to the Middle East, wonderful parts, excellent pay.'

'In a travelling company?' asked the other actor.

'To be met at the boat,' said the first actor, with heavy emphasis.

'And who has been offering them these marvellous opportunities?' asked Phryne.

'Jobs for All,' said the Shakespearean actor.

'I see.'

'I talked the silly mare who told me about it out of going,' said the Shakespearean actor. 'But there will have been others.'

'Without the benefit of good advice,' said the other actor.

Silence fell. Phryne was thinking, and did not speak. Neither did the company. They looked at each other and drank their coffee.

'There has been a loan application,' said the banker. 'For the purchase or lease of a passenger ship. Not a big one and not a lot of money. But from a Catholic charity called Gratitude. I thought it odd. I've held it up in paperwork. But it seems to be guaranteed by the Church. I haven't a reason for refusing it.'

'Why should the Catholic Church need to borrow?' asked the businessman. 'They've got pots of money. Something iffy about it, my dear.'

'I thought so. I've put an investigator on to them. Not one penny of my money do they get for white slaving. Think of the bank's reputation!'

'And the poor girls,' reminded the footballer.

'Yes, them too.'

Silence fell again. That appeared to be all that anyone had to say to Miss Fisher. And Dr MacMillan hadn't said a word. Interesting.

'I've seen you with that beautiful piece Lin Chung,' said the fancy-goods importer, desperate to break the quiet. 'I don't suppose he plays for both sides?'

'Sorry,' said Phryne. 'Do you deal with the Lin family?'

'For porcelain and jade,' said the importer. 'Now the Chinese would never engage in white slavery. They think white girls are ugly.'

'They do,' said Phryne. 'Round-eyes, they call us.'

'But the Middle East really like them pale. If you could find how they are getting them out . . . You've friends on the waterfront, I believe.'

'I have,' said Phryne. 'Well, gentlemen, thank you for a very pleasant luncheon. Unless there is something else? If there is, I am leaving my cards.' She did so. 'Please telephone me if there is something I should know. And I still do not know your names.' She smiled, bowed, collected Dr MacMillan and was escorted out.

'Blimey,' said the footballer.

The others agreed.

CHAPTER NINE

Prospero: The rarer action is in virtue than in vengeance . . .

William Shakespeare
The Tempest

Jack Robinson was having an annoying day, which was not unusual. He was hungry, thirsty, hot and cross.

He assuaged his hunger by sending his constable for hot pies from the pie cart, and tea from the office urn, which had been cleaned only last April. The tea, however masked by sugar and almost-off milk, tasted of tin. He attempted to cool himself by opening the window on hot, cross, dusty, noisy Russell Street. He shut it again. Bugger, he thought.

'Girls,' he said to his detective constable, Hugh Collins, 'are a mistake.'

'Sir?'

'Always trouble,' growled Robinson. 'Getting lost. Getting stolen. The commissioner's real ratty about these missing girls. And can we find them? Not a trace of the silly tarts. Nothing from the houses?' he asked, without much hope.

'No, sir,' said Collins, who was also feeling the heat. 'They seem worried, too. Let us in without a warrant, even Corsican Joe's. Even the Railway Inn.'

'Bugger,' repeated Robinson. 'Girls. I always said they were a mistake. We should have set our face against them from the outset.'

This was too much for Detective Constable Collins.

'But, sir, without girls the human race would not survive.'

'And what's good about the human race?' demanded his superior.

Collins could think of a few things, like beer and fishing and his fiancée, Dot, but wisely held his tongue. The day could only get hotter. Like Robinson's temper.

'Things are getting bad on the waterfront,' he said, hoping to distract the detective inspector.

'Something's going to crack soon,' agreed Robinson. 'Luckily that's not our problem. Open that window, will you? Perhaps there's a breath of air out there.'

'I doubt it,' said Collins. But he opened the window anyway. Orders are orders. The clang of passing trams, the horns of overwrought drivers and the ceaseless tramp of feet, plus a lot of ozone-laden dust, came in and he shut it again.

'Parents haven't heard anything?'

'No, sir. I spoke to those missing Reillys. They'd gone to her sister's in Shep. Skipped out ahead of the landlord. They haven't heard from their daughter Julie. Seemed a bit cut up about her, too. And they needed her salary—the old man's out of work. Said that if we find her she can come home provided she puts the baby out for adoption and promises to marry the bloke they chose for her.'

'Do they know who the father is?' growled Robinson.

'They got their suspicions,' said Collins, trying to loosen his tight collar. That had been an embarrassing interview. 'They think it was the union bloke at her work. He was asking after her. They didn't tell him they sent her to the convent. And there's been another of those odd assaults, sir.'

'The day just keeps improving,' groaned Robinson. 'Who is it this time?'

'That gentleman who's paying the O'Haras' rent,' said Collins delicately. 'Just like old man O'Hara. Someone came to the door, he answered, everything went black, and he woke up feeling like he'd been punched in the balls. Couldn't happen to a nicer bloke,' added Collins.

Robinson considered the assaults, rubbing a hand over his sweaty, unremarkable face. 'Ask around about about them,' he said to Collins. 'There might be more. But we still haven't found that pest of a reporter and we haven't got any more clues. I suppose no one's found the Ryans?'

'Not so far, sir,' said Collins carefully.

His superior stared bleakly into his tea. It stared back. It was not informative tea.

'We've got to find another avenue of enquiry.'

'You might tell Miss Fisher, sir, about those assaults,' suggested Collins. 'They might be relevant to her enquiries.'

'Yair, s'pose. Tell you what, you do some phoning and write me a report. Then you cut off to Miss Fisher's and have a cuppa with your beloved. Let Miss Fisher know about it. All this family stuff! It's enough to make a man swear celibacy, struth it is. Get out of here,' he advised his junior, and Hugh Collins got.

An hour on the phone garnered him some very coarse jokes and the information that four other men had been similarly assaulted. That made six. He wrote his report in longhand, with two carbons, and then departed with relief into the city street, which was marginally cooler and in slightly better temper. The odd thing about the case he kept for the moment when he and a long drink of iced lemonade sat down with Dot in Phryne Fisher's bijou garden.

It was very pleasant there. The bamboo fences kept off the worst of the salt wind. The jasmine was in flower. What air arrived was scented and almost cool. Hugh loosened his collar and wiped his face with his handkerchief. Then he took a long gulp of his lemonade. He was suddenly a very happy man.

'How are you, Dot? You look bonzer,' he said.

Dot blushed. Hugh took her hand. She was so lovely, his Dottie. Not like Miss Fisher, dangerous and beautiful, like a painting; but normal and human and a little rumpled. Her mousy hair was sweat-dampened on her forehead and curling a little. Her hand in his was hard with work. She belongs to my world, Hugh thought.

'I'm well,' said Dot. 'You look good, too.'

There the conversation stuck. They sat in silence for a while. Then Hugh recalled himself to his duty.

'I've got this report for Miss Fisher,' he said, putting down the envelope. 'I don't reckon you want to read it, Dot. Not nice for a lady. It's about various men who've been assaulted. But the odd thing, Dot, the strange thing . . .'

'Yes?' asked Dot.

'Them names,' said Collins. 'Here's the list. The ones who've been assaulted. Three of 'em are on Miss Fisher's list of missing girls, too. I mean, they're connected. Mr O'Hara, Mary O'Hara's father, and that Fraser bloke who pays their rent, and the foreman of that factory where Ann Prospect worked.'

'Odd,' commented Dot, filling up his glass with more of the icy lemonade. She knew where her priorities lay. Hugh looked hot, even though the air was mild and the jasmine sweet. 'What sort of assaults were they? Punched or kicked?'

'Er . . .' said Hugh, writhing with discomfort. 'More personal than that. More intimate, like. In a more . . . private place.'

'Oh,' said Dot, enlightened, and she blushed again. He loved the way she blushed. 'Oh, I see. Well, that sounds like revenge, doesn't it?'

'It does,' agreed Hugh, with enormous relief at having got over this difficulty. 'They answered the door, everything went black, and they woke up with . . . er . . .'

'Quite,' said Dot. 'They didn't see anyone?'

'Only one bloke said it was a nun.'

'A nun? I mean, only one nun?'

'Yes,' said Hugh. 'Oh, now you come to say it . . .'

'Exactly,' said Dot. 'Nuns come in pairs. I don't believe they are allowed to leave the convent unless they have a companion.'

'That's true,' said Hugh. 'So maybe this nun isn't a nun at all?'

'It would make a good disguise,' mused Dot. 'In the war they said German spies were dressing as nuns. The gown goes down to the feet.'

'Yes, and the headdress covers the whole head and chin. Unless he forgot to shave, a nun could be anyone. And you're right, you can't see the feet. We used to think nuns ran on wheels.'

'So did we,' said Dot. 'But it could be a woman. Those robes conceal the figure. I remember at school, Kitty told everyone that Sister Perpetua was a man, and we all believed it. She could have been, for all we could see.'

'Oh?'

'And she could hit as hard as a man,' said Dot ruefully.

'Too right,' said Collins, trying not to rub his rump, which had been frequently flayed by Sister Beatrice. The old scars still ached when he sat on hard chairs.

They drank more lemonade, freshly pleased to be out of range of the sisters' ruler.

'Growing up,' said Dot. 'It's all right, isn't it?'

'Too true,' said Hugh Collins, and took her hand again.

Phryne returned to her house with Dr MacMillan and fell indoors, battered by the weather, calling feebly for lemonade. She took the doctor, who must have been melting in her lounge suit, up to her own boudoir, where an ingenious arrangement of fans blowing over a block of ice made the air cold. Phryne stripped off her respectable garments and bathed in the cool breeze, and Dr MacMillan went so far as to take off her jacket and loosen her tie.

'You look like the nymph,' commented the doctor, looking from the lamp made in the shape of a lady poised on her toes holding up a globe to the white figure of her friend. Phryne sprayed her face and torso with rosewater and then donned a silk robe as she heard Mr Butler at the door with the cool drinks. He informed her that Hugh Collins was below and would she like to see him?

Phryne agreed that the sight of Hugh Collins was always amusing and sipped.

'God, what weather!' she exclaimed. 'How are you managing, Elizabeth? This is a bit different from Edinburgh!'

'I am thinking of adopting tropical dress,' said the doctor. 'But when I consider that at home I would now be wearing three layers of clothing, and freezing besides, I can cope with a little heatwave.'

Phryne giggled briefly at the idea of Dr MacMillan in a solar topee, khakis and mosquito boots, then sobered instantly.

'Something very bad is happening, Elizabeth. I notice you didn't say a word at lunch. Was it to spare the delicate sensibilities of the gentlemen?'

'It was,' said the doctor, stretching her limbs in the coolness. 'They have no truck with women, and would find gynaecological evidence upsetting. I was there mostly to hear what they had to tell you.'

'So, what do we know?' asked Phryne.

'That someone is enticing or stealing girls. That this appears to be carried out by an agency in Lonsdale Street called Jobs for All. That Mr Bates suspects white slavery and is angry with Miss Kettle for stealing his story. I believe it is called a "scoop",' said Dr MacMillan, pleased with her mastery of vernacular.

'It is. He certainly was,' agreed Phryne. 'Then again, he is usually angry. Being excavated from the ruined corpse of your only love can do that to a man. What have you to add?'

'Over the last month I have had several requests to test girls for virginity,' said Dr MacMillan. 'This is, as you know, not easy to ascertain. Not all women have a hymen at all and some break it by, for instance, horseback riding. It has always been my practice to give anyone who hasn't actually given birth the benefit of the doubt.'

'Because you don't like what may happen to them if you make a contrary finding?' asked Phryne.

'Precisely. Now I am beginning to wonder if I did them any favours.'

'Tell me about these girls,' said Phryne.

Doctor MacMillan produced a list. 'One was a Chinese girl, slip of a thing, brought in by a prospective mother-in-law. Ah Li, pretty little creature. Her mother-in-law elect had doubts about her chastity. I told the foolish bitch that the girl was as pure as the driven snow.'

'Was she?' asked Phryne.

'Oh, yes. I believe it was just a ploy to drive down the dowry, not uncommon in the more traditional families. Such ways will die out in time, I expect. Australia seems to have a leavening effect. But I issued a certificate in the usual form. So they will have to pay for Ah Li's virginity after all and the mother-in-law has had a loss of face, which should make the poor girl's life a little easier. Then there was Muriel Clay. Brought in by a woman about whom I had my doubts.'

'Why?' asked Phryne, drinking more lemonade.

'Just a feeling,' said Dr MacMillan. 'She had a sly glance, looking at me out of the corner of her eye. Gave her name as Smith. Sounded like one of the Dublin Smiths. Said the girl was about to work for a very saintly family and they needed to be assured of her chastity. Muriel was very blonde and very dim. Foetal alcoholism, I suspect. Orphan, her escort said, from the convent. Fourteen years old and never, as far as I could judge, been kissed.'

'All right,' said Phryne.

'Then Mrs Smith came back again.' Dr MacMillan leaned forward, both fists on her knees. 'With another girl. Another blonde, also fourteen, also lacking in the brain department, though I think Madge was just naturally daft. Also from the convent, but a bad girl from the Sacred Heart section which runs the Magdalen Laundry. I gave her a certificate also. I am wondering if I did the right thing.'

'Why?'

'Because a policeman came to the hospital looking for the two of them, and said they were missing.'

'Oh,' said Phryne. 'Oh, dear.'

'Quite,' said Dr MacMillan.

'You haven't seen Mrs Smith again?'

'I have not,' said the doctor. 'If she turns up I shall give her in charge. In view of the information from your lunch at the Blue Cat.'

'I still don't see . . .' began Phryne, just as Hugh Collins was shown in. He was uncomfortable in Phryne's boudoir, but was attended by Dot, who gave him confidence. However, despite her reassuring presence, he always felt that he was at least a yard too tall and weighed as much as an elephant in such surroundings. And he seemed to have reached new heights in clumsiness and was always afraid to move in case he broke something irreplaceable.

'Detective Inspector Robinson sent me to bring you this, Miss Fisher,' he said stiffly.

'Do sit down,' invited Phryne, but the officer preferred to stand. Phryne perused the report. Her eyebrows rose.

'Assaults?' she asked. 'Why bring this to me?'

'I thought you'd know the names,' said Collins, sweating in spite of the cool breeze from the new-fangled electric fan.

'I see,' said Phryne. 'Jack Robinson is wondering if I, or my minions, dropped in on those wife-battering child-raping men and booted them in the balls?'

'Er . . .' Hugh looked around wildly. His eye was caught and transfixed by an erotic ink drawing which Picasso had done of the youthful Phryne.

'There, there,' soothed Phryne. 'You can go back and tell Jack that it really wasn't me, or on my orders, but whoever did it has excellent judgment. Each of these men—or the ones I know about—would be vastly improved by a knee where it would do most good. Thank you for coming, Hugh. How is the investigation going?'

'It's not going,' replied Hugh. 'Commissioner's yelling, Boss is snarling and I haven't got a clue.'

'Then I'll give you one, free and for nothing,' said Phryne generously. 'Tell Jack that he might have a look at an employment agency called Jobs for All in Lonsdale Street. They are employing actresses for dubious jobs in the Middle East. That, at least, will give him something to do and stop him from fretting.'

'Thanks, Miss,' said Hugh Collins. 'And the assaults?'

'Leave the list with me,' Phryne replied. 'And thank you. You can go now,' she added.

Hugh Collins stood in the middle of the boudoir like Stonewall Jackson at First Manassas until Dot took his hand and gently led him away. Outside, he sat down on the top step and mopped his face again.

'I'm glad you're not like your employer, Dot,' he said.

'I'm not,' said Dorothy. 'I'd love to be that strong and that sure of myself and that beautiful. But I'm not,' she finished sadly.

'I like you just like you are,' Constable Collins assured her fervently.

'You were about to say?' prompted Dr MacMillan.

'I was?' Phryne was distracted.

'About the young women and Jobs for All,' the doctor reminded her.

'Ah, yes. I really do have an odd effect on poor Hugh Collins. No, I was thinking that I am looking for pregnant girls. Your Arab brothels wouldn't have any use for them. Not in view of those virginity tests. Such places set a high premium on virginity or the appearance of virginity.'

'Alum,' said Dr MacMillan. 'Or other such chemicals. Dries the vagina so that it bleeds when penetrated. Damages the tissue, of course, but they wouldn't worry about that. Or about the pain. The clients are paying for pain.'

'Erk,' commented Phryne. 'But to return to my point, I doubt Jobs for All and the sheiks would be interested in my heavily burdened ladies.'

'Unlikely,' said the doctor. 'I believe that I will have a wee drop of that single malt which your Mr Butler has so presciently brought to us, Phryne.'

'Glen Sporran it is, my dear. What do you make of these assaults?'

'Have any of the victims been examined by a doctor?' asked the older woman, breathing in the peaty scent of home. For a moment, the island of Barra, machair and daisies and seagulls, flashed across her eyes. Her dearest friend Dr Elspeth talking about sickly children. And a strange thought occurred to her. She paused, examined her mind, which boggled, and drank more whisky.

'I believe that Mr O'Hara was dragged off to some luckless medical practitioner,' said Phryne.

'Get his name. I would like to talk to him. Or her, of course. I have a theory which is so outré that I won't even mention it to you, Phryne. And can you find out if the other men on that list have been connected with a sexual assault or a pregnancy?'

'I can,' said Phryne. 'Why, in the name of Sappho?'

Dr MacMillan did not reply but just sat there, drinking single malt and looking, Phryne thought, Scottish. She gave up. 'All right, I won't tease you. Keep your secrets! To other matters. What have you heard about this Groves of Bilitis?'

Dr MacMillan chuckled. 'Nothing whatsoever, but I love the name. And something about Bacchus Marsh is itching at the back of my head. In a magazine, perhaps?'

'Do you take *The Woman Worker*?'

'I do,' said the doctor, taking another drappie.

'There was something in that about a socialist collective in Bacchus Marsh.' Phryne sorted the papers on her table rapidly, laying aside *The Australian Home Beautiful* and the *Hawklet*. She retrieved the gestetner'd manuscript and leafed.

'Aha. Isobel Berners. A fruit-growing collective on the socialist model. No name is given, but what do you want to bet it's the Groves of Bilitis?'

'No bet,' said Dr MacMillan. 'When you go out there, Phryne, would you see if they've got any apple jelly? I do like apple jelly and the commercial product is all pectin and no fruit.'

'I will get you some, if there is any to be had,' said Phryne. 'But first, I had better get on with my visit to the convent.'

'Try to keep your temper,' advised Dr MacMillan. Without a great deal of hope. The conjunction of Phryne, the Magdalen Laundry and a lot of nuns made her thankful that she operated a women's hospital and would not be needed to attend to blast injuries.

She drank her whisky, and chuckled.

CHAPTER TEN

Necessity is the plea for every infringement of human freedom. It is the argument of tyrants: it is the creed of slaves.

William Pitt
Speech to the House of Commons, 1783

The Abbotsford convent was impressive. The wall was suitable for a medium-sized castle and the gate was in the familiar dread portal style. Someone had scrawled in chalk on the wall beside it: *Lasciate ogni speranza, voi . . .*

Ch'entrate, she finished the quote. All hope abandon, ye who enter here. A very educated graffitist. Dante might have found a lot of material here, Phryne thought. The gatekeeper inspected the bishop's letter, opened the gate and allowed her to guide the Hispano-Suiza though. He directed her onward with a scowl. So there were some men here, she thought. She parked the car and got out.

Knowing that she might be facing formidable opposition, Phryne had armoured herself in very stylish clothes. A navy suit, grey stockings, grey shoes and a very fetching hat, in a strong shade of teal blue, with cock's feathers. She was liberally sprinkled with Jicky, an exotic and disturbing scent, redolent of Paris and chypre and chestnut blossoms. She had left Dot at home because Dot gave at the knees when she saw nuns. A relic of her childhood. Phryne's childhood, though poverty-stricken and stringent and sordid, had not included nuns. Besides, in some situations, Phryne felt stronger when she was alone, with no one to shock but herself. And she seldom shocked herself.

A plump nun rushed up to her, took her hand and exclaimed, 'What a beautiful car! Hello, welcome to the Good Shepherd, I'm Sister Perpetua, Mother Aloysius is waiting for you. Come this way?'

Phryne followed. Sister Perpetua kept talking.

'We take on everyone, you see,' she said. 'Orphans, the infirm aged, the cretins, the demented, the lost women.'

'And the bad girls?' asked Phryne.

'Oh, yes.' Sister Perpetua's smile broadened. 'Awful things might happen to them if they didn't have us for a refuge.'

Phryne suppressed the thought that awful things might happen to them if they did. Meanwhile, the walk was interesting. The gardens were well tended and blooming despite the heat. Buildings were clustered all around the central courtyard. Presumably when the sisters took on a new cause they just constructed a new building.

'From here,' Sister Perpetua directed Phryne's gaze, 'you can see the gardens and the farm. Goes right down to the river. We grow most of our own food, you know—eggs and milk and vegetables.'

'Commendable,' murmured Phryne. It all looked very bucolic; the sheep might have been freshly shampooed, the rows of cabbages were bright green, the low sheds had opened their doors and let all the chickens out. They scattered through the yards, doubtless pecking and clucking and gossiping in the manner of chickens and humans. Phryne could see them, like moving dots on the background. People in blue smocks were attending to them. The people seemed small. Phryne said so.

'Orphans from St Euphrasia's,' said Sister Perpetua. 'It's our duty to teach them skills. They love the animals and the chickens. They learn how to milk and churn butter and bake bread. They will need employment when they leave us.'

'And do you teach them to read and write as well?'

'Of course,' replied the sister, surprised. 'They do school in the afternoon and farm tasks in the morning. And we are lucky, of course, to have a river frontage and unlimited water. That's why the gardens are so green in this drought.'

Phryne had not noticed that there was a drought.

'And the bad girls? What do you teach them?' she asked idly.

'Oh, they don't go to school,' said the sister. 'Not with the orphans. We keep them apart.'

'Of course.'

'They work for their keep, and we hope for their repentance,' said Sister Perpetua.

'For the keep of the whole convent, actually,' murmured Phryne.

'Yes, we really need the income we get from the laundry. We have some very good contracts. The bishop is always interested in our work. And the laundry people are so envious. They say we are undercutting their prices.'

'Well, of course,' said Phryne. 'You don't actually pay your workers union wages, do you? And you get your water for free, from the river frontage.'

'We're exempt,' said Sister Perpetua, nettled at last. 'There was an act of parliament. Do have a look at our statue, and then I will take you to Mother.'

Phryne looked at a large statue of St Joseph, for whom she had always had an admiration. It can't have been easy, managing a girl with an inexplicable pregnancy. But he had accepted the word of the Lord and not put her away. Later generations had not been so forgiving.

'Very nice,' she said, and was led through several doors into a waiting room. It had a fireplace in Art Décoratif curlicues. It had stained-glass windows. The floor was tiled and cool. On a hot day, it was pleasant. On a cold day it must be icy.

Sister Perpetua, looking flustered, escorted Phryne into a parlour. Heavy plush drapes, Victorian furniture and another tiled floor, now covered with Turkish rugs. Mother Aloysius rose to meet her.

'Miss Fisher,' she said creakily.

'Mother Aloysius,' said Phryne, taking the old, fragile, dry hand.

'The bishop instructs me to allow you to ask my sisters questions,' she said tonelessly. 'I am, of course, under obedience. Whom shall I summon?'

'Those involved with the running of the laundry,' said Phryne. 'And I would like to look at the laundry, if you please.'

'No,' said the nun, still without raising her voice. 'I do not please. Nowhere does it say that I have to allow you a free run of my convent. You may speak to the sisters you have requested. Here. With my attendance, of course.'

'Of course,' said Phryne. She had expected nothing else. Her chances of getting anything even mildly secret out of the sisters was nil. But she had to try. This was a drama, with a beginning, a middle and an end. This was just the First Act.

Mother Aloysius summoned Sister Perpetua and sent her with a note to the laundry. Tea was not served. Homemade biscuits were not offered. Phryne sat in composed silence. She had come armed for combat in her teal-blue hat. She did not expect courtesy under those circumstances.

Poor Jack, she thought. This is how he must feel all the time. I wonder how long it takes to get used to it?

After perhaps ten minutes, Mother Aloysius said, 'Do you think that those girls have come to harm?'

'I fear so,' said Phryne.

'Dead?' she asked.

'Perhaps.'

'Or worse?' asked Mother Aloysius.

'Possibly. If there is anything worse than death.'

'Oh, there is,' said the nun. 'There is damnation.'

'That, too,' said Phryne, thinking of an Egyptian brothel full of terrified, captive blonde girls; unable to escape, unable even to make themselves understood. That would be a fair definition of damnation.

Sister Perpetua came back and announced that the laundry sisters were waiting. They came in and lined up before the desk.

Phryne looked at them. A tough lot, she considered. The smallest was carrying what Phryne identified from her youth as a pot stick—a yard-long, flat, two-inch-wide piece of seasoned timber used (in civilised households) for stirring the copper. The sister saw Phryne looking at it and tried to hide it behind her back. She received a glare fom Mother Aloysius which ought to have scorched her wimple. It was not the presence of the pot stick which was damning. It was the attempt to hide it.

Thereafter the interview went as Phryne had suspected it would. The three nuns identified themselves as Sister Dolour (who carried the pot stick), Sister Dominic and Sister de Sales. The missing girls, they told Phryne, were wilful and rebellious. They had been lazy and disobedient. Ann Prospect, here called 4781, had quoted the Factory and Shop Acts and said that the working conditions were against the award. She had refused to work and had stood, apparently, on a slab of concrete all day, to consider her sins. Number 4782, Mary O'Hara, had wept and fainted out of sheer impudence, while 4783, Julie Reilly, had had the nerve to burn her hand and make herself unfit for labour for a week. In all it was a relief, said Sister Dolour, when the time had come for them to deliver themselves of their children of shame and they had been sent to the pious widow, Mrs Ryan. Thereafter nothing had been heard of them and if they came back to the convent to beg forgiveness it might go hard with them.

'Did they have any friends amongst the other girls?' asked Phryne.

'Friends! We don't encourage friendships,' snorted Sister Dolour, who probably lived up to her name, sorrow.

'But nevertheless?' persisted Phryne.

'I never noticed any,' replied the nun.

'When Julie—I mean 4783—was in the infirmary with her hand, I recall her talking to her nurse,' offered Sister de Sales.

'Who was it?' demanded Mother Aloysius.

The sister winced. 'One of the auxiliaries, I believe. But I'm probably wrong. In any case, nurses do talk to patients, you know.'

'Who?' demanded Mother Aloysius, in the same tone.

'I believe it might have been Agnes,' said Sister de Sales.

Phryne got up and walked over to the sisters. Close up, they smelt of starch and sweat. The laundry must be hell on a day like this, she thought. She inspected them as if she were a visiting dignitary and they were soldiers. Mother sent Sister Perpetua for Agnes, and while they waited no one spoke.

Phryne sat down again as the black-clad woman was ushered in.

'Did you become friends with number 4783?' demanded Mother Aloysius.

The woman paled. 'I spoke to her a little; I was attending to her burnt hand. That steam presser really ought to have a guard.'

'It had one. I took it off,' said Sister Dolour. 'It made the work too slow.'

So much for Factory or any other Acts, thought Phryne.

'Did she say anything about an escape?' she asked.

'No, just how she would like to get away, be someone else. Everyone wants that,' said Agnes. 'Don't they?'

The faces turned on her were blank with displeasure.

'No idea of where she was going?' asked Phryne.

'Didn't know she was,' said Agnes. 'But I'm not surprised. She said she hadn't committed any sin—in her condition! She said she would go to her young man as soon as she could. So I expect that's what she's done.'

'Name of young man?' asked Phryne.

'Frank,' said Agnes. 'Forrest, I think. Some name which reminded me of trees.'

'Thank you,' said Phryne.

Agnes took her leave in a whisk of skirts.

'Is that all?' asked Mother Aloysius.

'Oh, yes, for the moment,' said Phryne airily. 'Though I may be back.'

She was escorted out by Sister Perpetua, and drove away secure in the knowledge that her little package of a ten-shilling note and her card had been accepted and instantly concealed by Agnes. She had prepared it in advance in case a suitable person presented herself. Agnes was unhappy about that Magdalen Laundry. Further developments might be expected.

Meanwhile, Phryne needed to get home and have a bath, to wash off the odour of—well, sanctity, to stretch a point. And dress for dinner. And phone Jack Robinson to get him to find Frank (probably) Forrest. Who might know where Julie Reilly was. And, by extension, the others.

Which still did not take her any nearer to the fate of Polly Kettle. Tomorrow, thought Phryne, Camberwell and an interview with the Kettle parents. Not precisely a destination as harsh as the Magdalen Laundry, but likely to be trying. Phryne had no time for the up-jumped middle class. And here she was about to plunge herself into the heart of them.

Bath, she thought. Dinner.

The bath scented Phryne with essence of freesia. Dinner with her family had been pleasant. Jane reported no progress in deciphering the code, but was not cast down. Tinker had been fishing again and had taken Molly for a long walk along the beach. The hound was lying on her back with her paws in the air, across a doorway as was her wont. She was exhausted but happy, returning covered in aged fish and having been laundered again. Ruth had been involved in the creation of a bombe Alaska which had neither sunk nor exploded and was a triumph: sweet cold ice cream inside a crisp hot meringue crust. It was much appreciated and Ruth blushed with pride. The dependants had then scattered to their own occupations and Phryne and Dot sat in the sea-green parlour, discussing the events of the day.

Dot seemed unsurprised when Phryne described the sisters, who would have been strong contenders for any Fitzroy stand-over gang.

'Some of them are like that. Especially at school. Angry,' said Dot, considering this for the first time.

'Vengeful?' asked Phryne, knowing that nuns were a touchy subject.

'Yes, now you say it. I never thought of it before. I suppose all that chastity and poverty and obedience must have been hard for them. Some of them were so sweet and kind. Sort of natural religious. Some of them seemed to hate us. Hugh says the same. Some of them were nice, some of them beat us black and blue. And it was no use complaining about it. My parents wouldn't have believed me. Or they would have said that I deserved it.'

'So, if you were saying that a priest had raped you, no one would believe it?'

'No!' exclaimed Dot. 'A priest wouldn't do that . . . a priest . . .' She subsided under Phryne's level, considering stare. She thought about her own past. About what her friend Kitty had told her. About Father Kennedy and his 'private devotional lessons'. The same one who had been the cause of that Jordan girl's pregnancy, or so she said. 'Oh,' said Dot in a small, sad voice.

'Priests are men, and men are fallible,' Phryne told her. 'If they were able to marry, there probably wouldn't be a problem.'

'Priests can't marry,' said Dot.

'Church of England priests marry,' said Phryne.

'Yes, but that—' began Dot.

'Isn't the one true Church?' teased Phryne. 'No, don't answer that. I'm just being mischievous. We are not going to agree on theology, Dot dear. But as I remarked, men are fallible. Otherwise they wouldn't be men. And women are fallible, too. We're humans. God made us like that, presumably for a purpose. Tell me, could you hide a female prisoner in a convent? Tucked away without any contact with the outside world?'

'Oh, yes, Miss, there are always devotional cells for sisters who need to contemplate . . . Miss Phryne, you aren't thinking that Polly Kettle is there? Held prisoner by the sisters?'

'I know, it's just too *Awful Disclosures of Maria Monk*, isn't it?' said Phryne. 'But I do need to search everywhere for her. And everywhere includes the convent. My chances of an unfettered look around there are very slim. Meanwhile, however, we need to consider where those girls have gone.'

'What about this Forrest man?' asked Dot.

'The sister might not have got the correct name; no, Agnes wasn't a sister, she was an auxiliary. What is that?' asked Phryne.

'A lay sister,' said Dot. 'A pious volunteer. They haven't taken vows. But they want to do good works.'

'That's why they dress all in black in a garment that is not quite a habit?' asked Phryne.

'Yes, they want to help, or they're lonely. Widows, you know. Or spinsters.'

'Agnes looked more like a tent fighter,' observed Phryne.

'Spinster, then,' said Dot.

'She seemed kind enough,' said Phryne. 'Actually talked to Julie Reilly while tending her burnt hand. Well, well, we will have to shelve the convent for the present. I might still receive some information. To other sources. I shall see Polly Kettle's parents tomorrow. I am not expecting this to be amusing. Would you like to come with me?'

'Are you driving?' asked Dot. Really needing to know.

'No, we shall go *en grande tenue*, with Mr Butler in his chauffeur's cap and livery.'

'In that case, Miss Phryne, I would like to go. I've never been to Camberwell.'

'It's nothing flash compared to London, but some of the houses are nice. For a colony,' said Phryne. 'Then I need to speak to poor Jack again. About Jobs for All and doubtful theatrical engagements in the Middle East.'

'White slavery?' asked Dot, and shuddered.

'It seems so,' answered Phryne. How would she herself manage, finding herself in a brothel in Cairo?

Like she would always manage, no matter where she was. Learn some Arabic from her clients. Seduce the doorkeeper. Manage her escape to the British Consul. It would not be amusing. But she could do it.

How would an innocent dimwitted fourteen-year-old cope?

Badly, Phryne decided. This was a terrible crime and needed to be stopped. She would, therefore, stop it.

On that thought, she took herself and her crime novel to bed. Mrs Christie was always amusing, if a little trite. Phryne thought that it would be nice to have easily solved problems, even if she didn't have Hercule's quantity of little grey cells.

She slept badly, dreaming of Polly Kettle crying out for rescue from a dark cell. Shadowy nuns looked in through the grating on the iron door. Phryne cursed the day she had borrowed *The Awful Disclosures of Maria Monk* from a prurient classmate and left the house for a fast, cleansing swim. She returned for a brisk shower and coffee and a croissant. She declared herself fit for the day. Which would contain, God help her, Camberwell. She dressed accordingly.

An extremely expensive couture-clad Phryne took her place in the back passenger seat of the big red car. Dot, dressed in beige with a terracotta hat which looked like an upturned flowerpot, joined her. And Mr Butler, in blue serge with piping, tipped his peaked cap to the postman as he drove carefully into the road and headed for Camberwell via Victoria Street. Phryne sighed impatiently. This car could do ninety miles an hour—had done eighty for twenty-four hours straight at the Indianapolis Brickyard, which was one reason she had bought it. Mr Butler stuck to the speed limit of thirty miles an hour as though it had been engraved on his heart. She smoothed down her silk skirt and started a conversation to beguile the time.

'Did you like the nuns at school, Dot?'

'Some of them. There were a few nice ones. Some of them would still scare the life out of me, I reckon. What sort of teachers did you have?'

'Mixed,' said Phryne, thinking back to her schooldays, something which she never did unless she wanted to make herself cross. 'They taught us to read and write, at least, and then when I was whisked off to England, Latin and a little Greek, French, geography, deportment, arithmetic, dancing and music. And how to endure cruelty, unkindness, bullying, isolation, loneliness and cold. That school was built on an iceberg, I swear. I had chilblains on my chilblains and the food was pure stodge. When I think of my education I smell boiled cabbage.'

'I always thought that rich people had good schools,' said Dot.

'Rich people happily send their children to places which the proprietors of Devil's Island would consider unduly severe. The only thing that frightful place had was books. A whole library of them and, since they stressed hockey and pure thinking, no one was there. That library was my refuge. I was a swot and gloried in the title. Once the bullies made me do their homework, of course, they were in my power.'

'Miss?' Dot did not follow.

'Because they didn't know anything about the subject, I could write anything I liked. And if they annoyed or oppressed me, I would write nonsense. They would hand it in as all their own work, and they could not say that I had written it for them under pain of torture. So their paters would be upset and cut off their allowance. Because they were such lazy, bone-idle bitches, I had them by . . . well, in the case of girls, the—'

'Indeed,' said Dot, cutting off the indelicate end of the sentence. 'That was clever of you, Miss.'

'Desperation lends the mind wings, Dot.' Phryne settled back. 'Nonetheless, if such situations arise at the girls' school, the headmistress is going to hear from me.'

'I don't think they have,' said Dot. 'Ruth looks after Jane. Jane's too clever to notice the other girls being snippy, and neither of them cares about what the other girls care about—clothes and boys and marriage. Jane says she can't see any point in marrying if you are not intending to have children, and she isn't, she's going to be a doctor, and Ruth wants to be a cook and can't be having with boys at any price.'

'Both independent young women,' said Phryne.

'And if they get real bullied, they just mention your name, Miss, and the bullies go away.'

'Really? How very gratifying,' said Phryne. 'Why?'

'Because you're an Hon, Miss. All their parents want to be friends with you.'

'Ah,' said Phryne, disappointed. 'I thought it might be the dangerous reputation and the gun.'

'That, too,' affirmed Dot.

'And Tinker is getting on better now he's got a bolthole,' Phryne observed. In Victoria Street outside she saw, on her right, the vast mansions of the wealthy and the green of Fitzroy Gardens. On the left was dirt-poor Collingwood and, soon, dirt-poorer Abbotsford. She could not see the convent from the road, but she knew it was there. Factories belched black smoke into the air. In summer, it stank, and she shut the window. Presently they crossed the Yarra. Up the hill and Barkers Road was sliding past far too slowly. Where were the bleats of narrowly missed pedestrians, the yells of outraged traffic cops? It was too tedious. On the left was the vast expanse of Xavier College. Phryne thought how strange, but oddly reassuring, that in such a very Church of England city, the Catholics had such extensive grounds and imposing architecture. The chapel even had a cupola.

'He's settling in real well,' said Dot. 'That was a real good idea, Miss. Every night he just takes his cocoa or his lemonade and locks himself in to read Sexton Blake, quiet as a mouse. He gets up at dawn and takes Molly out fishing. She's a lot less trouble, too; he tires her out. And he knows all those old fishermen on the pier. Even Ruth's beginning to like him.'

'Possibly because of the way he eats. Cooks adore a good appetite.'

'I used to be that hungry once,' said Dot.

'So did I,' said Phryne.

'It'll wear off once he knows dinner's going to come along tomorrow, without fail,' said Dot. 'Just like a stray cat.'

'Strays settle down in the end, Dot.'

'So we do,' she agreed.

Down the hill and crossing Glenferrie Road and the Methodist Ladies' College came into view, with giant Moreton Bay figs and a suffragette agenda to turn out clever gels. Then Carey Baptist Grammar, which made a trifecta of religions in one journey.

'What do we know about the blighted residents of this blighted suburb?' ask Phryne.

'Mr Robinson's report says they're respectable. He's a banker, she plays tennis every week at the social club and belongs to the lady mayoress's committee. Well off. Two children: Martin, a boy aged fifteen, still at Camberwell Grammar and one girl, Margaret—that is, Polly. She went to a local ladies' college, then joined the paper as a cadet. Last seen the morning of the tenth, which is the day she vanished. Ate her usual breakfast, seemed excited about something, wouldn't tell anyone what. They've heard nothing and had no ransom demand. If she is found her dad is going to make her stay home in future and give up "all this newspaper nonsense",' Dot read from Robinson's notes.

'I don't like his chances,' said Phryne.

'That's what he told the cops—I mean, Mr Robinson,' said Dot.

'Not that well off,' commented Phryne. 'Camberwell Grammar is not top drawer. Not one of the elite, like Melbourne Grammar or Scotch. Oh, dear, these will be the boring have-nots who want to be haves. I personally have no patience with them.'

'Because you're already a have, Miss,' Dot pointed out.

Phryne turned and looked Dot full in the face. Her voice was serious. 'No, Dot, really not. I am what I am and I have what I have, even when I was scouting for old veggies in the pig bins at the Vic market. And I never wanted anyone's place or their regard. They can like me or not; it is a matter of complete indifference to me.'

'Yes, Miss,' agreed Dot. Her employer had great beauty, learning, insouciance, a bijou house, a fortune, aristocratic connections and a (married) (Chinese!) lover. There really wasn't a lot Melbourne could do to her if it decided to be sniffy. So, of course, it had flung itself on its back with its paws in the air, licking Phryne's expensive handmade shoes and inviting her to tickle its belly. Occasionally she deigned to do so. This had always been met with whimpers of delight and photographs in the society pages. It was a mystery to Dot, who had always relied on being good to make her happy. Different rules, apparently, applied to Miss Fisher. She had always behaved as if this were so.

'If you get a chance to talk to the servants or the boy, Dot, do so. His sister might have confided in him, or he might have spied on her. Every boy wants to be Sexton Blake these days.'

'Yes, Miss,' said Dot.

The big car traversed Burke Road and stopped at a large iron gate. It was rather more over-wrought than was strictly necessary. Mr Butler honked the horn and a functionary opened it and let them in.

The carriage drive was miniature, but it was a carriage drive within the meaning of the act. The house was a three-storey monstrosity probably built during the Gold Rush, when red brick blushed for its presumption. It had verandahs and curlicues. It was in excellent repair, regrettably without ivy or wisteria to conceal its vulgar colour. Mr Butler conducted Miss Fisher to the door—another dread portal—and rang the bell, lest his patroness's expensive fingers be besmirched by touching the lowly possessions of the middle class. Mr Butler didn't like the middle class either. They marked their importance by being rude to servants. Many tiny stinging insults were about to be avenged.

The door was practically snatched open by a young man in a morning coat. Kitchen or yard boy pressed into service as butler to impress Miss Fisher, thought Mr Butler, a professional butler magna cum laude. Ill-fitting coat, too.

'Miss Fisher, Miss Williams, to see Mr Kettle,' he announced to the butler.

The reply should have been, 'To see Mr Kettle. Miss Fisher, Miss Williams,' but the boy just stood and gaped. Just like the frog in Alice, who come to think of it had been a porter, too.

'Go on, my son,' said Mr Butler in an undertone. 'Ask us in . . . No, ladies do not take off their hats. Put us in a room to wait for Mr Kettle, then go and tell him we're here. Then you come back and get us, and announce the names at the door. You'll get the hang of it. Off you go, now.'

The boy opened the door of the front drawing room in the mansion, and fled. Phryne and Dot examined the decor.

'Hasn't been changed since the house was built,' diagnosed Phryne. 'Plush and gold and Turkey carpets. A complete Victorian gem.'

'Must be awful to dust,' observed Dot, looking at a wedding bouquet under a polished glass dome. The glass was clean. The room had been freshly tidied. In honour of their visit?

'If you would come this way,' said the boy from the door, parroting what he had been told to say. Phryne and Dot followed the tight suit, were admitted through another door, and saw that Mr Butler was accompanying the young man beyond the green baize door. Good, he would come back with all the gossip from the servants.

Meanwhile, here was Mr Kettle, who looked just like a banker, and Mrs Kettle, dark hair, thin, not very good clothes worn with no élan. Phryne extended a hand. It was taken gingerly, as though she might bite.

'Do sit down, Miss Fisher, Miss Williams. Tea?'

'Thank you,' said Phryne, aware that this event had been agonised over and had probably caused the cook to threaten to give notice if the mistress didn't go away and let her get on. It would be pure cruelty to decline. This room, too, was untouched by artistic revivals, not to mention revolutions.

The Victorian plush and gilt were overpowering in the still, warm air.

'This hot weather is very trying, isn't it?' asked Mrs Kettle, sitting down.

Phryne obligingly talked about the contrast in climate between London and Melbourne as a trolley was wheeled in and tea was poured, sugared and milked as required. Mr Kettle took a cup. Dot took a slice of pound cake. The conversation wittered on through latest modes in hats and the newest sensation of the stage (Clarissa Cartwright in *Measure for Measure*) and was about to embark on the middle-class perennial, the Servant Problem, when Mr Kettle interrupted the feast of strawberry jam and the flow of tea to demand, 'Have you any idea where Polly might be?'

'Not at present,' said Phryne, very pleased at the intervention. She really had nothing to say about the Servant Problem. 'I am trying to find her, as is the police department. It appears that she was last seen in Footscray, but the account of her abduction may be false. I need to talk to her friends. I need to see her room.'

'Oh, Miss Fisher . . .' Mrs Kettle protested.

'Yes,' said Mr Kettle.

Interesting. Mr Kettle was seriously worried about the fate of his daughter. Mrs Kettle wasn't. Possibly she didn't like her daughter very much and didn't care what happened to her. Or possibly she knew where she was and was concealing this fact from her husband. Phryne tried to picture Polly as she had last seen her. Was that stomach swelled? Could she have been sent away to give birth to an unlawful child?

No, that girl had been plump, but not pregnant. Time to split these people up.

'So, if you do not object, Mrs Kettle, could you take my companion Miss Williams to see your daughter's room? Any letters, Dot, anything written. You know what to look for. And I will have a few words with you, Mr Kettle.'

This worked. Mrs Kettle led Dot away, and Mr Kettle, as soon as his wife was out of the room, crossed to the drinks trolley and poured a lot of neat brandy into his tea.

'I can't imagine how this happened to us,' he said, slumping into the plush chair.

'No one ever can,' said Phryne gently. 'You are very fond of your daughter. Can you think of where she might have gone?'

'No,' he groaned. 'She was always bright and clever. Got that newspaper job straight out of school. If she comes out of this alive I swear she's never leaving the house again.'

'Quite,' said Phryne. This reaction was not unusual. 'She is bright and clever. I met her. That's partly why I am looking for her. But the usual places where missing girls turn up have not revealed her. Something else is happening. Have you talked with her lately?'

'Just the usual—hello Dad, nice day, that sort of thing. She used to say "How's the millions?" because I'm a banker. It used to annoy me.' He wiped a hand across his eyes.

'And you haven't received any ransom demand?'

'Nothing. I'd pay, you know. I'd pay anything to have Polly back, chirping "How's the millions?" at me. But no one has asked for anything.'

'What do her friends think?'

'God, I don't know. I don't talk to them. I don't like those giggly girls and those stupid boys. Socialists all. I've got no time for them. I've worked hard for everything I've got.'

'I'm sure you have,' soothed Phryne. This man was really in pain.

'Do you . . .' he started, choked, coughed and then said, 'Do you think she's dead?'

'She may be,' said Phryne. 'But I don't think so. I suspect we'll find her. Meanwhile,' she went on briskly, 'tell me all about her.'

The portrait of Polly which emerged did not match the girl Phryne had encountered in Little Lon. Polly, according to her father, was bright, pretty, cheerful and artistic. Did the flowers for her mother. Had no boyfriend but lots of friends. Had a bee in her bonnet about this newspaper career which would, her father foresaw, speedily evaporate when the right man came along. Phryne doubted this, but said nothing.

Dot, meanwhile, was hearing about an entirely different Polly. As she leafed through papers and letters in the escritoire, Mrs Kettle related to Dot how her sweet little girlie, who looked so good in frills, had grown up insolent, cut off her curls, abandoned the tennis club and the garden parties and had actually got a position at a periodical. And not *The Australian Home Beautiful* or *Women's Own* either, but the *Daily Truth*. She had insisted on starting as a cadet journalist and Mrs Kettle had been terrified as to what her own friends would say. But they had approved, so Polly was allowed to continue.

'Lady Rose Winslow was so good as to tell me that young ladies should have a career, so I went along with it.'

Dot stifled a giggle. What Mrs Kettle didn't know about Lady Rose Winslow, a dear friend of Phryne's, was that she had been born Algernon Charles Winslow and her title was, like her gender, entirely self-endowed. Dot said nothing but kept leafing through slips, cuttings and notes. She put them all into the scrapbook which Polly had been keeping of her own writing and secured it with a ribbon.

'I should have forbidden her,' said Mrs Kettle.

Dot murmured something which could be taken to be agreement and kept searching. No love letters that Dot could find, and she knew where to look. Cards for parties and outings and theatre engagements. Letters from a friend called Cecilia. Dot took those. Her clothes were, according to Mrs Kettle, all there, except what she was wearing at the time. Nice clothes for a nice gel, undoubtedly bought by her mother. Her toothbrush and toiletries were present in the bathroom.

'Self-willed,' said Mrs Kettle. 'That's Polly.'

'How did she get on with her brother?' asked Dot. 'Could I speak to him?'

'He isn't here,' said Mrs Kettle. 'I sent him to Mount Martha, to his cousins, for the holidays.'

'So he wasn't here when Polly . . . er . . . vanished?'

'No,' snapped Mrs Kettle. 'He's a good boy and I don't want him bothered by all this. He's going to be solicitor. His grandfather left a trust fund for his education.'

'Oh, good,' said Dot. There was not much more to find in Polly's room, which had been cleaned and tidied. She hadn't been kidnapped from here, it was plain. Dot suggested that Mrs Kettle write Cecilia's address down for Miss Phryne.

'Of course, she may have lost her memory,' said Mrs Kettle hopefully. 'She used to sleepwalk when she was a child. One does hear of such amnesia cases. There was that soldier found by his mother after the war. Dressed like a farm labourer and only spoke French. But she knew him. A mother always knows.' She scribbled an address on a piece of headed stationery.

With that, they went downstairs.

Dot and Phryne made suitable farewells, collected Mr Butler and left in the big car, down the carriage drive and into Burke Road.

'The middle class,' sighed Phryne. 'I suppose they have a purpose in God's Great Plan.'

'That mother,' said Dot, worried.

'Yes, I know. Not concerned enough, was she?'

'No. But she did think her daughter might have lost her memory. How was the father?'

'Frantic,' Phryne replied.

'I didn't find anything strange in her room. And the little brother's been sent away. She says before the . . . er . . . incident, but I think she was lying.'

'Odd,' said Phryne. 'When we get home, we shall have a conference. I bet Mr Butler has wrung the servants' hall dry of information.'

'I did find them a chatty lot,' he said, never taking his eyes off the road.

'Oh, good,' murmured Phryne. She yawned. She closed her eyes. Really, that cupola was a bit above the odds . . .

CHAPTER ELEVEN

I must dance barefoot on her wedding day,
And for your love to her, lead apes in hell.

William Shakespeare
The Taming of the Shrew

Phryne was still chuckling about Dot's revelation of the high social position of Lady Rose Winslow, social arbiter of Camberwell, when Mr Butler brought in tea and, contrary to all custom, sat down and allowed his employer to pour him a cup. The children were accommodated with milk and one passionfruit biscuit each, so as not to spoil their lunch. Phryne had been so stuffed with scones and cake as to consider lunch an unappetising prospect.

'We have all been to see Polly Kettle's parents,' Phryne announced. 'As dire a pair as you might expect, but that's my prejudice. The father is a banker. He is very anxious about his daughter. He professes himself happy to pay any ransom to get his daughter back. But there has been no ransom demand. I think he would tell me if there had been. He's frantic with worry about his Polly, poor man.'

'The mother isn't very worried,' said Dot. 'She thinks Polly might have lost her memory. Or so she says. She's sent the girl's brother Martin away to Mount Martha—she says before the kidnapping, I say after—to get him out of the way of any questions.'

'I shall ask Jack to send . . . no, I actually do have a friend at Mount Martha. He could talk to the boy. I'll telephone in due course,' said Phryne.

'The young lady had nice clothes and a nice room,' said Dot. 'I've brought all her notes and clippings home with me, and some letters from a girl called Cecilia. No love letters. No pictures of a boy. She seems to have only been interested in her work.' Dot had a hand-coloured photo of Hugh Collins. She kept it in her bedside drawer and kissed it every night before she said her prayers.

'I spoke to the servants,' said Mr Butler. 'The cook and housekeeper, Mrs Johnson, a friendly plump lady with a small child of her own. War widow. The boy, Vern Jones, the yard man and gardener. The one inserted into that unbecoming jacket, Miss Fisher, is the boy's elder brother—called Bill Jones. They have no housemaid. A woman comes in to clean every morning.'

'I suspected that butler wasn't a butler,' said Phryne.

Mr Butler nodded magisterially. 'Miss Fisher has been received into the best houses,' he agreed. 'They told me that their employers were a bit silly but paid well and weren't too demanding. It isn't a big household even when the boy and girl are home. They like the girl. The housekeeper said that she fights with her mother all the time about clothes and the newspaper job. But she loves her father and gets on very well with him.'

'I got that impression, too,' agreed Phryne. Dot nodded.

'But the girl didn't demand service all the time, asking people to climb two flights of stairs to fetch her handkerchief, as her mother is wont to do. Then not even a thank you. But that isn't unusual. Daily women quit on a regular basis.'

'I bet they do,' commented Phryne.

'However, the housekeeper before Mrs Johnson quit without notice because of this misuse of authority, and Mrs Kettle was left with a dinner to cook—which she can't—and the vicar coming. After that she moderated her demands on the live-in staff.'

'Where do they live in?' asked Phryne.

'Nice rooms, Miss Fisher, on the ground floor. A girl employed by Mrs Johnson minds her child during working hours. They are in a position to note all comings and goings though the gates and both doors.'

'How useful,' said Dot.

'Indeed. On the day in question, Miss Fisher, the young woman had a screaming quarrel with her mother about her profession. Again. She took her brother Martin aside and confided something to him. The yard boy Jones didn't hear what she said. Then she left as usual and has not been seen again.'

'I knew that woman was hiding her son,' said Dot.

'She hustled the son out of the house to Mount Martha that very afternoon, Miss Fisher,' said Mr Butler.

'What did the staff make of the boy?'

'Apart from the fact that he hates his name, Martin, and insists on being called John, the staff say that he is a nice boy, keen on sport, not very bright or bookish. Likes making things. Wants to play cricket.'

'Oh, dear, his mother wants him to be a lawyer,' said Dot.

'Mrs Johnson says that Mrs Kettle dotes on Master Martin far more than is healthy. She adores the boy. She ignores or argues with the girl.'

'How does she get on with her husband?' asked Phryne.

'She rubs along with him,' replied Mr Butler. 'The cook says she's jealous of how much he loves his daughter. Says sometimes that he loves his daughter more than he loves her, goes into a tantrum and a sulk, and can only be brought out of it by gifts of expensive jewellery.'

'I see,' said Phryne. 'Not an unusual pattern. No signs that the father loves the daughter in anything other than a proper paterfamilial way?'

'None, Miss Fisher.'

'Good. I have enough deviant stuff in this case as it is. Anything more?'

'The household is prosperous without being rich,' said Mr Butler. 'Well run, well organised, the staff are happy enough to be there. I believe that is all, Miss Fisher.' He got up and started to gather teacups.

Dot announced that she was going shopping, and left. She had run out of scarlet thread for the waratahs on her glory box tablecloth.

'Clippings,' said Phryne to the minions, 'notes. Let me know what you find,' and walked into the garden. Behind her, there was rustling as of thousands of mice being admitted to their very own silo. She thought she heard a squeak of delight.

Having someone else to do the research was very pleasant. Clues appeared to be flapping around her like Loïe Fuller's ribbons. Though nothing like as decorative. She decided to call Cecilia Brown. She might know something about the multifaceted Polly Kettle. She would certainly know if her mother or her father was right about Polly's character.

She opened the packet of letters, found the most recent, and began to read. Cecilia was a breathless correspondent with a liberal view of punctuation. Her letters were spiky with exclamation marks. Mostly the letters concerned the extensive preparations for her forthcoming wedding to Lance, a young doctor. To judge from the number of times the phrase appeared, *really, my mother is so unreasonable!!* this was going much as one would have expected. Phryne had decided many years ago that marriage was for other people. She was freshly pleased about this.

In the middle of all this fuss I do wonder if I might have had a career too, wrote Cecilia plaintively. *But I wasn't any good at school and then I met Lance and it all seems to have just happened! I do like hearing your news about your investigations!!*

Irritatingly, Cecilia did not expand on this. She went on to discuss the relative merits of peach (her choice) or white (her mother's and Mrs Beeton's choice) for table napkins at her nuptial breakfast. Phryne very quickly lost patience with her. She combed through the remaining letters for mention of anything not marriage related, and found little about Polly's work except expressions of conventional regret for the writer's lack of a career and sympathy for the way Polly was being picked on by Mr Bates (*He sounds horrid!! and it about serves him right if you pinched his beastly story, he wasn't using it!!!*). And very little about the groom. He didn't seem to feature at all except for comments on his taste in buttonholes (*He was quite cross and said whatever I thought would be fine with him!*). Had Polly no other friend than this blithering idiot? Nevertheless, Cecilia would have to be hunted down and interviewed. As Phryne could not inflict Cecilia on anyone else, she had to do it herself.

Cecilia was at home, doubtless choosing tablecloths. She seemed quite pleased to be invited to the extremely respectable Hopetoun Tearooms in the Block Arcade and Phryne was resigned. At least she didn't have to endure another middle-class house. She set out in the big car for the city.

There were two types of young woman that Phryne found trying. One was the sullen or bohemian: painty hands, significant art, no stockings and dirty hair. The other was the frilly or gushing: immaculate hair, hat, stockings and gloves and the affectations of the 'little me' type. Cecilia was the latter.

Hopetoun Tearooms was the most exclusive and respectable tearoom in the whole city. Phryne always enjoyed the Block Arcade. She had found it on her first walk on her first day in Melbourne. Italian tesserae on the floor, arches and gilding, excellent small shops, bijou jewellers, a couple of intriguing milliners. Phryne calmed herself as she paced the Block with the young woman. The Block was, at least, neutral ground. Miss Cecilia was a healthy, strong young woman with a rosy face, clear eyes, blonde hair and a regrettable taste for pink. She had a faint, die-away voice, ending each sentence with a little questioning gasp, which would doubtless serve her well with the in-laws—she would never express a contrary opinion—but which was annoying Phryne quite out of proportion to the offence. Also, she could not approve of a cloche with quite so many roses on it, even if they were pink silk.

'Poor Polly,' sighed Miss Cecilia.

'Why do you say that?' asked Phryne, inspecting a window display which contained a daring confection of pink ruffles in which she would not be seen deceased.

'She worked so hard,' said Cecilia. 'She really wanted to succeed. They only gave her the job, she said, because there are so few men about. That's why I'm so lucky to have Lance. Most of the boys from his grammar school class are dead or missing or maimed.'

'It's a common problem,' observed Phryne, moving on to a green lace hat with two antennae which might belong to a giant ant. Who bought these things? And if they were so unwise as to buy them, who had the nerve to wear them?

'Yes, and I'm very lucky to have him, but this wedding is wearing,' said Cecilia. At all costs Phryne had to keep her mind on the problem.

'Suppose I tell you that I will give an hour of my undivided attention to your wedding problems as soon as I have found Polly Kettle?'

Cecilia clasped her little hands together in a reprise of *Her First Sermon*. 'Oh, Miss Fisher, will you? Everyone says you have the most exquisite taste.'

'I will, if you tell me everything you know about Polly and you do it now, over tea and ribbon sandwiches.'

'Deal,' said Miss Cecilia decisively. They secured a table in the wood-panelled tearoom, gave their orders, and Cecilia began to yield her knowledge forthwith.

'She's the same age as me. Twenty-one. Mother says that's a good age to marry . . . sorry, off the subj . . . but Polly has always been a brain. She was a shark at school. Good at sport, too. Could run me off my legs and used to play wing in hockey. We won a cup. But she wanted to be a newshawk, so she wheedled her father into letting her take the position as a cadet. She worked really hard, moving copy, talking to printers, proofreading, carrying messages, then they let her do garden parties and such, all names spelt right. They wanted her to do women's pages but she wanted what she called "hard news". They didn't like that. There was an awful man called Bates who made ever such a fuss, said she'd stolen his story. I said it served him right for being such a beast to her.'

'Have a sandwich,' offered Phryne. She had eaten far too many scones and cakes in the interests of manners and wasn't in the least hungry. The Hopetoun did a very good sandwich. Refined and tasty, an unusual combination.

'Thanks,' said Miss Cecilia, scoffing two and continuing her narrative. 'So she found that these three girls left the place the convent had sent them to and vanished. She thought that if she could find them she might have a scoop which would make her career. So she was searching.'

'Yes,' said Phryne. 'What did she tell you about her search?'

'I can't remember much,' said Cecilia vaguely. 'I wasn't all that interested. They didn't seem to be in the . . . the . . .'

'Houses of ill repute?' Phryne offered.

'Them,' said Miss Cecilia, covering her blushes by stuffing another couple of sandwiches into her rosy mouth. 'And then she said she'd found some connection between the convent and white slavery. They always warned me about white slavery and I didn't believe it.'

'Yes, me too,' said Phryne.

'She said there was some connection which she couldn't find. And they must have the girls.'

'In that state?' asked Phryne.

Miss Cecilia blushed again. 'That's what she said, Miss Fisher. Then she said something—oh, well, why don't I give you her letters? I've brought them with me.' She handed over a packet.

'Thank you,' said Phryne, with heartfelt gratitude. 'What can I do for you in return? A new hat, perhaps?'

'That would be nice,' said Cecilia. 'I just love that one in the milliner's window with the pink ruffles.'

Heartless little minx, thought Phryne. She deserved a frightful hat with pink ruffles in which she would look hideous. Not a word about her friend. No worries about her safety.

'How did Polly get on with her brother?'

'Very well,' said Cecilia, glowing with expectation of a new hat. 'They were rather thrown together. Mrs Kettle dotes on the boy, and he's a perfectly nice boy, but just a boy, you know? Likes sport and football. Not very good at school. Mrs K got him tutors and made his life miserable by saying he had to be a doctor or a lawyer. Polly knew him. She never expected him to be brainy. He really loves her. Mrs K packed him off to Mount Martha as soon as Polly went missing. Poor boy must be frantic.'

'And her father?'

'Nice old man,' said Cecilia. 'He knows where the brains in the family went. He really likes her. And her mum really doesn't like that. I expect it's a complex of some sort. Lance was telling me about complexes. He's a doctor, you know. Mother says I have to be a helpmeet. I'm not sure I know how to do that.'

'About Polly's mother?' prompted Phryne.

'Oh, yes,' said Miss Cecilia, who had been distracted by the lustre of her intended. 'She's always been a bit funny about Polly. Tried to get her to marry Herbert Grant, her second cousin. He lives in the country. Polly can't stand him but he really liked her. He's a halfwit, but owns a big house and lives like a gentleman in Castlemaine. I believe he's rich. Polly thought her mum was trying to get rid of her. Polly wouldn't even consider Herbert. Her mum was really angry about that. If Polly's Dad spends any time with her, Mrs K gets sniffy.

They used to play chess until Mother Kettle threw such a conniption that he didn't dare play anymore. He's been spending a lot of time at his club. Polly used to see him there. There's a ladies' part, you know, at the Athaeneum. She used to go there at lunchtime and play chess with him, or talk.'

Phryne found this sad. Miss Cecilia was unaffected.

'And since Polly has been gone Mrs K has been sweet as honey.'

'And her father?'

'He's spending even more time at the club,' said Cecilia. 'So if she got rid of Polly to have more of Mr K, then it hasn't worked. Do you read detective stories?'

'Yes,' said Phryne.

'If it was a detective story I'd say it was the mother,' said Miss Cecilia, swallowing the last gulp of her tea. 'Now, if you haven't any more questions, what about that hat?'

Phryne bought the hat, took the letters, and drove home.

There she found that her researchers had combed through the available evidence, made notes, drawn conclusions, and knocked off for a lateish sandwich lunch and a conference.

'She was interested in socialism,' said Jane. 'She took *The Woman Worker*.'

'She was interested in chess,' said Tinker. 'There's a lot of worked-out problems, mostly a player called Capablanca. "Technique is everything," he says. She's written it out. It looks interesting. I ought to learn this game.'

'I'll teach you,' promised Jane, delighted. Ruth had no talent for chess. 'And you'll admire Capablanca. I'll show you the moves this afternoon, if you like.'

'Grouse,' said Tinker.

'There's a lot of cuttings about the Abbotsford convent and the Sisters of the Good Shepherd,' said Ruth. 'Listen to this one. *A Fallen Women's Home. Centre of Sweating . . . The fact remains—and it is a fact that no church reclamation society seems to have risen above—that the women are sweated in return for such as they get—that they are compelled to toil to keep the institution going, and toil without wages. The proceeds from the laundry support the institution. The women receive no wages, no money at all, except the sum of one pound when they leave. This is absolute sweating of a sort confined to churches. It is a thing peculiarly aggravating to anyone not blinded by sectarian prejudice. It may be conceded, on hard material grounds, that the women should make some return for the beneficent work of preparing them for happier and more useful lives; but that they should be forced to toil for months and years without a penny of wages, without any other recompense than food and clothing, is repugnant to the sense that revolts at Sweating.*'

'Three cheers,' said Phryne. 'Couldn't agree more.'

'What's "sweating"?' asked Tinker.

'Slavery,' said Jane. 'And we know what sort of food and clothing you get from someone who's taken you on to work out of charity, don't we, Ruthie?'

'Cold porridge, bruises and rags,' Ruth summed up their mutual past.

'That's about it. He goes on,' said Jane. '*We bear no malice to the Sisters of the Good Shepherd; we fully recognise their motives are altruistic. But they cannot, however altruistic, be allowed to practise sweating. Their doing so is calculated to defeat the object of their ministrations no less than to injure a large body of workmen and workwomen, for to throw a reclaimed girl on the world with only a few shillings in her pocket is simply madness. This institution, like all other sweating church "reliefs" should be brought under the Factory Act. If this is not done, if the fallen women are still sweated and the general laundresses still exposed to unfair competition—the only thing for the anti-sweating public to do is to give the Home of the Good Shepherd a wide berth.* Gosh! Who does our laundry, Miss Phryne?'

'The Chinese, and they do not practise sweating except in the usual way, occasioned by high temperatures in the ironing room.'

'Hah!' exclaimed Tinker, who had just caught the play on meanings for 'sweating'.

'Good. What else?' asked Phryne.

'She seems to have been trying to find out about houses in the city,' said Ruth. 'She's got a 1922 government report on prostitution. It's a bit hard to read,' she confessed.

'Give it to me, and I shall skim it. Lots of things get left out of reports like that. Does it mention white slavery?'

'Yes, Miss Phryne, but it's all about shipping girls overseas. I didn't quite follow it.'

'Government reports are like that,' Phryne told her. 'Not altogether meant to be understood, thus easily denied. Well done for trying, Ruth. And the next?'

'Notes,' said Tinker. 'I got 'em because I used to have to read the boss's writing, and it was chronic. This girl scribbles and she don't—*doesn't* sharpen her pencil. There's stuff about the lying-in home, just the names and address, and there's notes of people refusin' to talk to her. A whole page of them. I copied it out fair, Guv'nor.'

'Thank you!' said Phryne.

'And there's that SS 5.10 BM. No explanation. Just all by itself in the middle of a page. Looks like it really is a clue, Guv.'

'Yes, Tink, and I still don't know what it means. Curses. Mr Butler? A drink for all,' said Phryne, who felt that she deserved a cocktail. If Polly's letters were anything like those of her little friend Cecilia, it was going to be a trying afternoon.

When faced with difficulty, spread it out. She doled out a letter to each of her researchers. There weren't many.

The room filled with the noise of rustling and sipping. Gin and orange juice, provided the orange juice is freshly squeezed and properly iced, was nectar on a day like this, Phryne thought.

The first letter was dated New Year's Day and must be the most recent.

Dear Ceccie, your dress sounds very good, wrote Polly, evidently trying to sound enthusiastic.

> *I'm sure that you'll look beautiful, you always do. I've found a link between the convent and this agency called Jobs for All. I'm going there to ask about it. Bates was foul to me again today. But the editor says there's no property in a story. It's mine if I can work it. And I have been. Mum's been on at me to go out with that idiot Herbert. I won't. I don't care if he's rich. He hasn't an atom of brain. He's good-looking if you like brawny men. I don't, and I won't go out with him when he's in town. Dad says I needn't. So there. I'm going to the Lonsdale Street agency tomorrow, and to this lying-in home in Footscray where some of the convent girls have been sent. That's where the three went missing. Watch the papers. This will be a front-page story. I think peach would be a good colour for napkins.*
>
> *Love, Polly.*

Tinker was giggling.

'What?' asked Ruth, grabbing at the letter.

'She's saying that the guv'nor rescued her in Little Lon,' read Tinker. 'And she's saying that she didn't need rescuing and it was high-handed. I saw that mob. She was gonna get a bad belting, all right. Guv?'

'She was,' said Phryne, 'but we are not in this business for the gratitude, Tinker.'

'We wouldn't wanna be,' snarled the boy. 'Nothin' else in 'ere. *Here*,' he said, recalling his diction.

'Jane?'

'Nothing we don't already know,' said Jane.

'Ruth?'

'Same. This Cecilia sounds very frivolous,' said Ruth. 'And she's dead wrong about game pie being incorrect for the wedding breakfast.'

'Ceccie's concerned only for her nuptials,' said Phryne. 'Poor Polly had a very inattentive correspondent. This is the last letter, I suggest you all read it. I am going to telephone Jack Robinson—no, actually, I shall leave that to Dot when she gets back; she can call Hugh. She likes doing that. We need to find out how the raid on Jobs for All went.'

'Yes,' said Jane. 'Miss Kettle might have been kidnapped from there, if she was making trouble.'

'And she would have been,' said Phryne.

But there was no need to call Hugh, for by the time Dot returned with not only the scarlet for her waratah but a new viridian art silk for the leaves, the detective constable was already at the door. Mr Butler conducted him inside.

'A hot day, sir,' observed the butler. 'Miss Fisher and Miss Williams are in the parlour, sir.'

He saw Hugh to a seat and provided a pint of soda water and then a bottle of beer, which vanished as though there were no sides for it to touch. He was panting. His brow was wet with honest sweat.

'For God's sake, Hugh, take off your coat and loosen your collar. We won't be shocked at shirtsleeves, will we, Dot?' asked Phryne. 'But we will be shocked if you expire in our drawing room.'

Mr Butler took the coat and provided more cold beverages. Hugh, who had felt that he was actually melting like an altar candle, began to solidify.

'Thanks!' he gasped. 'Outside's like walking through a furnace.'

'Like Shadrach, Meshach and Abednego,' said Jane helpfully.

'Yair, them,' agreed Hugh, engulfing more soda water and then more beer. He had not been a particularly attentive scripture scholar.

'Though a furnace temperature is about . . .' Jane began, then intercepted Dot's glance and subsided. Sometimes people just didn't want to know useful facts about the Bible. Dot especially. Jane found this strange.

Hugh removed a sheaf of papers from his coat as Mr Butler took it away.

'Messages from Jack Robinson, Miss,' he said, holding out the sweat-marked bundle to Phryne. 'Information received.'

'Oh, goody,' said Phryne. She leafed through, handing each page to a minion after she had read it.

'So, no Forrest called Frank at that factory?' she said.

'Not as we can find,' said Hugh, gulping more soda water in preparation for another heavenly beer. 'But there's the list of employees, Miss.'

'And how about Jobs for All?' asked Phryne.

'Oh, they're into some dirty work all right,' growled Hugh. 'Started off as a straight employment agency for genteel ladies, that was before the war. Then they got . . . er . . .'

'Less genteel?'

'Yair. But Jack Robinson says there ain't nothing we can get on them. They say they only handle the employment of the girls and their travel arrangements. They say they're only agents. Fair dinkum. I nearly punched the boss. Smarmy, la-di-dah bast— coot. English.'

'Is he?' asked Phryne. 'That's unusual. Upper-class voice? I'm just Burlington Bertie from Bow, doncherknow?' she mimicked. Hugh winced.

'Yair, like that.'

'I really must drop in and visit a compatriot,' said Phryne.

'Oh, no, Miss, that might be dangerous. These ain't nice men,' protested Hugh. He looked to Dot for help, but Dot merely shrugged.

'Didn't you know, Hugh dear?' purred Phryne. 'I'm not nice either. So there was nothing that Jack could do about Jobs For All?'

'No, Miss,' muttered Hugh, deeply unhappy. His boss would go crook about this, he just knew it.

'Closed 'em down for a couple of days while we go through the books. Best we can do unless they're smuggling. Which they might very well be, you know.'

'As you say. And this charity, Gratitude?'

'They send 'em girls, the agency sends the girls on.'

'I see. Neat.'

'Got 'im!' exclaimed Tinker, who was reading the employee list.

'Got whom?' asked Phryne grammatically.

'The bloke whose name reminded her of forests.'

'Well?' asked Jane.

'Here,' said Tinker. He exhibited the name.

Phryne chuckled 'Of course, how clever of you—you shall have some clever ice cream. Too hot for chocolates in this weather.'

'What's the name?' asked Ruth.

'Timberlake,' said Jane. 'That was clever,' she admitted.

'A word with Frank Timberlake would be advisable,' Phryne told Hugh. 'Also tell Jack I would like to know the city address of a certain Herbert Grant, who wants to marry Polly. Also anything known to the police about him. Now, you sit here until you are quite recovered. We shall consider these documents in my office. Come along, minions. We need to plot. And, Jane, I believe you were about to teach Tinker chess?'

Left alone with Dot, Hugh accepted another glass of fizzy water.

'She isn't going to do something rash, is she?' he asked uneasily.

'Probably,' said Dot.

They sat together and worried. After a while, Dot took up her embroidery, and Hugh took up her book and began to read to her. Soon, they were very content together.

CHAPTER TWELVE

I believe that . . . it is in the sterilisation of failure, and not in the selection of successes for breeding, that the possibility of improvement of the human stock lies.

HG Wells
On Galton, 1904

Dr MacMillan called just before dinner. She bustled inside, full of some discovery, and hardly waited to divest herself of her coat and drink the first pint of soda water before she exclaimed, 'Phryne! The oddest thing!'

'Tell all,' said Phryne. 'We're agog.'

'I talked to the doctor who treated that creature O'Hara,' she said. 'He had noticed the suture and thought it odd. Then I arranged for three more to be examined. Phryne, someone is chloroforming men and performing vasectomies on them!'

This rather fell flat. The faces of her listeners remained agog.

'And that would be?' asked Phryne.

'It's a small operation,' said the doctor. 'Yes, a little of the whisky would be lovely, Mr Butler. I never heard of such a thing! Each one still has his . . . er . . . virility,' she censored her discourse.

'You mean he still has all his reproductive organs,' said Jane.

'Exactly, but he cannot engender. He's been . . . well, not castrated, but . . .'

'I see. How difficult is this operation?' asked Phryne.

'Oh, it's easy. Just a little incision, draw out the vas deferens and snip it, then the same on the other side. Would take about ten minutes if the operator was experienced.'

'He or she is rapidly gaining experience,' said Phryne. 'And this would be when the nun arrived unannounced at the door and everything went black?'

'Precisely.'

'Goodness,' said Phryne.

'Have you observed a pattern, Dr MacMillan?' asked Jane.

'I have. Each one is responsible for a pregnancy. Mr O'Hara for thirteen of them.'

'And the girls in question?' asked Phryne.

'All of them—well, all that I know about, Phryne—were sent to the Convent of the Good Shepherd.'

'Well, well,' said Phryne. 'That really is odd. I must meet this eugenicist.'

'Eugenicist?' asked Hugh Collins.

'The science of eugenics. Scientific breeding,' explained Jane, who had just finished the book. She had thought it interesting but badly reasoned and illogical. The criteria for acceptance appeared to be fatally flawed by the prejudices of the writer.

'What, like cows and horses?' asked the bemused police officer.

'Yes, except applied to people,' Jane told him.

'That doesn't sound right,' he said. 'I can't believe it.'

'Believe it,' advised Phryne. 'Someone is doing it, eh, Doctor?'

'Yes, they do seem to be.'

'This isn't castration, you say?' asked Phryne.

Dot blushed. So did Hugh. The minions were unaffected. The doctor accepted a little more whisky.

'No, not at all. The operation itself is common; often used to treat various neuroses. In this case it appears that some, at least, of the victims have demonstrated that they are reproductively untrustworthy and have been removed from any chance of impregnating anyone again.'

'Some girls from the Magdalen Laundry?' asked Phryne.

'That I cannot tell you.'

'Hugh, can you find out?'

'I expect so, Miss Fisher.'

'Then do so. And I will take some legal advice. The motive cannot be revenge. If they wanted to avenge a rape, they would remove the offending organs. The man is at their mercy, he's unconscious. But they've stopped him not from raping anyone else, but from impregnating them. Strange, lucid way of thinking. Right. Can you all stay for dinner? If so we need to tell Mrs Butler.'

'I'd be delighted,' said the doctor.

'I got to get back to my chief,' said Hugh reluctantly. 'I'll find out those things for you, Miss Fisher. See you later, Dot.'

'I'll walk you to the door,' said Dot.

Dinner, which was cold and salady and delicious as always, was beguiled with interesting discussions on morbid psychology. With the ice cream and fruit Phryne remembered to ask a question.

'About this amnesia explanation for Polly's disappearance . . .' she started.

Dr MacMillan snorted. 'Very rare,' she said. 'Usually more of an alibi than a neurosis.'

'But what about the Tom Smith case?' asked Jane. 'His mother knew him, though he was dressed as a farm labourer and only spoke dialect.'

'Possibly,' said the doctor.

'What do you mean?' demanded Jane. 'I read about it. It seemed conclusive.'

'Well, my hinny, perhaps he was an Englishman. Perhaps he had forgotten all about himself. That war was enough to obliterate anyone's mind. The noise, for example, the big guns, the vibrations. Unhinges the thought processes.'

'So it does,' agreed Phryne, recalling the High Explosive raining down overhead with noises much louder than thunder. 'It sounded like the end of the world.'

'He learned English very fast, three months, and he had no French accent when he spoke,' argued Jane.

'Ay, well, imphm. As I said, real amnesia is rare. A blow to the head will produce a gap in the memory of the incident which produced the amnesia; the blow or fall is almost never remembered. As to more than that, who can say? Tom Smith certainly made his mother's heart glad, and that was a good thing.'

'So you do not think it likely that Polly Kettle is wandering around the city unable to remember her own name?' asked Phryne.

'Not very,' said the doctor dryly. 'Not unless she wants to be.'

'Ah,' said Phryne.

Phryne slept that night without dreams. When she woke she explained it by reference to a judicious amount of gin in her gins and orange. No word had come from Jack Robinson by the time breakfast was concluded, so she sat down in her parlour to think about what to do next. Jobs for All was closed for two days. That would require some preparations. Investigations were on foot about Polly. She had to wait for Agnes from the convent to call her. What to usefully do today?

Phryne pondered. She put her silk-clad legs up on another chair and sipped her second coffee. She needed advice. Legal advice. And to whom should she apply, given the extreme oddness of the crime which was being perpetrated?

Someone was noting which man had impregnated some of the girls in the Magdalen Laundry. Someone was ascertaining the whereabouts of their assailants. And someone was creeping into their houses, chloroforming them, and neatly, surgically, painlessly removing from them that which would allow them to engender any more bastards on unwilling prey. They had not been castrated. They had just been . . . removed from fatherhood. Which just about suited them.

A eugenic mission, but it had to be illegal. Phryne sipped again. Aha. Felix Pettigrew was in Melbourne. He had left his practice in England to follow the gorgeous Clarissa Cartwright to Australia. And she, gossip said, doted on him. A visit to Felix was indicated. Besides, Phryne hadn't seen him since he had escorted a blubbering ex-maiden, child in arms, along a line of sappers, identified from their shoulder badge, which was all the dazed young woman could recall of her lover.

'Two and six a week, and was she worth it?' he had remarked cynically and almost inaudibly, still bearing up the woman on his arm with perfect courtesy. And he had, of course, got his man.

Phryne rang and had Mr Butler call for an appointment.

Felix's Collins Street office was canonical, with leather chairs, a huge desk piled with files, a throne-like chair for the solicitor and the general air of a gentlemen's club. His bowler was hanging on the hallstand. He was clad in his pinstripes and correct lounge suit, with subfusc tie and discreet pearl pin. But he still had the sharp, acute, bony face, the air of subdued amusement, and those bright eyes which saw much further into the human mind than was quite comfortable. Phryne had never tried to lie to Felix and considered that it would not be a good idea. For one thing, he would instantly know, and for a second thing, he would find the attempt funny.

But he also had the well-fed aspect of Ember with his whiskers deep in the crème fraîche. That marriage really suited him was evident. Drat, thought Phryne, another one gone into matrimony; I might run out of men by the millenium at this rate.

He rose politely to meet her and took her hands. Felix's grasp was warm and dry, as always.

'Phryne, how very good to see you!' She recalled his voice: crisp, precise, English.

'And you too, darling, I can see that marriage pleases you. How is the law?'

'Human folly,' he told her gravely, 'is still flourishing, thank God. Tea?'

'Aren't you too busy?' she asked. The office outside was buzzing.

'For you, I have all the time in the world.'

'Too sweet of you. Thank you, tea, and I have a really strange problem for your delectation. I know how you used to love puzzles.'

'Unlikely to be one I haven't seen before,' he assured her. 'But in any case I promise not to be shocked.'

Phryne told him, over tea and imported Huntley & Palmers biscuits from a tin. Felix drank his tea. Then he ate his biscuit. Then he started to laugh. He laughed so much that he set Phryne off and his secretary came in to see if he needed anything. He waved her out, weeping with mirth, mopping his face with an immaculate handkerchief.

'Who is this person, that I may suggest a medal?' he asked. 'The world has needed one of them—many of them—for years.'

'My view entirely, but what crime has he committed?'

'Oh, well, there's the problem. Assault with a weapon—I assume a scalpel was used. Battery. Grievous bodily harm. False imprisonment. Five years' jail, perhaps eight. I cannot think of a judge who would be as enchanted by his actions as am I. Pity. Should he be charged, do instruct me. I know just the barrister for this case.' He laughed again.

Phryne left with another handclasp and an invitation to Clarissa's first night in *A Midsummer Night's Dream*, in which she was playing Titania. As she would be, of course.

Finding herself in the city, Phryne walked past Jobs for All. It was a small, neat shop with a genteel sign. Unexceptionable. Pleasant for the genteel ladies in distressed circumstances who had originally used it. Nice for the girls who crept in asking for a situation overseas, perhaps minding a prince's children. Who found themselves in quite another establishment. God rot them, thought Phryne, and decided to pay a morning call on Madame Paris, principal brothel keeper in Melbourne. Her establishment was at the top end of Collins Street. Phryne had always wondered whether the description 'the Paris end of Collins Street' was not a subtle Melbourne joke—only for those in the know.

Madame Paris had been one of Madame Brussels' 'girls'. Phryne remembered seeing a newspaper photo of them—in the *Truth*, she thought: an elderly lady and three young women in blameless swimsuits under parasols. It had been enchantingly captioned *Madame Brussels and her junketing Jezebels.* Now Madame Brussels was dead, her empire had been left to her three 'girls'—Madame Bristol, in Kew, Madame Leyden, in Caulfield, and Madame Paris, in the original house in Collins Street. Phryne was prepared to put good money on none of them appearing in the government report on prostitution in Melbourne. Very brave would the policeman have to be to raid a house in which he might encounter the commissioner, the mayor or the premier. Almost as brave as the loon who raided the Blue Cat. So far, no one had been foolish enough.

The house was quiet. A monstrous object uncoiled itself from his seat inside the door. A Maori about seven feet high and three wide, with shoulders like an ox. Oxen. He asked in an unexpectedly soft, cultured voice, 'Lady?'

'Miss Fisher, to see Madame Paris,' said Phryne to his second coat button. Someone like that should not have been wearing livery. He should have been wearing very little, so that he could flex his muscles for the visitors. Possibly he should be armed with a spear or a greenstone club. Reminding the oafs that they could always end up as the main ingredient in a dish of long pig, for which he had his grandfather's recipe. He grinned. His teeth had been filed to a point.

'If the lady will wait a moment?' he asked, and rang a bell.

'University?' asked Phryne.

'Pays my fees,' he said.

'Law?' she asked.

'Psychology, sociology, anthropology and science,' he replied. 'Going home as soon as I graduate to help my own people preserve their traditions.'

'And you remind the annoying that one of your traditions involves eating people?'

'Seems to work so far,' he replied, and grinned again. 'I don't see a lot of trouble.'

'I can't imagine why,' said Phryne, fanning herself with one hand. 'Melbourne is less endowed with the suicidally insane than I thought.'

A girl came down to conduct Phryne upstairs. She was perhaps twelve. Phryne's good opinion of Madame Paris took a blow. Surely this child wasn't one of the staff. She was dressed in a shift, with bare legs and sandalled feet.

'No, I'm not one of the ladies,' she told Phryne defiantly. 'I'm Madame's adopted daughter.'

'I have two adopted daughters of my own,' Phryne told her.

'My mother died in a car accident,' said the child. 'She was one of Madame's ladies. Madame took me in. She said she wouldn't send anyone to an orphanage.'

'Good,' said Phryne. 'I wouldn't either. You're better off here.'

The child smiled at last. She held out a hand. 'I'm Jonquil,' she said, and Phryne said, 'Phryne Fisher.'

'Ooh! You're in the society journals!' said Jonquil. 'I've seen your picture!'

'For my sins,' said Phryne.

'Madame's breakfasting,' said Jonquil. 'She said to go right in.'

'Madame Paris,' said Phryne, as she was ushered into a large, beautifully decorated parlour. No Victorian hangings or plush or gilt. Pure Art Décoratif and very soothing and cool. Madame put down her croissant and stood up to welcome her. She was a short plump woman with a wealth of greying brown hair and eyes of pure polished jet. A glance from them used to set men on fire in her prime. Now she could quell the irritating with a flick of her lashes. Madame Paris was a formidable person.

'Phryne,' she said. 'Would you like a croissant? These are really very good. There's a French baker in Little Collins Street, an artisan boulanger just out of Lyon.'

'Just coffee,' said Phryne, sitting down. 'How are you, Ann?'

'"What with the war, what with the sweat, what with the gallows and with poverty, I am custom shrunk",' replied Ann Thomas, quoting Shakespeare as she always did in moments of stress. 'Not too bad. Love always sells, Phryne dear. Nice to see you. Is this just a social visit?'

'Not entirely,' confessed Phryne. 'I have come across a very nasty white slavery ring and I would like to ask your ladies about it.'

'Ever since you found Pompey you know that you have my eternal gratitude,' said Madame.

Pompey, a beautiful orange tomcat, heard his name and spared a brief purr for the distinguished visitor before returning his attention to his dish of cream. Phryne had located him locked in the van which delivered the houses' fish. He had eaten quite a lot of premium flathead tails before he had been rescued, much against his will, and bathed, combed and fluffed dry, to his grave displeasure. The ladies of the house doted on Pompey.

'Drink your coffee,' said Madame Paris. 'The ladies will still be in the bath.'

'I see,' said Phryne. It was excellent coffee.

'We rise at nine, unless we have been up very late,' said Madame. 'We bathe, don shifts, and breakfast. Then we have physical exercise, dancing and music, and the schoolmistress comes for those who are not quite as educated as the rest. The others are at liberty to amuse themselves until lunch, then we have a nap until afternoon tea. After that we prepare for the evening—the hairdresser comes, clothes are tried on, and so on. Until seven o'clock the house is closed, unless a gentleman wishes to make a special arrangement.'

'Which would cost him a fortune,' said Phryne. 'Upsetting your arrangements as it would.'

'A small fortune,' conceded Madame. 'This is hard work. We need time when we are not expected to be charming or amusing or amorous. I always suggest that when they marry, my ladies impose a similar rule on their husbands.'

'And do most of your ladies marry?'

Madame smiled complacently. 'Or retire. Running pubs has been popular lately. When my ladies arrive they often have great beauty but no manners. When they leave me they are polished, still beautiful, and quite the best wife for a man of business. They know how to dress, how to please, how to conduct themselves in company, have some sort of respectable diversion and are unlikely to take lovers.'

'I can imagine,' said Phryne. 'They would have had any curiosity about men well satisfied before they leave here.'

'Indeed,' said Madame Paris. 'We do have specialists, of course. Some gentlemen have individual tastes. We can cater for most of them. But we are not a freak show. There are other places for the more outré pastimes. And for gentlemen of the other persuasion there is the Blue Cat, of course.'

'Is there much abuse of your ladies?' asked Phryne.

Madame Paris bridled. 'None,' she declared. 'Gentlemen who act unbecomingly are asked to leave and are not allowed to return.'

'Asked by, as it might be, your doorman?'

'Isn't he just adorable?' said Madame dotingly. 'We don't use his real name. He's called Pompey, too, like the cat. Yes, indeed, Pompey escorts the misbehaving client out of the door. Sometimes at some speed and with some force. The ladies and

I rely on him. It will be a pity when he finishes his degree and returns to New Zealand. I don't know where I'll find another like him.'

'In Melbourne he is unique,' agreed Phryne.

A small bell tinkled.

'Ah. The ladies will be at breakfast,' said Madame. 'Come this way, Phryne.'

She led the way into a large parlour, where the table was laid for fourteen. A buffet was laden with what smelt like excellent food. The coffee pot steamed. Around the table sat ten women in white shifts, three in plain black dresses, and Pompey. Both of them. They were contemplating white china plates piled with their favourite delicacies—in Pompey the cat's case, raw fish, whereas Pompey the man preferred his smoked and in kedgeree. Both appeared to be agreeably conscious that they were the acceptable males in an all-female household. They looked sleek and glossy.

The ladies varied in colouring and in body shape from the very plump to the very thin, the youthful to the mature. They also looked comfortable and clean. They were gossiping about their clients in words which would have brought no blush to a vicar's cheek, but was devastatingly frank all the same.

'He said that his young lady wouldn't kiss him,' giggled one. 'I gave him the card for our dentist and told him to do something about his foul breath and disgusting teeth and then everyone would want to kiss him.'

'That was daring,' said Madame.

'Yes, but he asked me for advice,' said the girl. 'And he stank like a rotten corpse, poor man. If a whore can't tell him, who can?'

'True,' said Madame. 'But it might have been more gently expressed.'

'Yes, Madame,' said the girl deferentially.

'Our gentlemen can get home truths at home,' said Madame. 'Here they should not have to listen to them. Unless, of course, as you say, Primrose, they have asked for advice. Now, Phryne, I would like to introduce Posy, Primula, Poppy, Peony, Pansy, Primrose and Petunia. And there are Mrs Smith, Mrs Smythe and Mrs Schmitt. The Hon. Miss Phryne Fisher is here to ask you some questions and I would be obliged if you will answer her. She is a friend of the house.'

Seven women called by a name starting with P put down their cups and gave Phryne their full attention. Also two rather unlikely variations on Smith. Phryne was reminded of the convent giving their workers numbers. But the names were more pleasant. She would ask about this convention later.

'Jobs for All in Lonsdale Street. Does anyone know anything about it?'

'They were putting out the word in the factory where I used to work,' said Peony, who looked like she hadn't done a hand's turn in all her plump, well-fed life. She had the velvet assurance of a Persian cat and, regrettably, the intellectual power. 'Jobs overseas, they said. In the theatre. A likely story! One of my mates went. May. No one ever saw or heard from her again. That was last year.'

'And you think that something bad happened to her?' asked Phryne.

'She was real fond of her mum and her little brother,' said Peony. 'She would have written, sent them a postcard, something. But not a word.'

'What do you think became of her?' asked Phryne.

Peony shrugged. Imagination was not her strong suit.

'Anyone else hearing anything about this agency? Or girls vanishing?'

'When I was in that Magdalen Laundry,' said Primrose, 'someone kept chalking SS five hundred and ten BM on the wall. No one ever caught her. Used tailor's chalk. I don't know what it meant. I got out of there fairly soon and found a place here.'

'And someone is collecting blondes,' said the redheaded Primrose. 'Three natural blondes in my street, they all went to Jobs for All and they all . . . went. Never came back, as far as I know. I went to the agency, and they didn't have anything for me. I ain't been back there,' she added, sounding thankful. 'Or to Fitzroy. And the blondes ain't—sorry, haven't—come home.'

'Where did you live?' asked Phryne.

'Brunswick Street,' said Primrose.

'Anyone else?' asked Phryne. Heads shook all round the table. Breakfast resumed. Clearly the establishment had told Phryne everything they knew.

Madame stood up and addressed the staff. 'Well, time is getting on. Any complaints, ladies?'

'Why do I have to learn arithmetic?' complained Poppy, the thin blonde girl with the fashionable bobby-cut. 'I'm such a dolt, I can't understand it. And Miss Thompson gets so cross with me.'

'If you don't learn arithmetic, when you have a household of your own—which will be quite soon, I expect, if that elderly lawyer plucks up his courage—then your servants will rob you blind, your husband will be unhappy and your dress allowance will suffer,' said Madame equably.

'You're not such a dunce as all that,' teased Posy, the plump dark girl. 'I've never seen you lose track of a sixpence, not so much as a farthing.'

'Oh,' said Poppy. 'Right. My household, of course. If only Miss T had told me that! Of course. I'll just have to try harder.'

'Splendid,' said Madame, and led Phryne back to her own parlour.

'What a well-run establishment,' said Phryne.

'I like to think of it as such. The work is not too hard, they are well fed and dressed, and I turn them out in a very marriageable condition. Some of them send me Christmas cards every year, with pictures of themselves and their children. Some of them, of course, never wish to think of us again. But they are a credit to me by the time they leave.'

'"Some polish is gained with one's ruin",' quoted Phryne.

'Thomas Hardy, yes? He was right.'

'Why the flower names?' asked Phryne.

'Oh, Madame Brussels established it. So no one used their own name and could leave their identity behind when they left the house. I'm Madame Paris so all my names start with P. Madame Bristol has Begonia and Butterfly and Bellflower and Bluebell.'

'And Madame Leyden has Lavender, Larkspur, Lobelia and Lotus?' guessed Phryne.

'Quite. When they are being called by those names, they put on their professional armour. Their feelings are not engaged. Ideally.'

'And what happens when, for instance, Poppy marries her lawyer?'

'Then a new Poppy will be found. I have a waiting list.'

'Where do you get your labour?' asked Phryne.

'Some come along from the trade,' said Madame. 'Some are naturals. I don't take any but the most enthusiastic volunteers, and they arrive in various ways. The present Primrose, in fact, came here by stowing away in a van. Oh, Lord, it's ten o'clock and I have an errand that won't wait. Will you come?'

'Where?' asked Phryne.

'To the alley,' said Madame.

Phryne followed her to the back of the house where the laundry van was drawn up. Large sacks of sheets were being hauled into the tray by a cheeky bloke with a bright eye: Phryne thought that he liked his job—this aspect of it, at least.

'G'day, Madame,' he said, tipping his cap. 'Prim decided to marry me yet?'

'She is still thinking about it, Terence,' said Madame.

He grinned. 'She'll come round to me in time,' he said. 'I'm building a house, you know. In Sunshine. The usual?' he asked.

Madame nodded. She took out her purse from an old-fashioned petticoat pocket and put a ten-shilling note into one of the washing bags. The driver mounted, chirruped to his engine as though it was a horse, and trundled off.

'Why the ten shillings?' asked Phryne.

'That is a terrible place,' said Madame. 'With ten shillings, a girl might survive a little while if she gets out. Until she finds a place.'

'Why, who does your laundry?' asked Phryne.

'The Convent of the Good Shepherd,' said Madame. 'It is well known that bad girls do the best sheets.'

CHAPTER THIRTEEN

Journey's end in lovers' meeting
Every wise man's son doth know.

William Shakespeare
Twelfth Night

Home again, Phryne asked for a considering cocktail. Which was unusual because it was two hours before lunch. But it had been an intriguing morning. How did the working conditions of Madame Paris's young ladies differ from any other professions? Better paid, better lodging, better food and opportunities for education. Admittedly, they had to spend their evenings making love to gentlemen who might be perverse or actively unpleasant, but how was that different from being a wife? Whores got paid for their services. And they had the company of other ladies in the same profession. In all, as a career choice, whoredom had advantages. If you left out love and children and family and social approval, of course . . .

What now? she asked herself. Events appeared to be overtaking her. What she needed was a solid lead. And apart from a cryptic message, she didn't have one and was required to wait for someone else to do something before she, Phryne, could manage the situation.

Her household, warned by Dot, tiptoed around her. She noticed this and was irritated. She wasn't going to explode. She was about to rise and find out what game they were playing in the other room when the doorbell rang, and soon Mr Butler informed her that a Mrs Timberlake was waiting and would like a word. Also Mr Timberlake.

'I don't know any Timberlakes,' said Phryne. 'Who are they?'

'I believe that Mrs Timberlake's maiden name was Reilly, Miss Fisher,' said Mr Butler, and was ordered to conduct the pair into the sea-green parlour as speedily as possible.

'Hello,' said Phryne, considerably surprised.

'Miss Fisher?' asked a young man. He was dressed in his best blue suit, was painfully and closely shaved, had a button-hole in his lapel and a baby in his arms. 'Saw your ad in the *Argus*. Can I present my wife?' He beamed with honest pride, blushing up to the tips of his ears.

'You certainly can,' said Phryne warmly. 'Do sit down, Mrs Timberlake. Tea, Mr Butler, if you please. I have been looking all over the place for you, Mrs Timberlake.'

'So have the cops,' said Mrs Timberlake, née Reilly. She was dressed in a becomingly loose cotton shift in a cheery shade of orange, with orange daisies in her straw hat. 'I didn't mean to cause all this!'

'You are not in any trouble,' said Phryne. 'But you vanished, you see, and that will cause comment. Will you have some tea and tell me all about it? And congratulations on your marriage,' she added, noting that Mrs Timberlake was displaying her left hand with its plain gold band as other women display diamonds.

'Just today,' said Mrs Timberlake. 'Poor Frank was looking all over for me but my bloody family wouldn't tell him where I was. Then . . .' She sniffed, groped for a handkerchief, and failed to find one.

'Here,' said Phryne, supplying one. 'Don't distress yourself. Ah. Tea. And these are Mrs Butler's extra-special passionfruit biscuits. Does the baby need anything?'

'Only me,' chuckled Mrs Frank Timberlake. 'I'd love a cuppa and a bikkie. Go on, Frank. Tell the lady what happened.'

'Well, me and Julie, we fell in love, and her family hated me on sight, 'cos I'm not a Catholic like them,' began Mr Timberlake. 'So they told her, get rid of him, you can't see him, we forbid it, and all the time her dad was taking her wages and giving her nothing but the Victorian father. She thought—I mean, *we* thought—that if she got . . . was expecting, they'd have to let us marry. But they wouldn't. They sent her to that . . . place. I didn't know where she was. I looked for her, I asked all her mates at the factory, no one knew.'

'It was cruel,' observed Mrs Timberlake. 'I knew Frank would take me if I could only get out, but there's no way out of that convent, and those bitches worked me almost to death and fed me nothing but gruel. I was that hungry all the time.'

She nibbled a passionfruit biscuit in memory of starvation.

'They beat some of the girls. Me, too. They told me every day I was atoning for my sin. I refused to work in their unsafe laundry and they made me stand on a concrete slab all day. My ankles swelled up so I couldn't walk and they made me crawl. Bitches. Then one of them was nice to me when I burned my hand on the presser.'

'Agnes,' said Phryne.

Julie raised her eyebrows. 'Yes, Agnes. She said I was being sent to have the baby in a hospital in Footscray. She smuggled me a two-bob bit. So I thought, I'll get out of the hospital; it can't have a wall like that foul convent. All I have to do is find Frank and I'll be sweet and I'll never see my family again, thank God. And I'll never go into a church again, ever. When I got to Footscray the two others had a plan. They were going to walk out before they gave birth. So I walked out with them, found a phone, called Frank out of his dad's garage and he came and got me.'

'Just in time, too,' said Mr Timberlake. 'I had to take her straight to the Queen Vic. Little Effie was born that same night. Isn't she beautiful?'

He exhibited the sleeping baby. Phryne thought it looked like all babies, as red as a newly skinned rabbit, vaguely unfinished and fragile. Considering that Effie's mother had been fed on pap all during her pregnancy, the child might find that being out of the womb was an improvement in her living conditions. Effie was sleeping soundly, which Phryne liked in babies. And the young man was holding it confidently. He at least had no doubt about the child or his new wife.

'Then as soon as Julie was up for it, we got married,' continued Mr Timberlake. 'In the registrar's.'

'My family has thrown me out,' said Julie. 'Thankfully. I never want to see any of them again. I bet that lazy bludger my dad misses my wages, but.'

'He does,' said Phryne. 'He has informed the police that you can come home provided you give the child away and marry the person of his choice.'

'Jeez,' commented Mr Timberlake. Phryne agreed with him.

'But that need not concern you now. Your own family is happy with this marriage?' she asked him.

Mr Timberlake grinned. 'Oh, yes, Miss, they always really liked Julie. She gets on real well with my mum. She always wanted a daughter, she says, but she was stuck with four sons. We've got the bungalow at the back of the house. I've done it up,' he said with quiet pride. 'Lined walls and plumbing and all. I knew I'd find my Jules again somehow, and she did it herself, she rescued herself, she's such a clever girl! I worked on the house every night while she was away. It was all I could think of to do.'

Mrs Timberlake leaned on her husband's arm and cried briefly—largely, Phryne thought, from relief. Then she mopped and sniffed and drank more tea.

'Now,' said Phryne, 'I need you to remember everything that Mary O'Hara and Ann Prospect said about where they were going.'

'Oh, Lord,' said Mrs Timberlake. 'It had to do with some numbers and letters. SS five hundred and ten BM. It was on the wall. But Ann already knew it. She wrote it. I asked what it was about and she said that she was leaving the message for other poor exploited women. Mary was sick, poor girl, very young even for her age, poor little mite. She kind of relied on Ann. But she was real clear that they were going to a safe place.'

'Where?' asked Phryne, really wanting to know.

'Somewhere in the country,' said Mrs Timberlake. 'I did wonder if it was some sort of religious thing, you know, BM for Blessed Mary. But Ann was a real fierce atheist. She read all them socialist papers, like I did. When I told her I was going to Frank, she didn't tell me anything else. The bitch in charge didn't like us to talk to each other. Threatened to chloroform us if we gave trouble. What's happened to the others?' she asked urgently.

'I don't know but I will find out. Do you remember the reporter coming to the house in Footscray?'

'Reporter?' asked Julie.

'Young woman called Polly. She's vanished, too.'

'I don't remember anyone coming,' said Julie. 'Except the tradies. And the bitch's awful son. Patrick, that was his name. A pig. Is that all?' she asked. 'Only I got to get the baby home on the bus and she'll wake up and cry pretty soon.'

'Mr Butler shall drive you home,' said Phryne. 'I will tell Detective Inspector Robinson that you are well and found, and here is a little wedding present.'

'Oh, no, Miss, we can't . . .' protested the young man, but Julie took the banknote and stowed it in the recesses of her costume.

'Thanks, Miss, that'll come in real handy,' she told Phryne. 'Being as I can't go back to work for a while.'

Phryne summoned Mr Butler and saw her visitors into the car.

'Minions?' she asked, coming back into the house. Jane and Tinker looked up from the chessboard. Ruth was reading the recipes in *Women's Own*.

'Miss?' they asked in chorus.

'Developments,' said Phryne, and retailed all she had learned from Mrs Timberlake, née Reilly.

'So now we're only looking for two of them,' said Tinker. 'Beaut. And Miss Kettle, of course.'

'And I've an idea about that message at last,' said Phryne, relieved that she hadn't lost her skills. 'Find me the train timetables, Tink.'

He duly produced them and she leafed through the lists of times. Finally her minions saw her exclaim, plant her finger on a line, and stand up.

'Right,' she said. Her eyes were bright, her cheeks pink, the picture of a woman on a mission.

'But, Miss, where are you going?' asked Dot, who was mending stockings.

'I'll be back soon,' said Phryne.

'Take me, Guv!' pleaded Tinker.

'I'm going alone,' said Phryne. 'Only way I can get to where I am going.' She told them about her destination, timing and suspicions. Phryne had never adopted the Gothic convention which had seen so many young women in flimsy nightdresses and high heels obeying instructions to burn the assignation and meet the writer in a disused barn on a distant estate. At midnight. Phryne considered that anyone silly enough to do that sort of thing had no right to expect to survive any adventure.

But now there was time to burn. Jane and Tinker returned to learning how knights move. Ruth went back to a recipe for fish pie which sounded promising. Dot picked up her mending.

Phryne, restless, went out for a swim. The prospect of action made her hungry and the exercise and the cocktail meant that she tackled her lunch with pleasure.

In the early afternoon Jack Robinson and Hugh Collins arrived, needing reassurance and tea. Mr Butler provided the tea. Phryne provided the reassurance.

'I'm going to find O'Hara and Prospect this afternoon. I am confident that I shall do so. So you just need to concentrate on Polly Kettle,' she told him.

'Where and how?' asked Robinson.

'I'll let you know,' said Phryne, who occasionally liked to follow the precept of Sherlock Holmes that 'Any problem, once expounded, seems simple' and would decline to explain. 'It will be all right. If I need any help, I'll scream for it. What about Jobs for All?'

'They're opening again tomorrow,' Jack said gloomily. 'Nothing to hold them on. I dunno. I wish I could lay hands on that wretched girl. The papers are nagging the chief and he's nagging me. And I'm nagging Collins,' he added ruefully.

'That's all right, sir, that's what I'm for,' said Hugh manfully.

'And there's more of those assaults,' complained Robinson. 'I tried to get a list of their inmates from that convent and they not only told me to go away, they complained to the bishop.'

'I'll get one, even if I have to go and see Mannix,' Phryne assured him. 'He owes me a favour.'

'How?' asked Hugh Collins.

'Ah,' said Phryne, and would not tell him any more, for she had promised that not a word of the strange affair of Jock McHale's hat would ever be spoken.

'Anyway, the ones we can find out about have all been involved in either an illegitimate pregnancy or had a real lot of kids,' said Robinson. 'And they're all in the area of the convent. And some of them can remember a nun.'

'Before it all went black,' said Phryne.

'Yair. But the nun's not high on my list,' he said. 'She's doing good work, I think.'

Both Dot and Hugh looked at him with identical expressions of horror, which Phryne and the minions failed to share.

'Indeed,' said Phryne. 'Well, I'll call you as soon as I've found out about Prospect and O'Hara. Dot, would you walk them to the door? Then come up to my room. I need some advice on costume.'

When Dot arrived in the sea-green boudoir, Phryne was looking at an armload of what she called her 'playclothes' laid out on her bed. They included disgraceful garments which Dot had had a hand in ruining, allowing her to appear to be eccentric, disturbed or very poor.

'Poor, desperate and pregnant,' said Phryne. 'The dreadful blue sacque?'

'Not blue,' said Dot. 'The convent would never let the bad girls wear blue.' Phryne looked her question.'The Blessed Virgin Mary's colour,' explained Dot to her pagan employer.

'Oh, indeed. What about that shabby grey sacque?' asked Phryne, inspecting a garment notable for its sagging hem and uncertain neckline. It had originally been charcoal but had run in the wash.

'Yes, that'd be good.'

'No stockings?'

'No, Miss. Socks and sandals. Or maybe those old shoes.'

'And padding?'

Six months ago, this request would have curled Dot's hair. Now she said equably, 'How pregnant do you want to be, Miss?'

'Very,' said Phryne.

Dot contrived a believable belly with a small pillow and some bandages. Phryne shook talcum powder over her hair to dull its shine, applied diluted shoe polish to her nails and neck, and picked up a roomy shopping bag made of unravelling pink raffia.

'Yes?' she asked.

'Yes,' said Dot, appalled. Even the way Phryne stood had changed. She leaned back on her worn-down heels, cradling her fraudulent belly. She looked beaten down by time and fate.

But Dot knew that Phryne carried her little Beretta and a wad of cash in her belly, which abandoned women seldom did.

'Good. I'll get a lift from Mr Butler. You hold the fort, Dot, and I'll be back as soon as I can.'

Phryne kissed Dot, bade the minions to be good if at all possible, and left, trailing mystery behind her.

'I don't like her goin' alone,' worried Tinker.

Jane patted his arm. 'None of us likes it,' she told him. 'But she'll see you if you follow her.'

'I know,' said Tinker in an exasperated tone. 'I've tried.'

'Come on, back to the chessboard,' urged Jane. 'Miss Phryne always falls on her feet.'

'Or someone else's,' added Dot.

SS, thought Phryne. Obvious, when you think of it the right way, which is not how I had been thinking of it. She boarded the train at Spencer Street station. The 5.10. For Bacchus Marsh. SS 5.10 BM.

What she would find when she got there would be interesting. The train would presumably be met, because from the map in the directory the station seemed quite a long way from the actual town. If there was a bus she hoped someone would tell her which way to go. Phryne had a copy of *The Woman Worker* in the raffia bag, which also contained a change of garments and other belongings expected of a woman who is running away to an unknown destination. Rat-tat, the train set off, carrying Phryne to an unknown destination.

Along with a lot of other people, of course; this was the Ballarat train. My Lord, thought Phryne, remembering another voyage in first class where the whole carriage had been chloroformed in order to kill an old woman who stood, unforgivably, between her assailant and a lot of money. Here in third class the seats were harder and the company less select, but no one chloroformed her, which was an improvement.

Mostly businesspeople, she noticed. A few definite farmers, in town on some agricultural errand, loaded down with presents for their families. One darling young man with a little box he kept taking out of his pocket and staring at and putting back again—Phryne diagnosed an engagement ring. Had he asked and been accepted? No, too nervous. If he didn't stop doing that he was going to drop the thing. Next to him two old women with shopping baskets. A long way to go to buy—what? The bags they carried seemed to contain clothes. They were eating cream cakes with a lot of flaking and enjoying their day out immensely. The woman sitting next to Phryne was eating toffees and offered her one, casting a pitying glance at her protuberant belly and her naked left hand.

Phryne took the point, but she also took the toffee. Clack-clack and the train pulled in at North Melbourne, where a lot of men in suits shoved their way aboard. Also an inspector of tickets, though Phryne could see no way that he could force his way through the throng unless he could discorporate. She fended off knees and briefcases.

Clack-clack and it was Footscray, a baroque example of Railway Architecture, where some of the suits got off to try their luck in another compartment, or risk the wrath to come by riding in second class on a third-class ticket. The rest of the passengers found a sitting or leaning or strap-hanging position and settled, prepared to defend it against all odds. Phryne knew that her seat was safe, even if she did move, because pregnant women, if they had the bad taste or the sheer necessity to travel, always got a seat. The social disapproval of a healthy man who kept his seat while a lady in a delicate condition stood would be crushing. Also there was a fair chance that the lady would fall on him or some censorious old lady would spike him with her umbrella or park her shopping on him, stepping on his feet the while. Some courtesies were absolute.

The inspector moved through the train, now that he was no longer crushed against the far wall, checking tickets. Clack-clack, and the inspector loomed close to a group of ticketless boys, who managed to escape at Sunshine, running away towards the massive Harvester Works, which covered several acres in every direction and had given the suburb its name. It was fittingly sunny today. The train pulled out on whistle and signal just as the boys reached the gate and leapt it.

And clack-clack as the outraged inspector crossly demanded tickets from the remainder of the population. And as the train clacked on, Phryne heard an altercation and looked up from *The Woman Worker* to find a scene around a very pregnant woman who was weeping freely and had no ticket whatsoever.

'I'll have to put you off, Missus,' said the Inspector.

'Oh, but I have to get to Bacchus Marsh,' she protested. 'I have to!'

'Why, hello!' said Phryne, struggling through the mass of people, who tried to part and let her through. 'There you are! Didn't you get the ticket?'

The woman stared at her dumbfounded. Her face was red and wet, she was clearly at the end of whatever tether she had. She could not say a word, which was fine with Phryne.

'I'm so sorry,' she told the inspector. 'This is my cousin and she lost me in the crowd. I thought she'd missed the train. Here's the money for her ticket. We can only say sorry, can't we, eh, Mary?'

'Yes?' whispered Mary, aware that she had just been rescued and totally at a loss about the means.

'Oh, very well,' grumbled the inspector, and condescended to issue a sixpenny ticket, which he punched himself with some violence and put into the clammy paw held out to him. 'Don't be so careless next time!'

Phryne assured him that she would be the soul of exactitude in future and leaned over the pregnant girl. The gentleman sitting next to her immediately rose. Phryne thanked him and told him to take her seat further back, if he could fight his way through the throng.

'SS 5.10 BM,' she whispered to her rescuee.

'Oh. We're going to the same place,' whispered the young woman.

'I believe we are,' said Phryne, settling. Her fraudulent belly was very uncomfortable.

'But how did you know my name was Mary?' asked the girl. 'Did the comrades tell you that I was coming?'

'No, I guessed,' responded Phryne. 'Which station is this?'

'Ardeer,' said Mary. 'There's the silos. It's where the grain comes in. Were they going to send you to the convent?' she asked.

'Yes,' said Phryne.

'They take the baby away,' said Mary. 'My bloke's dead. We was goin' to get married. Had the ring and all. Then he got killed. On the wharf. And me like this. My family said I was a shame and a disgrace. And they wanted to take the baby. It's all I 'ave of my bloke.' She started to cry again.

'Have you got the ring on you?' asked Phryne.

'Yes,' said Mary, pulling at a string around her neck. It bore a cheap, rolled-gold wedding ring.

'Then you have a perfect right to wear it,' Phryne told her as the train clacked into somewhere called Deer Park, which was perfectly flat and perfectly dry, except for boulders and thistles. It was entirely free of deer. 'Put it on.'

Mary obeyed. And she did feel better, visibly. Phryne was reminded of the charitable practice of the Queen Victoria Hospital. For reasons of hygiene during labour, every woman's wedding ring was covered with a strip of sterile sticking plaster. The white ring around the finger was immediately evident, separating the married from the unmarried. So every woman at the Queen Vic for delivery wore a sticking plaster ring.

'Where are we now?' asked Phryne.

'Rockbank,' said a shopping woman comfortably. 'Soon home, dear.'

'Good. I think Mary and I could do with a nice strong cuppa.'

'You'll be going out to Miss Isobel, then?'

'Indeed,' said Phryne.

'She sends my son Russ to this train every day,' said the shopping lady. 'I always gets a lift home with him. My house's on the way. You'll be all right with Miss Isobel, dear.'

'Good,' said Phryne.

'We didn't quite know what to think when she started changing the old Harrison place,' continued the shopping lady, introducing herself as Mrs Albert. 'But they're growing real good fruit there now.'

'Apples?'

'Apples and pears, of course, but peaches, apricots, nectarines, cherries. My old man said you couldn't grow them fruits in this climate; too hot and dry. Went on and on about it and bet my son Russ a tin of pineapple to a week's milking that it couldn't be done. He didn't enjoy all that milking, I can tell you.' Her satisfaction in her old man's error was palpable.

'But you can?' asked Phryne, as required.

'Miss Isobel's done it,' said Mrs Albert. 'My Russ takes the fruit to the Queen Vic market. Top prices, too. My old man planted a hundred apricot trees this year. Ah, here's Melton. Not long now, dear.'

'I'm a bit faint,' said Mary. She turned a chalk-white face to Phryne.

'Hold up, dear,' said Mrs Albert. 'Soon be out of the train and into the nice fresh air. I'll tell my Russ to get you a drink of mineral water. It's very good. Nice and cold, out of the ground.'

'Like Hepburn Springs?' asked Phryne, feeling the pregnant woman slump against her shoulder.

A change of landscape outside, more trees and fewer rocks, and then at last the train clanked into Bacchus Marsh and the crowd parted to allow Mrs Albert, Phryne and Mary out of the compartment and onto hard tarmac.

Few houses, lots of trees, pasture. Very idyllic, thought Phryne irritably, lowering Mary onto an unyielding railway seat.

A stringy, cheerful young man bounced through the gate and said, 'H'lo, Mum!' to Mrs Albert.

'Drop of water for the lady,' said his mother, and Russ went to a tap and drew a tin cup full of cold water. Mary gulped half and gave the cup to Phryne, an action comparable to that of Sir Philip Sidney. Phryne appreciated it and sipped. It tasted like earth, was faintly fizzy, and would be very nice with lemon cordial and gin, she thought. Mary breathed deeply of the unpolluted air and seemed to recover.

'Right-o,' announced Russ. 'Off we go, ladies. Got everythin', Mum? Into the old trap then.'

'Where are we going?' asked Phryne.

'Old Harrison place for you,' said Mrs Albert.

'Got a new name now,' said Russ. 'It's called the Groves of Bilitis. Sounds sort of foreign. Like Midnight of the Sheik. But that's what the boss says we have to call it.'

'It's the old Harrison place as far as I'm concerned,' sniffed Mrs Albert.

'Well that's what I gotta call it,' said Russ. 'They even renamed the old mare. Called her Rosa. She answers to it, but. Carm on, Mum, they're nice ladies and it's a good job and there ain't a lot of work around here, what with veggie prices so low.'

'I'm sure they're good women,' agreed Mrs Albert peaceably.

Rosa, thought Phryne as the mare walked faster. Rosa Luxemburg, of course.

Mrs Albert descended from the trap outside a farmhouse with all her belongings and told Mary, 'You cheer up, girl, my boy Russ'll look after you.'

Russ grinned. Rosa picked up her pace. A mile or so on to her destination and a mile further back, and she got to put up her hoofs and rest.

They paced through dusty bushes lining groves of fruit trees, some tall, some newly planted. Sheep grazed between the rows. Then they passed a gate with *Groves of Bilitis* emblazoned on it. It was open so Russ left it open. And there was the farm.

It was a very big old farmhouse, surrounded by sheds overgrown with passionfruit vines. Down the verandah steps came two women. Four dogs of indeterminate breed raced out, barking loudly to impress on any visitor that unpleasant people would be eaten. Russ said, 'Get outta it, ya mongrels,' and they fell back, abashed and wagging. Phryne clutched her unravelling raffia bag and inspected the duo approaching through the guardians.

'Alexandra,' said the short plump woman in men's clothes.

Phryne thought for a moment. Then she dead-heated Mary in replying, 'Kollontai.' Sign and countersign, indeed. Communists. They were almost as secretive as the freemasons.

'Names?' asked the short plump one.

'Mary and Phryne,' said Phryne, wondering how long this was going to go on.

'Well, now we've got that over with, Sophie, let's get them inside for a cuppa. They look ready to drop.'

A tall, commanding woman with the sort of grave beauty seen in statues of Athena took Mary's arm. Phryne followed.

Russ said, 'See ya termorrer!' and went back to the trap, unloading several boxes which had come on the train and then endeavouring to extract Rosa from a multitude of small children. They were feeding her apples and hanging around her patient neck. Rosa snuffled and crunched. She declined to move while there were apples on offer.

The principal scent of the kitchen was vinegar. It was strong enough to sting the eyes. Seven women were working at the final stage, which was packing the scalded onions into their jars and pouring the boiling pickling liquid over them. Hundreds of ranked jars of various concoctions (piccalilli, apricot, plum, cashmere chutney, sweet mustard) and bottles of tomato sauce gave evidence of their industry.

'Sorry, pickling day,' explained the tall grave lady. 'I'm Isobel, by the way. This is Sophie. Come and sit on the verandah. The smell will dissipate soon. They built these houses to cross-ventilate. Wendy, are you on teas today? Can you make some for us, please?'

This, though expressed as a request, was more of a divine command and the tea appeared swiftly. It was good, strong and bracing. Mary drank two cups and ate a slab of shearer's cake, a dense fruit cake made in a baking dish.

'Now, what can we do for you, Comrade?' asked Isobel to Mary.

'I just want to be safe,' said Mary. 'To have my baby in peace. Then I'll have to find a job. But they were going to take it away. No one's going to take it away.' She clutched her belly fiercely.

'No, no one is going to take it away,' said Sophie. 'You're safe here. You need to work for the good of us all while you can. We will look after you and then we'll find you a place, somewhere you can keep the baby with you.'

'I'll work,' said Mary fervently.

'Good. But you don't have to start today. I'll take you to Algie. She can show you to the bathroom and get you a comfy nightie. Then you can rest.'

Mary sobbed, mopped, and was taken away. Isobel Berners leaned back in her chair, lit a cigarette, and said casually to Phryne, 'Well, what brings you to visit us, Miss Fisher?'

CHAPTER FOURTEEN

We have nothing to lose by fighting but everything to gain. We want the right to live decently, to have comforts and pleasures and to give our children nourishment and care. The Master class have always encouraged the inactivity of women. We must fight! There is nothing that men can do which we cannot do.

The Woman Worker
7 January 1929

'Rats,' commented Phryne. 'And I thought I was doing well.'

'Oh, you are,' said Isobel. 'Very convincing. Stance and all. Took Sophie in. Would fool anyone except that I've seen you before. At the Socialist Women's Conference last year.'

'Indeed,' said Phryne, taking out a gasper and allowing Isobel to light it. 'You were very convincing about how a commune could never work once it got beyond a certain size. And that the Russian experience was thwarted by centralised government.'

'I am honoured that you remember my speech so well,' said Isobel.

'You were very memorable. And yet . . .' Phryne waved a hand at the surroundings. 'Here you are in the middle of what is definitely a commune.'

'Life is strange, sometimes,' reflected Isobel. 'When I was a nice doctor's daughter in Kent, I thought that my life would be very predictable. School, home duties, marriage. My brothers went to university to become doctors but that was never thought of for me. And my sister was indulged with clothes and so on, because she was pretty and taking and likely to Marry Well. But I was too tall, too definite, and far too prone to speaking my mind, so it was decided that I would be the one to stay home and look after my aged parents. A spinster until I died, full of good works and regretted by few.'

'Erk,' said Phryne. 'So, what happened to that nice little plan?'

'The Great War,' said Isobel.

'Ah, yes,' said Phryne. 'That changed my life, too.'

'What did you do?' asked Isobel.

'I ran away from school and became an ambulance driver,' said Phryne, swallowing tea and tasting horror and mud.

'I became a Land Girl,' said Isobel. 'You have to cast your mind back to the way that people thought then. I didn't know I was strong. I always thought men were the strong ones. I didn't know I was intelligent or competent. Only men knew how to run things. And I believed it all!'

'Quite,' said Phryne.

'They sent me to Lord Hamilton's estate, from which all the men had gone. I was there with a staff of girls and one very old man to teach us what to do. We had to plough, sow, cultivate, reap, stack, run tractors and look after horses and cows and carry manure. My parents were horrified and tried to get me exempted, but I gave them a speech (which still makes me blush) about patriotic duty and the motherland. This land work was my only chance to see anything else of the world.'

'So you went?'

'I went,' said Isobel. 'And for the first six weeks I was so hungry and cold and my body was one big ache and I swore that I'd run away, but somehow I never did, and it got easier. I found out I was strong. I could lift a cast ewe back onto her feet. I could swing a churn onto a truck. And I began to get the hang of the agricultural year. I made charts and diagrams. I kept the accounts. I managed to circulate my tasks so I tried everything—milking, butter churning, cheese making, clotted cream. Riding and the care of horses. Driving a truck. Slaughtering, butchery and cooking. Pickling and preserving. It was a wonderful education. Not that the old lord appreciated me or anything silly like that.'

'Of course not,' said Phryne. 'You're just a gel. And a stopgap gel at that.'

Isobel snorted. 'The old beast insisted on his imported wine and his Cuban cigars,' she said. 'I could only just squeeze the money for petrol and sugar and other useful things out of his steward, as old and crabby as he was. By the end of the war I was as good an estate manager as anyone could want, and even though the young lord never came home—he was killed on the Somme, poor boy—I was instantly sacked and couldn't find another job.'

'Of course,' said Phryne. 'But you really couldn't go home.'

'No need, my parents had moved into a boarding house run by one of their nieces, thankfully. So they were settled. Then I met Sophie Harrison.'

'That Sophie?' asked Phryne, gesturing to the house which a Sophie had just entered.

'Yes, she was looking for a place where she could be herself.'

'Harrison as in "the old Harrison place"?' asked Phryne.

'You are very sharp,' complimented Isobel. 'She said she was establishing a women's commune in her old family home, and she had the capital. So I sailed for Australia with her. No men, she said. Not even male animals. I managed to persuade her that we needed a rooster if we wanted more chickens and that drakes were very decorative, but that's the extent of it. The cows have to go to bull somewhere else and even the dogs and cats are all female.'

A cat sleeping on the verandah table near Phryne raised her head, blinked, and went back to sleep.

'That is . . . individual,' said Phryne.

'I've come across stranger ideas,' shrugged Isobel. 'When Sophie formed her commune she needed an estate manager, and I am she. Farms need an immediate authority. Much as it pains me to say, they really do need a boss. Large decisions go to the commune. Small day-to-day ones are mine.'

'For example?'

'The commune decides that they want to grow nectarines. I talk to some nectarine growers, find out the best type, locate and buy the saplings, and oversee the planting and nurture. And the picking and marketing. We have a stall at the Queen Vic Market and it is doing very well.'

'I thought fruit prices were very low?' said Phryne.

'Oh, they are. But not only are we selling top-quality fruit, we are making things from it which command a higher price. For example—we have a glut of tomatoes at present. The vines are overloaded and some of the fruit has been pecked or spoiled. So we make tomato sauce, with our own onions and vinegar. We only have to buy spices and sugar from outside. We collect the bottles for free. Just have to wash them and scald them in the oven. One bottle of our tomato sauce costs a halfpenny to make, and we can sell it for threepence, which is still cheaper than the commercial brand. And much tastier, as well. We can sell all that we can make—pickles, preserves, jams. Cheeses. Come and let me show you around.'

'And your labour?'

'All the members work,' said Isobel serenely. 'And the women seeking refuge, too, if they can. Some of them are so starved and ground down that all they can do is rest until their baby is delivered. Mrs Albert is our midwife.'

'Thus the SS 5.10 BM?'

'My aunt had a baby out of wedlock and they made her give it away. And she mourned it the rest of her life. She was always sad. She cried over that baby every night until she died. It's not right. Until there is a reliable way of avoiding conception, women take all the blame and then have the fruit of their wombs stolen from them. Fair enough if they don't want the child. But if they do, they can come through here.'

'Through here? Not to stay?' asked Phryne.

'Well, no, there wouldn't be room. We get them jobs or find them places.'

'You don't use Jobs for All, do you?' asked Phryne.

'Never heard of them,' said Isobel briskly.

'I'm so glad to hear that,' said Phryne. 'Shall I shed my disguise?'

'No, no, the others are used to pregnant women wandering around. You don't want to disconcert them.'

'Tell me, did a reporter called Polly Kettle ever come here?'

'No. She would not have been very welcome if she did. People think the oddest things about groups of women without men. I shall ask, of course. You are investigating her?'

'She has vanished,' said Phryne. 'And you were just one place that she might have gone.'

'You shall see the whole establishment,' promised Isobel.

Walking like a goddess, Isobel exhibited thc Grovcs of Bilitis with pardonable pride. Four Jersey cows grazed in their little after-milking paddock. Children had made wreaths for their necks, which they were quietly eating. The dairy was scrubbed sterile. Pans of milk sat quietly in the cool stone building, cream rising. Cheeses dripped through their cloths. In an adjoining shed, shelves held drying cheeses. The smell reminded Phryne sharply of Tuscany.

'We make two sorts: a soft cheese for cooking and a hard cheese, which takes six months to mature. If the soft cheese doesn't sell we can turn it into hard cheese. Have a taste,' offered Isobel. The cheese was reminiscent of Parmigiano, grainy and salty.

'These apricots are going to be jam tomorrow,' said Isobel, indicating an overloaded row of trees. 'Russ brought in the sugar. We make pectin out of lemon juice, from the trees over there. We tried oranges, but they did not do well. But lemons do well everywhere except on actual ice. We've got as much water as we want from the Werribee River. Now we've got pipes it's a lot easier.'

'How long have you been here?' asked Phryne.

'Since 1919. The first years were hard. Quarrelling and inappropriate crops. Several of the commune left. The rest worked very hard to nurture our soft fruits. Everyone said we couldn't grow them here. But they flourished.'

'So I heard,' said Phryne.

Isobel chuckled. 'I've never seen Mrs Albert so pleased. Now that we're making a living, we can employ people for the hard tasks—ploughing, fencing, picking, heavy lifting. We did it all ourselves in the beginning. We could do it all again,' said Isobel Berners.

Phryne believed her. This was a woman in her right place at her right time, and nothing short of catastrophe could stop her.

Actually, Phryne's money would have been on Isobel despite the worst that catastrophe could do.

She was shown the apple press for making cider. The racks of dried fruit dessicating in the sun. The rows and rows of fruit trees with their weed-control sheep grazing between. The olives from which the commune made oil. The spacious barn with a flock of chickens pecking through the litter. Two donkeys, a mare and a foal. Phryne caressed velvet ears and was nuzzled.

'Fortunately, the baby donkey is a jennet,' said Isobel.

'Isobel,' said Phryne, after an hour, 'this place is amazing. Now show me the mistakes.'

'If you wish,' said Isobel, taking Phryne outside. She waved a hand at a stand of straggly green sticks. 'Corn,' she said. 'We won't sow it again. Something lacking, perhaps, in the soil. We can grow our own barley. One year we had a plague of fowl pest and lost most of the chickens. Yes, Maisie?' she asked, as a small child dragged at her hand.

'Isobel, the bees are swarming!' shouted a little girl.

'Get the little kids out of the orchards, and run for Mr Bee. Quickly now,' she added, and the child sped off.

'Mr Bee?' asked Phryne.

'Mr Bairstowe, our local bee-man. Hence the Bee. The commune doesn't like employing men but he's the only bee-keeper around here. We are doing well with the honey. Our bees fertilise the fruit blossoms, so the honey is delicately flavoured. What were we talking about?'

'Mistakes,' said Phryne. 'Failures.'

'This year the foxes got a lot of ducks and the remainder haven't been able to keep up with the slug population so the cabbages have holes. And a bold experiment in making apple brandy exploded and took the shed with it. Other than that, we are doing well.'

'And the women?'

'The labouring mothers are in the back of the house, where it's quiet,' said the stately woman. 'Come and meet them, if you like.'

Phryne followed her through the cool house, past the scrubbed-clean kitchen where the seven picklers were putting up their feet and drinking cold cider, to a large room which had been made out of screening the back verandah with heavy mosquito netting. It contained a row of army cots made up with clean linen and blankets. Four of them were inhabited. One woman was breastfeeding a newborn, watched by a doting girl hardly into puberty, herself heavily burdened.

'Hello, Ann,' said Phryne. 'Hello, Mary. I've been looking for you.'

Both faces froze in terror. Ann Prospect clutched her baby so tight that it screamed. Mary O'Hara paled and sat down suddenly. Phryne kicked herself for her brutal approach.

'I'm so sorry, you have nothing to fear, I've just been looking for you to make sure that you were all right. Now that I can see you are, I can cross you off my list of missing girls and look for the others.'

The baby provided a useful pause by throwing up all over Ann. There was an interval while she was rinsed, dried and provided with a clean gown by a slender woman in blue overalls.

'Who sent you?' demanded Ann Prospect.

'I sent myself,' said Phryne, sitting down on one of the cots. 'I am helping Detective Inspector Jack Robinson with his enquiries. Girls are vanishing. You amongst them. We need to have a talk. You've fallen on your feet, ladies. Others might not have been so fortunate.'

'All right,' said Ann. She burped the baby and laid it in the haybox cradle beside her bed. 'Ask us anything you like.'

'Tell me how you came to be sent to the convent. Who is the father of that fine baby?' asked Phryne.

'Bastard foreman at the works. Got me against a wall one day as I was going home from the night shift. Said no one would believe me because he was a respectable man with three children and I was a factory worker. Bastard! But he was right,' she admitted. 'I told my dad and he called me a whore, and off to the convent I went. You been there?'

'Yes,' said Phryne. 'Though not in the laundry.'

'No, they wouldn't let anyone in there,' snarled Ann Prospect.

'But I will get in,' said Phryne. 'Because a reporter is missing and I have yet to find her. I've located you and Mary and Julie,' she told the woman.

'How's Julie?' asked Mary.

'Fine—married, a mother and very happy,' Phryne reported.

'Beaut,' said Ann. The baby mewled. She picked it up again.

'Someone dropped in on that foreman and made him infertile,' said Phryne, watching both faces closely. 'Surgically. Someone dressed as a nun.'

'Yer jokin',' said Ann, joggling the baby.

'No, true dinks,' said Phryne.

Both women grinned.

'Couldn't have happened to a nicer bloke,' said Ann. 'What about her Mr Fraser?'

'Him, too, and her dad.'

'Gosh,' said Mary O'Hara. 'Who did it?'

'There you have me,' said Phryne. 'Have you any idea who might want to revenge you?'

'No, but if I could meet her I'd shake her by the hand,' said Ann.

'Any of the nuns seem friendly?'

'Friendly? Those bloodless bitches?' demanded Ann with scorn. 'They told us all the time we were atoning for our sin with labour, and no labour could be too great to save our immortal souls. Didn't matter if we actually sinned, you know. Mary didn't sin. Neither did I. We were raped.'

Mary O'Hara winced and Ann Prospect patted her shoulder.

'Well, we were,' she said. 'Don't take on, Mary. It wasn't your fault, just like it wasn't mine. Your dad sold you, for God's sake. Therefore it wasn't our sin. It was their sin. But we paid for it, all right. By God we paid. We paid in beatings and sweat and injuries and pain. And no one's ever going to get me into a church again. Not till they carry me feet first. Even then I might fight me way out of me coffin to stop them.'

'Are the others all right?' Mary caught Phryne's faded sleeve. 'Have you talked to them? I didn't want to leave my little sister, she's about the right . . .'

'Age for Mr Fraser's attentions? I have spoken to them, and I am sure that Mr Fraser will behave with great propriety, because I shall have him killed if he doesn't.'

Both faces turned to her in astonishment. Then Ann Prospect laughed suddenly.

'Knew I'd seen yer before! You're Phryne Fisher, aren't you? The comrades told me about you. It's all right, Mary. Comrade Bert says she can do anything she sets her mind to. I reckon your Mr Fraser will keep it in his trousers all right. And there's always the chance your bastard father will drink himself to death. Cheer up. It's all gonna be all right.'

'If you say so, Annie,' said Mary.

'I do say so. Have I ever led you wrong? Got us out of that hell-hole, got us here, didn't I?'

'Yes, Annie,' whispered Mary.

'Right, then.' Ann seemed to consider the matter settled. So did Mary.

'Have you thought about what you are going to do after you leave here?' asked Phryne.

'I'm going up country,' said Ann. 'Grazier's wife wants a housekeeper. I can keep house. I can take little Isa with me. Comrade Isobel arranged it. It's hard for the outback stations to find staff. I like the wide open spaces. It can't be harder than working in that rotten factory. Mary wants to stay here. She's good with children. Barely more than a child herself,' she added. 'It's a crying shame. When the revolution comes those child-raping bastards will be hung from the nearest lamppost.'

'Live the day,' said Phryne. 'Travelling money,' she said, handing over some of her stash. 'Always good to have a pound or two in hand. And I'll let the comrades know that you're all right.'

'Thanks,' said Ann.

'Anyone else here from the convent?' asked Phryne.

'Nah,' said Ann. 'Poor cows come from the gutters. Gimme a hand, Miss. I got to sit up and drink me veggie broth. Tell you one thing,' she added. 'The food's better here.'

Phryne helped her to sit up, then wandered through the large house. In one room, children were pasting labels on pickle jars while a young woman read to them from *The Condition of the Working Class*. At least it wasn't *Das Kapital*, thought Phryne. Engels had a much more readable style.

'*Do not believe that you can ever rely on the bosses*,' read the lector. '*Their interests and yours are diametrically opposed . . .*'

Phryne passed into a large living room where other women were resting, reading, knitting, kissing, playing cards and drinking tea. They looked up when she came in, then returned to their recreations. Phryne asked if they didn't work as well.

'We're day shift,' one told her. 'Afternoon shift's come on. Three shifts a day. Gotta always have someone awake when you've got a house full of women.'

'Of course,' said Phryne. 'Have you had any trouble?'

'Some of the local oafs thought they'd see if we could provide them with any fun,' said a stalwart woman, rippling a few muscles. 'We didn't and they ran home with their bums on fire. Some idiots decide to try to scrump fruit or steal livestock. We've got noisy dogs and shotguns. They've largely given up.'

'Though you didn't mind the little kids pinching fruit,' said another, putting down her copy of *The Social Revolution*.

'Poor little scraps,' said the first woman. 'They don't take much and they don't hurt the trees. We've got a lot,' she added. 'We can share.'

'So we can,' agreed the first woman, and went back to the matchless prose of Alexandra Kollontai.

A third woman was sewing a sampler. Phryne wondered what text could possibly suit a wall which already had a banner proclaiming *The Workers Revolution* tacked to it. She asked to examine the text, which was being surrounded with very conventional cottage flowers.

If no one ever marries me—
And I don't see why they should,
For nurse says I'm not pretty,
And I'm seldom very good—

If no one ever marries me
I shan't mind very much;
I shall buy a squirrel in a cage
And a little rabbit hutch.

I shall have a cottage near a wood
And a pony of my own,
And a little lamb quite clean and neat
That I can take to town.

And when I'm getting really old—
At twenty-eight or nine—
I shall buy a little orphan girl
And bring her up as mine.

'Very pretty sentiments,' she told the embroiderer.

'I found it in a book,' said the woman.

Phryne kept walking. The house was orderly, if not very neat, comfortable, and felt welcoming. Only an iron will and a delicate hand could keep all this running without exploitation and complaint. And she knew who had both of those.

'Isobel,' said Phryne, when she located her in the fowl yard, mediating a dispute between two factions, one of which wanted chicken for dinner (aged about twelve) and one of which (aged about six) opposed the killing of her favourite hen. 'You have accomplished great things.'

'Daily,' agreed Isobel. 'Everyone stop crying. Just this once, Milly, you can go over to Mrs Thomas and buy three of her boiling hens, cleaned and plucked. Here's the money. You, Janice, shall tie a ribbon round the leg of your favourite hen so that everyone knows about her and she doesn't get sacrificed by mistake. And I want you both to meditate on this. If you want to eat flesh, you must kill to get it. For you to eat chicken, a chicken has to die. Either accept this or don't eat chicken. All right?'

'But not Henny,' declared the six-year-old.

'No, not Henny,' said Isobel.

All parties dried their eyes.

'All right,' they agreed. They decamped. Peace returned to the chicken yard. Phryne gently dislodged a hen which was attempting to repose on her shoe.

'So you find jobs for women in outback stations?'

'Yes, they find it hard to get staff. It's a long way from anywhere in those places. But our women select themselves for intelligence and ingenuity. That's why we use the cipher. They have to be bright to work it out. I only deal with women I know or who are vouched for by women I know. I wouldn't want to run the risk of sending our women into slavery. Again.'

'That is just what I am investigating,' said Phryne.

'That's why you mentioned the name of that employment agency?'

'Yes. Can you ask if any of your comrades have heard of it?'

'Of course. Stay to dinner. It'll be ready in an hour or so.'

'After Milly gets back with the chickens?'

'No, they're for tomorrow. City children don't know where milk comes from, or eggs, much less that eating meat involves killing something. They are almost always shocked. We used to do our own slaughtering until we acquired so many children. Now we send animals to be slaughtered to the next farm. It isn't so upsetting. In any case, we don't kill much, except the occasional chicken. Half the commune are vegetarians.'

'And the other half?'

'Are carnivores like me.' Isobel grinned. 'I buy a lot of rabbits from the local kids. They're pests. And depending on who's cooking, they can be very tasty. You can meet the commune at dinner. What would you like to do in the interim?'

'I'd like to meet your pig,' said Phryne. 'I like pigs.'

'Pigs, at present,' said Isobel, leading the way. 'She's just farrowed.'

'You don't kill your own bacon, either, do you?'

'No, I buy a cleaned carcass from Mrs Gargaris. She's got good stock. Then we cure it ourselves. We can always sell the piglets when they are a little bigger. And when they are loosed in the barley field, they eat all the grubs and bugs and weeds and churn up the soil so it's easy to plough. I only keep them penned when the piglets are very young. There are eagles around here that could carry off a small pig.'

The pig pen was well appointed. The sow lay on her side, a huge breadth of breathing pink flesh, while her piglets suckled and walked across her. She raised her head and grunted when she heard a step. Isobel spoke to her.

'It's all right, Belinda,' she assured the creature. The sow subsided, laying her head on her straw pillow with an almost human sigh.

'Lord, seven piglets,' marvelled Phryne.

'I know. Poor creature. Another thing which makes me glad I'm human.'

'Isobel,' said Phryne, 'that old lord who sacked you?'

'Yes?'

'He was *such* an idiot.'

Dinner was held in the biggest room in the house. In the original farm it had probably been three bedrooms. Now it held long trestle tables, which during the day were dismantled and stacked against the wall. Here was the commune, sitting down on a variety of chairs and picking up its soup spoons.

Twenty-five people and an indeterminate number of children. The noise was appalling.

Then the soup came in, carried in a galvanised-iron bucket, and was ladled into bowls. Phryne took some. It was a thick hearty vegetable broth. The servers moved around the table and, once everyone was served, moved around again with refills until the bucket was empty.

'They start at a different place every day,' said Isobel. 'So no one is permanently disadvantaged when the food runs out. We work hard: everyone is hungry. Have some bread. Homemade. Home-churned butter. Rabbit stew to follow. And Ernesta is in the kitchen today. It will be good.'

It was. Phryne would have said it was *coniglio alla cacciatore*, heavy with garlic, tomatoes and herbs. With it were tender new potatoes and a melange of green vegetables: beans, peas in their pods, spinach. The vegetarians had the *cacciatore* without the *coniglio*. Phryne ate enthusiastically, even though she had sworn she would never eat rabbit again. This was excellent food for an institution. She noticed that the children were actually eating their greens. Most of them ate them first. She asked Isobel about it.

'If they eat their greens they get cooked dessert,' said Isobel. 'If not, only raw fruit. It seems to work for all but the most adamant, and those have just drunk vegetable soup. We are not bound by the outmoded conventions of child-raising that saw them fed on nothing but starch,' she added proudly.

'They do you credit,' said Phryne.

They were bright-eyed, rosy and noisy. One child had smuggled a kitten into the room and was feeding it cooled bits of rabbit. No one banished her.

'Where do they go to school?'

'At Bacchus Marsh. There are enough of them so that they are not much bullied. Some of them are very bright.'

Plates were cleared away. There were few leftovers. Then large platters of raw fruit were brought in, accompanied by apples baked with honey and sultanas, and fruit crumble and pitchers of cream, for those who had eaten their greens. There was sweet cider for the children and alcoholic cider for the commune. It was reminiscent of Cornish cider: cloudy and potent.

'We use the apple pulp to feed animals,' Isobel informed her. 'Pigs, goats and donkeys love it.'

'Very good,' said Phryne. 'The old lord's steward trained you well. No waste. And you have adapted beautifully to local conditions. What happens to the ones who will not work and want to lie about all day, discussing important political questions and painting mediocre pictures?'

'Oh, you mean men?' asked the woman next to Isobel. 'We don't have any of them.'

There was a general laugh. 'All right, yes, we have had people like that,' said Isobel. 'But they get bored easily. We don't have any amusements like cafes and pubs and galleries, their natural habitat. You can't wear pretty clothes here, not with gumboots. No point in putting on makeup to attract the cows. And we get up far too early. We just set the whiners to heavy work, like mucking out stables and weeding. If they do it, fine. If not, then they're out. We get Russ to take them back to the train. Just because we're socialists doesn't mean we're a soft touch.'

'So I see.' Phryne stood up and banged on the table with a spoon. Conversation about Lenin died away. 'Hello, Comrades. Bert and Cec send their fraternal greetings. I'm Phryne Fisher and I'm missing a reporter. Can anyone help me? Has anyone seen anything of Polly Kettle?'

General denial and a buzz of speculation.

'And does anyone know anything about Jobs for All in Lonsdale Street?'

'You stay away from them,' said a stout, ruddy, good-looking woman in an apron. 'They're collecting blondes, they say. Girls.'

'Do you know anything more, Mrs . . . ?'

'Comrade Levin,' said the woman. 'I got a letter from my sister. She just says that someone from Jobs for All was telling little blonde schoolgirls they could get them a theatre job overseas. My sister's daughter was approached. Luckily my niece told her mum and her mum sorted them out, smartish. Got rid of the bloke with a clip around the ear and told all the neighbours about him. He didn't come back!'

'Any name? Description?' asked Phryne.

'I got the letter here . . .' She groped in the apron's capacious pocket. 'Yes, here it is. She says he was a good-looking, flashy bloke with patent-leather hair and a gold tooth. A rat, she reckons.'

'He sounds like one! Did he give a name?'

'Bill Smith,' said Comrade Levin, with a world of scorn in her voice. 'Somethin' ought to be done about rats like him.'

'And I shall give the matter my earliest attention,' Phryne assured her. 'If not Polly, has anyone seen a reporter? Someone interested in your endeavour?'

'Only that Rachel from *The Woman Worker* a few months back. We gave her tea. Nice girl. But we know her. She's been here before.'

'Ah, well,' said Phryne. 'She's either been shipped to Beirut or is locked up in the Convent of the Good Shepherd. Poor Polly!'

'There's not a lot of ways out of that convent if they don't want to let you go,' said one of the comrades, feeding mashed vegetables to a toddler. 'Only one, apart from being dead.'

'And that is?'

'I'll whisper,' said the young woman.

Phryne stooped. 'I see,' she said. 'Thank you. Now, I really must go if I'm to catch the 8.10. Can I order a case of your white peaches, Comrade Isobel, when they are ready? Here's the money and my card for delivery and also—Lord, I almost forgot—do you have any apple jelly to sell?'

CHAPTER FIFTEEN

But whoso shall offend one of these little ones which believe in me, it were better for him that a millstone were hanged about his neck, and he were drowned in the depth of the sea.

Matthew 18:6
The Holy Bible

Having arrived home, given her large jars of premium apple jelly to Mrs Butler—half for herself and half for Dr MacMillan—shed her disguise and taken a bath, Phryne dressed in a silky robe and sat down at her window. Where are you, Polly? she thought into the soft darkness of the St Kilda night.

The darkness, as was usual, yielded no answer. Just drunks singing, the splashing of the sea, the almost unheard whicker and gossip of homing fruit bats overhead. I do like Australia, thought Phryne, and put herself to bed. Tomorrow would produce some answers, or her name was not Phryne Fisher.

Tomorrow, however, produced a pre-dawn downpour in which Ember had been caught. While Jane and Ruth were in the kitchen drying him, much to his displeasure, and Mrs Butler was contemplating the ruby light of early morning through her new jars of apple jelly—which she would be enjoying on English muffins any moment—someone lifted the latch on the back gate and slunk into the garden.

The intruder was promptly bailed up by Tinker, who had been out fishing, barked at by a damp dog, marched dripping wet into the kitchen, and plunked miserably into a chair next to a spitting angry wet cat, who was shredding an old towel.

It was not a conspicuously joyous advent. However, since the intruder clearly posed no threat and was really wet, cold and weeping, Mrs Butler provided dry garments and a towel and laid on a good breakfast, though she did not feel that she had to offer trespassers any of her apple jelly.

'Did you leave the back gate unlocked?' demanded Mrs Butler.

Tinker hung his head. 'I didn't think I'd be long; they were really biting,' he muttered, holding up a string of cleaned fish for evidence.

'Good boy for the fish, bad boy for the gate. Always lock it. We could all be murdered in our beds!' exclaimed Mrs Butler. 'You never know who might sneak inside!'

'I meant no harm,' began the shiverer in a whisper.

'That's as may be. Now drink your tea,' ordered the cook. 'Toast, eggs, bacon, fish, porridge?'

'Not porridge . . .' whispered the invader.

'All right, then. Tinker, put those fish in the sink. Get the girls to set the table. Bustle along,' she said, and they bustled.

Breakfast was just getting into its swing when Phryne made her usual entrance, in silk gown and with her second cup of coffee in her hand. Only the iron self-control of years ensured that she did not drop it when she saw who sat at her table, wearing Mrs Butler's dressing gown and nibbling toast with (shop-bought) strawberry jam.

'Good morning, Agnes,' said Phryne, sitting down and ordering more coffee.

'Guv?' asked Tinker, confessing before anyone could tell on him. 'I left the gate open when I went out fishing. I'm sorry, Guv.'

'And that's who walked in?'

'Yes, Guv.'

'No matter. Lock it in future. Agnes will cause us no harm but someone else might.'

'Yes, Guv.'

'Good fish, though,' said Jane. 'Ember's forgiven us for drying him.'

'That cat would forgive a lot for fish,' said Ruth.

'Especially fresh fish,' agreed Tinker. 'He meets me at the gate when I come in each morning, and the look he gives me if there ain't, *isn't*, no, *any* fish. Like my old schoolmaster.'

'Cross cats are good,' said Ruth dotingly, embracing the purring black creature.

'I like cats,' said Agnes timidly. She was a plump, pop-eyed woman of indeterminate colouring, aged perhaps forty. 'They have cats at the convent. For the mice. But not black ones. They won't have black ones. Black cats come from the devil.'

'Yes, I expect so, but that's cats for you,' said Phryne soothingly, suppressing her minions. Any moment now Agnes would tell Ruth that they always drowned the black kittens and she would be upset. Phryne disliked upsets in the morning.

'Leaving matters feline aside, why have you come to see me? Not just for breakfast, surely, since you didn't come in through the front door?'

'That laundry,' said Agnes, putting down her cup.

'The Magdalen Laundry at the convent?'

'Yes. Things go on there . . .' She stuck.

Phryne looked at Dot.

'You tell the lady,' said Dot bracingly. 'I'll sit here and say a rosary for your intention.'

Dot was so patently and transparently sincere, and already had a rosary in her pocket. Agnes took a strengthening gulp of tea and said, 'It's the girls, Miss. My lady. They're worked too hard in their condition. If they won't work then the sisters stand them on a concrete slab all day. Their legs swell so they can hardly walk. They feed them nothing but porridge. It's a scandal.'

'Yes, it certainly is,' said Phryne. 'Who can we tell?'

'No one!' wailed Agnes. 'No paper will touch it, even if I dared to write it, and anyway I never learned much about writing.'

'Is there anyone hidden in that laundry?' demanded Phryne.

'Well, no, my lady, I don't think so, I know all of them.' Agnes was surprised by the question. 'There's thirty eight of 'em at present. No, thirty-seven.'

'What happened to thirty-eight?' asked Jane, who gravitated to numbers but did not think they should apply to humans.

'She's in the infirmary, real sick; she miscarried. Poor little mite. Not a day over fourteen. They left her there on that ironing-room floor for three hours, until the shift changed. She coulda bled to death. She'll be all right now, though.'

'Do new girls come in every day?'

'Often, my lady, not every day.'

'So I could join them?'

'Oh, no, Miss,' said Dot, dead-heating Agnes, who objected, 'No, my lady, you don't look right. They'd know you wasn't never a tart. Nor a factory girl.'

'You should have seen me yesterday,' said Phryne, 'But you're right, I need to get in and have some freedom of movement, which the laundry girls don't have. Could you get me a nun's habit?'

'They don't own their own kit, so it wouldn't be noticed if it didn't fit right. But they all know each other, my lady. You'd never get away with it.'

'And you'd never pass,' said Dot firmly, her rosary almost falling from her nerveless fingers. 'You'd never pass as a nun, Miss! You don't know how nuns are supposed to behave. Even in the right clothes. There's the walk. They sort of glide. And they never look you in the face, not even when they're hitting you. And you don't know the prayers.'

'All right, then, how am I to get in? Because if Polly Kettle is there, I need to find her. I have arranged a way out for her.'

'How?' asked Agnes.

'Never you mind,' Phryne told her. 'What about the black gowns you wear? They would be very disguising.'

She had noticed that each auxiliary looked like a sackful of wet spaghetti tied up ugly, as Bert would say. No shape could be discerned under all that black cotton. The hair was covered by a cap and a veil, all black. A cheerful costume.

'I'm an auxiliary, my lady, a sort of helper, not a sister. I'm a widow. They pay me and I get free lodging and food at the convent. And I help out with the nursing—my brother was a doctor and I used to help in his practice. My old man left me nothing. He was a gambler and a drinker. I had to sell his best suit to get him buried proper,' said Agnes bitterly. 'But it's a big risk, my lady. What if Sister Dolour catches you?'

'What can she do to me if she does?' asked Phryne lightly. 'I shall be scolded and thrown out. That won't raise a blister. It wouldn't be the first time, either. I can offer you a pound for general expenses, and if you do get sacked, come and see me and I'll find you something equally holy to do which doesn't involve oppressing children.'

'And you'll expose them?' asked Agnes eagerly.

'Oh, indeed, if I have to start my own newspaper.'

'Good,' said Agnes. 'It's not right.'

It was dawning on the audience that Agnes wasn't very bright. However, once she had an idea, she worked it to death. And she had been kind to Julie Reilly with her burnt hand.

'Now, is there anywhere in that convent where they could hide a prisoner?' asked Phryne, conscious as she asked that the question smacked of melodrama. The minions pricked up their ears. Tinker had just finished *The Awful Disclosures of Maria Monk*, recommended by Ruth and not to be mentioned to Miss Dot, and was ready to believe anything at all about convents.

'I suppose so,' admitted Agnes. 'They have punishment cells. But they're only for sisters. I couldn't get to them, my lady.'

'Ah, but I shall. Now, if you've finished your breakfast, you shall sit down in the parlour with Jane, our best draughtsman, and draw a map of the convent for me. Ruth will do the labelling. Tinker will examine the map and work out the best route from the laundry to these punishment cells. And you, Agnes, can assure me that you will bring me a set of those dreadful black rags this afternoon, and show me how to put them on.'

'All right,' said Agnes, a little breathless, an effect which encounters with Miss Fisher often had. 'All right! I will!'

'Bravo,' said Phryne, and took a piece of toast.

While the drawing was going on, Phryne was summoned to the telephone. It was Jack Robinson.

'So you've found those three missing girls,' he shouted into the receiver. 'Bert said.'

'Yes, all happy and healthy. No need to worry about them anymore,' Phryne assured him.

'And the reporter?'

'Still looking, and you don't actually need to shout, Jack dear, I'm not at all deaf.'

'Nothing on them assaults?'

'Not a word, just a lot of rather unseemly amusement and hearty cheers from every woman I have asked. I can't get the records. How have you been proceeding with getting them?'

'Stymied,' said Jack gloomily. 'The commissioner said I can't even ask.'

'Catholic, is he?'

'Yes.' The firm note indicated the end of that line of enquiry.

'Oh, well, I may have another way of finding out.'

'Are you doing to do something unwise?' he asked suspiciously.

'How well you know me,' purred Phryne in a tone which Ember might have produced on being presented with smoked salmon within easy claw reach. 'Unwise but not dangerous. On the other hand, Jobs for All is downright inadvisable and I will need some reinforcements. Come to a conference about them tomorrow? I'll ask Bert and Cec. Would lunch suit or would you prefer one of Mrs Butler's dinners?'

'I'd love one of Mrs B's dinners, but I promised the wife I'd be home tomorrow night—got to finish tea early because it's the orchid-growers' meeting. Lunch? Twelve?'

'Twelve it is. Will you bring your constable?'

'Collins? He's enough to turn a man's stomach at the moment. He's gone all moony over your Dot.'

'I think it's sweet,' Phryne told him. 'Bring him. I might need his assistance. Twelve sharp, and cold steak and kidney pie shall be yours.'

'Deal,' said Jack Robinson, who could bear even the presence of a romantic policeman for steak and kidney pie.

Phryne arranged by phone that Bert and Cec would come to lunch, informed Mrs Butler of the same, and went back into the parlour.

'That's about the best we can do,' said Jane. 'The place is huge. We're a bit vague about the edges but it's pretty correct.'

'You're right, the place is huge. I think we can discount the farm,' said Phryne. 'Too many people go there who wouldn't be in on the secret. And the orphanage, St Euphrasia, that's too populated as well. And the laundry is, you should forgive me, a closed shop. Same goes for the old ladies and the school. No, if she's really in durance vile, she'll be here, where the nuns live, or in the actual laundry itself. Now, before you go home and fetch me some garments, Agnes, tell me under what circumstances one of the auxiliaries might leave the laundry during working hours.'

'If there's been an accident,' said Agnes, thinking it through. 'Someone has to report to Mother if there's an accident. Didn't help that poor little girl, though—didn't get her up off the concrete any sooner.'

'Terrible,' said Dot sympathetically. 'Go on, Agnes.'

'If something breaks down. We've got gas irons, we've got big boilers and mechanical mangles and pressers. And we've got contracts. If something goes wrong, we have to tell Mother about it so she can get it repaired fast.'

'Because the most expensive brothel in Melbourne is waiting for its pristine sheets,' said Phryne bleakly.

'What?' demanded Agnes, shocked.

'Never mind,' said Phryne. 'Any other time you might be loose in the convent?'

'Just coming from our lodgings and going home,' said Agnes. 'And going to church, of course. We can go out any time we like,' she said proudly.

'Wonderful,' said Phryne, in such a flat tone that Dot took Agnes to the front door herself, told her she was doing the right thing and that God would approve, and gave her sixpence for the bus.

'I,' said Phryne, 'am going out for a long walk,' and she rose, ran up the stairs, dressed and, descending, slammed her way out of the house.

'What's wrong with the guv'nor?' asked Tinker, worried that it might be his mistake in not locking the gate.

'Miss Phryne,' said Jane affectionately. 'She wants to fix everything, and it makes her cross when she can't. I don't think even Miss Phryne can fix that convent.'

'It'll know it's been in a fight, but,' said Tinker admiringly.

Agnes, whatever her private misgivings, arrived at about two with a bundle of black cloth. The garments were, indeed, very disguising. With a baggy shift (black) belted around the waist with a cord (black), a cap (black) and veil (black), which was pinned firmly to the scalp (ouch)—the ensemble would have reduced Theda Bara to a nonentity. All to the good, thought Phryne.

'Now, Miss, you have to remember that you're in a holy place. Don't shout, don't raise your voice, don't touch that skirt except to go up steps,' instructed Dot, who was torn between excitement and the distinct feeling that she was going to do penance for this. 'Do whatever Agnes tells you to do. And if you see awful things in that laundry,' she said uncertainly, 'don't do anything. You can't help them by making a scene.'

'I know,' said Phryne softly.

'And when a nun speaks to you, do exactly as she says. Without a word.'

'That,' said Phryne, looking at her face in the mirror, surrounded by unrelieved mourning, 'ought to be interesting.'

Dot's feeling of disquiet increased.

'Can we come too, Guv'nor?' asked Tinker, viewing her with great interest. 'You look real different, Guv.'

'That was the idea. I'd take you anywhere, Tink, but you'd rather stand out in a nunnery.'

'Like a dog's balls,' he agreed.

Dot blushed. Tinker's lessons on Polite Conversation had not advanced to any great extent.

'Mitigate your language, Tink dear, you're embarrassing the innocent. Dot, ask Mr Butler to bring the car around. Here is a note. If I am not back by dinnertime, you will take it, yourself, to Raheen, and give it into the hands of Dr Mannix. Only him. Take Jack Robinson with you.'

'Why?' asked Dot, clutching the letter.

'Because it will mean that something is extremely wrong in that convent, and he had better come along himself and get me out. Or when I do get out his church is going to have a lot of very loud questions to answer. But I don't for a moment think you will need it,' she said. 'While I am away, minions, I want you to consult everything we know about Jobs for All. Don't go and look at them because I don't want them to recognise you. Formulate a few ways we can get in and nail the bastards. Bye.' And she was gone.

The minions looked at each other, then trailed down the stairs to inspect the mass of information on Jobs for All. And, in Tinker's and Dot's case, worry.

Phryne had Mr Butler drop his passengers at the end of St Helier Street. It would never do to swan up to the front gate in the Hispano-Suiza, wearing these clothes. Phryne found the black garments cumbersome, but found a way of walking in them without treading on the hem. They were also hot. She mentioned this.

'Wait till you get into that laundry,' said Agnes. 'Especially in the boiler room with all them coppers. Come on. The guards know me.'

The gates were huge and moved very slowly to allow a van to go out. Phryne and Agnes went in. The guard waved at Agnes and let them pass.

'This way,' said Agnes. Her voice was shaking.

Phryne took her arm. 'Agnes, if you can't control yourself, then let me go on alone. Anyone could tell you were scared. You'll get us discovered.'

'Oh, no, my lady, you don't know the way. I'm all right. I'm usually nervous, they won't see any difference. They don't look at us much, anyway.'

'All right,' said Phryne, not at all sure. She was not concerned at being detected and flung out neck and crop, had she brought a crop with her. She was concerned about being flung out before she found Polly Kettle.

Agnes led her to the laundry.

It was a large annexe, built onto the side of the convent quadrangle presided over by the statue of St Joseph. Phryne wondered which saint would preside over this building. None occurred. The big doors by which trucks came and went to load and unload led into crooked corridors, stinking of disinfectant and bleach, almost sticky with starch. The noise was acute. Machines rumbled and rolled and squealed.

The first room held the clean, dry and folded laundry, each in its own pile, being packed into clean calico bags by women in grey smocks. No one spoke. No one even looked up. They consulted and ticked off lists and pinned each one to the completed orders.

'This is where the good obedient girls are,' said Agnes. 'Light work.'

'Light, I see,' said Phryne.

'This is ironing.'

A large number of lines ran from a central point in the middle of the room, each attached to an iron. Inside this monstrous spiderweb more grey-smocked women were working, ironing sheets, shirts, clear-starched doctors' and waiters' coats, watched over by a sister whom Phryne had seen before. Sister de Sales, eyes everywhere, walking behind every ironer in a manner guaranteed to disconcert.

Phryne had seen every face so far. They were blanched, exhausted, weary beyond bearing. Not all of them were pregnant. Some were very young. And none of them were Polly Kettle.

Out of the ironing room, and Agnes hitched up her skirts. Phryne did the same.

'It's always wet in here,' she told Phryne. 'The girls work barefoot. It's easier. Shoes don't last long.'

Neither, thought Phryne, would humans. The huge coppers—fifty gallons, Phryne estimated, at least—boiled continuously, filling the air with steam. Women in those same smocks, barefoot and bare-legged, shoved sheets in and pulled sheets out, wringing them between two pot sticks until the slimy stone floor was swimming with hot water.

'Bad girls,' mouthed Agnes. The sour stink of soapy filth and sweat was overwhelming. Phryne managed to see each face. Pull, haul, twist, wring, endless sheets, endless hard, hot, heavy work. Severe labour for any strong man. Iniquitous for pregnant women.

Still no Polly. Out of the boilers and into the rinsing, not as hot or as foul but just as hard. Still no familiar reporter. Then further, into a room which was occupied by a gigantic mangle, broad enough to take a double bed sheet, into which more slaves were poking the wrung-out sheets from the rinsing. Still barefoot; the mangle squeezed out more and more water.

Agnes nodded to the auxiliary in charge as she conducted Phryne into the drying yard. The warm wind struck chill. What a way to catch pneumonia, thought Phryne, out of that fug into cold air. A new meaning to the term 'catch your death'. More grey-clad servants of the laundry, busily pegging the sheets, under the malevolent eye of Sister Dolour. One girl saw a friend on the other side of the yard and spoke. Sister Dolour slapped her across the shoulders with her pot stick. There was a distinct 'thwack'. Phryne froze. The urge to remove the weapon from that bitch of a woman and beat her to death with it was very strong.

Phryne did not move. The girl didn't even react. She expected Sister to hit her. Sister expected to be able to hit anyone she chose. Agnes dragged at Phryne's arm. No Polly among the dancing linens.

And inside again to another room, where wrung, almost-dry coats and fine linen tablecloths, gossamer wedding veils and delicate laces were starched. No face that Phryne knew.

And in the middle of the next room, which contained benches and tables and might have been meant to be a place of rest, stood a woman in a grey smock, standing on an uncarpeted square of concrete. She swayed. Only pride was holding her erect. She was very pregnant. Her arms embraced her belly. A penitent who had refused to work.

Not Polly. Phryne dragged Agnes across the room to speak to her. Agnes fought her every inch of the way, and lost.

'If they send you out to give birth, catch the five-ten to Bacchus Marsh,' she said, bending down as if to wring out the hem of her dress. 'If not, tell Terry to take you out of here with Madame Paris's sheets. Remind him about a girl called Primrose. And if I were you, a graceful faint about now might be politic.'

The girl's eyes opened wide. 'Who are you?' she asked.

'Phryne Fisher,' she replied.

'Right,' said the girl, and slumped.

Agnes and Phryne took her up and bore her away, out of the room, into the corridor which ran into the convent itself.

'Agnes?' asked Sister de Sales, as they passed the ironing room.

'She's fainted,' said Agnes with some heat. 'How long's she been there?'

'I don't know,' said the sister. 'Dolour must have ordered it. All right, take her away, I'll explain.'

'Thank you, Sister,' said Agnes.

Phryne, who would not have put good money on the timbre of her voice, kept silent.

The infirmary was not palatial, but it was quiet. Agnes indicated a bed and they laid the girl down on it.

'Just lie still and I'll get you some water,' said Agnes. 'How long you been there?'

'Since dawn,' said the girl. 'My legs bloody hurt.'

'Get a pillow and put her feet up,' ordered Agnes, secure in her own domain. 'I got some aspirin. Why don't you just do the work?' she demanded.

'I wouldn't work for those bitches if they killed me,' said the girl, faint but clear.

'They just might if you don't learn,' scolded Agnes.

'No,' said the girl.

'You should have said that before,' sneered Agnes.

'Didn't have a choice,' said the girl.

'Enough,' said Phryne. 'Recriminations will not help us here. What's your name?' she asked.

'Faith.'

'Have you seen anything of a woman called Polly?'

'No. We're all numbers here. Thanks,' she said, as Phryne lifted her swollen ankles onto a folded blanket.

'She was a reporter, here to expose the conditions in the laundry,' said Phryne, as Agnes propped Faith's head on her shoulder and fed her a paper of aspirin and a long drink of water.

'No, never heard of her. But I wouldn't be her, if the bitches knew why she was here.' Faith closed her eyes.

'Right, I'm off,' said Phryne. 'Give me a note about Faith and I'll be back as soon as I can.'

'You don't want me to go with you?' asked Agnes, scribbling on the back of a bill and trying not to sound as relieved as she felt.

'No. Back soon,' Phryne said, and stepped out into another corridor.

The trouble was, she considered—after walking for too long, according to the map she had memorised—was that all these passages looked the same. No signs, no pictures, all painted an institution grey. The only light relief were some very realistic oleographs of the Sacred Heart, gory and unsettling. Still, not a lot of point in going back. By what she could recall, most of them led back into the quadrangle. There were only four possible sides. One had to lead somewhere.

So far she had seen few nuns, and no one had challenged her. This could not continue. She picked up her skirts and ran to the end of the present passage and emerged into what must be the nuns' quarters.

They were sterile. Clean, grey, stony, and even on a warm day, cold. Each little cell had a door, and all were open. Each nun had a bed, a blanket, a prie-dieu, a book of prayers, and that was about all. Not a bauble, a lolly, a family picture, even a toothbrush.

The last two doors, though, were firmly shut and when Phryne tried them, locked. There were slots in the doors, as one saw in the best prisons. She looked in.

Two sad countenances. Two tear-streaked penitent faces.

No Polly Kettle.

Few people have been happier to leave a building than Phryne Fisher at that moment.

She went out into the courtyard, navigated her way back to the infirmary, bade farewell to Agnes and Faith, then stalked out to the gate.

'Leaving us so soon?' asked the guard, with something that resembled a leer.

'Let. Me. Out,' ordered Phryne. Eyes as cold as emeralds glared into his, clearly prophesying what would definitely happen if he didn't do exactly as ordered and that right speedily. An old soldier, he had last seen that look in the eyes of a German soldier, who had been bayoneting him at the time.

'Right you are, Miss,' he said, and swung the gate open.

After that he knocked off early for a drink. He had had a shock. Females at the convent were usually real biddable.

Phryne stalked down St Helier Street, got into the car, tore off her veil and cap and threw them out the window.

'Home, Miss?' asked Mr Butler, very gently.

'Home,' said Phryne. 'Now.'

The convent had been searched, and Polly Kettle was not there.

CHAPTER SIXTEEN

We console ourselves with the flesh for all the iniquities in the world.

Anaïs Nin
A Spy in the House of Love

Phryne had walked sadly into the house, taken herself off for a shower and a change of clothes, and was sitting, staring out the window, in her boudoir, having refused food, drink and company.

The minions were gathered in the parlour, worrying.

'What did she say?' asked Dot of Jane, who had actually spoken to Phryne.

'That Polly Kettle wasn't there,' said Jane, who had an exact memory of that cold speech, muttered through a frozen mouth. 'That the convent was as she thought it would be, but worse. That she wanted nothing. Then she told me to go away. So I went.'

'She didn't even want a drink,' said Ruth. 'Or anything to eat. And Mrs Butler's made her favourite *petits bouchons de quiche lorraine.*'

'She didn't even have a nice hot bath with lots of perfume,' said Dot. 'Just a shower with pine soap.'

'Did she tell you to go away, too, Miss Dot?' asked Tinker.

'Yes,' said Dot.

'So what do we do?' asked Tinker.

'We leave her alone,' said Dot. 'Until dinner. Then . . . I have to make a phone call.' She hurried away.

The minions looked at each other.

'What do we do now?' asked Tinker.

'Come on,' said Jane. 'Want to try some more chess?'

'Bet you don't beat me in two moves anymore,' he responded.

'What do you bet?' asked Jane. Tinker didn't own a lot.

'I got . . . two crown caps, three fishhooks stuck in a cork, a button, four pretty shells and this nice bit of string,' he said, dredging his pockets. 'Bit of string's always useful.'

'I like the shells,' said Jane. 'Come along, and remember to watch out for the way knights move.'

'They're tricky,' he agreed.

Ruth took her cookbook into the garden. Jane carried the chessboard. Tinker carried the box of chessmen. Dot, returning from her telephone call, brought her embroidery. It was a pleasant day out under the vines, shielded by the bamboo fences from the hot salt winds. Mr Butler provided lemonade. It was a very quiet, comfortable afternoon. And they heard not a word from the first floor, where Phryne had shut herself in.

Seven o'clock, and there was a knock at her boudoir door. Phryne, who had been sitting on her window seat, staring out to sea, started. She had given orders that no one should even consider approaching her. Whoever was at the door was either extremely brave or extremely foolhardy.

Actually, he was Lin Chung, carrying a tray. She stared at him.

'Silver Lady,' he said in his gentle voice 'May I come in?'

'And if I say no?' she snarled.

'Then I will go away,' he replied. 'Taking this cocktail which Mr Butler has compounded, these little pies which Mrs Butler has prepared, and this copy of Sexton Blake which Tinker has lent you.'

She looked at him. He was, as always, immaculate, elegant, beautiful, foreign. And very patient. She had the feeling that if she chose not to speak he would stay there, holding the tray of offerings, until she did or the world ended, whichever came first. She let the door fall open.

'Come in,' she said.

Downstairs, the household breathed a collective breath of relief. Then they went on with dinner. Dot's gamble had paid off. Suddenly everyone was very hungry.

Lin Chung put down the tray and poured two glasses of the iced drink. Phryne took one. She sipped. It tasted of mint and tonic water and gin and elderflower cordial. It tasted, indeed, wonderful. She drank it. Lin refilled the glass. He surveyed Phryne. She was wrapped in her least favourite dressing gown, and she had tied the cord very tight, binding herself closely. Her hair was disordered and her face was pale. She had been weeping.

'These little hors d'oeuvres are very acceptable,' he said, offering the plate. Phryne ate one. Her throat, which had been blocked with outrage, relaxed enough to swallow. Lin did not venture to touch her, as she seemed primed to explode. Dot's phone call had been instructive. Phryne had been to a dreadful place which she could not amend. She had withdrawn and forbidden all contact. And she had a conference on the morrow which was very important to a number of shanghai'd girls. Therefore, Dot thought, Phryne needed Lin Chung. He knew all about misery, war, starvation and captivity. Lin had come to do what he could. He was not at all sure that he could comfort her, but he could provide an educated auditor.

'Shall I send down for some more food?' asked Lin.

'Yes, please. And some more of that cocktail. Mr Butler always knows what is going to be acceptable.'

'It's a supernatural gift,' agreed Lin gravely. He picked up the house telephone and gave the order. Phryne nibbled another *petit bouchon*.

'Probably learned at butler's college,' she added.

'Where he graduated top of his class, gold medal and magna cum laude.'

'Indeed,' said Phryne. When the tray of appetisers appeared and a refreshed jug, she said, 'Dot sent for you, didn't she?'

'She did,' he confirmed.

'I didn't ask her to,' said Phryne.

'She has the audacity of love,' said Lin. 'She was concerned about your state of mind.'

'It was dreadful,' said Phryne, putting a hand on his hand. 'Not the hard work or the slavery or the conditions, though they were bad enough, God knows. Have you ever been in a convent?'

'Not likely, Silver Lady,' he said with a smile. 'Monasteries, yes.'

'I bet yours weren't like this one,' said Phryne.

'Probably not. Buddhism works on the theory that all humans are sinful, due to being made of flesh. But the flesh makes its own punishment. Monks generally do not take it on themselves to punish us further.'

'Nuns do,' said Phryne. 'They beat the women and starve them and misuse them and scold them continuously because they are wicked.'

'Yes?' prompted Lin. Phryne had not told him what he needed to know. He had not yet discovered the core of her disquiet and pain. He waited for her to disclose it

'A girl spoke to a friend. That was against their rules. The nun beat her.'

'Yes?' Lin repeated.

'The girl accepted it,' said Phryne, her voice rising. 'She accepted it! The nun knew she could hit her with impunity. The girl didn't resent it. She didn't even think of fighting back! Not even an angry look. Nothing.'

'Ah,' said Lin Chung, enlightened. 'A story?'

'All right,' said Phryne, shaking with fury.

'A slave in the old Imperial days, working on the Great Wall. He and hundreds, thousands of similar slaves carry and build all day until they die. One day a guard throws him down and beats him. The slave cries out, "Why are you beating me?" and the soldier, kicking him again, says, "Now I am beating you because you asked why."'

'Your point?' asked Phryne.

'That slave, should he have survived, would not ask again,' said Lin imperturbably. 'Cruelty teaches the slave about the death of hope.'

'Those girls have no hope?'

'Not that one, certainly,' said Lin. 'Others, perhaps. Dot told me there had been escapes.'

'Yes, there have,' she said.

'Successful escapes?' he asked, daring to approach and sliding an arm around her waist. She did not flinch. She did not knock him unconscious with a decanter. He was getting somewhere.

'Yes, I found at least three who got out in one piece.'

'So hope is not dead and cruelty does not always triumph. And you cannot save everyone,' he added.

Phryne embraced him. His heart beat comfortingly under her cheek.

'I still have some I can save,' she murmured.

'And I am here,' he said simply, 'to carry out your every wish.'

Phryne grinned wolfishly. 'Begin by taking off those clothes,' she said.

Lin woke at dawn. He was hot, sticky, extensively bitten and scratched, and felt as though he had spent the night with a very amorous female tiger, or possibly dragon. Eye to eye with him on his pillow was a large, dew-spangled black cat.

'Quite a night, eh, Small Tiger Mau?' he murmured. Ember butted his head into Lin's chin. This human smelt agreeably male, but was clearly no rival for the local female cats' affections. Phryne rolled over, pulled the other pillow over her eyes, and sank back into slumber.

'I think if we are very careful,' Lin told the cat, 'we might be able to get up and have a wash and some breakfast before anything else is demanded of us. What do you think?'

Ember stepped delicately off the pillow. He had just heard Tinker come in through the back gate, delivering his very own fish. Lin slid out of the moss-green sheets without awakening Phryne and padded into the bathroom. He had been, he thought complacently, more extensively ravished than any man in the history of China, even the oversexed protagonist of *The Carnal Prayer Mat.* But some hot water would be pleasant. And some food. And some tea. And then perhaps another little nap. It had been an eventful night.

He took a shower with the pine soap, which stung in his claw marks, and dressed in a gown, then descended the stairs very quietly, barefoot.

Unsurprised, Mrs Butler provided him with tea and toast with apple jelly, a mark of gratitude, which he carried back to the boudoir. He did not want Phryne to wake alone. She slept heavily, however. He finished his breakfast and lay down beside her again. In her sleep, she embraced him and laid her head on his chest.

When she woke she heard his heartbeat as she had the night before, and saw a dozing, golden countenance as she sighted over the muscles of chest and upper arm. His eyelashes were black and absurdly long. They fluttered as she watched, awoken like a cat by her glance falling upon him.

'Silver Lady,' he said.

'Oh, Lin,' said Phryne. She rose on one elbow. 'Did I hurt you?'

'Minor flesh wounds,' he replied.

She sought out and found and kissed every scratch and bite. This took some time, and would have led into further activities had not Phryne noticed the clock.

'Rats,' she announced. 'Bath. Breakfast.'

'Lunch, actually,' said Lin.

'Yes, I know,' she told him, kissing him again. 'Thank you,' she said. 'Saved my life. Or my reason. Again.'

'My pleasure,' he replied. No one could doubt that he meant it. He went hunting in the wardrobe for a replacement shirt. His previous one had been ripped off his body and shreds of it decorated the bedroom. Phryne, when roused, was really very strong.

•

The Phryne who descended to lunch with her co-conspirators was a different Phryne from the crushed woman who had crept up stairs to be alone with her misery at the cruelty of the world. She bounced into the dining room.

'Everyone here?' she asked Dot.

'Yes, Miss, the buffet's ready. Mrs B made two steak and kidney pies, in case one wasn't enough.'

'Very kind of her. Bert, Cec, how are the comrades? Jack dear, how nice to see you. Hugh, you are looking in the pink. Dot, that dress really suits you. Hello, minions. What's for lunch?'

'A good feed, however you look at it,' replied Bert.

'Wonderful, I'm starving.'

She grabbed a plate and loaded it with food. Bert and Jack Robinson met over the first steak and kidney pie. They divided it in half with mathematical exactitude. With Mrs Butler's sister's homemade tomato sauce it was, as always, magnificent.

Dot hovered over Hugh Collins, supplying him with food. Ruth fed Bert. Tinker and Jane were still discussing chess. Lin ate distractedly. He knew what had worried Phryne the night before. But her present high spirits made him instantly suspicious. What wildly dangerous thing was she contemplating now to stagger humanity, or at least his part of it?

Well, he would know soon enough, and for the present there was a banquet to be eaten. He was Chinese. He knew about the importance of food.

When the feast had concluded with a beautiful fruit sorbet and the company were nibbling dry biscuits and cheese and sipping their coffee, Phryne called the meeting to order.

'Polly Kettle,' she said, 'has not been found, but we know where she isn't, which is an advantage.'

'I don't call it progress,' grumbled Jack Robinson.

'Then you're a very silly policeman indeed. To find where something is, you must look in all the places where it isn't. Stands to reason,' said Phryne briskly. 'Now, she isn't in the commune. She hasn't even been there. She isn't in any of the brothels. If so, Madame Paris would know, because she knows everything which concerns her. At the . . . upper end, you might say, of her trade. And Jack and his policemen have covered the lower end.'

'No sign of her,' confirmed Jack Robinson, as gloomy as a man could be who had a stomach full of very good steak and kidney pie.

'She isn't in the convent,' said Phryne. 'I am sure. I searched it. Every loathsome part of it. There ought to be some law against what they are doing there, Jack.'

'But there isn't,' he said. 'I wish there was, if it's as bad as they say.'

'It's worse,' said Phryne.

'All right,' said Jack. 'Miss Kettle isn't in the convent, she isn't in the houses. I've laid hands on that precious pair, Mrs Ryan and her thug of a son. I've got 'em in custody for fraud, theft, assault and recklessly causing grievous bodily harm. They left one poor girl in a state where she might have bled to death. They didn't give a f—' he looked at Dot and censored his speech '—fig about the patients. Mrs Ryan's been fleecing the Welfare department for years. She lied about being a nurse, too. She'll go to jail for a long time.'

'How nice,' said Phryne. 'Just what I would have wished for her. And her son?'

'Him, too,' said Jack Robinson. 'The house is up for sale, to defray debt. I don't reckon they'll get a penny, them debtors. The place was mortgaged up to the hilt to pay off sonny's gambling debts. He had a real eye for a horse, that one. He just had to look at it and it fell down.'

'Excellent! I am very pleased. Well done, Jack dear!'

'Just routine police work,' muttered Robinson. 'The odd thing is that they did see Polly Kettle that morning, but she was never kidnapped. She just went away. No one at that address laid a hand on her. That fool was just romancing.'

'I suspected as much,' said Phryne. 'But that leaves us with very few clues. She left the house in Footscray, presumably caught a tram or a train back into the city. What was her next port of call?'

Jack consulted his notes. 'Jobs for All,' he said.

'Right,' said Phryne.

'Oh, by the way . . .' Jack passed a piece of paper across the table 'This is the town address of that bloke you asked me about. Miss Kettle's intended. Got a house in Toorak, as you might have expected.'

'That must be why the family wanted her to marry him,' said Phryne, putting the paper aside. 'Right, now, all of you minions, what do we know about Jobs for All?'

'Nothing good,' growled Hugh Collins.

'But nothing we can nail them on,' said his superior.

'Searched the place,' said Collins. 'Looked through the books. They seem to charter small boats for their girls. Two of 'em, the *Thisbe* and the *Pandarus*. Funny sorts of names. They seem to be looking for blondes at present. Younger the better. Say they're sending them out to theatrical appointments or to be maids or nannies or nurses.'

'And you think their destinations are going to be less respectable?' asked Jane.

'Yes,' said Collins. 'I think that an awful fate awaits the poor girls.'

'When does the next boat sail?' asked Phryne.

'Tomorrow night,' said Hugh. 'But we've got nothing we can stop the boat with.'

'Yair, we have,' said Bert.

They all looked at him.

'You been keepin' up with the wharf news, Comrade?' he asked Phryne.

'No, I've been otherwise occupied. What's happening?'

'They won't get a small boat loaded with slaves out of Melbourne River at the moment,' Bert told her.

'Why not?' asked Phryne.

'Port's closed,' said Bert. 'There's war on the waterfront. Pickets around all the gates. Ever since the Beeby judgment. The smugglers are real crook on us,' he added.

'Because?'

'Place is swarming with cops and bucks and scabs,' he told her. 'White wingers. Reporters. Harbour Trust, Seamen's Union, Carters' and Drovers', all pokin' their noses in. Not a mouse gets in or out without some bugger noticin'. They won't be takin' them poor tarts out of port.'

'Where, then? They can't get them to Beirut on a train,' objected Dot.

'Willi, I reckon,' said Bert, consulting Cec with a look.

'Too right,' said Cec.

'Williamstown?' asked Phryne.

'Too right,' said Cec again. 'That's the Naval Dockyard, the Royal Yacht Club, Gem Pier, Blunt's Boatyard, lots of small vessels, nothing carryin' cargo.'

'Or we'd know about it, eh, Cec?' said Bert. 'Thanks, Ruthie,' he added, as she refilled his beer glass. Bert had rescued Ruth from domestic slavery and brought her to Miss Phryne. She would never stop loving him.

'Too right,' said Cec.

'All right. Can you find out where those two little ships are moored and when they are going to set sail?' asked Phryne.

Cec nodded.

'And now, what about that employment agency?' asked Dot.

'They're registered,' said Hugh Collins. 'Two directors, one that smarmy bast . . . man I told you about—his name's De Vere. Vivien De Vere. What sort of name's that for a man?' he asked.

Phryne smothered a giggle. 'No sort of name,' she told him. 'The chance that he is actually called De Vere is very limited. Vivien, eh? I wonder if I've met any Viviens. Not lately, to be sure.'

'The other one's called Bill Smith,' said Collins.

'Just as likely to be a nom de crime,' said Phryne. 'But that need not concern us here. How long have they been operating?'

'Eleven years,' said Collins. 'Pay their taxes, too.'

'Indeed. How very law abiding of them.'

'If you're drivin' a stolen car, don't run no red lights,' said Bert philosophically.

'Quite.'

'Miss,' said Dot, looking worried.

'Dot?'

'I asked around about that Catholic charity, Miss, the one called Gratitude who's supposed to be sending the girls.'

'And?'

'I couldn't find out anything,' confessed Dot. 'Bishop's office never heard of them. None of the priests I talked to knew about them. They're in the phone book, but when I rang the number it didn't answer. I asked Hugh—' she blushed '—and he sent a constable to the address in the directory. It doesn't exist.'

'Bodgy,' said Bert.

'Too right,' said Tinker. 'I went and did a bit of a lurk around there. In me old clothes, Guv'nor. It's a vacant lot. But there's a phone box. The phone rang and blow me down but a bloke jumps out of a parked car and answers it. Smarmy-lookin' goat with slicked-down hair. I got the number of the car,' he said, and produced a carefully lettered page out of his notebook.

'Good boy,' said Jack Robinson, which was not something that any cop had occasion to say to Tinker before. He was flattered, but he looked to Phryne for approval.

'Yes, very good,' agreed Phryne. 'Chocolate ice cream for you, also a small addition to your pocket money.'

'And for me and Ruth,' said Jane. 'We went through their books. Jobs for All, I mean. Mr Collins lent them to us for the afternoon,' she said. 'And we were curious. Don't be cross, Mr Robinson.'

'Tell you what, you tell me what you found and I won't be cross with a constable who mislays evidence in a criminal case,' replied Robinson. He sounded serious so Jane handed over several sheets of lined paper.

'You see.' She pointed out several entries, copied in Ruth's careful hand. 'Payments which don't have a donor or a double entry. Only designated by G. G for Gratitude, perhaps?'

'Blimey, you're a shark of an accountant,' said Jack, impressed. 'I missed that. And that's a good half of their income. Quids and quids.'

'Ice cream for all,' said Phryne, very proud of her family.

They beamed.

'So, we've got Gratitude collecting girls who're in trouble or can't make a fuss,' summarised Lin Chung. 'Having no families, or none which want them back. We have an agency who is also collecting—or trying to collect—pretty little blonde girls. We have two ships, *Thisbe* and *Pandarus*, and we do not need to think about which one holds the slaves.'

'We don't?' asked Bert.

'Trust me that it will be the *Pandarus*,' said Phryne. 'It's another name for pimp.'

'Right-o,' said Bert.

'You said that this De Vere was English?' asked Lin Chung.

'Yair,' said Collins, who still loathed the man.

'Then a university education has clearly been wasted on him,' he said calmly. 'Both ships are named from Shakespeare. *A Midsummer Night's Dream* and . . .'

'*Troilus and Cressida*,' said Robinson, who doted on Shakespeare. A man you could sit down and buy a beer for, should he still be extant.

'So, we have all the facts,' said Phryne. 'This is what I plan to do.'

She expounded. Only Lin Chung and Dot were not very, very shocked.

CHAPTER SEVENTEEN

What is a ship but a prison?

Robert Burton
Anatomy of Melancholy

Tinker played white and moved his king's pawn two squares forwards. Jane did the same, and Tinker moved his bishop out three squares on the diagonal. Jane smiled. 'This would be the Boden Gambit I was telling you about? All right, Tinker, but I'm not going to move my knight. I'm going to do this instead.'

She moved her own bishop out next to Tinker's. Tinker frowned, and moved his queen's pawn out two squares. Jane looked disconcerted, and moved her queen out to the very edge of the board. It was Tinker's turn to frown. He had expected that Jane would take his queen's pawn. He moved out his king's knight to attack Jane's queen. Jane clapped her hands together gleefully and moved her queen down to take the pawn next to Tinker's king. 'Checkmate!' she exulted. 'See, your king can't move anywhere.'

'You got him,' said Tinker, lying the piece down.

'That's called the Scholar's Mate. We've all fallen into that trap at some stage. Remember it for next time.'

'Still,' he growled, 'you didn't win the bet. Took you four moves.'

Jane conceded that this was so and showed him the Scholar's Mate again, slowly. Tinker was getting the hang of chess. You had to think several moves ahead and guess what the other person was going to do. This made the game really difficult. Rather like fishing. A lot of fish in the sea, his father had said, but an awful lot of water mixed up with 'em. You had to out-think the fish.

'What do you reckon about the guv'nor's plan?' he asked. 'She's only going to be on her own for a lot of it, but.'

'What have you learned about chess, Tink?' asked Jane. He looked at her. 'The queen is the most powerful figure on the board,' Jane told him. 'Now, you try to mate with that move. It works just as well for black or for white.'

Phryne was sitting in Clarissa Cartwright's dressing room, looking at herself in the brightly lit mirror.

'Felix has told me all about you,' said Clarissa. Her face appeared in the mirror besides Phryne's. She was as beautiful as a porcelain doll, but much more animated.

'Indeed?' murmured Phryne.

'You're just as beautiful as he said you were,' observed Clarissa. 'And he says you're doing something very hush-hush and I ought not to ask about it.'

'Does he?' asked Phryne. Felix's discretion was legendary. Phryne's was not.

'So tell me all about it as we work,' said Clarissa cosily, and Phryne did. Felix was not the only person with discretion. One reason that Clarissa was a star was that she was very intelligent.

And she was pleased to help Phryne wreak vengeance on any low hound who preyed on actresses. Clarissa had been in the theatre since she had first appeared as a slightly wobbly (but enchanting) fairy at the age of four. She loved the theatre almost as much as she loved Felix. And she had a delighted, wicked inkling that any vengeance wreaked by Phryne would be satisfying to the soul, if not positively Jacobean.

A stout, middle-aged woman was dragging Phryne's hair back under a stockinette cap. Her name was Elsie and she had been Clarissa's dresser for her whole career, picked out of the chorus by the rising star. Elsie might have dreamed of being a leading lady herself, once. Now she was entirely devoted to Clarissa.

'I don't know about this Tait,' she mumbled.

'Which one?' asked Clarissa. 'CogitTait, HesiTait or AgiTait?'

'Very funny,' muttered Elsie. 'I dunno about the arrangements for the New Zealand tour. You only got a small cabin.'

'The others will have smaller,' said Clarissa, with the certainty of someone who was used to being a star. 'Now, Phryne, you want to look like an aspiring but down-at-heel actress who might accept a dubious engagement which might end in a brothel?'

'That's the idea,' said Phryne.

'Isn't that dangerous? What if these men really seize you?'

'I will have protection,' said Phryne.

'Well, I think you're very brave,' said Clarissa, and kissed her gently on the cheek. Her skin felt like the softest buds of a pussy-willow or a kitten's paws. 'Good luck! Now, on with the slap. This is greasepaint,' she explained, as she mixed it in the palm of her hand. 'You have lovely pale skin, so you will be wearing too much makeup if you put anything but rice powder on it. Therefore, prepare to be plastered.'

Phryne looked at the face appearing in the glass. Clarissa was an artist. Phryne's startling green eyes were subdued by an orangey underlay over which was painted a bright blue crescent. Her own eyebrows were blocked out and others drawn in a good deal higher on her forehead. Her mouth was outlined in greasy red crayon. The whole was dusted over with fine powder. She looked shabby but aspiring. She puckered her lips for an appreciative whistle and Clarissa put a hand over her mouth.

'Don't,' she warned. 'Or Elsie will make you go outside, turn around three times and swear before you can come back in.'

Phryne looked at Elsie, who nodded portentously. She unpuckered and Clarissa applied more red paint to her lips.

'That'll last twelve hours, and you can only get it off with cold cream, remember. Oh, dear, what a picture. Elsie! The wig!'

'Oh, my,' said Phryne, as a wig of tumbling golden curls, almost metallic, was fitted over the stockinette cap. She had always wondered what it would be like to be a blonde. So far it had no advantages. Elsie thrust in a number of hairpins, apparently straight into Phryne's skull. Then she grabbed the wig with both hands and pulled at it. Phryne's head rocked under the tension.

'That'll do,' said Elsie.

'Once Elsie sets a wig, it stays through everything short of a hurricane, and my money would be on the wig anyway,' observed Clarissa. She extended both soft, scented hands. 'Stand up. How does it all feel?'

Phryne rocked on heels higher than she normally wore and resolved to shuck them if she had to run. She looked at herself in the full-length mirror.

Oh, dear. Scuffed heels, stockings with one artful ladder, art silk shift in a distressing shade of teal, navy blue hat pinned onto the golden wig.

'Perfect,' she said, sketching a kiss towards the smooth cheek.

'You'll be careful?' Clarissa had retained a grip on her hands.

'I will,' said Phryne, who wouldn't.

'You'll let me know how it goes?' asked the actress. 'This is a very good thing you are doing for us, you know.'

'I shall have a party,' said Phryne. 'At the Windsor. If this works,' she added, conscious of the number of things which might go wrong. And of the St Christopher which Dot had hung, that morning, around her neck.

Jobs for All proclaimed the sign, and Phryne went boldly inside. She knew that several of the children playing skippy in the street were watching. It had been a long totter on those heels to Lonsdale Street and she sank into an office chair with a sigh. The man at the desk looked up as she came in.

'Need a job,' said Phryne, reverting to the accent of her childhood, overlaid with some affectations.

'What sort of job?' asked the man. This must be the bloke with the slicked-down hair reported by Tinker. Not a prime specimen of manhood, Phryne thought. Bill Smith—or could this be Vivien of the caste of Vere de Vere? No, Australian accent. Must be good old Bill.

'The girls say you've got a tour going to England,' said Phryne, stretching out her legs as though her feet ached—which, as it happened, they did.

'Which girls?' asked Bill.

'The chorus at the Maj. I sprained an ankle, can't dance like I could. But I can act. Done all sort of parts. The *Maitland Gazette* loved my Juliet.'

'That would have been a while ago,' commented Bill.

Phryne bridled at this suggestion that she was too old to play Juliet. 'Only a few years. Come on, you got anything?'

'Might have,' he grunted, consulting his books. 'What's yer name?'

'Fern Williams,' said Phryne.

'You got any family?'

'Not here. We didn't see eye to eye about my career in the theatre, you see. They wanted me to marry and settle down. Anyway, what's that to you?'

'Nothing,' he said.

He stood up and surveyed Phryne, then pulled her to her feet, groping her body and closing a hand on her buttock.

'Get off!' She struggled, but not too much.

'All right, you'll do, I think the client can use you. You'll meet the rest of the company in London. Chorus and small parts. Two quid and allowances. Where's your trunk?'

'Lodgings in Carlton,' she said.

'Right. Here's a train ticket. Get yourself and your trunk to Williamstown Beach by ten o'clock tonight. Train'll be met by my partner, Mr De Vere. Sign here,' said Bill Smith.

Phryne signed *Fern Williams* at the bottom of a very closely printed contract and then grinned, creasing her greasepaint.

'Good-o!' she said. 'See you then.' She tottered out of the office, walked to the corner, and Mr Butler collected her, Jane, Tinker and Ruth.

'May God have no mercy on my soul if I ever wear high heels again,' she said, snatching the offending footwear off. 'Home, Mr Butler, we need to fudge up a suitable trunk. Dot may need to go to the second-hand shops.'

'Are they bodgy, Guv?' asked Tinker, smearing his already smeared face. He had bought an ice cream as cover and it had melted faster than he had anticipated. Ruth gave him a handkerchief.

'Oh, they are bodgy all right. Did he ask for my clippings?' asked Jane.

'Clippings?' enquired Jane.

'All actresses have clippings. Reviews of their performances. They're like references,' explained Phryne.

'Well, did he ask for them?'

'He did not. All he wanted to know about me was whether I had a family who would miss me. And he groped me. Mr Bill Smith is a pimp. And I am hoping to get a chance to punch his face. Several times,' she said firmly.

'Miss Dot would say we ought to be sorry for the poor soul,' observed Ruth. 'Coming up against you and all of us.'

'Are you?' asked Phryne, interested.

'No,' said Ruth. Tinker and Jane nodded.

'Right,' said Phryne. 'War to the knife.'

The trunk had been purchased from a middle-range second-hand shop, and Dot had half filled it with shabby clothes, scuffed shoes and almost ragged underwear. She had added a couple of sprightly novels in yellow paper covers, some cosmetics, a bottle of cheap brandy, a toothbrush and seven cabinet photographs of someone's relatives obtained from the same source. Phryne carried a shapeless handbag which contained Fern's passport, a lipstick, some coins and a packet of Champion Ruby Twist, papers and matches. She also had some franked postcards of Australian Views and a small Vest Pocket camera, popular with soldiers.

Her Beretta was holstered in her garter worn high on her thigh, under the shapeless blue dress. She had donned shoes in which she could run. The high heels had done their work and could be presented to the poor, assuming that they wanted to court a broken ankle along with their other problems. Along her forearm, covered by the loose sleeve, her throwing knife was strapped. Phryne, as a helpless victim, was a complete failure.

But the golden wig cascaded factitious curls down her shoulders and the makeup was immoveable.

She sat down to a dinner at which she ate sparely and drank nothing but lemonade. This was going to be an evening where she needed every single wit about her, as plate armour was No Longer Worn in polite society.

Then Mr Butler drove her to the station, and she took the train for Williamstown Beach: coat, trunk, down-at-heels actress and all.

She sat in the third-class compartment—Jobs for All had a fine sense of guarding their client's money, curse them, or perhaps it was their own—and attracted no attention. The train was nearly empty, except for a group of local girls going home from work, who glanced at her, shrugged, and turned back to their own concerns. This was the second-to-last train on this line, and by the time Phryne arrived at Williamstown Beach, she was alone in her carriage. She got out, dragged her trunk from the guard's van, and stood on the platform, looking as forlorn as she ought to have felt.

What she mainly felt was cold and annoyed. Had they suspected something? Had they refused the bait? She went through the turnstile and gave up her ticket. The guard gave her the second leer in two days. It would have been more effective if he had cleaned his teeth in the last year.

'You waiting for Mr De Vere?' he asked.

'Yes,' said Phryne. 'His partner said he'd meet me here.'

'He'll be along,' said the guard. 'You wanna sit there on the bench, or come into the guard's room with me?'

'I'll just sit out here,' said Phryne. 'I might have been born in Collingwood,' she told him, 'but it wasn't yesterday.'

'Just trying to be friendly,' muttered the guard. 'Can't blame a man for tryin'. Most of 'em ain't as stand-offish as you.' He went into his little office, and slammed the grilled window shut, taking his huff with him.

Phryne sat down on the seat. Nothing to see in the dark but little lights in humpies. This was not the select part of Williamstown where she had been wont to dine. The place smelt of frying, dirt and despair. She heard a baby crying. Another two joined in.

Phryne felt for her tobacco and rolled herself a smoke. A girl materialised at her side.

'Gimme a drag?' she asked.

Phryne handed over the pouch, keeping a close eye on it in case it was snatched. The girl was fifteen, perhaps, thin as a lath and dirty in that ground-in way which would take several hot baths, a gallon of yellow soap and a city-council broom to eradicate. The girl rolled a thin smoke and handed the tobacco back. Phryne struck a match for both of them.

'You waitin' for Mr Smarmy?'

'I expect so,' said Phryne.

'You wanna run,' advised the girl. ''E's no good.' She began to sidle away.

'I know,' said Phryne.

'Oh. Right then. Just thought I'd warn yer. None of 'em come back,' said the girl.

'It's all right,' said Phryne.

The girl took a close look into Phryne's eyes.

'You're not like the rest of 'em,' she said.

'No, I'm not, but don't give me away.'

The grimy hand came out, crooked into a claw. Phryne put a penny into it. The fist shut.

'Good luck,' whispered the girl. 'Here 'e comes. I c'n hear his bloody truck.'

And Phryne was alone again.

Dirty sand sprayed up against her legs as a battered van screamed to a stop. A classic flash cully got out and opened the door for Phryne, ordering a man in overalls to load her trunk into the vehicle.

'Milady's carriage awaits,' he said. Phryne was interested. She had not seen such a paragon among con men since her Paris years. Cheap, smart suit, purple socks, patent-leather shoes, flamboyant tie, very large cubic zirconia tie pin, fedora. He sat beside her, just a little too close. She did not move away. He smelt of Bay Rum and cheap Egyptian cigarettes, just as she had known he would. She herself was scented strongly with Night of Passion, a steal from Coles at sixpence a flask. It had an unfortunate overscent of cabbages, but this man would not notice that.

'What's your stage name, Princess?' he asked, sliding a hand up her thigh. As she did not want him to find her armament, she pushed his hand away and held it in both of her own. He was wearing far too many rings.

'Fern,' she said. 'Where's the ship?'

'Not far,' he said soothingly. 'Just enough time for you and me to get acquainted.'

'I ain't that sort of girl,' said Phryne, with complete accuracy.

'Come on,' he said. 'Be nice! You're on your way out tonight to a new life! Could spare me a kiss.'

'Perhaps,' said Phryne. 'Are you coming on board with me?'

'Yes, but not for too long. You're the last. They're leaving tonight.'

'And you're not coming too?' asked Phryne, striving to sound disappointed.

'No, so you better take me while you've got me, eh?'

'I might at that,' said Phryne, raising hope in his heart. Had he but known what Phryne was thinking of doing to him, he would not have felt so sanguine.

The van rumbled along an unmade road to a dock. There the flash man conducted Phryne out and ordered the overalled worker to carry the trunk. The worker obeyed, shouldering the piece of luggage as though he had been carrying things all his life. They walked along a wooden pier, Phryne picking her way across the uneven surface. Meanwhile the De Vere arm had slid around her waist, and a De Vere hand was groping for her breast. Phryne did not mind what he might find on her torso: it was all hers. Was this part of his payment or gratification? Phryne wondered, bumping into him to fit a breast into the hand. Getting to take advantage of the girls before they were sent away to a vile fate?

The nasty little leech, she thought. I do so hope I get a chance to drown him.

The ship was small and dirty and very uninspiring, but it did not look like sinking just yet. The gangplank was down, the worker was carrying her luggage aboard, so Phryne followed. A man in a greasy cap, who must be the captain. Another man in overalls, who leered. It is my week for being leered at, Phryne thought, and I hope that next week won't be.

'Milady's cabin,' said De Vere, conducting her down through a maze of companionways to a small door. He opened it. Inside were two bunks, a porthole and a chair.

'I'm sharing?' she asked.

'No, the other girl hasn't turned up. She'll miss her chance of a new life.'

Clever girl, thought Phryne. 'Do you miss London?' she asked De Vere.

'All the time,' he said, and there was an actual trace of truth in his affected voice. His accent veered from cockney to county. 'Now, how about that kiss?'

Phryne pulled him into the cabin and shoved him into the chair. Then she sat herself on his knees. He was laughing until he felt the sharp knife which had miraculously appeared in her hand and was pricking his throat.

'You gotta shiv!' he whispered.

'Yes indeed,' said Phryne. 'And now you are going to tell me about this operation, about the little girls, and many other useful and beautiful things.'

'Or?' he asked.

'I'll cut your throat,' said Phryne flatly. 'This dress will have to go in the rag bag anyway. Your choice, Mr De Vere. And if you're a De Vere I'm Gef the Talking Mongoose. However, this is your chance to save your miserable life. I don't like pimps and slavers and rapists so I might kill you anyway—no, don't move. Talk or not talk. Which is it to be?'

'Talk,' he decided.

'Very wise.'

'Wotcha want ter knaow?' Pure cockney now.

'The girls. Where are they?'

'Below.'

'Do you know what happens to them when they leave here?'

'Port Said. They don't come back. That's all I know.'

'Your contact in Port Said?'

'Jim Simmonds in the High Commission.'

'Where are the documents for these transactions?'

'In me pocketbook,' he said. 'Don't kill me!'

'Anyone else in this with you?'

'Just Bill.'

'And the little golden-haired girls?'

'Special order. We only got four.'

'Are they on this boat?'

'Nah, the *Thisbe*. This boat's only got the tarts.'

'Right,' said Phryne, and struck him hard and scientifically behind the ear with the hilt of the knife. He collapsed very satisfactorily. She got off his knee, searched him for his pocketbook and stuffed it in her shoulder bag, arranged him neatly in a bunk, and cracked open the door. Someone was right outside.

'You seen Viv?' asked a man in overalls.

'In here,' said Phryne, and crowned him with the chair as he came in. She could not get him onto a bunk so she left him on the floor, tying his hands and feet together with his belt and his unsavoury handkerchief. Two.

Phryne had crept through ships before. Her cabin was not in the depths, below the waterline, where the engine crew worked. The tarts would be on this level or the one above. She needed to subdue the captain, then she could unload the prisoners.

Then she heard someone weeping desolately behind a door and decided that she could just as easily do it the other way round.

The door was latched on the outside. Phryne opened it. The woman inside tried to knock her down.

'It's all right, I'm your rescue party. Gather your wits and let's get out of here.'

'What about De Vere?'

'He's out of it,' said Phryne.

'And Harry?'

'I suspect I may have got him too. Who else is here?'

'I dunno. I heard someone crying last night.'

'Unlatch all the doors and get them all out,' Phryne told her. 'I'll keep watch. What's your name?'

'Lily.'

'I'm Phryne. Get on, I can hear the engines getting faster.'

Lily unlatched and soon ten women were in the narrow way.

'That bastard locked me in!' swore one. 'I'll rip 'is balls off!'

'No time for pleasures, ladies—climb,' instructed Phryne. 'I'll go first, Lily will go last. Any other women on board?'

'They said there were ten of us,' said the thinnest young woman.

'Right. Up we go. When you get to the deck, get ashore and run. Into the street, not the beach. Someone will meet you there. Don't panic and don't fall.'

'What about the captain?' asked Lily.

'Leave him to me,' said Phryne.

They climbed.

Phryne was just about to emerge on deck when she saw the greasy cap turn suspiciously, this way, that way. He had heard something, sensed something. She took a penny out of her pocket and flicked it onto the deck, towards the bow. It clinked as it fell. He turned towards the noise. Instantly Phryne was out of the companionway and in front of him. Behind her, women streamed up to freedom, leaping ashore, running towards the town lights.

'Stop!' he yelled. 'I paid good money for you!'

'Unless you want to die where you stand,' said Phryne, 'you revolting specimen of something resembling humanity, you'll shut up and put your hands on your head.'

'You! You bitch! Who are you? Where'd you get that gun?'

'It's mine,' said Phryne. 'I brought it with me. Look on me as Spartacus. This is a slave revolt.'

He grabbed for her. She shot him in the foot. As he lay groaning, she said quietly, 'You wouldn't make a noise like that if you knew where I really intended to shoot you.'

Thereafter he was quiet and compliant as the police came to take him away.

'Good pinch,' said Jack Robinson. 'We'll gather up the ladies and get statements.'

'Here's De Vere's pocketbook with all his transactions in it,' said Phryne. 'He's rather tied up downstairs, as is another sailor. The contact in Port Said is Jim Simmonds at the High Commission. Now, Jack, we have to hurry.'

'Why?' asked Robinson, disapproving of this modern tendency to hustle.

'Because four little girls are on the *Thisbe*, and she's just started to move.'

'Get the harbour master on the phone!' yelled Jack to Collins. 'Call the pilot boat. I need an arrest warrant for a ship!'

Phryne had already left him. She had run to the *Thisbe* and scrambled aboard, golden curls and silly blue hat and all, and in a moment the boat was out of range.

Jack Robinson swore for so long that even the attendant wharfies were impressed.

Aboard the *Thisbe* Phryne was seized, disarmed, and carried below to see the captain.

CHAPTER EIGHTEEN

Come, friends, who plough the sea
Truce to navigation
Take another station
Let's vary piracy, with a little burglary!

Gilbert and Sullivan
The Pirates of Penzance

Phryne, as she was being dragged down into the depths of the *Thisbe*, admitted to herself that her actions had been silly, reckless, foolish, precipitate and likely to lead to her early and unpleasant demise. Then she charitably forgave herself and took a deep breath. She did not struggle, so the sailor who was holding her did not discover the knife attached to her arm. She was put down into a chair and the same sailor tied her hands behind her back. At least she would now meet the mastermind behind this frightful operation.

The boat was moving. Phryne was alone. She occupied herself while waiting by attempting to remember the flex of muscle which would bring the hilt of the knife down into her hand. She had practised it enough. But she was shaking with shock, and her arms felt like they were made of noodles.

The cabin was luxurious, in a 'Midnight of the Sheik' style. The owner clearly travelled to the Middle East. There were many pillows, hangings, a full-sized double bed about which she preferred not to speculate, a hookah from which she could detect the scent of kif, and paintings of the sort sold on postcards in the street in Cairo. Known to the vendors as 'feelthy pictures'. They all concerned children. Though the animal kingdom was represented, in several sentimental pictures of dogs, and of course the woman and the donkey.

The odd picture out was a cabinet photo of a stern-faced woman in severe black. The only point of relief in the picture was a large crucifix on her breast. His mother? That might prove a useful chink in Mastermind's armour. There was a surge and the boat rocked. Phryne seemed to remember Bert telling her that boats couldn't get out of the river until the turn of the tide, which was usually about three am. There was some maritime reason for this. So Mastermind would have time to play with Phryne before any serious sailing happened.

Not a nice thought. She returned to flexing and loosing the muscles. Something was happening outside in the corridor, if ships had corridors. Men were running and shouting. Perhaps Jack had already organised a pursuit. Which would mean that she would be rescued and have to be grateful, and Phryne had always failed at that. She wriggled with more effort.

'Scared, aren't you?' asked a voice from the door.

Ah, the Mastermind. Just the tone of voice she had expected. A sadist who liked tormenting small animals and little girls.

'Should I be?' she asked coolly.

He came into the room and closed the door. An ordinary devil of about five foot six, quietly dressed in a good suit (though she detected Cairo tailoring) and neat: small hands and feet, clean-shaven, mid brown as to hair and eyes. I bet he's got pairs and pairs of perfect kid gloves, thought Phryne, staring into his eyes.

'Oh, yes,' he said. His voice was educated and had a faint Irish lilt. Attractive, if he hadn't been a monster.

'I'll try,' she promised.

He stared at her. Her gun was dangling from his hand.

'Once I tell you what I am going to do with you, whore,' he said to her, 'then you will be scared.'

'And you feed on fear, don't you? I shall try to oblige. Tell me, how long have you been in the slave trade?'

'Why should I speak to you?' he asked, disconcerted.

'It will while away the time,' said Phryne. 'I'm not going anywhere else at present. You have my full attention.'

He giggled. 'All right. You just sit there,' he said. 'Don't get up.'

Sadistic and nasty with it, thought Phryne. That tone must have made little girls cry. I bet he loved that.

'The trade?'

'I cornered the market,' he told her, lounging against the corner of his desk. The movement of the ship did not unbalance him. He must do a lot of sailing. 'The others are all sending worn-out old whores like yourself. They only last a couple of years. But I can sell a blonde virgin for a hundred pounds—English pounds, not dinars. One of them pays for the voyage and the rest are pure profit. I love my work.'

'Simmonds from the High Commission put you up to this profession?' asked Phryne, trying to bend her fingers in ways which fingers are not meant to move.

'It was my idea,' he said. 'Simmonds . . . shares my tastes. Easy to slake in Port Said but blondes are a rare treat.'

'It must be trying,' she said conversationally, 'to have to deliver those little golden-haired girls virgo intacta.'

'I control myself until we get to the port,' he said. 'Then I can buy as many of the little dark-haired darlings as I wish.'

'But they aren't the same, are they?'

He came closer. He had put her Beretta on the desk. Phryne wriggled again and at last felt the hilt begin to slide. She couldn't do anything with the knots—they had been tied by a real sailor. If she pulled, they got tighter, and they were beginning to cut off her circulation.

Jack Robinson was still in deep and furious negotiation with a harbour master who woke up slowly and cross when Bert looked at Cec. All the policemen were on the *Pandarus*, except the ones who were guarding the prisoners or providing blankets, tea, brandy, cigarettes and consolation to the freed prisoners and taking statements. No one was looking at them.

'Which one you reckon, Cec?'

'That one,' said Cec, pointing his chin at a shiny white pleasure boat. 'Got a fair turn of speed. Ought to catch that old tramp.'

'Before the tide turns?'

'Too right.'

'Fancy a bit of piracy, mate?'

'Too right.'

They strolled along the pier. Jane, Tinker and Ruth were not deceived and fell in behind in approved sheepdog fashion.

'Oh, no, I'm not takin' you kids,' Bert protested. 'This is real dangerous and real illegal.'

'Too right,' said Tinker, copying Cec. 'You'll need a crew. I been on fishing boats all me life. And Jane and Ruthie can learn fast. And meanwhile that boat's getting away.'

'All right, a man can't stand around all night arguing. Can you all swim?'

They nodded.

'Then come on,' urged Bert.

A brief conversation with the watchkeeper on the shiny new yacht, a member of the Seamen's Union and a comrade, and they were starting the engine. It was new and caught immediately. The yacht was drawing away before anyone noticed, and then it was too late.

Jane leaned into the darkness, feeling her short hair ruffle in the wind of their speed. They were moving very fast. Bert yelled at them to hang on to the rail, because he was about to put on pace.

Then they moved faster. It was wonderful. Tinker had never been on a new yacht. He was delighted by its cleanliness and shiny paint, and by the revving of the heavy engine. He had not realised until that moment that he had missed the sea more than he missed his mother.

Ruth felt sick. She found a place downstairs where she wouldn't be in the way and regretted her very good dinner.

'You haven't introduced yourself,' Phryne reminded the Mastermind.

'Oh, I do beg your pardon,' he said automatically, then bit his lip. He hadn't had a polite conversation since—he couldn't remember when. 'O'Rourke. Declan O'Rourke. And you are?'

'Fisher,' said Phryne. 'Phryne Fisher.'

'English?' he asked.

'As much as you are Irish,' she replied. 'I was born in Australia. I thought I detected a trace of the brogue in your voice. Dublin?'

'Yes,' he said.

'And your mother must have been so proud when you were admitted to the priesthood,' she said. 'Father Declan!'

'Don't you speak about my mother!'

'You keep her picture on the wall,' observed Phryne. 'You must still have feelings for her. How did she feel when you were thrown out? Or were you actually caught in flagrante with one of those little golden-haired tots?'

'Shut up!' he yelled.

'She must have almost died of shame. Her sweet clever boy, educated and intelligent, had a fatal flaw. Lust, sinful lust.' Phryne was watching him like a hawk. 'Or did she actually die?'

'Be quiet!' he screamed.

He fell onto her, grabbing her breasts bruisingly tight, and forced his mouth down onto hers. What he wanted was the flinch, the fastidious wincing, Phryne knew. So she leaned forward as her cut ropes fell away and kissed him as passionately as she could, forcing her body into his embrace and her tongue into his mouth. He tried to get away from her but she clung and kissed, then her hands dropped and she found the right place, grabbed and wrung, and he collapsed to the floor, crying and clutching his crotch.

It was not then difficult to use the ropes he had thoughtfully provided to truss him as tightly as a parcel.

'Beware the kiss of the vampire woman,' she breathed into his ear, a line she had always wanted to say.

She stood up and staggered. The boat was moving faster. She surveyed herself in the full-length mirror. Shocking. Her dress was in rags, her stockings ditto. Her golden wig, however, was still immoveable.

She was thirsty and shaking. But she had conquered the Mastermind. Now it remained to hold up the ship.

First, though, a drink of something to take the taste of sadist out of her mouth. She rummaged. She found a perfectly acceptable Irish whiskey. Not as good as Glen Sporran, but Phryne was not of a mind to be picky. She gulped. The spirit burned all taste of maniac out of her mouth. She would now be able to kiss other people, which was good. Her Beretta was on the desk. She reclaimed it.

It was no use attempting to wash her face. Her greasepaint was a strange, lopsided mask. She smeared as much as she could onto a linen washcloth. Mr O'Rourke had dainty tastes. She dragged him into a sitting position, but he wept so much that she let him lie on his side again.

'How many men on this ship?' she demanded.

'Oh, you've killed me,' he whimpered.

'No, if I'd wanted to kill you, you'd be dead. Don't think I didn't want to kill you, you child-raping monster. But I want you alive to stand trial. They'll hang you. I shall watch.'

He snivelled. Phryne was disgusted. 'Here, drink this,' she said, hauling up his head and pouring whiskey down his throat. 'Now, talk. How many crew?'

'Ten,' he said.

'You're lying,' she said dispassionately. 'You're not very good at it.'

'Thirty,' he said. 'Don't hurt me again!'

'And where will they all be at this time?' she asked.

'Twenty below, ten to man the ship,' he replied, all resistance broken.

'And the cargo?'

'Next cabin,' he whispered. 'I like to look at them every day.'

'Thank you,' said Phryne. 'Who looks after them?'

'Mrs Donnelly.'

'And she knows their destination?' asked Phryne, deeply disgusted.

'Of course.'

Clearly, Mrs Donnelly had to be added to the bag. And what seemed to be an increasing crowd on the gallows. It was going to be like Tyburn Fair Day. Phryne would have to buy a new hat.

'You don't use a pilot?'

'No, my man Phil knows these waters like the back of his own hand. We didn't want to attract attention with so much trouble on the waterfront.'

'Of course.'

Phryne sat down to think. She could hold up Mrs Donnelly, collect the little girls and bring them into this cabin, then barricade the door and wait for rescue. Sticking up a whole ship might prove beyond even her powers. But didn't she remember something from her rescue of Lin Chung? Bert said that those lid things could be closed and barred, locking the crew in. That might prove possible. If she could reduce the odds, she might be able to stop this boat, at any rate.

She stowed Father Declan under his own bed, gagging him with a gay Tunisian scarf. Then she took the gun and crept out of the cabin. The crew would be under orders not to interrupt the ex-priest at his little pastimes. She should be able to find at least some of the hatches and batten them down. Ah, yes, that was the word.

She found the first and examined it. She didn't want to make a noise and bring trouble boiling up out of the depths. The hatch lowered on a hinge. She pulled and pushed until she found the catch, released it, and lowered it gently into place. One. How many were there?

As many as there were companionways, she thought, creeping onwards. She had secured two of the possible four before she encountered anyone at all. But they had a rifle.

Bert yelled at Cec 'You're flogging that engine, mate!"

Cec grinned. 'She's a beaut!' he yelled back. 'Can you see *Thisbe*?'

'Yair, mate, comin' up on the starboard bow. You're right about this toothpick of a boat. It's real fast. Mind you, that tub is mostly held together with baling twine and spit.'

'Tink on deck?' asked Cec.

'With the watchkeeper. They look good.'

'Too right,' said Cec. 'You want 'em to speak to *Thisbe*?'

'Yair,' said Bert. 'Is Janey up there too?'

'Yair,' said Cec. 'She's a natural sailor, our Janey.'

'I gotta plan,' grinned Bert, and hurtled up onto the pilot deck.

'Aub, you sing out to 'em that they left one of their cargo behind,' he ordered the watchkeeper. 'Janey, you look scared.'

'Like I'm about to be sold to a brothel?' she asked calmly.

'Yair, like that,' said Bert, disconcerted. Jane put her hands over her face and began to sob. She was quite convincing, in the dark on a fast-moving ship.

'*Thisbe*, ahoy!' yelled Aub. 'You left one of your girls behind!'

Thisbe slowed. Orders were yelled. Bells rang. Slowly, the *Thisbe* came about.

Tinker threw a line and it was secured. A boarding ladder was shipped.

'Send 'er over,' yelled a sailor. 'Another hundred quid in the bank!'

'I'll have to carry 'er,' said Bert. 'Stand aside.'

He grabbed Jane and slung her over his shoulder. 'When we hit the deck,' he whispered, 'run. They'll chase yer. You scared?'

'No,' said Jane, after thinking about it.

'Over the top, then,' said Bert. The last time he had said that, he had run into a Turkish machine-gun. He hoped this time might be slightly less bloody.

He gained the deck of the *Thisbe* and stumbled slightly, letting Jane go. At once she was off like a rabbit. Three men chased after her. Bert hit the remaining one very hard with what was admitted to be his best punch, a right hook to the jaw. The man fell to earth he knew not where.

The yacht lay wallowing beside the *Thisbe.* Cec climbed over the boarding ladder.

'Two of us now,' said Bert. 'Who's got the helm?'

'Tink and Aub,' replied Cec. 'They'll be apples. Clear the decks first?'

'Might as well,' said Bert.

Methodically, trained in many a mud hole and pitiless cliff, the two wharfies hunted down and negated the three crewmen on deck. They hadn't even managed to catch Jane, who was perched on a lifeboat just out of reach.

'Good girl,' said Bert. 'Down you come, Janey.' She leapt into his arms. 'Now, what about the rest of this old scow?'

At that point, they heard a shot from below.

The man with the rifle, who was supposed to be on shark watch in case any of the cargo threw itself overboard, missed. The shot pinged off a metal wall and ricocheted before it fell. Phryne drew herself back behind a wall. Damn, she thought. Now Mrs Donnelly will issue forth demanding to know why someone is shooting, and the rest of the crew will rush up from below, and I've only managed to lock two of the hatches. What to do?

She jumped out from behind her wall and tried a shot. It hit something. She heard a yelp. The door behind her opened and a woman stuck her face around it.

'What's all this noise? You'll wake the devil!'

'Oh, no,' said Phryne, presenting her little gun. 'The devil was already here. Look on me as an angel.' She pushed Mrs Donnelly back into the room. 'Though I admit that is difficult in my present guise. So this is your cargo?' she asked, as four little girls sat up in bed, round-eyed, horrified.

'Sit in that chair,' she ordered.

'I will not,' said Mrs Donnelly.

'You will,' Phryne assured her. 'Or I will shoot you.'

Mrs Donnelly decided to try outraged innocence.

'Who are you, bold as brass, and you with a gun, comin' in here to me very own cabin, frightenin' me daughters . . .'

'We're not her daughters,' said one of the golden-haired children. 'She's going to do something awful to us. I heard her talking to the captain. They stole me! Shoot her!'

'I'd love to,' Phryne assured her. 'But for the moment we will leave her to the law. Now, tell me your names. Then tear up one of those sheets and we shall tie her up.'

'Are we rescued?' asked a second child, naming herself as Madge.

'You certainly are. Strips of linen, please. It's cheap. It'll tear.'

The children found that it did indeed tear. Phryne trussed Mrs Donnelly securely, gagging her with more strips. Then she motioned the children to sit down again on their beds and went to the door.

'I want to go home!' wailed one child, whose name was Marion.

'So do we all,' said Phryne. 'But there's a man with a rifle out there. I'm expecting some help any moment,' she added. Surely Jack must have overborne the harbour master by now.

The first golden-haired child, Muriel, went to Mrs Donnelly and kicked her as hard as she could in the shins.

'I see your point,' said Phryne. 'But we are not allowed to torture prisoners. Let the law do the revenge. Now, everyone, quiet. I need to listen.'

Phryne pressed herself against the door. She heard footsteps. Then she heard the clang of one of those lids. She opened the door. And there was Ruth. Of all people, she had been the one least expected.

'Ah, Ruth,' said Phryne. 'Could you sit here with these girls and make sure this beastly woman doesn't escape?'

'Can I have the gun?' asked Ruth.

'No, I've only got one and I'm going to need it. But feel free to hit her with whatever you like if she tries to get away.'

'Right you are, Miss Phryne,' said Ruth. 'Find a weapon, ladies.'

Mrs Donnelly did not move a muscle. She sat tied to a chair in the midst of her victims, every one of them with some weapon—a hairbrush, a chamber-pot, a curling iron, a table knife—and every one of them watching her like cats watching a mouse.

Phryne emerged from the cabin to find Bert latching the last lid, Cec licking his knuckles, and Jane looking ruffled.

'How very nice to see you, darlings,' she exclaimed.

'You didn't need no help,' said Bert, grinning.

'Oh, yes, I did. There was the man with the rifle, for example. What happened to him?'

'We had a bit of an accident with that rifle and he sorta fell overboard,' said Bert artlessly.

'And the others?'

'All under hatches except for the ones tied up in the lifeboat,' said Cec, fighting down an urge to salute.

'How did you get here so fast?' asked Phryne. 'Where's Jack?'

'Still contendin' with the bloated bureaucracy,' said Bert. 'We borrowed a boat. Tink and Aub's looking after it.'

'And you're sure that the owner would have freely donated it to the cause if he had been around to ask, which, as it happens, he wasn't?'

'Yair, like that,' said Bert.

Phryne kissed him. 'I'll square him, whoever he is,' she said. 'You realise that we've taken up piracy, my dears?'

'Yo ho ho,' said Jane, who was beginning to feel very pleased with herself.

'And a bottle of rum, with any luck,' added Bert.

In all it was something of an anticlimax when Jack Robinson arrived in the pilot boat with his warrant. He arrested the ship by nailing said warrant to the mast. He also took into custody Father Declan, Mrs Donnelly (who was considerably bruised), twenty-nine crewmen (all protesting that they knew nothing about any white slavery), four rescued girls and a lot of documents from the safe in the main cabin. He did not enquire as to how the safe had been opened, nor what happened to the sheaves of banknotes which Father Declan swore should be there. After all, Jack had won a considerable victory, a wonderful case, and he had the girls, the crew, the Mastermind and the ships.

He didn't need the money, and he knew wharfies.

CHAPTER NINETEEN

Virtue is bold, and goodness never fearful.

William Shakespeare
Measure for Measure

Phryne, who had sent Jane to knock up a local chemist and buy some cold cream (at twice the price for the inconvenience) had finally cleaned her face and, at the price of considerable ouching, removed the golden wig and the blue hat. Her head felt curiously cool and light.

The waterfront at Williamstown was a buzz of noise, activity and relief. The Black Maria had been sent for to carry the prisoners. Jack Robinson had actually accepted a kiss on the cheek. Aub and Tinker had brought the yacht safely back to her mooring without a scratch. The foreshore was loud with lamentations, laughter and policemen shouting. Engines revved in the quiet streets, a stream of them coming along the Esplanade.

As it was so late, or early, no pubs were open. Though Bert boasted that he could find a drink in any port at any time, the local hostelries were nervous about the Licensing Act, seeing that the town was seething with policemen.

Phryne wanted a hot and luscious bath. She had been groped and handled by people she didn't like, and wanted to wash off their contaminating touch. It was black dark, the very deep of the night. Not even seagulls cried.

'Tide's turning,' observed Bert, taking a deep sniff.

Phryne listened to the sirens as the moored ships in the river farewelled their friends, who were going out, escorted by tugs, to dare the Rip at Queenscliff and thence to any port in the world. She felt a strong urge to get on a ship and go somewhere. Anywhere. Even though she was very pleased with where she was. She shook herself.

'Home, darlings?' she asked.

Heads nodded. Bert and Cec did not seem to want to stay and be hailed as heroes of the hour, so she loaded her whole family into Bert's taxi and took off for St Kilda. They had coped with adventure very well. Ruth, though seasick, had been reassuring to the kidnapped girls, who had to go into police custody until their doting parents arrived. Tinker had managed very well with danger. Jane had not turned a hair. Bert and Cec had dropped into their comradely action as though they had never left the army. And she was pleased with how close she had come to sticking up a whole ship by herself.

'I want a bath,' said Phryne.

'And I want a drink,' said Bert.

'We shall have both,' Phryne reassured him.

The bath was deep, hot and scented with chestnut blossoms. Apart from a reasonable number of bruises, Phryne was unhurt. She washed herself and her hair and drank the little glass of green chartreuse which Dot brought her. Phryne would not rouse Mr and Mrs Butler at four am, and they did seem to be able to sleep through anything, which was fortunate. Ruth was foraging in the kitchen. Bert had found the bottle opener and the store of beer. As far as he was concerned, this constituted breakfast. Cec agreed.

'So you found all the girls, Miss?' asked Dot, who was remarkably tidy for someone who had been awake and embroidering and worrying for so long. She had finished her waratahs. And started on the banksias. And pricked her finger, which she hadn't done in years. It had been a long night.

'Ten women and four little girls, saved from the bonfire. The little girls had been actually kidnapped, Dot.'

'And were they . . . unhurt?' asked Dot.

'Yes, because to do otherwise would reduce their sale value. That man was a fallen priest, Dot.'

'I hope he hangs,' said Dot, clutching her rosary, which was wound around her wrist. 'And after he hangs, I hope he burns in hell.'

'As to that,' said Phryne, standing up in the bath and reaching for a towel, 'I cannot say. But I should think it most likely. And we could hardly have any more evidence against him, Dot dear. As we left I heard that hag Mrs Donnelly denouncing him as a son of Satan.'

'Sounds about right,' said Dot.

'Both of them,' said Phryne. 'All of them. Well, we've put a crimp in the trade. Good enough for one night. Put that blue dress in the rag bag, and those stockings can go to tie up the jasmine. Give me the scarlet gown, Dot dear, I must go down and tell the troops how well they did.'

The troops had settled down in the parlour. Bert and Cec had beer, the rest had tea, and a scrambly, delicious kind of dormitory feast of leftovers. Mrs Butler always cooked for a regiment, as she could keep things overnight in the American Refrigerating Machine. It was now looking rather empty. Phryne accepted a piece of cold egg and bacon pie and a cup of tea. Dot, relieved that it was all over, allowed Bert to pour her a glass of sherry to celebrate a notable victory over the forces of darkness. In her previous respectable hard-working life, Dot had never thought she would be drinking confusion to the devil at four in the morning. She liked it.

Tinker was above himself with delight. He had been useful. He had been pivotal! He sat next to Bert and listened to him talking about ships. Tinker knew all about fishing boats, but had never met anyone who knew the big ships. Bert was a deep-water man. Jane was thinking about chess again. Ruth was more than a little shocked and still felt a bit nauseous. She leaned on Dot and closed her eyes. It was so nice to be home. Dot hugged her. Keeping up with Miss Phryne was wearing on the nerves.

'Right,' said Phryne, who caught herself in a yawn. 'I'm going to bed. Better leave a note for Mrs Butler, Dot. Don't let anything save house fire or earthquake wake me until noon, please. Good night. You all did wonderfully well. But did you notice one thing about our rescued ladies?'

'They seemed like ordinary tarts to me, Comrade,' said Bert.

'Yes. But none of them was Polly Kettle,' said Phryne, and she trailed up the stairs, half blind with exhaustion, and fell into bed.

She woke and every single bruise made itself felt. Even her scalp hurt. She got out of bed on legs which wobbled, sat down at her dressing table and looked at her face. A little pale, but no bruises visible. Overstretched muscles twanged and cried. Ember, who liked Phryne's dressing table because he could look at himself in the mirror—a fine figure of a black gentleman cat, he considered—put a paw on her hand and allowed her to caress his ears.

'We have been seeing life lately, Ember dear,' she told him, stroking Milk of Roses into her skin. Ember liked Milk of Roses, too. She allowed him to lick her wrist. 'The cure for an overworked body is a slow, decorous stroll,' she told him. 'Down the stairs for lunch will do for the present.'

Dot appeared with a cup of Hellenic coffee and a croissant. It was not until Phryne had finished eating that she said, 'Inspector Robinson is downstairs, Miss, and Hugh. Constable Collins, I mean. They're looking very pleased.'

'Oh, good, that means Jack is not going to get cross about all that money,' said Phryne.

'Money?' asked Dot.

'Nothing to concern you, Dot dear. Bert has Views on spoiling the Egyptians and it wasn't as though it was a difficult lock. Right, what sort of day is it?'

'Bright and shiny, Miss. Warm but not hot.'

'Good. A cotton shift, please, and sandals. I am not doing anything energetic today.'

'I should think not. Jane says you held up two ships!'

'Not alone, Dot, I had very valuable assistance. How is everyone this morning?'

'Mrs B was a bit huffy about the mess in the kitchen, but Ruth, Tinker and Jane came in to help her with the washing-up. There were no fish for breakfast, because Tinker slept in. He says he wants to be a sailor.'

'Then so he shall,' said Phryne. 'He is very adept when it comes to ships, Dot.'

'But not washing-up,' said Dot. 'He broke one of your Clarice Cliff coffee cups.'

'Then we shall buy another,' said Phryne.

•

Jack Robinson was as close as that subfusc man ever came to being puffed up with pride. He had broken a white slavery ring, captured all the main players and a lot of very chatty accomplices, all eager to secure their own skins. He had actually arrested a ship. He had rescued ten actresses and four innocent girls. He had been congratulated by the commissioner. His own chief had shaken him by the hand.

The fact that Phryne was the one who had actually done all these things was what stopped him from being really puffed up. Phryne wished for no acclaim. She disclaimed recognition. He knew that. But still, he felt like a fraud.

He was kibbitzing on Tinker's chess game when Phryne came in.

'I reckon you want to move that knight, Tinker,' he advised.

'He's pinned,' said Jane patiently. 'If he moves the knight either way, he's lost. I'll take him with either the pawn or the bishop.'

'Oh, right, I see,' said Jack. 'Well, son, I think you're in trouble.'

'But I can do this,' said Tinker, sweeping his queen across the board to attack Jane's bishop.

'So you can,' said Jack.

'The queen is the most powerful piece on the board,' said Jane, with a suspicion of a grin.

'So she is,' agreed the policeman. 'G'day, Miss Fisher. How do you find yourself this afternoon?'

'A bit creaky but very pleased,' said Phryne, sitting down carefully in a padded chair. 'How are you?'

'Likewise,' he replied. 'We got all the bad men in custody, all weeping and wailing and calling for their mothers. It's pitiful. Talk about no honour amongst thieves! There's even less honour among slavers. The ladies have retrieved their trunks and are back where they came from. Someone seems to have given them a fiver each. I can't imagine who that would be,' he said with elaborate innocence.

'Probably some person with a socialist conscience,' said Phryne. 'Only a wild guess, you know. What did you find out about Gratitude?'

'A front for their foul trade,' said Robinson. 'They'd send that harridan Mrs Donnelly—she's Father Declan's aunt—out to orphanages and so on pretending to be a pious widow, Mrs Smith. She'd collect the girls, drug them, and when the poor little mites woke up it'd be at sea. Been doing it for years. Only attracted attention when they snatched some from the street. Or they bought them, of course. Mostly from their fathers.'

'Charming,' said Phryne, glad that she hadn't eaten much breakfast. Dot, who had been sitting with Hugh Collins, missed a stitch in the stocking she was repairing.

'The four on the ship all have parents,' said Robinson. 'All of 'em reported missing as per regulations. All of 'em very pleased to get their little angels back. I've never been hugged and wept over so much in all my born days. Poor Collins was one big blush.'

'Rather you than me,' said Phryne.

'You really mean that, don't you?' he asked.

'Certainly.'

'Well, anyway, came to thank you,' said Jack.

'My pleasure,' said Phryne. 'I haven't had a chance to be a pirate before. Any trouble with the owner of that yacht we borrowed?'

'Never knew it was gone,' said Hugh Collins. 'We didn't see it as our duty to tell him.'

'Excellent.'

'So most of it is solved,' said Robinson. 'You found the girls from that lying-in home and they're all all right. You foiled the white-slavery ring and the victims are all right, too.'

'But still—' Phryne leaned forward '—Polly Kettle is missing.'

'Oh,' said Robinson, damped. 'So she is.'

'And I mean to find her. She isn't in the convent, I searched it.' Robinson decided not to ask her about that, as her face had become as stern as a white marble Justice—without the blindfold. 'She isn't in the Bacchus Marsh commune. She wasn't and hadn't been on the *Pandarus*. Those creatures kept quite careful records. So she's still somewhere.'

'If she isn't dead,' commented Tinker, and was immediately hushed by Ruth.

'Usually would have found a body by now,' Robinson told him with matching bluntness. 'They'd ha' nosed her out behind the arras.'

This meant nothing to Tinker, but he got the point, and went back to playing chess.

'So I shall spend today and tomorrow recovering and thinking. Then, if I need some help, Jack, can I call you?'

'For anything, at any time,' said Robinson. 'With everything I've got.'

She rose with some effort and held out her hand. Greatly surprising himself, he kissed it.

Then he collected his detective constable and left the house. Reporters were eager to interview him. He began to think that Miss Fisher was right about keeping in the background.

'Polly Kettle,' said Phryne. 'We need to review everything we know about her. But now, who's up for a gentle stroll *au bord de la mer* before lunch?'

•

They all joined her. It was a lovely day and a charming walk. A gentle breeze stirred the palm fronds. Tinker talked about being a deepwater sailor. But it brought Phryne no nearer to finding Polly Kettle.

With their usual inducements to thought—lemonade, ginger beer, a cocktail, a sherry cobbler—Phryne and her minions sat down in the shady garden with all available notes and considered the problem.

'She did visit Mrs Faceache in Footscray,' said Phryne.

'Ryan,' corrected Jane, to whom an inexactitude was a pain under the pinny.

Phryne waved a hand. 'As I said, Ryan. I've been meeting a lot of harridans lately. She left that house and was supposed by that disgusting pair to be headed for the city. Except that Patrick told a pretty story. Right so far?'

'Right,' said Jane.

'And then she fell out of the world,' said Ruth, who loved a florid phrase.

'Exactly. No one can disappear. She is somewhere. Just not where we have looked. Yet. Not in the convent,' said Phryne. 'Not on the *Pandarus*. Not captive in that lying-in home. So where can she be?'

'Inspector Robinson says she isn't in any of the . . . houses,' said Dot.

'And they let him search, which argues both fear and a clear conscience,' responded Phryne. 'And it stands to reason. Brothels at present have no need of uncooperative women. There are a large number of hungry volunteers. Madame Paris has a waiting list, for heaven's sake. And they wouldn't tolerate Polly hanging around seeking a story. Though there was a saint, wasn't there, Dot, who sat on the steps of a brothel and converted the inhabitants?'

'Yes, Miss,' said Dot. 'But that was a long while ago. I don't reckon that'd work nowadays.'

'Indeed. Now, what do we know about Polly?'

'She's silly,' said Jane, her strongest term of condemnation. 'She takes foolish risks.'

'She's bl . . . very ungrateful,' said Tinker. 'She lied about you rescuing her, Guv'nor.'

'She doesn't have a boyfriend,' said Dot. 'Her best friend Cecilia's a silly young miss who's only concerned with her wedding. I'm sure that Cecilia would have mentioned a boyfriend if there had been one. Miss Kettle doesn't seem to have been interested.'

'She wanted a career,' said Phryne. 'Everyone in that newspaper office was spitting on their hands and bending to the task of discouraging her. So she seized on a good story which she thought would make her name and convince her editor to put her on to reporting the news, rather than the garden parties. And she stole the story from the crippled and extremely angry Mr Bates.'

'He sounds like he might bear more investigation,' said Dot.

'Did he fancy her?' asked Ruth. 'It might be a tale of forbidden love.'

'I swear, Ruth, one day I am going to make a little bonfire of all the romance novels in the world,' said Phryne without rancour. 'Actually, it would have to be a very big bonfire. Perhaps I could rent a volcano and drop them in from the air. Honestly. No, he wasn't.'

'How do you know?' asked Jane.

'Because he's a member of the Blue Cat Club, and that fact does not leave this garden.'

'Blue cat?' asked Tinker. 'Cats don't come in blue. They're black like Ember or stripy or white or orange . . .' Ruth whispered into his ear. 'Oh, one of them blokes,' said Tinker. 'Bloke who runs the ships' chandlery in Queenscliff's one of them blokes. Lives with another bloke. But he's all right. Always pays his messengers, never whinges about the trade, has a drink down the pub with the rest. I got nothin' against queers,' said Tinker.

'Good, because some of my best friends are. Queer, I mean.'

'You mean like Dr Mac?' asked Jane, athirst for knowledge.

'Yes, but back to the subject,' Phryne recalled their attention. 'I interviewed Mr and Mrs Kettle. Her father was desperate to have her back. Her mother . . .'

'Not so much,' said Dot. 'Mr Butler talked to the staff. They said the mother was jealous of the father's regard for the daughter, threw tantrums when he paid too much attention to her. But surely . . .'

'The mother wouldn't have arranged the abduction of her own daughter?' asked Phryne. 'You heard what Jack said. Some of those little golden-haired girls were sold by their parents to the Port Said brothel trade.'

Dot was shocked. 'But they were poor people; I bet that—'

'Doesn't happen in the best of households? Perhaps not. Anyway, what was the name of that putative boyfriend? Herbert Grant, that was the name. A halfwit with a lot of money. Jack left us his address. Mr Grant says he hasn't seen Polly. I think I would like a word with him.' Phryne smiled in a way which made Dot very uncomfortable.

'There's another possibility,' offered Jane, who was reading Ruth's notes.

'What?'

'The brother. His name's Martin but he likes to be called John. It says here that Cecilia said that Miss Kettle said something to him before she left that morning. He got packed off to Mount Martha that afternoon. If she left him a message to deliver, he wouldn't have had a chance.'

'I wonder if he knows that his sister is missing?' asked Dot.

'He shall,' said Phryne, and went inside to telephone.

Ruth followed to eavesdrop.

'Hello, darling, how are things in the outback?' she heard Phryne ask. The telephone protested. 'All right, not as out back as all that. And Chloe? In her usual good health? Excellent. I have a favour to ask.' The phone made a quacking noise and Phryne laughed. 'No, it isn't trouble, really not, not for you. I just want you to go and interview a boy. His name is Martin Kettle, he likes to be called John, and he's in Mount Martha at present at the Kettle relatives' house.' There was a patter of words. 'No, darling, I don't know their name. How many people are in Mount Martha? Precisely. Get weaving and find the little darling, and find out what his sister said to him before she disappeared. He may not know she's vanished. Break it to him gently, if possible. I'm trying to find her.' More protests. 'I'm sure you'll manage. Tell him to phone his father if he wants more information, not his mother. There's something very odd going on in that family.' More words. The telephone appeared to be expostulating. 'No, I don't think it's incest. Just something odd. Nor do I think she is dead. No body. I tell you, darling, I have scoured the brothels for this girl and she's not there. Also sneaked into a convent. Not one of my more fragrant experiences. And held up a ship—no, two ships. Piracy is a lot of fun; you should try it. Please—this is important.' The telephone sounded much less annoyed. Phryne smiled at the receiver. 'All right. Call me tonight. Love to Chloe.' She hung up.

'Is Chloe his wife?' asked Ruth, not hiding her presence.

'No, she's his cat,' said Phryne. 'A beautiful, fluffy, very silly tabby on whom he absolutely dotes. I fetched her out of a tree and since then Charles has always said that he owes me a favour. I'm calling in my favours. I must be at my wits' end.'

'Would this Charles qualify to join the Blue Cat Club?' asked Ruth.

'Why do you ask that?'

'You were talking to a man as if he was a girlfriend,' explained Ruth, 'and he hasn't got a wife.'

'You are very acute. He'd be a foundation member,' said Phryne. 'I met him during the war. You forge close friendships when you share a shell hole. Come along. We need to look up that address in Toorak in the directory.'

Phryne had attended many expensive parties in the most expensive suburb in Melbourne. Herbert Grant owned a mansion in St Georges Road.

'Very exclusive,' commented Phryne. 'Anything known about him?'

'I asked Mr Bert,' said Jane, 'and he just said one of them bloated capitalists. When I asked what his business was, he told me Mr Grant would curl up and die if asked to do any work but had been a football player. For Melbourne, I think; a centre half forward. Retired when he hurt his knee.'

'So he's big and strong and fit,' said Phryne.

'Mr Butler says the Kettles' staff think Herbert Grant is a fool. The housekeeper said he was just short of being a moron and he'd inherited all his money from his father, who was in building.' Dot was reading ahead. 'And he's twenty-eight.'

'And not married?' asked Phryne. 'I wonder why?'

'The Blue Cat?' asked Ruth mischievously.

'Possibly. But why, then, would he want to marry Polly Kettle?' asked Dot.

'Anything about the rest of the family?' asked Phryne.

'Not much,' said Dot, scanning the page. 'He's got a house in Castlemaine, he goes hunting and shooting and fishing and looks after his estate. He doesn't come to Melbourne often. Here's a picture that Mr Robinson sent.'

Phryne looked, then passed it round the circle. It was of a large, stolid man in good tailoring.

'Dumb as an ox,' opined Tinker.

'Why oxen, I wonder? Is it because they allow people to attach them to drays? I would have thought oxen were quite smart. They know everything they need to know about being oxen. It's like saying "as weak as a kitten". Kittens are very strong and spry for their size,' said Jane. 'I don't know why people say these things.'

'That's people for you, Jane dear,' said Phryne absently.

'What do you want us to do, Miss Phryne?' asked Ruth, who wanted to get back to the kitchen where Mrs Butler would be starting dinner. She was on peeling duty this week. As a consolation, she got to watch the construction of the meals and was on tasting duty, as well.

'All this is best done during the light of day,' said Phryne. 'Start creeping around at night and people in that neighbourhood will call the cops. We'll drop in on Mr Grant at a nice respectable eleven in the morning, just in time for tea. Should he offer us any. Which I doubt.'

'Just you, Guv'nor?' asked Tinker uneasily.

'No, this is going to take all of us. Break out the playclothes, darlings. Not too poor. This is a very rich neighbourhood. You, Jane, will dress in your complete school uniform, with hat and gloves. Take a notebook and pen. You are doing a school project. I am escorting you. Dot is escorting two poorer children, her sister and brother. She is a housemaid, headscarf and apron. She has to take them to work because it is school holidays. Tink, I might need the housebreaking stuff; you can carry it. We will consult tomorrow. Now, everyone find something amusing to do. Tomorrow will prove to be really interesting. By the way, did Jack give us Grant's telephone number?'

Yes, Miss Phryne, it's here.'

'Good,' said Phryne, and took herself and her stiff limbs off for a soothing recline on her favourite sofa, with a copy of *Bleak House.* Dickens, she thought, had the right ideas about Justice.

CHAPTER TWENTY

Once there, I'll frighten her into marriage.

John Benn Johnstone
The Gipsy Farmer

Phryne had decided to sleep in until ten o'clock, and for once no alarums or excursions disturbed her rest. She was not concerned about the confrontation with Grant. After all, she had stuck up a ship almost on her own. How hard could it be to hold up a house? Charles had called and said that he had interviewed the boy, who seemed very distressed at hearing that his sister was missing. What she had told him was simple: that she would never marry Herbert Grant if he was the last man on earth. That seemed conclusive. The boy had told Charles that his mum was funny about Polly. She liked him all right, in fact Charles had received the impression that she was somewhat suffocating in her regard and far too demanding. Charles had summed the boy up as perfectly ordinary, make a good craftsman, not very bright, and much oppressed.

Which accounted for Martin-called-John and allowed Phryne to sleep in peace, which she did.

As she was nibbling her croissant, Dot told her that the rest of the minions were all prepared. Jane in her school uniform, crisp white shirt, demure cotton skirt and blazer, hat and gloves, notebook in hand. Tinker and Ruth in their shabby genteel finery. Phryne dressed in a severe blue suit with an azure hat which was not too daring.

'Good,' she said as she descended the stairs and surveyed them. 'Very good.'

Dot straightened her headscarf, then darted into the kitchen.

'What?' asked Phryne.

'Dab of lysol,' said Dot. 'Got to smell right.'

'You are a gem amongst women,' said Phryne affectionately. 'Now, off we go. Dot, you three go to the kitchen door. I have been told by Mr Butler that the housemaid and cook is a poorly paid slavey from an agency. She is not, luckily, an old family retainer who carried Mr Grant in her arms when he was but a puling babe. Bribe her and she will go away and that gives Dot the kitchen. If you've got the kitchen, you've got the house. You take charge there. Tink, you and Ruth search the rest of the house. Quietly, secretly. You know how to move. Open all the doors. If you find one that is locked, then come and get me.'

'How?' asked Ruth.

'Dot will bring in tea. I'm told that Mr Grant is very proud of his family, especially his father, who was apparently a big loud bully. The son will doubtless try to emulate his pater. I will then ask for the amenities, and you will lead me to the locked room, which I will open. Now, this all depends on confidence and timing. If he rushes upstairs and discovers you, wail and blubber and tell him that you're the maid's siblings and you're lost.'

'What's a sibling?' asked Tinker.

'A sister or brother,' said Phryne. 'Dot's too young for you to be her children. Now, I'll just leave a message with Jack Robinson so he'll know where we've gone. Always secure your retreat.'

They set off in the big car for Toorak. Traffic was light at this time of day. Fitzroy Street was almost empty, even the nightclubs had emptied out and were washing the detritus of the night away. Phryne zoomed up Punt Road until she turned the big car into Alexandra Avenue, which followed the curves of the river until it magically transformed itself into St Georges Road.

'Gosh,' said Tinker. 'I never saw such big houses before. And all those high hedges.'

'Don't want the working classes to get anything for nothing,' said Jane, quoting Bert. 'Not even a glimpse of their front door. I don't know I'd want to live in anything that big.'

'My feeling exactly,' agreed Phryne.

They passed decorously through avenues of majestic trees.

'Here we are,' said Phryne. 'I'll have to leave the car in the street. Though the chances of anyone pinching it in Toorak are fairly low. Some of these people hire their own guards, you know.'

'In case of the revolution happening?' asked Ruth.

'Indeed. In which case they will hang from their own elms. There are some nice stout branches up there,' said Phryne.

Dot muttered a prayer. Miss Phryne could be outrageous, sometimes.

'Good luck, darlings,' said Phryne, and put a hand to the front gate. Dot and her siblings took the tradesman's entrance.

The path to the front door was long and winding, meant to impress. The path to the kitchen was short and straight. Dot tried to remember something about roads to hell and was therefore unprepared to be bailed up by a very large fierce dog, the approximate size and heft of the Hound of the Baskervilles, and seemingly composed of teeth.

Phryne's path to Mr Grant's mansion was less fraught with danger. She rang the front doorbell and knocked the huge brass knocker in the shape of a Gorgon's head. The sound echoed. She waited. Finally, there was a footstep and a girl in an apron hauled open the portal.

'Yes?' she asked, fumbling for the card tray which was kept on the hall table.

'Miss Fisher,' said Phryne. 'The Hon. Miss Fisher. To see Mr Grant.' She put her most elegant card on the silver salver.

'Come in, Miss,' said the girl. 'I'll ask if you can see him.'

Phryne and Jane were led into a parlour. It was dusty, unused, and smelt stale. Phryne longed to pull back those heavy plush curtains and open a window. But she and Jane perched decorously on the least dusty chair and waited for the maid to come back.

They heard a voice roaring in another room. Soon the maid returned, hurrying slipshod in her kitchen shoes, and led them into a large room which did show signs of being inhabited. It had far too many stags heads on the wall—in fact there was also a lion, good Lord, and a thing with spiral horns which might be an ibex, perhaps, and a forest of antlers besides. This man had slaughtered his way around the world. Fond of wildlife in the same way as a cook is fond of guinea fowl, quail, chickens, cornish hens, pigeons and ortolans. Ah, yes, Phryne made a mental note. Must ask Mr Featherstonehaugh about those *ortolans en brochette.*

'Mr Grant,' said Phryne, holding out her gloved hand. 'I am Phryne Fisher, and this is my daughter. She is doing a school holiday project on our great families, and she has chosen the Grant family and would like you to tell her about your father.'

'The pater? He was a great man,' said Mr Grant.

My, he was big. Running to fat now that he was not exercising but six feet tall at least. Blue eyes, fair hair thinning at the temples, florid complexion ruined by the sun and probably whisky. Big hands, innocent of callus or blister. Nicely dressed in flannel bags and a sporting blazer, probably his old school, Scotch by the candy stripes. He held out a huge hand to Jane and crushed her fingers. He did the same to Phryne. She winced. Doesn't know his own strength or doesn't care. Not likely to be treating Polly well, if he had her.

'Well, well, sit down, ladies, I'm on my own here,' he said. 'I'd be glad to tell you about my father. Where would you like to start?'

'At the beginning,' said Jane, taking up her pencil. She had three others and a sharpener in her pocket.

'He came here from Home in 1891,' Mr Grant began.

Jane wrote busily.

Tinker liked dogs, but this one seemed to want to eat him rather than make friends with him. Dot put her back against the kitchen wall and prepared to kick. Ruth, however, sank down onto her heels and wreathed her arms around the mastiff's thick neck.

'Good dog!' she cooed with complete conviction.

The dog stopped barking so fast it almost bit its tongue.

Dot watched the dog's confusion. Good dog. Good dog? He knew that he had heard good dog before. Yes, good dog, good dog meant ears down, ruff down, open mouth to pant, wag tail. He did that. Ruth felt in her bag and brought out a packet of dog biscuits. She had wondered why Miss Phryne had added them to the equipment. 'Here you are, there's a good doggie then,' said Ruth, patting all the expanse of massive canine that she could reach. 'You don't want to hurt us, do you?' She fed him a biscuit, which vanished immediately into a fanged red maw. 'Have another,' said Ruth. The dog accompanied them to the kitchen door, which was open.

'Hello?' called Dot.

'Yes?' asked a skinny maid, turning from the stove. 'He's ordered tea, I can't stop.'

'No, you can take a day off,' said Dot, holding out a pound note.

The maid examined Dot. Then she examined the pound note. 'You robbers?' she asked.

Tinker laughed. The dog nudged Ruth, suggesting another biscuit for the really extraordinarily good dog sitting next to her and leaning heavily on her knee. She obliged.

'What've you done to Snap?' asked the maid. 'You've drugged him? He usually bites people who come to the back door without ringing the bell. He nearly tore the trousers off the postman yesterday, when he forgot.'

'No, he just likes me,' said Ruth. 'Have another bikkie, Snap.'

Snap gulped and wagged.

'You don't mean Mr Grant any harm?' asked the maid. 'He's all right, really. He's just not very bright. His stepmum and that other woman push him around. They wouldn't do it if I was in charge,' she added fiercely.

'No,' said Dot. 'Miss Fisher wants to fix everything without scandal.'

'You reckon she could? 'Cos I really like him,' said the maid.

Ruth understood immediately. 'You're in love with him, aren't you?' she asked gently.

'Ever since the agency sent me here,' confessed the maid.

'Dot, Tinker and Ruth,' Dot introduced them.

'Phoebe. But he never even looks at me,' said Phoebe. 'I cook his favourite dinners, make his bed, polish his boots. But he never sees me.'

'Tell me about yourself,' said Dot, as the tea making went on, and Ruth fed more biscuits to Snap.

Phryne was not surprised to see Dot bringing in the tea. But she received no signal from her as she handed and poured. Herbert Grant, meanwhile, hadn't even noticed that there had been a change of maids.

Phryne was learning about Mr Grant from his narrative. His father had been a loud, opinionated, moderately cruel bully. Had beaten his son every day and thus 'made me what I am today', which was regrettably true. His mother had been pretty and sad and had pined away and died of consumption at an early age. Thereafter he had had nannies and then boarding school. Then a stepmother with whom he did not get along. His pater had taught him to shoot anything which stood still long enough or breathed heavily in the bushes. Not an unusual upbringing, but far from ideal for a not-very-bright boy. The only thing in which Mr Grant had pleased his father was his football career, which had been cut short because of the knee injury.

Phryne began to feel sorry for Mr Grant, which was absurd. He was rich. He had a house of his very own and a country estate. She kept listening, wondering what the rest of the minions were doing and wishing that they would get on with it. Jane's hand must be getting tired and Phryne was bored.

The kitchen was silent as Phoebe considered Dot's outrageous suggestion. Tinker beguiled the time by thinking about big ships. Ruth patted Snap and was ravished by the King Cophetua story unfolding in front of her eyes.

'I'll try it,' said Phoebe. 'And if he sends me away, I can always get another job.' She sounded forlorn.

'Come along,' said Dot. 'Upstairs.'

Phryne was just reaching screaming point when several people entered the den. One was Polly Kettle. She was clean and well dressed and well nourished, so her captivity had not been too stringent. She was, however, panting with stress and release. The others were Dot and a pretty woman in an old-fashioned tea-gown, flanked by Tinker and Ruth.

'No!' cried Mr Grant, leaping to his feet.

'Sit down,' said Phryne, in that voice of female authority which promised tears before bedtime. 'You knew you couldn't keep her.'

'She's mine!' he said. 'They both said she was mine!' But he sat down.

'Yes, you might think that, but she doesn't,' explained Phryne patiently. 'Now, I am here to resolve this situation neatly and quietly and without scandal. Shut *up*, Polly Kettle. You've caused me enough trouble as it is. Not a word. You can scream later. You can now consider yourself rescued. Also I have a scoop for you which will make your name. All right?'

'All right,' conceded Polly.

'I traced you as far as Footscray,' said Phryne. 'Where did you go from there?'

'I was on the way to the train when this . . . creature . . . pulled up and offered me a lift. Then he said he had to go to his house for some papers and would I mind coming along. I agreed. Then as soon as we got in the house he told me I had to marry him and he already had the licence. When I said that I wouldn't ever marry him, he dragged me into a suite and locked the door.'

'Window?' asked Tinker.

'Barred. It used to be the nursery. So it had a bathroom and so on. But no one could hear when I screamed out the window for help. I threw paper aeroplanes out but none of them landed anywhere useful.'

'Neighbours too far away,' commented Phryne. 'How did he press his suit?'

'Came every day, talking, talking,' said Polly bitterly. 'Said my mother had agreed so I have to agree. He left food in the outer room. He kept saying that I had to marry him and now he couldn't let me go because his stepmother would be cross with him. And my mother.'

'Aha,' said Tinker, then shut up.

'Indeed,' said Phryne. 'I did notice that your mother was not worried about you, whereas your father was frantic.'

'Oh, poor Dad, he must be really worried!' exclaimed Polly. She glared at Mr Grant. 'Let me out of here!'

'You're mine,' he said violently.

'Sit still,' Phryne advised him. 'I am getting quite good at shooting people. Did he rape you, in which case he is going to jail?' she asked Polly.

'No. He tried to kiss me. I fought him off,' said Polly proudly.

Phryne looked at her. Nine stone, perhaps, and fought off the fifteen stone of athletic Mr Grant? Not likely. Not without special training. This man was simple. He had been told that Polly was his for the taking, and did not know what to do when she failed to cooperate.

'Mr Grant, who told you that you could have Polly?' asked Phryne

'Mrs Kettle. And my stepmother. They agreed it would be a good match.'

'I see. Mrs Kettle has no right to give Polly away with a pound of cheese, Mr Grant. She's a person. And she doesn't want to marry you. Therefore she doesn't have to marry you. Isn't there another girl?'

'No!' he roared. 'Girls don't like me. Girls laugh at me. They said . . . they said if I . . .'

'If you raped her she'd have to marry to save her reputation?' asked Phryne calmly.

He nodded. 'But I couldn't,' he confessed.

'You're a good boy,' said Phryne, in much the tone Ruth had used to calm Snap.

'And we can find you a nice girl,' said Dot, pushing Phoebe forward. 'This is Miss Phoebe Taylor. Her father was the vicar in Castlemaine. She already loves you and is willing to marry you.'

Phryne looked at Dot in astonishment. Dot grinned. Phoebe had been quickly stripped, washed, and arrayed in one of Mr Grant's late mother's dresses. It draped over her thin frame and reached to the ground, covering her stout boots. Dot had dragged her light brown hair out of its bun and combed it out so it fell gracefully over her thin shoulders. She looked very much like the illustration of the Beggar Maid in Ruth's fairy book, as seen by Arthur Rackham.

'Hello, Miss Phoebe,' said Herbert Grant. He took her hand

with care. Phoebe looked into his eyes with huge affection. 'You look beautiful in that dress.'

'Thank you, Herbert,' she replied.

'Will you really marry me?' he asked in a small, ashamed voice.

'Today,' said Phoebe.

This is turning into a Gilbert and Sullivan ending, thought Phryne. 'If that is so then derry down derry we'll merrily marry when day is done!' Where did Dot find that very pretty rabbit to pull out of her hat? she wondered. I underestimate that girl.

'Come on, Polly, we're leaving,' she said as she drew the young woman to her feet, and led her towards the door.

'But isn't this a maiden sacrifice?' asked Polly. 'How can she really love him? I'm sure I was alone in the house—no other lady there.'

'She's his housemaid,' said Phryne. 'Do you have things to collect? Got your handbag and your notebook? Yes? Right. Come along while the magic lasts.'

'His housemaid?' asked Polly, as they swung the big door shut behind them.

'No, Ruth, Snap needs to stay behind to guard the house,' said Phryne, as the huge dog showed signs of accompanying them.

Ruth farewelled the mastiff with the remains of the biscuits.

'His *housemaid*?' repeated Polly, shocked and elated and a little nettled at being supplanted so easily.

'And she'll give his stepmother a run for her money,' said Dot. 'Strong-minded young woman. And she knows all about him, and really dotes on him.'

'So romantic!' exclaimed Ruth.

'So, do we take you home?' Phryne, loading her family into the Hispano-Suiza, asked Polly.

'Yes, I have to see my father. He'll be frantic. And then,' she said grimly, 'I have to see my mother.'

Fortunately, though Dot would not agree, Phryne drove fast. They arrived in Camberwell just in time to prevent a murder.

The front door was open. A flying housemaid just avoided them as she ran down the drive, cap awry, apron sailing. When they entered the house at a run, they heard raised voices and headed for the sound.

It was an arresting tableau. Mr and Mrs Kettle were bailed up against a wall by their son. He had a shotgun, a weapon to be treated with extreme caution due to its tendency to massacre anyone within range. Polly gestured to the minions to spread out around the walls as they approached Martin-called-John from behind. Mr Kettle saw Phryne. Mrs Kettle's gaze was fixed on the boy with the gun.

'What have you done with her, Mum?' he yelled.

'She's here,' said Phryne, forcing the gun barrel up and shoving Polly into the boy's arms. The gun fired and brought down nothing but plaster.

Then Polly embraced her brother, Mrs Kettle sank to the floor in hysterics, and Mr Kettle tottered into a chair.

'It's all right,' said Phryne clearly. 'It's all fixed. Polly's back and she isn't hurt. She isn't hurt. Tell him, Polly.'

'I knew she was plotting,' sobbed Martin. 'I knew she sent me away for a reason. Then when that friend of Miss Fisher's told me you were missing, I knew it was her. I pinched some money and got the first train.'

'Yes, yes,' soothed Polly. 'But I'm all right, Johnnie. I'm really not hurt at all. I've just been held captive and very bored. That man has never read a book in his life; I've been putting myself to sleep every night with the volumes of Victorian sermons from his library. Sit down, John. Miss Fisher came and got me just now.'

'Ruth,' said Phryne, 'a large glass of whisky for Mr Kettle. Dot, can you go and sort out the kitchen and countermand the cops if someone has called them? Tink, go out and retrieve that housemaid—you'll probably find her having the vapours in the street. Jane, are you too tired to take some more notes?'

'No,' said Jane.

'Good, have a chair. Clear some of the plaster dust off the table. Polly, would you like a little whisky?'

'No,' said Polly. 'I'd like a lot of whisky. Mother . . .' She turned to the woman sitting against the wall, wailing. 'How could you?'

'I did it for your own good!' she whimpered. 'He was a good match and your father wanted you to give up all this newspaper nonsense.'

'Me?' demanded Mr Kettle. 'What have you done?'

Ruth supplied drinks for all. Mr Kettle hauled his wife to her feet and plumped her down into a chair. She cried aloud at his handling and seemed about to rocket into hysterics.

'Ruth, just pick up the house phone and ask the housekeeper to bring in a large bucket of cold water, will you?' asked Phryne.

Mrs Kettle eyed her with loathing.

'This is a mess,' said Mr Kettle, gulping his whisky.

'Certainly, and I cannot abide messes. They're taking up time which ought to be spent on amusing occupations,' Phryne told him. 'Now, I will summarise, and Jane will note down what I say. Ready, Jane?'

Jane nodded, pencil in hand.

'Good. Mrs Kettle was jealous of her daughter. She resented the attention and love lavished on her by her father. She wanted to get rid of her. So she hatched a plot with poor, simple Herbert Grant's stepmother to have her kidnapped and forced to marry him. He's rich. It would be a good match. And that would get the annoying daughter out of the house forever. Right?' Phryne pierced Mrs Kettle with an icy stare. Mrs Kettle winced. 'True?' demanded Phryne. 'I can always give your son back his shotgun.'

'Yes,' muttered Mrs Kettle. 'Yes!'

'You didn't!' exclaimed Mr Kettle. 'And you let me worry all this time. I nearly went mad!'

'Excuse me,' said Phryne in sub-zero tones. 'You can recriminate later. Polly told her brother that she'd never marry Herbert Grant, and you packed him off smartish to Mount Martha where he would not hear about Polly's abduction.'

'Yes,' Mrs Kettle said. 'He's going to be a lawyer. He can't afford to have any scandal . . .'

'Herbert Grant picked Polly up and tucked her away and I came and rescued her this morning.'

'So it seems,' said Mrs Kettle.

'And he is even now marrying a very suitable girl from a respectable background, so your matrimonial ambitions have come to naught, as they deserved. You will not try to marry Polly to anyone again.'

'No,' said Mrs Kettle.

'And you will allow your son to pursue the career of his choice. What'll it be, John?'

John, sensing a never-to-be-repeated opportunity, said, 'I want to be a carpenter. I'm good at making things.'

'Your great-grandfather was a carpenter,' said Mr Kettle. 'It must run in the family.'

'Grouse!' said John.

'You will cease pestering your husband with your attentions, foreswear hysterics, be an angel of the house, and donate your next six months' dress allowance to the charity of my choice. Sign, please,' said Phryne.

Mrs Kettle looked up at her family. She could not see a way out. Her son, still white with anger. Her husband, shaken and appalled. Her betrayed daughter, incandescent with freedom and disgust.

She signed.

'Thank you,' said Phryne. 'If I hear a word about you again, this goes to the *Hawklet*. Good morning.' And she swept out, carrying her minions with her.

Polly caught up with her at the door. 'My scoop?'

'Tomorrow at eleven,' said Phryne. 'Come to my house. Now I think you had better go to your father.' She beckoned Tink, who was escorting the maid up the drive.

Inside, the shouting had begun.

'The middle class,' sighed Phryne as they all piled into the big car. 'I should *never* have got involved with the middle class.'

CHAPTER TWENTY-ONE

This is the very womb and bed of enormity . . .

Ben Jonson
Bartholomew Fayre

Phryne rang the Blue Cat when she got home, then went for a swim with the minions. Even Dot so far unbent as to take off her shoes and stockings and paddle. It had all worked out beautifully. Polly Kettle was home, all the lost girls were rescued and Miss Phryne hadn't had to shoot anyone important. Jack Robinson was pleased and this extended to Hugh Collins. And it was a lovely day. Tinker, who could swim like a fish (having been thrown into the sea at the age of six by his father, in an experimental mood, to see if he'd drown) was teaching Jane how to duck-dive for shells. Ruth, who still had her long hair, preferred to float. Phryne rolled and luxuriated in the waves. She had always admired seals, but early attempts at swimming like one always left her human sinuses full of water.

And tonight she would tie up another loose end. Mr Featherstonehaugh had agreed to her proposal to admit her again to the Blue Cat for drinks before dinner.

How did he manage to put *ortolans en brochette* on his menu in Australia, a country entirely without ortolans? Surely no one bottled the poor little birds? Even for the French, a country that elevated cuisine to the heights usually enjoyed by religion, that seemed to be extreme.

Phryne and her minions returned to the house. Jane and Tinker resumed chess. Ruth and Dot sat reading in the garden. Phryne took a long nap. It was so nice to have it all worked out. Except for a few minor niggles.

At about five Dot came to Phryne's boudoir and said that a nun was waiting for her below. Phryne got up, donned a silky gown, and went down to the smaller parlour, away from Tinker and Jane's chess game, which was getting noisy. She asked Mr Butler to bring lemonade, but the nun disclaimed any need for refreshment.

The nun was small and thin. The robes were shapeless and the wimple and band concealed the face. But Phryne knew who she was.

'I thought it was you, Agnes,' she said. 'You were the only person who knew all the real names of the pregnant girls in the convent.'

'Other people could have known that,' said Agnes.

'Yes, for a while I wondered if it was a socialist lady from Bacchus Marsh with decided opinions,' answered Phryne. 'But she didn't know who those defaulting fathers were. Then I wondered if it might be Sister de Sales, who seemed sympathetic to the poor inmates.'

'It could have been her,' said Agnes.

'But real nuns are never let out alone,' said Phryne. 'Only in pairs. And your brother was a doctor; doubtless he performed the operation many times. You used to help him. My friend Dr MacMillan says it isn't difficult.'

'No. Just two tiny incisions and two little snips. Then no more girls to be tortured by Sister Dolour.'

'When did you begin your sacred mission?' asked Phryne.

'Six months ago,' said Agnes. 'Some of those poor little girls are barely fourteen. It would be better if the fathers were castrated, but that's too dangerous in an unsterile environment. They might easily bleed to death. And God does not condone murder.'

'Well, that solves that little problem,' said Phryne, standing up.

Agnes looked up at her in astonishment. 'Aren't you going to call the police?' she asked. She sounded a little disappointed, like a martyr who had been informed by the Coliseum authorities that the lions were off their feed today.

'No, why should I?'

'But I thought that policeman wanted you to solve the crime,' said Agnes.

'Then want must be his master. It isn't good for Jack Robinson to rely on me to solve all his problems. I consulted a lawyer and I am sure that you know how illegal your operations are. I don't think you'd like prison. So try to avoid being caught. Jack can't obtain the list of inmates from the convent, so he might not connect these assaults. Or he might not connect them to you. And I'm not going to tell him.'

'Then you don't mean to stop me?' asked Agnes, cheering up.

'Go to it, Agnes dear, and if you get arrested, don't say a word and call Felix Pettigrew. Here is his card. He will arrange suitable representation for you.'

'It's God's work,' said Agnes, lifting her black bag. Phryne preferred not to speculate as to the contents.

'You may well be right,' said Phryne. 'By the way, take Mr Timberlake off your list. He's married his Julie and they are very happy.'

Agnes took out a notebook and put a black line through a name. There were pages of them, Phryne noticed, but did not speak.

'God go with you,' said Phryne quietly, and showed Agnes out.

The Blue Cats' guardians let Phryne in without any delay, and Mr Featherstonehaugh came to meet her, taking her hands and drawing her into one of the smaller rooms, which was decorated with Beardsley *Yellow Book* drawings. She had always found the Spartan ambassadors overdrawn.

'Now, my dear sir, I need but a few words with one of your members, and then we shall be square. Is he here?'

'He is,' said the manager.

Her interviewee sat scowling in a padded chair, glaring at a cigar as though it had insulted his mother.

'I have rescued Polly Kettle,' Phryne told him. 'Someone set her up to be abducted. I am sure that you will be delighted that she is unhurt and will be back at the newspaper soon. With a scoop relating to the white slave scandal.'

He grunted.

'I shall take that as a "yes",' said Phryne. 'You see, Mr Bates, I did wonder how the abductor knew where Polly Kettle would be on that morning. Her mother could possibly have read it in her notebook, but she always carried her notebook with her. Who would know? Why, her newsroom colleagues. And who would tell the vile Mrs Kettle, hoping to get rid of a bothersome girl and her annoying ambitions? Why, I believe that would be you, Mr Bates.'

'You got me,' he said.

'If you were about to tell me that she would be happier married to a moron and not getting in the way of your ambitions and littering up your nice clean newspaper, don't.'

As he had been about to say something like that, he adjusted it to asking, 'What're you going to do to me?'

'Me? Nothing. I will just extract a promise that you will be as polite as you can manage to that silly, but fundamentally decent, young woman in future, and cede her the white slavery story.'

'It was mine,' he muttered. 'She stole it!'

'Yes, so she did. You will have to forgive her. However, I have a story about the Magdalen Laundry which will curl your hair. Are you game to offend the Catholics? Dr Mannix may denounce you from the pulpit. You may be excommunicated. It will be very noisy and very, very public.'

'Try me,' he said greedily.

He got out his notebook and wrote busily as Phryne detailed the conditions in the Magdalen Laundry and Mr Featherstonehaugh supplied Veuve Clicquot and *brie petits bateaux*.

At the conclusion of her narrative, Phryne stood up and extended a hand. 'Deal?' she asked.

He looked up into her face. 'Thank you,' he said. 'This is hot stuff. Deal.' He shook her hand.

'Do finish up the Veuve,' said Mr Featherstonehaugh to the scribbling reporter. 'I have a debt to pay also.'

He led Phryne into the kitchen, where chefs were shouting in a routine fashion, and out into a pocket garden, which had a small fountain, a turf seat, a grapevine and a set of tables and chairs. It was alive with wild birds. There was a large cage of sparrows. Common, city, gutter-feeding sparrows.

'Oh, no,' said Phryne, breaking into a huge grin. 'Really?'

'The practice of eating ortolans is barbaric,' Mr Featherstonehaugh told her, allowing himself a small, well-controlled smile. 'Also, we may well run out of ortolans; they are wild birds. And they don't have them in Australia. I could not bring myself to cook budgies or finches, the equivalent. But there are plenty of sparrows. I keep them in their cage for a month, feed them on figs and grapes and grain, and then when someone demands the dish, take out three and drown them instantly in cognac. They are then plucked and cooked. In a grape leaf. No one has ever complained.'

'You are a remarkable man,' said Phryne.

'And you, Miss Fisher, if I might be allowed the liberty,' said Mr Featherstonehaugh, 'are a remarkable woman.'

Arranging a party was, for Phryne, a matter of picking up the phone and conversing with the maitre d' at the Windsor. Once the details were discussed, Phryne set the minions to filling out invitation cards for a really quite wide acquaintance.

Some of the invitations enclosed banknotes to allow the attendees to pay for, as it might be, a new dress or a taxi fare. Jane was excused addressing envelopes because her handwriting was so illegible. She was reading aloud from a book of fairy tales. Phryne was listening to 'King Cophetua and the Beggar Maid' rather absently while she assembled her props for her interview with Polly Kettle.

List of times and dates. Names of ships and fellow prisoners. Fairly accurate account of police action which rescued them. Details about Gratitude and Mrs Donnelly and ex-Father Declan, with a few notes on what constituted sub judice. And the golden wig with its silly blue hat still skewered to it with Elsie's hatpin.

Polly arrived on time, notebook in hand. She was bouncing with joy and still getting a great deal of pleasure out of not being in a room with bars on the windows.

'Isn't it a beautiful day!' she enthused. 'I really like St Kilda, the seagulls and the sand and the palm trees. You have entirely squashed my mother. I owe you a great debt, Miss Fisher! Dad's put his foot down about her extravagance. She's put us in debt. John's starting a carpentry apprenticeship, so that saves his school fees. Dad signed the papers this morning. We ought to manage on Dad's salary and mine. My mother has sent me with this cheque for you.' She handed it over. Being threatened by her son and disapproved of by her whole family was one sort of pain, but being deprived of her dress allowance for six months was another, and possibly deeper, agony for Mrs Kettle. Phryne smiled and took the cheque.

'Right, now I promised you a scoop,' she said. 'This is how it was. You went to Jobs for All in Lonsdale Street, wearing this wig and hat, impersonating an out-of-work actress. You were picked up from Williamstown Beach station by a smarmy creature called De Vere and stuffed aboard a tramp steamer called the MV *Pandarus*, bound for Port Said and a dreadful fate. Here are the notes about the times and places. You will have to interview the ladies yourself: here are their names. I know one was going back to New Zealand, but you should be able to find some of the others. You were there when the heroic Jack Robinson broke down the door and set you free, and when the police arrested the other boat, the *Thisbe*, and brought the four little golden-haired girls ashore, arresting all and sundry.'

'I was?' asked Polly, dazed.

'You were, and you were very brave. People are going to wonder where you were for the last week, Polly dear; it doesn't do to give them ideas. This will be a full and acceptable explanation and I expect your editor to fall on your neck, weeping tears of joy. Make sure you get a photo taken of you in your disguise before you return the wig and hat to Clarissa Cartwright at the Maj, with my compliments.'

'Miss Fisher,' said Polly humbly. 'This was all you!'

'Yes, but no one else knows that who might object. You can interview the parents of the rescued children. They were unharmed, by the way. You might try having a word with the revolting Mrs Donnelly and the even more repellent ex-Father Declan O'Rourke, but be sure to take some strong anti-nausea medication before you do. They are both in custody, along with twenty-nine sailors and the stenographer and bookkeeper from the agency. Of all of them, I suspect she is the only one who isn't as guilty as sin.'

'Everyone is trying to find out about this story,' said Polly, awed. 'Robinson won't say anything. My God. This is the story of lifetime!'

'You paid for it by being abducted,' observed Phryne. 'If I hadn't been looking for you in all the wrong places, I would never have found it out.'

'I'd spend a week in prison reading Victorian sermons any time for this story,' whispered Polly.

'Right. Go to it. I will give you this note for Jack Robinson. He will give you an exclusive. Be nice to him. He isn't used to being famous.'

'I will. But what about Mr Bates? He thinks I pinched his story.'

'You did,' said Phryne. 'I would like to hear you admit it.'

'Well, yes, I did,' Polly conceded.

'Good girl. If you work in a man's job, you have to be both manful and gentlemanly. Tell him you are sorry. He will not cause you any more trouble.'

'Did you manage that too?' asked Polly.

'I had a word. He has a scoop of his own. Now, off you go, I have a party to arrange. Sunday, at the Windsor? Just a little gathering to celebrate—I haven't quite decided yet. But do come.'

Tinker handed over an invitation. One less stamp, he thought. He did not approve of Polly Kettle. She was ungrateful. And, as Jane said, silly. And now she would get all the glory which rightfully belonged to the guv'nor. It didn't seem fair.

'Never mind, Tink,' Phryne told him. 'Everyone who needs to know, knows.'

Sometimes it was real eerie, the way she read his mind. He went back to addressing envelopes. And he didn't approve of this Beggar Maid and King Cophetua lark. What if she liked being a beggar? What if she didn't want to be forever beholden to a king?

Perhaps he could go fishing at dusk, when the water cooled and the fish rose. Molly needed the exercise, and so did Tinker. He was getting grumpy from being indoors so much. Jane moved on to the story of 'Snow White and the Seven Dwarves'. Much more to his liking. He'd some across a lot of women like the Wicked Queen lately.

Polly Kettle possessed herself of wig, hat, notes, addresses and letters and was shown out of the house. She ran for the bus, hugging her scoop to her bosom. Another woman on a mission.

Phryne was about to consider all her debts paid as she addressed a cheque to her sister Eliza's educational centre for unfortunate women for half Mrs Kettle's reparation and another to Isobel Berners for her own work for the other half, when she remembered an outstanding obligation. Cursing, she went to the phone, sat down on the hallstand, and called Cecilia for a promised consultation about her wedding.

Cecilia was delighted to hear that Polly was home from a dangerous secret mission, but soon got on to more important matters. She and her mother had reached a deadlock over the table napkins. Cecilia wanted peach. Her mother insisted that white was the only canonical colour. Hair was being torn, pillows bedewed, doors slammed. Her father had taken Lance and gone to Portsea, ostensibly to fish. Matters had reached a crisis.

'Simple,' said Phryne. 'I have attended many county weddings and one royal one. Colours are now considered proper. But not peach,' she added. 'If you want to walk down the aisle with a glad heart, you will take my advice. Scatter the table with frangipani blossoms. The tablecloth is white, but not bright white. It will be the same shade as the blossoms, a pale ivory. And the napkins shall be frangipani yellow. Not buttercup. Not orange blossom. That yellow with a squeeze of lemon juice in it. Your bouquet will be of frangipani and gardenias. It will look and smell divine. And that,' she said, 'is my last word on the subject. If your mother does not agree, tell her to ring me. I hope you will be very happy, Cecilia. Just as happy as you deserve to be.'

'Oh, I shall,' said a vastly relieved voice on the other end of the phone. 'I shall!'

For the rest of the week Phryne did nothing but amuse herself. It was such a change. She went dancing with Lin Chung, dining on the strange but delicious fare of Little Bourke Street. She lunched with Dr MacMillan in the buttery near the

Queen Victoria Hospital. She visited the Adventuresses Club. She continued to breakfast on fresh fish, caught by Tinker. She read with interest the scandalous tale of the brave girl reporter who had got herself kidnapped for a story. Polly looked quite indescribable in that wig. The Magdalen Laundry was in the news. Dr Mannix denounced the reporter.

'The Magdalen Laundry turns out girls who are demure and meek, fitted for their station in life!' he stated. 'Anyone who prints these outrageous lies has allied themselves to the forces of darkness!'

Which must have made Mr Bates very proud. Ever since the Somme, he and the forces of darkness had been close personal friends.

The party was going well. The jazz band was playing dance music. Felix Pettigrew had arrived with Clarissa. She was wearing an Erté jade-green crêpe de Chine dress with just the suspicion of a train lined with steel and silver tints. She was loaded with diamonds: fingers, wrists, neck and a creditable crown.

'Out of the tat box,' she confided to Phryne. 'They're Titania's jewels from the *Dream*. They're good fakes, though: zirconias, not rhinestones. Thanks for returning the wig. Elsie gets so cross if anything's missing.'

Felix bowed. He was not only dressed in faultless evening costume, but wore a gold watch and chain and a quizzing glass on a velvet ribbon. He was perfect. There was something very eighteenth century about Felix.

'Phryne, you look delightful,' he said. 'What happened to that . . . er . . . assailant?'

'Still undiscovered,' said Phryne.

He read her face, as he always did.

'Very good,' he replied, and led Clarissa out onto the floor.

Everyone was dancing. Hugh was dancing with Dot, Tinker with Ruth. Isobel Berners, in a leaf-green brocade gown patterned with apples, was dancing with Charles, Phryne's friend from Mount Martha. Mr Featherstonehaugh was dancing with Dr MacMillan, both wearing well-tailored gentlemen's evening dress. Bert was dancing with Eliza. Cec was dancing with his Alice.

Clarissa swept past in the arms of a scion of one of the Best Families. Phryne heard her say to the eager young man, 'The prince gave them to me? Oh, no, I can't *say* they came from the prince. I promised his mama.'

Actresses.

Mr Downey of the newspaper office danced with his intended. He did not seem too downcast at the loss of his promised scoop.

Madame Paris had brought her young ladies. They were a general hit and all had dance partners. She was sitting at a small table, holding court with the ones who did not dance—Mr Bates, Jane and Jack Robinson. They were getting on surprisingly well. Madame, however, seemed likely to lose Primrose, who was dancing cheek to cheek with Terence the delivery man. There would always be another Primrose.

Phryne had not invited the Kettle parents. Polly seemed to be enjoying a conversation with Peony and Poppy. That ought to ensure that her hair stayed curled. Herbert Grant was dancing with his Beggar Maid, Phoebe, and they seemed very comfortable together. After all, if she had been his housemaid, there was nothing she did not know about him. If she still loved him after that, then she really did love him. Herbert had the slightly dazed look of a man who has won a lottery for which he did not recall buying a ticket.

'Pleased?' asked Lin Chung, extending a hand.

'Thinking about slavery,' said Phryne. 'All sorts of it. Marriage, whoredom, servitude.'

'Stop thinking about it,' advised Lin. 'Tonight is for celebration. Have you decided what you are celebrating?'

'Freedom,' said Phryne, and took his hand.

AFTERWORD

I found the poem 'If No One Ever Marries Me' in a Children's Encyclopedia written by Miss Laurense (sic) Alma-Tadema (daughter of famous painter Alma-Tadema). No one ever married her, or perhaps it is better to say that she never married anyone. She seems pleased about that. She died in 1940 at an advanced age.

The Awful Disclosures of Maria Monk (reprint Senate, London, 1997) bears as much relation to a real convent as *The Protocols of the Elders of Zion* bears to Judaism. It was passed hand to hand by Protestant schoolgirls (including my grandmother) in the 1920s, along with Havelock Ellis, *Married Love* by Marie Stopes and *Psychopathia Sexualis* by Krafft Ebing, which at least made them practise their Latin translating the rude bits. Oh, well, I suppose it could be worse. It generally wasn't De Sade or Walter's *My Secret Life*. That was reprinted when I was at school . . .

•

For conditions in the Magdalen Laundry I have read the Sisters' views in their own book *Pitch Your Tents on Distant Shores*, and the views of their inmates on their websites and several essays. The laundry supported the good works of the convent, and it was the hardest labour required of prisoners since the law gave up the treadmill—and they weren't even prisoners. It was unconscionable by the standards of the day, and by any standards. Women working in outside laundries had their hours, conditions and breaks fixed by legislation. The convent was exempt by an act of parliament. They got everything from water to labour for free. I have the highest respect for nuns—some of whom are related to me—but those laundries were unforgivable.

This isn't to say that the convent didn't do good works. Their charity was exemplary, their orphans well fed, their old ladies well tended. Except for the Magdalen Laundry. The children were told never even to look at the inmates.

Besides, I walked past the only window in that laundry one night, now that the Abbotsford Convent has writers' festivals. I didn't know that was what I was passing, then. I was thinking about the panel I was about to be on. I have never been afraid of the dark. And I walked into the most dreadful concentrated suicidal despair I have ever felt. Someone had stood at that window and really wanted to die. I ran. I later found that I had skirted the Magdalen Laundry. It's not evidence. But it felt very real. Email support@clan.org.au for the inmates' stories.

Once I found out that the Collins Street establishment which used to be Madame Brussels' was run by a Madame Paris in 1920, I wondered about that statement that the top end of Collins Street was 'the Paris end' as it does not greatly resemble Paris. I suspect it was one of those sly in-jokes of which

Melbourne is so fond. Like the assessment of someone's chance of success as zero being 'Buckley's and None', referring to the department store Buckley and Nunn and the stalwart survivor, the convict William Buckley (no relation). Information about brothels is hard to find, unless they are the basic ones which are raided by the police, which Madame Paris and indeed the Blue Cat Club never were. I have had to extrapolate a little about them, but they existed. Gay history is even more subterranean. I have read the available archives and done the best I could, knowing a bit about the subculture as a foundation member of GaySoc at Melbourne University in my youth, when we thought—as my friend Dennis Pryor noted—that we had invented sex. Such was not the case.

Isopel Berners is the eponymous heroine of a novel by that strange gypsy-loving polyglot George Borrow. My copy is Hodder & Stoughton, London, probably about 1925. She is a marvellous character, especially for her time. She travels alone and engages in serious fisticuffs with anyone unwise enough to attack her. 'I loved to hear her anecdotes of people (on the road) some of whom I found had occasionally laid hands upon her person or effects, and had invariably been humbled by her without the assistance of either justice or constable.' If you have never read Borrow, I do recommend him. A true eccentric.

BIBLIOGRAPHY

Abrahams, Gerald, *The Chess Mind*, Penguin Books, London, 1960.

Bacchus Marsh Historical Society, *Bacchus Marsh Heritage Guide*, Bacchus Marsh, 2007.

Camm, George (compiler), *Bacchus Marsh: An Anecdotal History*, Shire of Bacchus Marsh with Hargreen Publishing Company, Melbourne, 1986.

Craig, Elizabeth, *New Standard Cookery*, Odhams Press, London, 1933.

Ebbutt, Blanche, *Don'ts For Wives*, AC Black, London, 1913.

Farrell, Frank, *International Socialism and Australian Labour*, Hale & Iremonger, Sydney, 1981.

Kollontai, Alexandra (ed. Alix Holt), *Selected Writings*, Haymarket Books, London, 1980.

Kovesi, Catherine, *Pitch Your Tents on Distant Shores*, Playwright Publishing, Caringbah NSW, 2006.

Li, Yu (trans. Patrick Hanan), *The Carnal Prayer Mat*, Arrow Books, London, 1990.

Monk, Joanne, *Cleansing Their Souls: Laundries in Institutions for Fallen Women*, Lilith Collective, Fitzroy Vic., 1996.

Nin, Anaïs, *A Spy in the House of Love*, Penguin Books, London, 1954.

Pescott, Mrs N (compiler), *Early Settlers' Household Lore*, Raphael Press, Richmond SA, 1977.

Spry, Constance and Hume, Rosemary, *A Constance Spry Cookery Book*, Pan Books, London, 1951.

Terrington, William, *Cooling Cups and Dainty Drinks* is worth downloading from Google books. I cannot find an extant copy.

Willett, Graham and Arnold, John, *Queen City of the South: Gay and Lesbian Melbourne*, *Latrobe Journal*, no. 87, State Library of Victoria Foundation, Melbourne, 2011.

Willet, Graham, Murdoch, Wayne and Marshall, Daniel (eds), *Secret Histories of Queer Melbourne*, Australian Lesbian and Gay Archives, Parkville Vic., 2011.